The Afflicted Saga
Defiance
Tale of the Fallen: Book IV

Katika Schneider

For Mom and Dad
You always encouraged my creativity, fostered (and funded) my dreams, and taught me to give my best in all I do.
Thank you for the bedtime stories.

ACKNOWLEDGMENTS

As always, thank you to my beta readers for helping me craft this book to its best potential, especially to fellow author, J.R. O'Bryant for helping me fine-tune one of what I consider Defiance's most memorable lines.

Thank you to my amazing street team and those of you who so graciously spread knowledge of Abaeloth's existence to others—you are all pretty much my heroes.

A special thanks to Sarah of Sarah Miller Creations for this beautiful cover, as well as to Cynthia and Nodus Astra for their time and talent in making my characters more tangible.

My continued appreciation to the Superstars Writing Seminar Tribe for all of their insight and support.

And a massive heap of gratitude to every single reader I've met at conventions and signings. There are days when your enthusiasm is what keeps me pursuing this path. You are the best.

ONE

Annin had known from the very first time Kol declared his intention to bind himself to Nessix that it was a mistake. As the oraku trudged through the overgrown forest of Elidae's foothills, wings uncharacteristic to his demon subclass catching on lower limbs, he realized it was *his* mistake for helping the alar achieve this stupid objective. He glanced down at the orb in his hand and stopped walking.

"Blood's run cold," he said as Kol stopped beside him, their detail of half a dozen demon soldiers halting a respectful distance behind them.

Kol shifted his weight impatiently, orange eyes darting around their surroundings with a manic frequency, left hand tapping his sheathed dagger against his thigh. To a casual observer, the alar appeared frightened for his life, and part of him likely was, given Grell's expectations. Someone who knew Kol as well as Annin did, however, would easily recognize a much deeper fear. Kol jutted his right hand forward, not reacting when Annin stuck his index finger with a thin pick.

"I told you we'd find her." Annin hushed his voice to veil that he was comforting his friend. Everything about speaking that promise—especially the fact that he genuinely meant it—made Annin doubt his own intelligence, but an increasingly influential part of him knew his personal well-being hinged on finding their renegade creation. He grasped the end of the pick between his teeth and squeezed Kol's blood into the opening at the top of the orb. "Calm down before you generate more suspicion than you've already got."

It wasn't Annin's instruction that gained Kol's compliance, but the subtle flare of light which illuminated the glass ball as his blood warmed it. "It's been a week," Kol said. "How long can this thing track her?" Annin sighed and rolled his head away from Kol's anxious snip. "That's what I thought. Lecture me after we find her. I'll listen to you then."

"Will you?" Annin muttered. He peered down at the orb, squinting his pale eyes as he struggled to decipher its readings, and resumed walking.

Frowning tightly, Kol hastened after the oraku, trusting the rest of the unit to follow. He'd nearly bled dry once to bring Nessix to him, and he was prepared to do so again. The sliver of her soul he wore around his neck had settled in a dull glow, no longer giving him insight to her activities or whereabouts, and so he relied on his own blood, the same blood that had been used to raise Nessix in the first place, to lead him back to her.

And when you find her, you can remind her what trust is…

Even with skills as ancient as those Annin possessed, tracking a week-old trail via blood magic was slow and tedious and drew out the headache only Kol and his terrible decisions knew how to create. Difficult or not, they moved through darkness and hunger and doubt. Limited by time, stopping wasn't an option; even the underlings who had come along to support their superiors in this search knew returning to the hells without Nessix in tow was not an option. After all, Grell only stayed calm when he was truly furious.

They'd searched for nearly two days when the smell of death put an abrupt end to their hunger pangs, and neither Kol nor Annin bothered so much as a glance at the other before following the stench to a peaceful bed of pine needles. The corpse they came across had bloated, juices of decomposition seeping from between the seams of its armor. Its face had been peeled clean by scavengers, one eye missing and the other ruptured and oozing

2

over exposed bone. If not for the style of armor, the body's origins would have been unidentifiable.

Kol stared down at the remains of the dead demon, Grell's suspicions and Annin's terse warnings echoing in his mind.

"That one of yours?" Annin asked.

The alar processed the question slowly and nodded.

Annin sighed one of those reluctant sighs that conveyed just how much he wanted to go back in time to never get himself involved with Nessix or the akhuerai or even Kol. Silently, he grabbed Kol's hand to let more blood into his orb. It glowed to life and led them to the next demon's remains.

"An accident, right?" Annin asked.

Kol's lips were numb and the warmth had begun to drain from his extremities. Based on the armor he wore, this demon had been the elite of the two guards, the one who should have carried Nessix's sword belt. It was missing and none of the demon's weapons had been drawn. He hadn't fallen victim to any sort of organized attack—the only way a group of flemans or the few members of Zeal's Order of the White Circle here on Elidae would have been able to defeat both demon guards—and he'd been taken down by surprise. By someone he'd underestimated. Someone he'd been assured was not a threat. Annin stopped beside Kol, silently staring at the corpse as identical thoughts ran through his mind.

Kol turned his head toward Annin, the demon who had stood beside him through all of his reckless theories and experiments, the smartest demon he'd known, and his last chance at being spared from the punishment Grell was gleefully choreographing for him. Quietly, to himself, Kol had to finally admit that Nessix had chosen to run. She'd deceived her guards just as she'd deceived him, and now she was in the wind. Admitting this out loud, with witnesses, wasn't an option for Kol. He was an elite, an ancient. He didn't make mistakes, because no demon who did survived long enough to face their consequences. Overwhelmed by a cold confusion he didn't understand, missing the rage that once came so naturally to him, Kol held his breath to wait for Annin's reaction.

A sensible demon would have been outraged. He'd have spun on Kol and knocked him out, shredded his wings, and bound him to be delivered back to his lord. A sensible demon would have found a way to appease this lord with gifts or distractions while he figured out a way to solve the greater problem. All his life, even as a mortal, Annin had been sensible—and powerful enough to execute the necessary requirements to keep himself safe. But as he met Kol's pleading eyes, that sensibility wavered, reminding him that he had told Grell that the akhuerai were the demons' means to conquest, that Kol was reckless but not wrong to bind himself to Nessix. He hadn't spoken up when the idea of sending her to the surface was presented. All of those factors added up to his own hefty responsibility for this catastrophe. And that didn't even touch the fact that he genuinely liked Kol.

The rotting demon at their feet told the tale of Nessix's escape just as clearly as if she'd dropped from the trees to share it herself. Kol and Annin had come to know her mannerisms well, but that advantage would only buy them a few minutes before the demons they'd brought along put the events together for themselves.

Kol hadn't been able to relax in the vaguest sense of the word after he first realized Nessix wasn't coming back. Spent in every fashion, the alar wasn't in an ideal frame of mind to make important decisions, and since Annin had foolishly let himself be drawn into this mess, it was up to him to initiate a solution. At least the six footmen they'd brought along had been meant to serve as decoys in the event of an ambush. If they didn't make it back, nobody would question it.

Annin knelt beside the corpse and carefully placed his orb in a bed of leaves, nestling it close to the dead demon's shoulder to protect the magical artifact from accidental destruction. He took a moment to gather his strength, closing his eyes to concentrate on the steady pulse of his threads and take into account how many he was prepared to sever. An oraku's mind was considered too valuable for him to be kept fit for physical combat, so Annin was only armed with a jagged knife reserved for emergencies. This met all his criteria. Hoping Kol's anxiety hadn't robbed him of his ability to provide support, Annin leapt to his feet.

Nobody in the group registered what was happening the first time Annin reached forward and snapped his fingers, but the moment the first of the six guards gasped and stumbled backwards, frantically rubbing his eyes, he quickly figured it out. By Annin's second snap, Kol spun around to see the soldiers scatter. By the third, he realized Annin was eliminating dangerous witnesses.

With three more soldiers left to immobilize, the oraku would risk depleting too much strength for self-defense if Kol didn't assist. A strange sensation washed over Kol, a feeling he'd seldom experienced after he'd become a demon. Gratitude, and the desire to act in Annin's defense as much as Annin was acting in his.

Without a word, recognizing the cold determination in Annin's eyes, Kol pulled his dagger free and rushed toward the fleeing demons. He pushed past the three Annin had blinded, shoving one to the ground in the process.

The three soldiers who still had their sight ran desperately to escape the radius of Annin's magic. Kol sprang forward and grabbed the nearest by the arm and plunged his knife into his target's side where the seams of leather armor came together. The strike might not have killed the demon, but it did slow him down. Kol didn't wait to assess the results of his attack as the other two demons steadily gained ground away from him.

A gargling scream sounded behind Kol, and he hoped it belonged to one of the blind demons rather than his friend. He'd tend to that concern after he disposed of the two witnesses he was after. He had a visual on one and the other revealed his position as he crashed through the trees ahead. In such thick cover, Kol wouldn't be able to track them through the sky, and they'd distanced themselves enough that he'd never catch them both on foot. Dusting off his knack for deception, Kol ran ahead and called to the fleeing demons.

"Annin's lost his mind! Regroup to me! I know how to fight him!"

The demon in his sights slowed enough to turn and look back at him, but the strain of exertion and terror contorted his face too much for Kol to determine if he believed the claim. Up ahead, an abrupt rustle of dried leaves and snapping twigs—accompanied by a startled curse—suggested the other demon had tripped himself to a stop. Kol didn't have their compliance, but he did have their attention.

"We'll be stronger and safer together," Kol shouted. "From Annin and the Order both. Do not forget they now have a presence on Elidae."

At last, sense penetrated panic and the demon ahead of Kol slowed to a jog, then a winded halt. Kol shoved his dagger back in its sheath and strode forward as the demon doubled over, hands on his knees as he panted for breath.

"We have to stay together if we want to stand a chance." Kol threw his voice hard to ensure it reached the last witness. "Annin's likely made quick work of those he blinded. Hurry!"

Moments later, the last demon staggered toward Kol, wild-eyed and face scratched from thorns. "You really know how to fight an oraku?"

"I know how to fight that one." Kol reached an arm out to beckon the demons close. "I haven't worked alongside him this long without learning his weaknesses."

Seduced by Kol's certainty and conditioned to respect his authority, the soldiers nodded through their panting and flanked him with no further encouragement. Disappointed at how easy the general population was to manipulate, Kol's flimsy grasp on compassion pitied their willingness to condemn themselves. Taking them down wouldn't be a simple task, as they were already seized by adrenaline, but that experience Kol had just claimed to have working alongside Annin also declared that the oraku was counting on him. And in doing so, Kol was counting on himself.

Kol struck in a flash, popping his left wing open in a forceful snap and catching the scraped up demon in the head. The strike flung his target to the ground, adding a second blow to an already dazed head. That demon was managed, but only for a moment, and Kol spun to grasp the feistier of the pair by the wrist as he tried to scramble away. Kol was strong and an experienced fighter, but the soldier's desperation countered a great deal of that skill.

The demon flailed at the end of Kol's arm, swinging his free hand to his hip to grab his sword. It was an awkward, unbalanced draw, giving Kol the chance to jerk his opponent forward and drive a knee into his abdomen. Protected only by hard leather armor, the strike didn't cripple the soldier, but it did succeed in pushing the air from his lungs, and Kol's hold prevented him from doubling over to gasp against the blow.

While Kol had acknowledged the risk of turning his back to the other demon, he hadn't anticipated retaliation from him until pain pierced through the webbing of his left wing.

"You son of a whore!" the offending underling shouted.

A surge of agony followed the blade's path through Kol's wing, cleaving a two-foot long laceration through the tender membrane. Kol howled, the cry contorting into seething rage as the demon's insubordination processed in his mind. He'd used all of his excuses for disobedience on justifying why Nessix had run off, and spewed that previously contained fury at this unfortunate outlet. Kol quickly rammed his knee into the first demon once again, resulting in the sword falling to the ground, and spun on the second demon, slamming his good wing into his opponent's head.

The soldier was better prepared for a wing strike this time around and only staggered from the impact, but staggering was all Kol needed. Before his prey could shake off his daze, Kol swept forward and grabbed his arm, giving it a yank so stout that the limb pulled free from the shoulder with a satisfying pop. The bloody knife dropped from the demon's hand as he shrieked and tried to retreat, but Kol held fast to the dislocated limb and prevented his opponent from moving more than an inch.

A furious roar sputtered from behind Kol as the remaining witness found his footing, and Kol cursed his luck. Still confident he'd walk away from this fight, he was no longer certain he'd do so with grace. Locking down on the current demon's arm, he twisted to fling him toward the oncoming attack. In flight, the demon wailed in agony as his tendons stretched from the sudden departure, but his cries met an abrupt end as the charging demon's sword sank into his back.

With the odds now balanced against him, the soldier swore viciously and jerked his sword free of the last ally he'd had. He continued his charge, eyes steeled over with a look Kol had once known well, the recognition that he'd likely never see the results of his actions. If sympathy still had a place in the alar, he'd have felt it now, but determination and the degree his morals had degraded prepared him to intercept the attack. That option never came, either.

Two strides from engaging, a choke bubbled in the charging demon's throat and he jerked to a stop. Throwing his shoulders back, a massive tremor shook him as his sword slipped from his limp fingers. Instincts interrupted, Kol struggled to comprehend what happened until blood seeped from the demon's eyes, nose, and ears. The soldier sucked in a breath that instantly sputtered out as a mouthful of frothy blood, and then he collapsed forward, a puddle of bodily fluids growing around his head.

"What weaknesses were you speaking of?"

Annin's voice was strained, but Kol had never been so relieved to hear it. If not for the pain pulsing in his wing, he would have laughed. He turned to face his companion, meeting drooped shoulders and exhausted eyes to accompany the spent tone.

"Convincing you to overexert yourself seems to be one," Kol said. "The others? I wouldn't know."

Annin's worn gaze eased with what could have been a smug smile, but the expression never made it to his lips. He slumped to the ground. "You made quite a commotion. How long do you suspect we have before some mortal comes to investigate?"

Kol grimaced and took a moment to look around. There were no signs of civilization within shouting distance, but he didn't know what sort of patrol schedule the Shade had established since taking up residence on Elidae. His grimace developed into a full-fledged frown as Sazrah crossed his mind. Neither he nor Annin had it in them to engage her in their current conditions. He crossed his arms, injured wing twitching.

"How long do you need?" Kol asked.

Annin shook his head and waved Kol closer. "Give me that wing."

Kol complied readily as Annin groped at a pouch on his hip to produce the tracking orb. As long as Kol was bleeding, they might as well take advantage of it. "We're not reporting what happened here," Annin said.

Kol flinched as Annin squeezed blood from his wound. "Of

8

course not."

They paused their discussion as the magic within the orb settled. Annin raised it into the air and slowly swept his arm until he found its strongest glow.

"Damn it all..." he growled.

Kol looked down at the orb, straightened, and traced the path it suggested Nessix had taken. He, too, growled his dissatisfaction.

Though he didn't understand magic the way Annin did, Kol had learned to trust the results the oraku achieved with his powers, and the orb implied Nessix had moved toward the temple after she'd taken out her guards. Kol had never doubted Nessix's intelligence; she'd gone to the temple intentionally. There would be no sanctuary for demons there, and that desperation Kol had forgotten in the heat of combat returned in a flood of anxiety. Unless they could find a way to lure Nessix away from the temple, she was protected from them. Kol glanced at the demons he and Annin had just defeated, wondering if silencing them so hastily had been a mistake. They'd have made useful scouts for what would be a most unpleasant task.

Annin looked up at Kol, and the alar silently helped his companion to his feet. "Even if we were in fighting shape, that is not a place I wish to go." Annin's voice didn't bear the same warning Kol had gotten used to, but it did carry a degree of ridicule, constantly reminding Kol that his desire and attempts to own Nessix had been terrible decisions.

Kol's heart beat heavily, still aching with the pain of Nessix's betrayal and now enhanced with dread of what Grell would make of it. "We'll need fresh forces to go after her," he said, pleased to discover that his acclimation to panic had resulted in a greater degree of confidence in his voice.

"And what story are we going to tell?"

Kol looked at the trio of dead demons around him, assuming the results of Annin's handiwork wouldn't look much better. "We're going to say evidence showed that Nessix was rescued by her people. Both of her guards had been slain and she was taken. When we came upon the scene, we were assaulted by the Order, which is how our men fell. I've got an injury no sane alar would inflict on himself simply to bend a story in his favor. We'll be able to petition for a greater force, one that will coax Nessix free from hiding."

Annin's frown persisted. "You're assuming that her remaining commander here on Elidae won't believe who she is. With what she knows"—that was spoken with a heat Kol didn't appreciate— "she'll be too valuable for them to risk losing again. We can attack all we'd like, but the rebel army, the Order, and whoever Elidae's new leadership can rally will be the ones who march out against us, not Nessix."

Cursing Annin's practicality and logic, Kol rubbed the back of his head and looked toward the temple again, contemplating the ever-decreasing options at his disposal. "If we began to raze townships, she wouldn't let any number of knights or commanders hold her back. Strike her people, and she'll come charging in their defense."

A bitter chuckle left the oraku and he shook his head. "The faith you have in that woman, Kol…"

"Yeah. I know," Kol seethed. "I understand you think I'm a fool for it. And maybe I am. But you cannot deny that I know Nessix better than anyone else does."

"Not better than she knows herself," Annin said. "And she's got one advantage over you now."

Kol furrowed his brow and jerked his attention back to Annin. "And what's that?"

"She's got your memories in her, doesn't she?"

Those drawn brows wavered and tilted toward uncertainty. Annin was the only person Kol had discussed Nessix's dreams with, an unavoidable circumstance given the way she'd disclosed that she suffered them in the oraku's presence. At that time, she'd been confused by what she'd witnessed, the one comfort the demons had enjoyed.

Over the following weeks after that disclosure, though, her dreams had become more vivid and had uncovered details she'd asked Kol about. She hadn't spoken outright that she knew she was living his past in her sleep, but the degree of certainty she'd had when asking him to elaborate on the details she didn't understand confirmed it well. What was worse, this understanding had built on its own accord, organically developing in Nessix's mind as she continued to experience Kol's distant past. How long would it be until she was able to see past the terror of the Divine Battle? When would she find out about the road to the demons' downfall?

"That's what I thought," Annin said, interrupting Kol's fretting and driving the point home all the better. He shook his head, lips twitching as he held back his chastisement and curses at what Kol's foolish obsession had caused. Venting such thoughts at the alar wouldn't accomplish anything; it hadn't any time in the past. "We have to get a hold of her before she puts it all together."

Kol wouldn't mention that he was afraid she was well on her way to doing just that. "I know we do," he spat. "That's why we're out here."

"I thought we were out here so Grell didn't skin you and force you to eat your entrails."

Kol glared at his friend, wishing there would have been some amount of jest in those words. Instead, all he found looking back at him were stern eyes every bit as apprehensive as he felt. "That's an added bonus." Kol sent one more loathing glare in the direction of the temple, then turned toward the path that led back up the mountain and to their entryway to the hells. "If we can keep our story straight, we can postpone judgement until we have time to find her. There's nothing Grell likes more than war, and any chance to launch one will overshadow his desire to torture me. Are you able to travel?"

Annin stared at Kol for long moments, hating the alar for what he'd gotten them into. At this point, even if Grell didn't hold Annin responsible for Nessix's disappearance, he was certain he'd take collateral damage. Annin had committed himself to this path, a decision he'd reluctantly made when Kol first sourced himself for Nessix, a decision he'd continued to make as he went along with the idea of not ending the rebellious akhuerai when she first showed signs of disobedience, and a decision he'd sealed now that he'd slaughtered his own warriors to cover up damning evidence against Kol. Annin was every bit as responsible at this point. He'd learned to trust Kol as much as demons ever trusted anyone, but it had been lifetimes since he'd last relied on another so strongly.

"What choice do I have?" Annin asked. "You won't be able to lift me anywhere with your wing like that, and the longer we dawdle, the more likely our chances one of the Shade's puppets shows up to finish the job."

Together, the two demons, risen from mortal men who had served alongside each other in the most trying time in Abaeloth's history, set a resigned course back to the hells, reciting their story until even they believed it.

TWO

Sazrah hated using blood magic as much as she hated everything else that reminded her of her heritage. She'd learned to justify most of the attributes she'd been born with—her natural resilience, increased strength and perception—since they assisted her in combat, but the darker parts of her blood? No matter how adept she'd become at using it, she still felt filthy and unworthy of Mathias's confidence for it. Which was ironic, considering how hard she'd been trying to reach him using these same methods.

It was the fourth consecutive day Mathias had failed to reply to her blood scrying. While a lifetime of bitterness and regret had conditioned Sazrah to throw her antipathy about freely, Mathias was among the few living beings she'd never looked down on, though she was as close to it now as she ever would be. In the absence of immediate peril, Mathias was notoriously easygoing and mischievous, and he knew how Sazrah loathed her inherent talents. He often pressured her to accept these traits as unique blessings, and though she didn't want to disappoint him, she'd never accept what she was.

Heel bouncing at the opposite end of toes aggressively planted into the floor, Sazrah glowered into the shallow bowl of her blood. She didn't know why she was trying so hard to reach Mathias, besides Sulik's insistence and her annoying sense of loyalty to the paladin who she considered a troublesome father. Her fruitless efforts nodded sagely as justification of her impatience. Regardless of who that woman actually was, Sazrah would believe one thing— if a demon warned her that demons were coming, then demons were coming. And with that, she had more important matters to address right now than trying to play messenger with her distracted mentor.

The blood she'd let had nearly lost its viable heat when a ripple traced across the surface, and Sazrah perked up. The gentle disturbance settled, revealing Mathias's face, and Sazrah cursed sharply.

"Good to see you, too, Saz."

"No..." she muttered, drawing a knife against her fingertip to drop fresh blood into the bowl. "It's not that..."

"Have I kept you waiting?"

Sazrah met Mathias's eyes, expression stony as she searched his for how serious he'd been. "Is that an honest question, or are you testing me?"

"Ah," Mathias said. "Seems I did. Sorry about that. I've been busy."

Sazrah recoiled her hand from the basin and pressed her thumb against the wound on the tip of her finger. The fact that Mathias hadn't responded with the comforting levity he often did jarred her calm, and she wished even more that she'd found an excuse to avoid this conversation. "Not that it's any of my business, but where are you?"

Mathias chuckled and looked past the scrying bowl's surface, his eyes growing deeper with dampness as his upper lip fought not to curl. "You're happier not knowing."

Sazrah tilted her head, caring for his ominous tone even less. "That usually means you're preparing to do something stupid."

"Oh, I am preparing to do something stupid. Necessary, but stupid."

Mathias had learned to tolerate the demons over the years, a lesson he'd systematically and unsuccessfully tried to impart on Sazrah, but there had been a time when he'd loathed them with the deepest fiber of his being. Right now, that same detestation was in his voice, and the firmness of his resolve told Sazrah exactly where he was and what stupid action he was preparing to take. Sazrah was a brave woman, but she frowned, not envying Mathias his position. All of a sudden, her desire to protect him from the report she had to deliver was overshadowed by her fear of what might happen to him if he entered the hells. Fate, it seemed, had made up Sazrah's mind for her.

"Mathias, we—" She stopped suddenly, hesitating as his eyes flicked back to hers. She'd known Mathias long enough to reliably predict his reactions to most situations, but this was new territory for her. If she was to trust Mathias, trust Sulik, trust that *thing* that had come claiming to be Mathias's lost lover, her news could very likely pull out a side of Mathias she didn't know how to address.

"You what?" Mathias asked when she failed to complete her statement. He frowned as her eyes met his once again. "You've never had the patience to be anything but blunt, Saz. What's happened on Elidae?"

Sazrah curled her lips between her teeth and released them with a sigh. "A... woman—demon... *something* came to the temple, claiming to be your Nessix—"

The image of Mathias wavered violently, and for a moment, Sazrah was afraid he'd drop his bowl and they'd have to start over. Slowly, the scene settled to reveal Mathias gazing off absently, his jaw slacked in stupefied shock. His breath came quick and shallow, ripping away that composure in which Sazrah often found so much comfort. She withheld the rest of her report as Mathias digested the information she'd barely managed to deliver. Finally, he closed his mouth to swallow and shook his head, clearing his throat.

"On Elidae?" His voice trembled the request.

"Yes." At this point, Sazrah was afraid to mention her reservations.

"And what did she say?"

Mathias was a dreamer and had been since he and Sazrah first met at the onset of the Age of the Undead, but seeing the tortured hope in his eyes, the cascade of relief and disbelief and sheer joy, squeezed the confidence out of Sazrah's heart. "She came to us, asking about that general you killed and this civil war you started and about... about Brant. She asked about you." Sazrah watched Mathias's reaction closely, ashamed of what she was compelled to speak next. "I'd intended to slay her, but Sulik stopped me. She knew who he was before he had the chance to address her. Mathias, I... I don't know what this means, but she knew too much that she shouldn't, even for a demon. I thought you should know that I may have found you a lead."

It took Mathias a moment to slow his thoughts enough to speak. "Where is she now? Can you bring—"

"I've sent her by transport ship to Gelthin."

Mathias's hope and enthusiasm drained from his face. "Sazrah, finding Nessix is all that matters to me." The impression of tears rattled his voice, but they didn't escape him. "Why didn't you bring her—"

Sazrah held up a hand, unaccustomed to correcting Mathias, but unable to stop herself. There were more important matters she had to address before she could take the time to listen to his heartsick laments. "The only thing I found believable about her story was that her soul was twisted. Tortured. There was something not right about it, just as you told me there'd be. I had doubts of her travelling the divine pathways and figured you'd prefer whoever she actually is to reach you as unharmed as possible."

Mathias's eyes drifted out of focus as he nodded. He blinked once and looked back at Sazrah. "There's something else you haven't told me. A reason you're being so cold about her."

Sazrah hefted a sigh and glanced away. "She didn't just come with a few names to throw around. She said demons would come after her once they figured out she was gone, that they'd come in force, and that she had to reach you before they caught her. Mathias, if she surfaced here, so will this hunting party that's after her."

Mathias drew a slow breath, his excitement carefully closed away. "And have they surfaced?"

"There's been increased activity reported, but nothing to suggest any degree of organization." Sazrah hesitated to keep her personal impressions at bay, knowing Mathias would not look kindly on them. "I'm ready for them when they come, and so are my troops. But if this *is* your Nessix, she may have brought more trouble than you bargained for. I need you to think that over."

The irony of this news struck Mathias hard, and if he'd been less overwhelmed and slumped on the ground anywhere other than an entry point to the hells, he'd have allowed himself a good laugh over it. Nessix had once accused him of leading the demons to Elidae, and now she might have launched them across all of Abaeloth… It wouldn't be a problem he'd soothe from her easily. "We'll sort that out if it happens. This isn't my first fight with demons."

Sazrah creased her lips tightly to keep her thoughts to herself. *Yeah, but you're blind this time…* "Just… be careful. Please?"

It wasn't often that Sazrah allowed herself public displays of concern, though it wasn't the first time Mathias had seen her worried for him. The sentiment warmed his heart, but he would spare Sazrah's pride and not let that show. "I always am," he said, aiming to restore the typical lightness to his voice. She didn't reply, likely bogged down by her memories of Mathias's experience with demons, and he rubbed his chin, searching for a way to change the subject and spare them both from dwelling on their miserable pasts. "Did Sulik stay on Elidae or go with Nes?"

Sazrah frowned at Mathias's casual insistence that the woman she'd sent his way was indisputably Nessix, but she wouldn't waste her energy trying to correct him for it. "He's still needed here, Mathias. The transport I've sent out is to retrieve reinforcements to prepare for war. Sulik's *needed* here."

Mathias nodded absently. "Yes, I suppose he is." He glanced up at Sazrah's uncomfortable eyes. "The crew of this transport you've sent, they're trustworthy?"

Relieved that Mathias indicated a willingness to proceed down a mature path, Sazrah sighed. "Completely."

"To you or to me?"

Sazrah shook her head in insulted disbelief. So much for maturity. "I told you she would reach Gelthin safely. They have orders to deposit her in Seaton before picking up troops from Shadeskeep."

At last, that chuckle escaped Mathias, though it was a weaker expression than Sazrah remembered. "Alright, I'm sorry. You just have a certain track record when it comes to demonic connections and you've done an admirable job conveying what you think of Nessix."

Sazrah looked down at the cut on her finger that had already scabbed over and was beginning to fade back into heathy tissue. Demonic connections... "You gave me two missions when you brought me to Elidae," Sazrah murmured. "The first was to protect the island from the demons, which I'm trying to arrange. The second was to help you find Nessix Teradhel. I don't have to like what I found, but I trust Sulik's judgement."

"More than you trust mine?" Mathias asked, his tone provoking a depth of consideration Sazrah had always been reluctant to dip into.

"You weren't here." Her eyes snapped up to his until she saw the intelligence watching her. "And it took four days for you to answer my scrying. If this woman is to be trusted as you say she is, getting her on the move was more important than asking you where to send her. All things considered, I worked as quickly as I was able."

Mathias bowed his head, conceding to Sazrah at last. She wasn't the most patient woman, and she put up with Mathias far better than most ever would. "If what Nes said is true, she may have started a fresh surge of the same war. You were wise to investigate. You are wise to be wary."

Sazrah pinched her lips together, uncomfortable receiving Mathias's praise. "I suspect the demons will hit hard and fast when they come, assuming she's as important to them as she claimed."

"She must be."

Sazrah looked into Mathias's eyes again, frowning at the sturdy structure of his certainty. "I've notified both kingdoms here on Elidae of the potential danger, not that they'll listen. I suspect the Order and I will be neck deep in work in the coming days. We are preparing accordingly."

Mathias's expression softened in the fatherly way in which he often approached Sazrah when distress lurked so near her. He was the only man on Abaeloth brave enough to try to coddle her, and her current dismay was palpable even through these shallow pools of blood. "Are you doing alright?"

"I will be once my transport returns, but I've made do with less than I have now."

Mathias shook his head and retained his melancholy smile for Sazrah's benefit. She'd gotten more defensive since Brant's death and he knew better than to bring it up directly. That wouldn't stop him from prying. "That's not what I meant, Saz. Are *you* alright?"

She set her jaw stubbornly—a family trait if Mathias had ever seen one—and looked away from the scrying bowl. "The blood's cooling. Do you have anything else you need to talk about?"

Mathias frowned, her redirection speaking painful truths. "I'd change the past if I could, you know that. Keep your head low, Sazrah. Let me know if you need anything; I'll do my best to be more prompt responding in the future."

A significant side of Sazrah gently urged her to take up Mathias's unspoken offer, to open up to him about how much she struggled with her grief, how afraid she was, how tired she was of not seeing a difference from all of the effort she'd invested in trying to save these people. But she'd been taught from a young age that acting strong was more important than actually being strong, and her instinct to hide her weakness thrived even in front of Mathias. It was an unusual response, considering he'd seen her torn down close to death and defeat more times than one woman should ever face, but maybe it was because he'd seen her at her worst that she never wanted to burden him with it again. The troubles before her now were her own. She'd opened herself up to them, and she'd bear the consequences. Besides, Mathias had enough to worry about.

She nodded at last. "Yes, sir. Find a way to notify me when she's in your custody?"

Mathias was through trying to correct Sazrah's implications that there was something inherently suspicious about Nessix and let this instance slide. He'd already pushed harder than it seemed she was willing to handle. "Of course. I'll stay in touch."

Sazrah stared through the cooling blood at the man she'd idolized her entire life, wanting to beg him for comfort or guidance, but too afraid to do so. She'd taken every necessary step to prepare for war, he clearly had his own problems to sort through, and there was nothing to be accomplished from prolonging this conversation. Foregoing a formal farewell, Sazrah discarded her blood onto the stone floor of her room in the temple, wiped the bowl clean, and stood. Closing her eyes, she took a slow breath to settle her emotions, squared her shoulders, and turned to go begin assigning patrols.

THREE

Despite the flemans' ocean-faring origins, it had only taken until the coasts of Elidae had disappeared from sight for Nessix to be convinced that Inwan had never intended his people to travel over the seas again. Five days confined to a cramped cabin without access to her weapons or freedom made her feel like a prisoner, a sensation she'd vowed to never fall victim to again. The inconsistent rolling of the ocean—and its effect on what little food she'd managed to consume—only ensured that ships had reached among her least favorite places to dwell. At least her preoccupation with not getting sick kept away her nightmares of Kol's past. If she never had to set foot on a ship again, Nessix would depart Abaeloth a content woman.

Beyond illness and instability, Nes's needs during the voyage were met just shy of satisfaction. Sazrah had briefed the crew of the situation and they'd responded by keeping Nessix confined and relatively unbothered. Her rations were a bland, stale bread with a thick porridge of unknown composition. Even the akhuerai's fare was superior to this, and it wasn't until Nessix was a tiny bundle of nerves as the ship heaved through the ocean that she wondered when she'd be able to replenish her meager supply of dream stop. The root was grown in the hells and was the only method she knew of to keep herself from folding to chaos under moments of stress, and all she'd been able to pilfer from the demons she'd slain in her escape were three chunks.

The ship's crew never warmed up to her. Had Nessix had less experience being looked down upon by the demons, their suspicions and callousness might have hurt her, but as it was, Nessix kept her chin up, constantly reminding herself that she was closer to salvation than she'd ever been.

They anchored just off Seaton's port late in the day. The captain assured Nessix that they'd made good time, something about brisk winds she didn't know what to make of. With the least appealing element of their contract fulfilled, the crew handed Nessix her sword and shuffled her onto a ferry to deposit her on the docks so they could be rid of her and return to their mission of collecting Sazrah's reinforcements.

Drawing on what little grit had survived the voyage, Nessix collapsed onto a crate on the middle of the pier to give her legs the chance to remember how to hold her upright. Living among the akhuerai had introduced her to a vast array of different races and cultures, but Seaton presented Nessix, in her sheltered upbringing, with sizes and shapes of people she hadn't imagined. Other travelers comprised of elegant elves and nimble halflings passed her, and burly human and dwarven dock workers hefted their loads between ships and horse drawn carts.

Even in its dull hours, Seaton was a busy city, as Nessix had been warned it would be. Under normal circumstances, crowds didn't bother her, but they did now. It had been just over a week since she'd escaped the demons, and Kol must have been hunting for her. Sazrah had sworn not to divulge Nes's destination to the demons, but Nessix didn't have a great deal of trust in the woman, given their introduction.

A familiar ache panged in Nes's heart, scolding her for what she'd done. Her escape had opened her homeland to a new war, one centered around finding her. She'd single-handedly thrust the people she'd vowed to protect—the ones she'd given her life to protect—into danger she was certain would be more violent than the war which had claimed her. Maybe this Sazrah the Shade was fierce enough to stop the demons, but after experiencing the tenacity of the likes of Kol, Nessix wouldn't hold her breath. Demons didn't take kindly to having their toys taken from them. She found limited consolation that the Elidae she'd fled was no longer the same one she'd sworn to watch over. The governments had deteriorated into corruption, and the only just people remaining had been exiled to the cave temple. Maybe war was for the best. Maybe.

The shaking left Nes's thighs, replaced by the sharp ache that came from muscles protesting neglect, signaling to her that she'd sat around long enough. During one of her brief phases of clarity aboard the ship, she'd requested a map of Gelthin, but the only maps the captain had were of waterways and coastlines. Nessix had no idea where Zeal was in relation to Seaton, only that Sazrah had said she'd be able to reach it from where they deposited her. Groaning, Nessix pushed herself to her feet and walked away from the noise of the pier.

In the past, she'd entered townships with confidence and a sense of authority, meeting people's greetings warmly. Now, an uncomfortable tremor of wariness beat in her heart, and she rapidly scanned the crowded streets, always on the lookout for danger. She tried to tell herself that it was ridiculous, that the demons—or even word of her escape—wouldn't have reached Gelthin ahead of her, but the guilt and risk of what she'd done clenched its jaws around her neck, threatening to shake her until she snapped in two. With her hand close to her hilt and her chin tucked against her collarbones, Nessix moved stiffly through the crowds, surveying her surroundings for something more useful than danger.

Whatever magic had taught Nessix common tongues allowed her to catch snippets from the conversations held by those she passed, and she was pleased to note that none of them included anything other than the mundane. No talk of wars. No fear of demons. All the people spoke of was when the fishermen were due to return, what they thought of the new bar maid at the local tavern, and who was coming as entertainment for an upcoming festival. Comforted by the citizens' peace, Nessix lifted her chin to discover that the only looks she received were from people making sure they didn't bump into her as she passed. Her heart slowed, and she breathed a bit more easily.

Understanding the tongue of the locals didn't do much to help Nessix with the script on business signs. She identified street vendors based on the visibility of their wares, and suspected she found the tavern by the graphic of a stout, frothy mug next to a tangle of words she couldn't read, but other than that, she was painfully lost. That ripple of uncertainty returned, telling her that she wasn't safe until she knew where to duck in an emergency, and her attempt at casually strolling through the city deteriorated into a frantic search for something she understood.

Nessix shouldered her way through the crowd, straining to read the signs around her. When she was certain she'd investigated all of them on a given street, she squeezed through alleys to find the next. The town guards were little more than young, burly men in pretty coats holding polished polearms; she wouldn't be able to count on them for help against demons. Three streets later, the sun began to retire, and Nes's hope of finding shelter for the night sank when her eyes caught a sign that briefly offered her a glimpse of familiarity.

"Library," it read.

She stopped to stare at the sign, jaw gaping. It was written clearly in her native fleman script. Pulling her shoulders back, Nessix turned to scan the storefronts around her, finding that none of them made the slightest sense to her. She spun back to face the library, sucked in a deep breath, and entered.

A quaint exterior made the building look more like a cottage than a scholarly establishment, yet the inside sprawled far larger than logic suggested was possible. Shelves crammed with books and scrolls lined the walls and formed aisles that towered over Nes's head. Despite the fact that the sign had been written in fleman, she could only understand the occasional word on the spines as she passed through the stacks. Her mind tugged back to Kol in that annoying way it was so fond of doing, wondering why he hadn't bothered to teach her to read more useful languages than those of his obscure, ancient texts. Frustrated with the alar as much as ever, Nessix crept through a central aisle, peering down the rows as she passed.

"Hello?" Several heartbeats passed in silence, not even the whispers of shuffling paper answering her. Walking farther in, Nessix tried again. "I'm looking for a map."

Still no answer. No workers or patrons. It was as though this library had been constructed solely for her. Unsettled, Nessix paced up and down the shelves, comforted at least by having found shelter. She hadn't thought being in a library would make her as restless as being trapped aboard the ship or imprisoned by demons, but the longer she searched through the towering shelves without encountering another person, the tighter her nerves coiled. She reached the end of the row and turned to face the back corner of the room.

Poorly lit, it might have deterred other people, but Nessix had learned to find some degree of comfort in shadows, and the corner drew her nearer. A single window sat high on the wall with its curtains drawn, a narrow sliver of light peeking through to shine against a worn wooden door. It wasn't until reaching this shadowed door that Nessix realized she hadn't passed any other apparent light sources while wandering through the library. She looked back at her path of progression and still couldn't find anything obvious lighting the room, yet a warm, golden glow illuminated each shelf and table, everywhere except this corner.

Dread returned as a fat lump in Nes's stomach and she shrank in on herself, deciding the benefit of shelter might not be worth facing whatever powers looked after this building. She threw a final glance at the shadowed door, and a quick flash of light snagged her attention, as if she'd been struck in the back of the head.

Nessix blinked to clear her vision. Perhaps she suffered exhaustion from her harrowing week. Sighing, she was about to leave when the flash caught her eye again, this time presenting as a clear plaque centered on the door.

Forgotten Histories. Restricted.

They composed the first complete statement Nessix had been able to read inside the library, and besides the intrigue loaded in them, she couldn't help but feel that it was meant as an omen.

What was more forgotten to the world than Nessix? Elidae had been an afterthought to Abaeloth. *She* had become an afterthought to Elidae. And this Berann who lurked unseen in her dreams? He'd become such an afterthought that Kol had beaten her for mentioning his name. Curiosity justified by her circumstances, Nessix sent a hasty glance over her shoulder to ensure she was still alone, and gave the door a shove.

It opened without protest, and Nessix bit her lip with one last bout of reluctance. She needed to find a map and get on the move, not play around with old books, but curiosity tempted her down the narrow flight of stairs. She stepped forward and let the door thud shut behind her.

The stairwell was clean of dust and cobwebs, the glistening wooden steps stained a rich cherry. As with the rest of the library, the stairwell glowed with its own mysterious illumination. Common sense and deeply ingrained combat training should have screamed to Nessix that this was an elaborate trap she was falling for. Even if nobody dangerous lurked below, a silent person above would only have to bar the door to trap her down here. Those essential survival instincts never kicked in, hushed by an overwhelming thirst for knowledge which soothed all of her worries and urgent objections into nothing. Pulled forward by this unexplainable force, Nessix reached the landing and stared ahead.

A desk was centered in the room, surrounded by a ring of ten bookshelves. Situated with their ends facing the desk like spokes on a giant wheel, asymmetrical shapes had been carved into the fine wood of the shelves she faced. Stacks of yellowed scrolls which stretched clear from floor to ceiling lined the perimeter of the room, not a speck of dust flawing their aged parchment. Suddenly, that sense of awe and wonder chilled as Nessix took in the sheer volume of knowledge loaded in this room. If she was meant to conduct her own research, it would take lifetimes to make it through the scrolls alone. She walked closer to the desk to look over the carvings on the shelf ends more closely, and gasped.

They were maps, each depicting a continent, complete with notches taken out to mark major cities and fine crevices etched into place to show main roadways. Nes's hope was dashed soon later as she realized she had no idea what Gelthin was shaped like, and the fact that she couldn't read the labels on these maps left her right where she started.

Heart falling, she looked past each foreign carving until she found the shelf depicting Elidae. She already knew everything about the island that would have made it to Gelthin, but seeing her home represented—and thoroughly so, based on the number of volumes on its shelves—warmed Nessix. Her fingers traced over the impression of the mountainous coast, followed the Bastin River to the Great Spring. A sorrowful smile tugged at her lips as she raised her foot to step forward, but she stopped before letting it fall.

Due to Elidae's seclusion from the rest of Abaeloth, Nessix knew little about world history and geography, but she knew there were eight continents. She stopped and turned around to count the shelves again, and after each of the continents had been accounted for, two more shelves remained. The first carried a carving of a lily, the symbol she'd learned to associate with Etha. The image of a comet run through by a spear adorned the last shelf. Nessix had never seen this symbol before, but as her heart stilled, she recognized it on a level deeper than she could comprehend.

Drawn to this mystery, Nessix turned from Elidae's shelf and approached that last one.

"What business do you have trespassing in the Forgotten Histories?"

Nessix had been so absorbed by intrigue, so intent on unearthing the information held in these tomes, that she hadn't heard anyone approach until a man's voice boomed through the room, stifling the air so she could hardly breathe. Normally, Nessix would have grabbed her sword, instinct having conditioned her to assume she'd need to defend herself. Instead, that voice scolded her very soul, chastising her as though she was a disobedient child, and Nessix instantly cringed and scampered to duck behind the nearest shelf, sucking back an unusual urge to cry.

"So bold to invite yourself into places you don't belong, yet you hide from me like a frightened mouse?"

Too shaken by the simple notion of being caught where she

didn't belong, Nessix couldn't form a reply. This response was absurd—she knew it on every level but the one which allowed her to react—after the trials she'd lived through. She'd survived combat with dire odds against her. She'd been a captive of demons. She'd had the foolish idea to *run* from those captors. Yet the idea of being found snooping in a place that was off limits flashed her back to such childish remorse and fear? Knees trembling, Nessix tried to fight this response and regain authority when she was finally able to latch on to a very peculiar aspect of this interaction. She'd understood this man flawlessly. Brows furrowing, it took Nessix two attempts to bundle up the courage to peer around the bookshelf to appraise him.

He was middle aged, face weathered and eyes elaborating on stories Nessix had yet to hear. A squatty top hat sat off center on his head and he wore a wool overcoat with patches wrapped around the buttonholes and one on his right elbow. One button didn't match the others. Ink stained half of his right hand and he was built lanky and tall. As Nessix looked him over, her combat expertise asked her why she'd been so afraid of him. No matter how experience teased her, Nessix remained tucked behind the bookshelf as she asked her question.

"You speak my tongue?"

"Obviously." He puffed the word out with a casual arrogance.

Nessix narrowed her eyes and leaned farther from her hiding spot. The man's hair and skin were too pale for him to be a native of Elidae, and only a scant few humans and demons had any way to know her language. "Who are you?"

The man's eyes lost their stern edge at the notion of playing a game. "Who are *you*?"

An immense urge to spout her lineage and life history struck Nessix so hard she thought she'd choke on it, but that overwhelming willingness tripped her caution. She'd quit questioning the reaches of magic after she'd been brought back to life—repeatedly—by the demons, but that didn't mean she understood it. This man's voice was somehow influencing her, and she was determined to fight it. Clenching her teeth, she buckled down on her stubborn silence. If he wanted to escalate this, she'd draw him to her and take him out the quick way.

The faintest hint of a smile joined those eager eyes, and when the man spoke next, it was with a lighter tone. "These *are* restricted stacks, child. You'd be wise to answer me before I'm forced to send for the authorities."

Considering Nes's appraisal of this city's peacekeepers, that threat meant little to her. "Even though I've got the impression the authorities aren't aware of this part of the library?"

The man raised his chin—an approving gesture—and crossed his arms. "You are an impossible one to read and you seem rather disinclined to cooperate. So I'll ask you again to save us both the trouble. What are you searching for?"

Nessix gnawed on the inside of her cheek, weighing what to do next. Her suspicions of this man ran high, but she had entered the library specifically for information on how to reach Zeal. "I take it you're the librarian?"

"I am," the man said. "And my job is to keep the information of Abaeloth in order and help inquisitive minds find what they seek."

Nessix cast a hasty glance back at that mysterious shelf she'd been drawn to, hungering for what was hidden in those books. She looked back at the man, found his brow half cocked, and sighed. Her mission was an urgent one, and if the librarian was willing to help her, she'd be a fool to anger him.

"I need to reach Zeal," she said. "A map or directions to guide me would be greatly appreciated." She grimaced and gripped the strap of her pack, realizing she had a problem she'd never had to deal with before. "I… I have no way to compensate you—"

The librarian burst into buoyant laughter that brought a shamed flush to Nes's cheeks. "This is a *library*, child! We don't *charge* for information."

Completely out of her element in the day-to-day functions of the civilian world, Nessix floundered for an excuse that wouldn't give her away. "Oh." She winced at how ignorant she sounded and tried again. "That's not how libraries on Elidae are run."

The weak excuse was reflected in the laughing glitter of the librarian's eyes. "Is that so?"

That same, childish shame washed over Nessix, flooding her cheeks with red, and she lowered her eyes and gave a wobbly nod.

The librarian gave her a moment to alter her story but when she kept her mouth clamped shut, he allowed her to stick to her fib. "I would be happy to transcribe a map for you." He smiled as Nes's eyes, sparking with gratitude, flew to his. "It will take a day or two to get it just right, but it will be free of charge."

Dismay mingled with that gratitude as Nessix fought back her urge to demand he find a way to work faster. She couldn't tell him she was on the run from demons, not for his safety or her own. Besides that, she didn't know where else she'd find someone willing to simply hand her such a valuable resource. She had no way to tell how long it would take Kol to investigate Elidae and figure out that she'd run, but she didn't doubt his intelligence or tenacity. He would expand his search for her the moment he suspected she'd left the island. With her limited resources, Nessix resorted to praying that she had the time to spare.

"I've got a modest scholar's chamber in the back upstairs, if you're worried about room and board," the librarian said, intercepting the panic gaining momentum in Nes's core.

His words calmed that maelstrom, though her fear lingered, and as Nes's heart settled, so did her mind. This was as safe a place as she could hope to find, and she had to take advantage of it. "Thank you…"

"Zenos." The librarian held his ink-stained hand forward, glared at it, then swapped it out for his left.

Nessix accepted his hand with a sheepish smile. "I'm…" Giving her name to strangers was a terrifying concept when she expected the demons and their torturous interrogations to come storming after her. "I'm Cora," she said, delivering her late mother's name.

Zenos hesitated once more as he let Nessix decide if that was her final answer before gesturing toward the stairs. "Well then, Miss Cora. Let me show you to the most average cot in all of Seaton, get you some warm food, and let you sleep away the stress of your travels while I get to work."

Nessix narrowly caught her frown from escaping, tactically

keeping the appreciative smile on her lips. She didn't *want* to eat or sleep, no matter how her weary body delighted in the suggestion. She wanted to read what was hidden in these books. As it was, she owed Zenos obedience for the favors he was doing her. Breathing out her disappointment, Nessix sent a longing glance at the last shelf, then followed Zenos up the stairs. A full night's rest would do her good.

FOUR

Kol couldn't put a name on the ache in his heart or the nauseating void plaguing his gut, and he knew better than to try. He was comfortable with the story he and Annin had fabricated, even if his mind still reeled with stubborn disbelief that they'd had to fabricate a story at all. He carried what he could of this confidence, fueled by it to keep from screaming to the sky for Nessix to come back to him, all the way to the foothills of the mountains and during a substantial part of the climb home. As Grell's lumbering form became clear, standing on the rocky outcropping before the portal, all of that confidence shriveled to dust. Kol balked and sucked in a sharp breath, second guessing his decision to come back empty handed.

"Keep steady." Annin's even tone suggested he'd spotted the inoga and that he had more faith in their plan than Kol did.

Of course he's calm... Kol thought bitterly. *He still has a chance to talk his way out of this...*

"Our report is solid."

Kol couldn't motivate himself to look at his companion. "But Grell's response is still an unknown."

Annin squinted to fight the glare of light coming off the mountains. "He won't kill you. He can't afford to, at least not yet. Let me put the idea of launching an organized force in his head, and he'll settle before any permanent damage is done."

That did little to comfort Kol, but it was too late to turn back. Running from Grell would only confirm his guilt, and then he'd be too busy staying on the move to look for Nessix. Damn, he missed her…

"Will you be able to sort yourself out enough to deliver the report? Grell's going to expect it from you."

Truthfully, Kol doubted he'd be able to, but he had no other option. He'd survived the Divine Battle—or at least came close to it. He could survive delivering a lie to a simpleton such as Grell, provided he remained calm.

Kol concentrated on doing just that as they climbed the rest of the footpath. If he tried to speak, he feared he'd fall apart, and he used the steady throb of pain in his wing to ground himself. For now, that pain would remind him how badly he wanted to stay alive. It would remind him of what he could overcome. It would remind him, a bitter corner of him thought, that Nessix was due for her own dose of pain the moment he got his hands on her again. Kol breathed out a relieved sigh as anger found him at last.

Grell didn't speak as Kol and Annin reached the landing, though his domineering presence prevented them from doing anything other than stop in front of him. Winded and worn, neither had made any effort to clean themselves up in favor of illustrating the struggle they'd allegedly suffered. Annin, in an unusual bout of selflessness, was the first to look away, hanging his head and hunching his shoulders as though he was a dog expecting to be whipped. Kol kept breathing, though the air didn't feel like it would sustain him for long. He swallowed his fear and doubt, and raised his chin as high as he was able. After all, he and Annin had just survived harrowing combat.

The inoga's eyes seared the sorry pair, his lip curled in disgust that they'd taken a beating which hadn't been delivered by his hands. "The two of you are alone."

Kol dug into the story he and Annin had concocted and unflinchingly answered the accusation which lurked in Grell's words. "We were ambushed by the Order. The troops were lost, and we were lucky to escape with what little damage we took."

"Lucky..." Grell spat to the side and cocked his head, sneer suggesting he'd have preferred both Annin and Kol to have perished rather than return to him without Nessix. "So you *ran*?"

This was a scenario they hadn't discussed, but it wasn't Kol's first time twisting the truth—or in this case, a lie—to ensure Grell heard what he wanted. "We found where Nessix's guards had been slaughtered, the scene of a struggle, and no sign of her. We were returning to report to you when the Order struck."

Grell's eyes narrowed to slits as he contemplated Kol's tale, but the alar held himself with the calm confidence he'd conditioned into himself. Perhaps, this time, Kol was telling the truth, and the truth was something Grell couldn't argue with, no matter how badly he wanted to. He grunted his opinion of this fact, and Annin raised his head at last.

"If I might make a suggestion, my lord?"

Kol held his breath as Grell's attention snapped to the oraku. Annin had claimed he'd be able to tiptoe around Grell's ire, but Grell was anxious to vent his anger on someone.

"Will it fix this?" Grell asked.

"It can lead us in that direction," Annin said.

Grell scoffed. "Then talk."

"I suggest we organize a task force, something more powerful than a handful of guards, to attack Elidae and distract the Order. A secondary force can infiltrate the townships and fortresses to search for Nessix." He was careful to avoid any mention of the temple, knowing that if anyone so much as reminded Grell that Etha's holy sanctuary existed, they'd have a riot on their hands.

"A task force, huh?" Grell crossed his arms and craned his head from side to side. "Yeah. I think I could arrange that."

Annin nodded respectfully and interjected with the smoothness he often used against inoga. "Whatever fighters you assign to the assault can be as disposable as you'd like, but I'm requesting to personally select those sent to infiltrate."

To this day, Kol admired the way Annin so fearlessly contradicted Grell's will, even more so that Grell seldom caught that he was doing it. It was a trait Kol envied, but one he'd never have the chance to achieve. After all, the reason Grell was so strict with Kol was because of insecurities tied to their past, when Kol was in charge and Grell subservient to him. Annin had never held power over Grell in their mortal life, and somehow, that had granted him power in this one.

Grell's brows shot upward with the spark of an idea, an unusual expression to see from the brute. "As disposable as I'd like! Ha!"

Kol glanced at Annin, whose pale eyes were suspicious at the sudden change in Grell's demeanor. Neither of them spoke, waiting for Grell to cease his self-satisfied chuckling and explain himself.

"Those akhuerai of yours." Another chuckle interrupted his words and he let his arms fall to his sides. "They came back safe and sound from their first mission. Tore up Heiligate *and* razed a village. You were right. They've got promise."

In his concern over finding Nessix, Kol had let the akhuerai's past mission completely slip from his mind, and he looked away. That army owed its success to Nessix's influence, and he was certain they'd long for her now more than ever after the acts the demons had coerced them into committing. There would be no delicate way for Kol to raise that concern, at least not one that didn't risk reigniting Grell's anger. As simple as the inoga had let himself become, however, Kol's awkward avoidance to meet his eyes poked a stick at that fire.

"You know…" Grell reached a hand out to slap Kol's shoulder. "I'd venture a guess that they're wanting to see that general of theirs awful badly."

Out of all of the times for Kol to lose his confidence, this was quite possibly the worst, but try as he might, he couldn't lift his head high enough to meet Grell's eyes. "That is what we promised them." Beside him, Annin shifted his weight, and Kol could only hope that he wasn't preparing something foolish.

"I suspect that after their success, their confidence is running high. Possibly high enough for us to send them to Elidae, tell them they can have their general back if they can find her."

"Sir," Annin said. "I don't think—"

"I wasn't asking anyone's opinion on it, oraku." Grell still kept a conceited tone that rang of how clever he thought he was, and

Annin pinched his lips together to keep from exacerbating a situation that was best left untouched.

Kol sighed out a slow breath. He suspected Annin had been about to argue against sending them out where the Order could get a hold of them. Based in chaos or not, each of the akhuerai were still in tune with their mortal pasts and it was possible they'd reach out to the Order for help—assuming the Order would be willing to listen. If those noxious knights got a hold of even one of these soldiers and reported what they found to Zeal...

But Grell hadn't been asking for opinions. Kol snuck another glance at Annin and found his friend's head bowed, though this time it wasn't with a feigned sense of submission. This time, it was with a coarse anger that only his desire to stay alive kept him from expressing. This project had been too intense to waste on something like Grell's impulsiveness, but if either Kol or Annin tried to stop him, it would be put to a more abrupt end by their deaths.

"Come, gentlemen." Grell swatted Kol's shoulder once more and turned with the expectation that he and Annin would follow. "Let's go have a chat with those soldiers you've made."

Grell sauntered off and after a moment to gather his bearings, Kol stepped after him. He didn't reach out to Annin, sensing that the oraku was unreceptive to such empty reassurance or even encouragement, but before he'd cleared the portal, Annin's footsteps followed after him.

The three walked in silence through the halls, demons of every faction scurrying out of their way as they passed. Kol caught the looks shot their way, some pitying, others amused. It seemed as though word had gotten around that Kol's days might be numbered. He couldn't gauge how much of this was based on rumors and how much had been declared by Grell's tongue, and he didn't let himself inquire anyone about it as they passed.

Kol was weary from his anxiety, weary from his frantic search across Elidae. The fight he'd had with his soldiers had drained him physically, the wound on his wing sapping his strength, and the trek to the akhuerai's chasm passed slowly on legs that burned in protest at the idea of moving. After an excruciating journey down halls he might never see again, what remained of Kol's confidence dragged bloody on the stone floor behind him, the three demons stopped at the chasm's edge. Grell turned a judgmental eye to Kol.

"That tattered wing able to carry you or do I have to?" he asked, the hint of a laugh on his voice.

At any other time, Annin would have snorted over the jab, and the fact that the oraku kept still ruffled Kol. Beyond risking humiliation, not one part of Kol trusted Grell right now, and he'd much rather take his chances on a crash landing than whatever the inoga's depraved mind had come up with. "It will carry me fine."

The humor flashed from Grell's eyes and his smirk shrank at Kol's crisp reply, confirming his intentions. "Then let's get down there." Grell dove off the ledge, plummeting toward the crowd of startled akhuerai.

Attempting to understand the way Grell thought had always given Kol headaches. The perversions which came from becoming demons only intensified that effect. Kol looked to Annin to see if his sharper mind had any ideas of Grell's intentions, but Annin shrugged and briefly shook his head. Watching as the creations he'd invested everything in scattered helplessly at Grell's imminent arrival, Kol sighed and leapt into the air.

The tear in his wing burned as it beat against the air, the pain pulsing so brightly it threatened to cripple him. He wavered in his flight, the stomach-seizing threat of an uncontrolled drop igniting his reactions at last. He wouldn't cry out from pain or that brief wave of terror that came with the idea of falling. Not to spare himself the humiliation of the akhuerai or Annin hearing, but solely to rob Grell of the pleasure. His descent was graceless, and he was certain he'd need to take the stairs back up, but he landed safely, keeping his distance from Grell. Moments later, Annin landed nearby and walked over to offer what support he could.

"*This* rabble tore up Heiligate?" Grell grunted once the two were within ear shot.

Weary from their march and emotionally drained, the akhuerai didn't even pretend to not fear Grell. Kol didn't have a valid reason to be disappointed in the akhuerai's reaction, because there was a generous part of him that wanted to join them in cowering. As he scanned the pathetic group, he noticed an unsettling pattern—while their eyes remained locked on Grell for the most part, waiting for an attack, they flicked to Kol, full of a grudging trust that he'd do something to aid them. The pathetic longing he had for Nessix… his shameful fear of what Grell might do to him… and now the akhuerai were looking at him with the fringes of hope? As if Kol wasn't taxed enough by uncertainty.

"Which one of this lot is in charge?" Grell asked, granting Kol the briefest reprieve from the discomfort that came with his wavering resolve.

There was so much Kol couldn't control right now, but drawing out one akhuerai was something he could handle. He stepped forward. "Auden," he called, relieved at the authority that filled his voice. "We need a word with you."

"A word about that general of yours," Grell added.

Kol's lips pulled back in a slight grimace, but Grell's blunt enticement worked in their favor. Where Kol had expected to have to grease the wheel of Auden's compliance before the akhuerai summoned his nerve, Grell's bait pulled him out immediately.

The last time Kol had seen the makeshift commander, the akhuerai had been uncertain of his position and authority, riddled with self-doubt. The man who emerged from the group today, proudly armed with a hoe as if it were a spear, had grown tremendously from the single outing he'd been sent on, carrying himself with a degree of confidence Kol was unfamiliar with from the bulk of this crowd. Auden still met Kol's eyes no longer than half a heartbeat, and he didn't look at Grell at all, but he strode forward with erect shoulders and a steady gait. It was a change Kol had wanted to see in the akhuerai for some time, but it was more poorly timed than anyone could have hoped for.

"You spoke of my general." Auden's voice didn't quite demand his request, but neither did he beg or grovel for his answer. "Where is she?"

Grell took a step forward to stand beside Kol, and gave a gentle hum of intrigue at Auden's demeanor. "She's gone."

Auden's jaw dropped and he speared Kol with a loathing glare, one reeking of the betrayal Kol himself was still trying to come to terms with. The concepts of fear and respect and obedience escaped Auden as he carelessly flung that accusing snarl in Kol's direction. "We were told she'd come back to us if we obeyed!"

It was Kol's place to correct this matter, but admitting Nessix was gone was still more difficult than he'd thought it would be. Besides, he had no idea what Grell had planned, and the thought of further irritating the inoga wasn't one Kol was pleased to entertain.

"We'd love to give her back to you," Grell said, deep voice soft and scheming. "Only we don't know where she's run off to. Would you have any ideas?"

Auden's eyes widened and the outrage tapered from them, replaced by something Kol couldn't help but recognize as the faintest glimmer of victory. Before that glimmer caught fire, Auden snapped his jaw shut and glanced away from the demons. "I don't even know where you took her. How would I know where she is now?"

Grell chuckled and slapped his hand on Kol's shoulder, a gesture Kol was getting tired of accepting. "Kol, would you like to share with these wretches what you did with your pet?"

The hope and rebellious glint quickly flashed from Auden's expression at the words Grell had selected, and a surge of hatred welled up around him. Kol would have delighted in toying with that emotion if he'd have been able to control his own to relax enough to do so. Grell's fingers dug into Kol's shoulder, forcing his participation in this interrogation. The alar gulped down his reservations, hoping for his lies to stick.

"I escorted her to the surface of her homeland so she could see the same desperation you did. It would have been a successful mission, had her guards not fallen victim to an ambush that resulted in her abduction."

Auden's cheeks rapidly drained of color, but his eyes darted aside in consideration. His stunned reaction eased for the slightest moment, betraying a fact that Nessix couldn't have wanted uncovered. Grell patted Kol's shoulder and gave him a look so firm that the alar shrank an inch of stature from that force alone.

"Do you know something the rest of us don't, Commander?" Grell asked, his tone increasingly pleasant, though far more demanding than inviting.

Auden sucked in a quick breath as he attempted to reinforce his meager fortifications. "I don't remember the last time I saw Nessix," he said. "How could I know anything you don't?"

Grell chuckled and withdrew his hand from Kol so he could take a step closer to the akhuerai. "You may not have seen her last, but you knew her better than anyone but *that* cretin." He jerked his head in Kol's direction and crossed his thick arms as he glared down his nose at the frightened man before him.

"I don't know what you mean."

Kol had to give Auden credit for managing to stand against Grell's imposing stature without crumbling. This was a newfound strength he considered rather valuable, assuming he'd make it to the other side of this debacle to put it to use.

"So you know nothing?" Grell asked.

"Nothing," Auden declared.

Grell narrowed his eyes. "Nothing at all?"

Kol and Annin both held their breath. It was unusual for Grell to use this much patience with anyone, and this miserable fool was taking it for granted.

Auden shrugged and shook his head. "No."

Grell picked at his teeth with his tongue, nodding slowly as he looked first to Kol, then threw a shoulder back to look at Annin. Neither of his subordinates offered any complaint or desire to interfere, which suited Grell just fine. He couldn't do away with Kol quite yet, not when he truly was the best route to seeing this army to fruition, and he'd been eager to satisfy his frustration for a week now.

"That's a shame," Grell said. "You'd have liked to have known something."

Auden shifted his weight as if to call for reinforcements, but any attempt to do so was too slow. In a flash, Grell reached forward and grabbed him by his collar, yanking him forward to fling him to the ground. The hoe bounced from Auden's hands. Accustomed to Grell's methods of dealing with problems, Kol and Annin calmly stepped aside to clear a place for Grell to carry out his whims, thankful someone else was on the receiving end of it.

Auden scurried forward and groped frantically for his polearm. Before he found either his feet or his weapon, Grell's massive foot connected with the akhuerai's side, cracking his ribs and propelling the breath from his lungs. Auden rolled to his side, arms gingerly wrapped around himself, as Grell loomed over him. With a casual swat, the inoga flung Auden to his back then tore open the wheezing akhuerai's shirt.

Kol had seen this frenzied madness in Grell once before and suspected the inoga had fantasized about ending an akhuerai since the time Kol had convinced him to spare Nessix. Even as weak as the akhuerai were, the act of physically ripping the soul out of a living being enticed Grell past his usual cruelty, and though Kol had no attachment to any of them other than Nessix—and had personally ended several unruly early trials—he couldn't tolerate Grell's blatant abuse of power. With Nessix gone, the akhuerai needed Auden. *Kol* needed Auden. He was the only person this army had learned to follow in Nessix's absence, and Kol doubted there'd be many volunteers to step forward to fill that role after this disaster. Kol leaned his weight forward and drew a breath to address Grell when Annin reached a thwarting hand against him.

He kept the gesture subtle and low, his jaw clenched and upper lip curled with thoughts identical to Kol's. Grell was making a terrible mistake, one that would fall back on them to fix in the long run, but the inoga had lost himself in his frenzy. The results of his actions could be balanced out if Kol was smart and Annin was careful, but if either of them attempted to stop him, they'd never have that option.

Grell didn't waste any time, didn't bother to savor the moment. Massive fingers pinching the metal ring, he plucked the soul vessel from Auden's chest. The man's scream bounced off the chasm walls, dropping the weaker willed of his peers to their knees in devastation and chasing those with weaker spines into hiding. Grell cringed at the shrill tone and slammed his fist into Auden's face to silence him. Pain from the strike wouldn't have registered through the shock of losing his soul, but the snap of his jaw adequately reconfigured the structure of his mouth enough to change the pitch of his wailing to something slightly more tolerable.

41

Blood spurted freely from the hole in Auden's chest as he gasped for breath. His frantic hands instinctively clawed at the wound, but Grell swatted them away until the akhuerai commander's eyes glazed over with the loss of coherence and his body sagged in a heaving, limp mass.

Grell stood and turned with a grand flourish, dangling the precious pendant that contained half of Auden's soul before him for all to see. "Annin, Kol. Haul this bastard to his feet."

Neither demon was surprised by Grell's brutality, but both were alarmed enough to obey without debate. Auden—or what was left of him—wouldn't die in the conventional sense of the word until both portions of his soul were freed from their vessels. Until that happened, he would be a walking corpse, a mindless shell moving through preconditioned habits and involuntary actions. Grell meant to make an example of Auden, and as the stunned and sobbing akhuerai quaked where they stood, it seemed he'd succeeded. Kol and Annin rushed over to hoist Auden to his feet before Grell felt the need to make examples of them, too.

"Is anyone else here going to tell me they have no idea where their general's gone?" Grell asked, the eerie warmth returning to his voice and demeanor.

Not so much as a breath was heard from the terrified masses as they gawked at their drooling commander where he slumped between the two demons they'd previously feared more than anything else.

"*Nobody*? Not even one of you has the inkling of an idea where she's gone?"

Still no answer, and Grell heaved a sigh. Kol opened his mouth to gently encourage Grell to let him try to find the akhuerai's compliance, but Annin swatted him with a wing to silence him. A generous moment passed while Grell gave the crowd the opportunity to comply, but he didn't receive a response until he released his grip on Auden's soul vessel and let it clink on the ground.

A communal gasp filled the chasm as everyone watched in horror for Grell's next move.

"Hold him good, boys."

In the silence of the chamber, Grell raised his booted foot above the soul vessel and Auden watched on with the ignorance of a newborn. Grell raised a brow and carefully scanned the tense crowd for anyone who appeared willing to talk. Nobody moved. Nobody spoke. It was questionable whether or not anyone breathed. Grell shrugged and, with a grunt of exertion, slammed his foot down on top of the pendant. Reinforced by veins of the god spear Affliction, the bauble didn't give with the first stomp, irritating Grell even more. Snarling, he raised his foot again and concentrated the bulk of his weight on the impact.

A glimmering mist swirled around his foot and Auden cried out, not in pain this time, but with the heartbroken strain of an unfathomable loss. His legs buckled, and Kol and Annin struggled to support the rapid plummet of his weight.

Grell smirked in satisfaction and lifted his foot, expecting to see tiny crystal shards crushed on the floor. The vessel held its shape, but fine cracks split through its surface to allow the soul to seep free. The cloud hung close to the blessed bauble, reaching confused tendrils out into the air. Grell figured another two strong stomps would finish it, but before he could lift his foot again, a trembling voice rang out through the muffled sobs.

"Wait! I know! I know where that bitch went!"

Kol nearly dropped Auden as hope slammed him so heavily in the chest he choked on a gasp. Betrayed glares tried to stop the former fleman, but nobody made any physical attempts to restrain him as he scrambled through the crowd. He threw the shovel he'd been armed with to the ground and held his hands open before himself, terrified eyes wide, pleading, and painfully honest. Grell smiled and placed his foot down beside the damaged pendant.

"And where is that, friend?"

The man balked at being labeled a friend of the demons, but as hatred from the rest of the akhuerai beat against his back, he knew he had no friends left among them. His frantic eyes looked at Auden's vessel as it bled out his soul, flicked to where the commander mumbled incoherently, slumped between Annin and Kol, and realized how dangerous the hatred of his peers had become now that they knew what their rings were for. He'd once criticized Nessix for suggesting she was going to try gaining the demons' trust, tried to rally the others against her for it, and now, he was going to do the same. He stepped closer to Grell than he'd ever willingly gotten to a demon in all of his pathetic existence.

"Zeal, my lord. She's seeking the White Paladin."

Grell's nostrils flared, his eyes engulfed in fury, and the fleman man hit the ground, groveling for his life. The rage, however, wasn't directed at him. Grell spun to face his subordinates, and Kol gagged on a brisk influx of bile. With the ocean no longer imprisoning Elidae from the rest of Abaeloth, Nessix's quest was not impossible. With connections to the Order currently residing on Elidae, getting her to Zeal was not improbable. And with the determination which had so enticed Kol still thriving inside of her, reaching Mathias, if that was truly Nessix's intent, was a grim reality. Grell let that guilt settle in Kol a moment longer before turning back to look over the akhuerai army.

They gaped at the trembling fleman at Grell's feet, faces pale as they struggled to grasp how and why he had turned on their courageous leader and confirming the man's words as truth. Grell wasn't the kind to keep pets or take pity on the weak, and it was well within the realm of his character to sign this snitch over to the punishment of his peers. His groveling proved his cowardice, an unforgiveable trait in the mind of a demon, but Grell might be able to find more uses for the traitorous fool. He crammed his toes beneath the akhuerai's chin and tilted his face upward.

"Do you know more about that woman's intentions?"

The man gulped, painfully aware of his vulnerable position, and nodded.

Grell grunted and moved his foot so he could crouch and retrieve Auden's cracked soul vessel. On his way back to standing, he grabbed the fleman's arm with his free hand and dragged him to his feet. "Let that miserable lump go. His loyal friends will see to his well-being, I'm sure," Grell told Kol and Annin.

Still trying to come to terms with the fact that Nessix had not only run from him, but had done so with such devious intentions, Kol released his grip on Auden from muscle memory alone. Auden wobbled on legs that no longer remembered how to manage a man's weight and yelped as he toppled to the ground. Kol made no reaction, too preoccupied with how quickly his own peril was compounding to care about anything else.

Grell tossed Auden's vessel to Annin, who scrambled to catch it. Disobedient or not, no akhuerai had been raised without tedious effort on Annin's part and he considered them investments he'd prefer to get his full value from. "See what you can do about closing that up again, then bring that magic bowl of yours to my quarters."

Annin cleared his throat to keep from yelling at Grell's carelessness, focusing all the energy and concentration he could spare on containing this portion of Auden's soul. "Sir, we cannot scry her—"

"Bah! I don't plan to scry her. But if she's heading to Zeal, I've got to make sure there's a proper welcome waiting for her."

Annin might have felt a degree of possession over the akhuerai as a whole, but Nessix still belonged to Kol. Reaching her was the only thing that mattered to him, and if he'd had a way to do so, he'd have already taken it. "Logistics won't allow for us to—"

Grell snapped his attention to the alar, darkness returning to his eyes. "Stop your bitching, Kol. I've got connections beneath Gelthin that can see it done. This project of yours has gained quite a bit of attention among my peers. I'm sure any of them would be pleased to trade their efforts for yours."

There were guarantees with Grell, certainties Kol had learned how to work with for the most part. A quick glance at Annin's wide eyes told him he was thinking the same thing. As if they weren't serving enough of a death sentence, being sent to work under a foreign inoga, one who recognized them solely as resources to exploit, would seal their fates for the worse.

Kol couldn't stop himself. "But sir—"

Grell swung his massive shoulders around, a victorious smile hanging on his face so obnoxiously that Kol had to hold back the urge to punch it off of him. "But *what*? Are you frightened to work under someone else? Afraid they won't be as good to you as I am?" When neither Kol nor Annin answered, fists and shoulders trembling in poorly executed restraint, Grell's grin broadened. "My new friend and I are going to go get to know each other. He's going to tell me some interesting stories, and Annin's going to bring me that bowl so I can do things *right*. If all of this scares you, Kol, you'll just have to figure out a way to find that pet of yours before anyone else does."

And before she finds Mathias.

The implication was in Grell's eyes and whispered in Kol's heart, but the inoga was content to simply leave it hanging over them. Digging his fingers into the fleman's skin, Grell launched into the air. The fleman shrieked in terror as he dangled from Grell's grasp. His screams didn't fade until well after they'd reached the top of the chasm, echoing the fear that threatened to devour Kol.

"I should kill you here and now," Annin said once the screams had tapered down the hallway.

Kol looked out across the stunned akhuerai as a trio of burly men crept forward to tend to their crippled commander. Auden voiced a cheerful sound at them, flailing an uncoordinated hand in greeting. Kol's army, the war machine he'd spent the past hundred years designing and accumulating, was falling apart. And Nessix was still gone.

"Please do," he murmured.

Annin was used to Kol's cryptic nature, but not this air of defeat. Witnessing such weakness awakened an unsettling discomfort in the oraku, and he knew only one way to combat it. "I have to obey Grell. You know that."

Kol sneered, but didn't criticize Annin.

"I have to obey him for our safety and for the safety of our objectives. If it makes you feel any better, I have to obey him for Nessix." He hissed her name with a loathing that caught Kol's attention in the worst ways, though he allowed Annin the opinion. "Go back to your quarters, tend to that wing, but don't let yourself fall asleep."

Kol shook his head and blinked. This lecture had flowed exactly the way he'd foreseen until that last remark. "Are you afraid Grell will kill me in my sleep?"

"No. I've got another plan, but I need you exhausted for it to work."

Annin had served Kol across lifetimes, and while Kol didn't always understand his reasoning, he seldom questioned it. Past experience had proven Annin a competent and clever companion, and if he said he needed Kol tired in order to locate Nessix... Exhaustion tugged at Kol at the notion of sleep, but the desire to live, to see Nessix again, pulled even harder.

"I guess I'm staying awake," Kol said.

"Good. Let's not wait around for the akhuerai to get over what just happened."

In full agreement, Kol and Annin hastened to the stairs and climbed out of the dreary chasm.

FIVE

Nessix couldn't remember the last time she'd enjoyed restful sleep, but when she woke in the modest scholar's chamber, she felt warm and strong for the first time in weeks. For Zenos's claim of offering only average comforts, Nessix had no complaints as she stretched and rose to find a simple breakfast of bread and fruit waiting for her. Stomach rumbling, she contented herself with eating the offering and quietly opened the door to peek into the library.

It was busier this morning than it had been the previous night—if Nessix could consider two visitors and the librarian's active presence as busy—and seeing normal people go about normal activities settled part of what Nessix had considered wrong in her world. Shoving the last bite of food in her mouth and wiping her fingers on the legs of her filthy breeches, Nessix left the room to search for a way to occupy her time and prevent her pressing worries from taking root in the day's peace.

As pleasant as the entire experience was panning out, the first true sigh of relief Nessix had been allowed in months, she didn't cope well with boredom. As a mortal general, people had jumped to serve her. As an akhuerai, she'd immersed herself in the plight of her peers so deeply that she hadn't had time to herself. Surrounded now by an immense load of knowledge—none of which she could easily read—Nes's options consisted of fretting over how each second Zenos took transcribing her map brought the demons closer to her or sitting in dull silence. In this case, silence was preferable. Barely.

Besides the dull atmosphere, Zenos made good on his offer to provide Nessix with her basic needs as she waited. He kept her fed and sheltered, and he checked often to see if she wanted anything other than her map. He respected her reluctance to speak of her past, but that left little for them to discuss. Nessix made it through half of that first day like this before breaking down to scour the books in Zenos's collection for something she could understand more than an occasional word from. She gave up after an hour of searching and settled on a book filled with faded illustrations of bizarre creatures.

Zenos looked up as Nessix brought her selection back to the table she'd previously been tapping in agitation and smiled. "Ah, *The Encyclopedia of Abaeloth's Living Wonders.* Excellent selection, Miss Cora."

Nessix sat down with the book and sighed. Her mother's name didn't suit her, and she was grateful she wouldn't have to use it much longer. She flipped the book open and studied the first picture. "I do hope the author was a better writer than he was an artist," she said absently.

Zenos lowered his quill to glower at Nes's blunt critique, but she'd already absorbed herself in studying the physical attributes of the creatures illustrated within. "It was one of the author's earlier works," he said. "He improved immensely over time."

Nessix didn't return the banter, imagination engaging with the beasts awkwardly depicted on the pages. The less she distracted Zenos, the faster he could work, and so Nessix tried hard to entertain herself with the sketches. She finished looking through the pictures with an hour remaining of the day. Having spent lengthy time and frustration locating this single volume, the thought of resuming the tedious task of finding another didn't please her. Hushing her grumbles beneath respect for the man who had agreed to help her, Nessix flipped back to the first page to begin the headache of studying the script the way Kol had taught her.

It was between the pages of what Nessix interpreted as a tree-climbing fox and a thirty-foot-tall woodpecker that Zenos allowed himself a loud yawn and stretched his arms out in an obnoxious fashion. Jarred from her studies, having not quite realized how deeply she'd been concentrating, Nessix blinked and looked up at him with a start.

"It's getting rather late, child." Zenos pushed his seat back to stand. "Your book will be here in the morning. You should get to sleep."

As if by magic, Zenos's suggestion weighed Nes's eyelids and the effort it took to keep them open hardly felt worth the effort. She rubbed her eyes with her wrist and stood. "And my map?"

"You can come take a look at it, if you'd like." Zenos stepped aside from his desk and gestured to the map.

Nessix accepted the offer, each step dragging more than the last. She'd never gotten this worn from studying before. Then again, her mortal studies had been fueled by tactical development and those she'd done in the hells had been driven by an earnest need to soak in as much information as possible. Never before had Nessix been able to simply sit down and enjoy a book—even if she'd been unable to actually read it. For all she knew, exploring the realm of fantastic possibilities truly was this exhausting. She reached the desk and her eyes widened in awe.

Elidae had talented cartographers, and she'd kept several in her employ during her time as General. She had grown up exposed to all kinds of maps, from ancient relics left from her ancestors' lives on Drailged, to sea charts that had been retired due to Havoc's ceaseless watch over the island, all the way to those she carried with her on campaigns. She'd never had complaints of her cartographers' skills until she gazed down at the perfection created by Zenos's hand.

The map depicted the continent as a whole, identifying Gelthin as the one Nessix had seen on the second bookshelf in the Forgotten Histories. The coastlines seemed to glitter where waves would crash against the shores, and Nessix had to hold her hands together to keep from touching the illusion of the mountains rising from the parchment, afraid the ink hadn't yet dried. Even the forests and grasslands appeared to nod about in a gentle breeze. She must have been more tired than she thought. Several small marks were scattered across the land, and Nessix assumed they indicated where cities stood. She was too overtaken by the map's perfection to fuss at Zenos for how much time he'd taken.

"Are my artistic skills better than the author of the encyclopedia you were browsing?" Zenos asked from behind Nessix.

Weariness limited Nes's expression to little more than a smirk and softened eyes. "Much better." She turned to Zenos to meet his warm smile. "And you'll have it done tomorrow?"

"It will be done tomorrow," he confirmed proudly. "And then I'll be able to send you on your way, if my company has been so dull to you."

Nessix let her eyes close with a soft laugh, the move nearly knocking her from her feet, and she jerked awake as Zenos's gentle hand pressed against her shoulder to keep her from falling. "You've been lovely company," she said. "More accommodating than most I've dealt with in my past. Thank you for your assistance."

"Helping the curious find knowledge is my vocation. Now. Go get your sleep. If you plan on reaching Zeal, you have a lot of walking ahead of you."

At peace, soaking in the intoxicating sensation of safety and warmth for the first time in months, Nessix thanked Zenos once again and trudged back to the quarters he'd set aside for her. By all her recollection, Nessix fell asleep before she'd even pulled the quilt around her shoulders.

* * * * *

The following morning, Nessix woke with a start, battle sense scolding her for sleeping so deeply. She'd been so desperate for help when she'd first arrived in Seaton, so weary from worry, that she hadn't questioned Zenos's intentions after he'd promised her a map to Zeal. In just over a day's time, she'd somehow grown comfortable enough with this stranger that she slept soundly through the night, despite being on the run. That was terribly out of character for her, which meant that there had be something more to Zenos than she'd first expected.

Nessix passed on the offer of breakfast this morning, satiating herself with her own rations and an inch of dream stop. A handful of patrons milled through the shelves, quietly keeping to themselves when Nessix left the tiny room. Zenos was back at his desk, working on her map, and he didn't even glance at her as she entered the main body of the library. She slowed as she came up behind him, doing her best to compare the map he was making her to the image he copied it from. They matched identically, easing the whisper of paranoia that suggested he was trying to set her up. Ashamed of herself for such thoughts, blaming them on her limited access to dream stop and the mistrust the demons had fostered in her, Nessix sighed and returned to her table from yesterday.

The encyclopedia of foreign beasts waited right where she'd left it, but the idea of subjecting herself to wading through the text, even if she was beginning to understand bits and pieces of it, did little to excite her.

Or, curiosity poked at her, *you could find a book from the Forgotten Histories.*

Nessix quirked her lips in a stubborn pout. She *had* been able to read several of those spines, most notably those on that last shelf bearing the comet and spear, written in the scripts Kol had taught her. Suspicion of Zenos returned and Nessix looked up to stare at him as he contently worked. As much as he spoke of assisting those who sought knowledge, he'd certainly gone out of his way to keep her away from those books. For what reason? What sort of information did those volumes hold that Nessix was forbidden to read about? The pressure of her contemplative stare wore through Zenos's concentration and he looked up, meeting her eyes with a silent question.

Yes, child?

Flushing, Nessix dropped her head to feign interest in her book once more. She had to find a way to get down there. The obsession consumed her, as strong as her need to uncover Berann's identity and role in Kol's past. But as badly as she yearned to get her hands on those books, Zenos was willing to protect them just as fiercely, leaving Nessix to wonder if, in addition to all of the other uncanny quirks about him, he'd be able to. Nessix fidgeted in her seat and flicked a longing glimpse at the closed door. Did she dare risk sneaking down there again? As hospitable as Zenos had been, she doubted he'd take kindly to a second offense.

Nessix sighed, missing the power and influence of her old station, and thumbed through the pictures. Between each page, she'd glance up to study either Zenos or that attractive closed door before resigning herself to ignorance and turning her attention back to her book.

After her first review for the day, Zenos asked if she was bored, and she said no. After the second, he suggested she step outside for some fresh air, and she declined. In the evening, as Nessix came close to finishing the day's third pass through the same book, the crisp click of Zenos slapping his quill down on the desk interrupted the flip of Nes's page and she mentally rolled her eyes.

"I appreciate your concern for my sanity, but I assure you, I'm fine looking at these pictures until you're through." When Zenos didn't answer her, Nessix blinked away her eye strain and looked up.

The librarian sat tall and straight, no longer lovingly hunched over his work, his eyes wide and focused sharply at the wall in front of him, as if he saw straight through it. Nessix glanced around the library to see if the other patrons considered his behavior unusual, but found that she and Zenos were alone. His eyes slowly scanned the wall, their intensity growing until the weight of the danger they sought seeped into Nessix, and his lips worked in quick murmurs that never left his mouth. Nessix regretted not bringing her sword out with her this morning.

Zenos's focus was trained so intently on this disturbance that Nessix suspected she'd have been able to sneak away, but as the muscles in his arm began to twitch, an old, forgotten side of Nessix recognized his energy at last. Zenos bore the same aura as Inwan had. Nessix had been found by a god.

Panic hit first, though her initial responses couldn't decide if she was more afraid of what powers he had over her or whatever it was he held in his divine sights. She sprang to her feet, knocking over her chair in the process, and Zenos spoke, still staring at the wall, before Nessix could bolt.

"Who *are* you?"

There was no warmth in the question this time around, only a crisp demand that the tiny part of Nessix that still registered as mortal trembled at. Lying to him would no longer work, especially if she hoped to make it to Zeal before the demons found her. She'd never learned anything about the children gods other than Inwan and had no way of guessing Zenos's true alignment or motivations off their limited interactions. He'd been cordial and kind to her so far, but that had been when they'd both pretended to be mortals. Nessix gulped at her gamble.

"My name is Nessix Teradhel. I am the late General of Elidae."

Zenos's lips puckered and his entire frame trembled, freezing Nessix where she stood. She'd expected some sort of divine lashing from his response, but what came instead was a misting of tears rolling free from his eyes.

"Blessed Mother…" He gave a vicious shake of his head. "You should have told me," he said with the same displeasure of a parent scolding their child. "Come with me. Come quickly!"

He pushed himself from the desk and hurried back toward the chamber he'd assigned to Nessix. Pursuant to the power she remembered from Inwan the few times he'd demanded her obedience, Nessix had no desire to argue, no inclination to even question why she followed him. She simply obeyed the order, pulled along by Zenos's urgency and a deep trust that he knew something terrible that she didn't. By the time Nessix made it through the door of the room, the god already had pieces of her armor in his hands and he didn't wait for her permission to begin strapping it onto her.

"You need to get out of town," he said curtly, investing twice the concentration on dressing her as he had on creating the map she needed.

Still overcome with the realization that she'd been

54

contemplating engaging in a battle of wits against a god, Nessix shook the tension from her hands and joined his efforts. "Have I done something to offend you?"

"Offend—" Zenos paused his actions to look up at Nessix from where he knelt on the ground securing a cuisse to her left thigh, brows furrowed. "No, child. Offense is the last thing you've done. You've brought answers. You've brought hope. But you've also brought danger."

"...Danger?" Nessix shook her head and her fingers froze on the buckle at her right thigh. That couldn't be. Not yet. Kol had left her on Elidae and hadn't expected her back for a week. He couldn't have been so close on her trail.

Zenos resumed his work. "Demons are coming, General. In force. For you, and anyone who tries to stop them."

Jarred back into action by the nearness of this alleged threat, Nessix rejoined Zenos's efforts, but her head kept shaking. Kol *couldn't* be there. It wasn't feasible. She followed Zenos with her eyes as he sprang upright to help with her breastplate. There was something greater behind his urgency, something she suspected he wouldn't tell her even if he owed it to her. His opinion was that she had to run, and the longer that idea hung in Nes's mind, the more she agreed with him.

"How much time do I have?" Nessix cursed herself for having been lulled into such comfort.

"A few hours at most. They're after you in earnest, and they haven't sent their usual soldiers."

Nessix shivered at the thought. Mortal men, if they kept their calm, were more than enough to take on an average demon soldier. Those trained in combat against demons could handle most alar on the ground, and a decent archer could shoot them from the sky. Master combatants and the lucky were equipped to face aranau troops, and a skilled magic user could neutralize an oraku. But demons a god was afraid of? That was reserved for the one class of the fiends Nessix had never been able to bring to their knees, and one she didn't even want to see Mathias try to take on. What had she done?

"A few hours..." she murmured. "Is that enough time to get

me to Zeal?"

Zenos stopped again and stared at Nessix in shock. "Zeal is halfway across the continent, child. That's why you must run."

All of that hope, all of that relief that this madness was near its end blew from Nes's grasp as she thought over the logistics of how to clear half the continent while staying ahead of these demons. Inoga were too temperamental and impatient to chase one objective for long, but if they'd already reached Gelthin, there would be proper search parties out for her soon. And all she had was a three hour lead on them. Zenos stood back and appraised the stability of Nes's armor, gave her a firm pat on the shoulders, and snagged her pack and sword belt. Handing them to her, he strode from the room, grabbing her wrist as he passed.

Conditioned from childhood to take a god's word without question, Nessix followed Zenos, his agitation breathing life into her fear. She'd been a fool to get so comfortable here, a fool for getting so distracted by those forbidden books. She still stood by her decision of withholding her identity from Zenos, but she did wish she'd have requested a more immediate solution to her map problem. Even while struggling to balance these regrets with her urgency, Nessix found a strange vein of peace from Zenos's words.

You've brought us answers. You've brought us hope.

Her plight, whether or not it was understood, was known beyond Mathias. That meant a solution might exist. That might mean Mathias hadn't given up on her.

Zenos led Nessix to a chest tucked beneath his desk, tapped the lid twice, and opened it. As he frantically dug through the bits and baubles, Nessix slung her sword belt around her waist, trying to draw on the familiar comfort of its weight. "What is the best way to get out of the city?"

"There's a gate at the eastern wall, after passing through the slums. Travelers don't use it, but the locals do for foraging in the woods. You won't be stopped there." A quick sigh streamed from Zenos, relief flickering in his eyes as he seized a bronze ring from the chest. He fogged its red stone with his breath and deftly buffed it on his palm before handing it to Nessix. "Put that on and never take it off."

Frowning, Nessix complied for no other reason than the fact that Zenos—who she'd blindly trusted this far—stood right in front of her. The ring was too big for her petite fingers and it spun loosely, even on her thumb. "May I ask what it's for?"

"Protection. Heed its warnings and it will keep you safe."

"Heed its—" Nessix stopped, fidgeting with the artifact. She knew better than to question a god.

Zenos turned from her to face the map. He tapped his thumb in ink and placed two prints on the previously precise image, one on the southern coast, the second two thirds of the way to the northern border, toward the eastern coast. "I'd have made it prettier for you if I'd had the time." He blew on the map to dry the ink then rolled it up and shoved it into Nes's hands, wrapping her fingers snuggly around it. "Forgive me for its imperfections. I've marked where you started and where you'll find Zeal. Other towns are only sketched in place, but the roads are all accurate. Now, child, run!"

Nessix balked at the order, fear launching up her throat. She didn't know where she was or how the roads to Zeal fared. She'd never had to travel anywhere by herself. Her entire life had been full of confidence and bravery, and now that she needed it most, she trembled at the concept of not being fast or strong or good enough to survive.

"You won't be if you don't get moving," Zenos said, extracting those unguarded fears the way gods were so adept at doing. "Be swift and know that you are being watched. Prove to Abaeloth you are a fighter, Nessix Teradhel. Reach Zeal and spite the demons. Go!"

It was an unconventional rallying speech, but it hit the right notes with Nessix. Clenching her fingers around the map, she made one final appraisal of her weapons and slung her pack over her shoulder. "Thank you, my lord," she said. Before fear had the chance to take her nerve away again, Nessix turned and ran, just as the god had ordered.

Zenos watched Nessix burst from the library. She disappeared down the street before the door fell shut, racing like any sane person who had an organized pack of inoga and their underlings on their heels would. Worn from the rush of his urgency, Zenos sat at his desk and stared at the wall once again.

He'd been asked to keep an eye out for the woman he'd just urged from town, told that she was of great importance, and now he'd just encouraged her—an untraceable soul, as far as his senses had been able to tell—from his reach. Etha would forgive him for the oversight, considering the circumstances, but Mathias would be livid. Zenos sighed.

There were still a few hours before the demons would arrive. Calming his mind in preparation for his sacred duty, Zenos pulled out a piece of parchment to begin recording the twilight of the current age.

SIX

Mathias strode into Seaton more content—more *hopeful*—than he'd felt since before Nes's death. Not only had he been spared a most unpleasant trip to the hells, but he was one conversation with the port master from a direct path to Nessix. The past year of torment and despair seemed lifetimes ago, and the fear that he'd never find answers or save the souls the demons had so blasphemously claimed flit from his mind. His spirits soared so high that his inner nag ridiculed him over how hard he'd tasked himself over this quest. Nessix was a crafty woman, a determined one; Mathias never should have doubted her ability to save herself.

Despite his brightened outlook, Sazrah's relay of the warning Nessix had given remained centered in the front of Mathias's mind. Nessix might be crafty and determined, but the demons were, too. Mathias had no doubt that she was of great value to them and that they'd stop at nothing to find her. If he was careful and kept a low profile until he got Nes to the safety of the Citadel, there was a chance he'd go unnoticed by the demons, sparing the collateral damage that would come from their retaliation to his involvement with whatever they had planned.

By the time Mathias made it past the city guards and into the bustle of the city, the sun had already begun its path to retirement. Mathias hurried through the crowds of last minute shoppers and eager tavern patrons, the longing for his life to be complete once again dragging him along blindly. He was so excited for his reunion with Nessix that the evening hour slipped his mind, and when he reached the port master's rickety station, a faded sign hung in front reading, "Gone home for the night."

Mathias's shoulders slumped as he craned his neck to peer down the dock to see if anyone was still active, but the workers had gone to the taverns and the sailors to their cabins, leaving Mathias alone and wanting on the shore. He debated trespassing for a moment, prepared to throw around his station if necessary, but that was bound to cause a scene he preferred to avoid. In all probability, Nessix hadn't arrived yet or, if she had, she'd have checked into the inn before getting on the road. Taking the honest route would be a rewarding change of pace after the amount of fast talking, brown nosing, and flat-out begging Mathias had carried out during his search. He'd waited this long to find Nessix. He could stand one more night.

Mind made up, but heart no less heavy, Mathias turned to seek the inn. Even if Nessix hadn't checked in, getting a sound night's sleep would do Mathias good. Most of the passersby kept to themselves as storefronts closed to the general public. Content that his plan of not standing out or gaining notice was working rather well, Mathias spotted a square, three-story building that must have been the portside inn, and made his way toward it.

The quick scamper of feet rushed his direction from an alleyway to his right, and Mathias stopped. A grunt and a gasp came next, followed by the thud of a body hitting the ground, and Mathias turned to face the alley. Seaton was sprawling and busy, but not known for violent crimes. He hung back against the wall of an adjacent cobbler's shop to gather what else he could.

A man's undertones rumbled menacing threats through the pressing darkness, though his words were unclear. Not long after, gasps and seething protests of a woman's voice answered. It was a shame this woman feared her attacker so much that she was unwilling to scream to alert anyone in the streets, but fortunately for her, Mathias had heard her subtle objections and didn't need to know anything else.

Mathias peeled away from his hiding spot and stood in the middle of the alley's entrance as the man dragged the woman to her feet by a fistful of dark curls. Her petite hands wrapped around his wrist and she flung her slight weight against him as he towed her deeper down the alley. Besides her frantic gasps and a gait irregularity Mathias assigned to a sprained ankle, the woman kept reasonably still, as though resigned to the fact that she had no choice in what was going to happen to her. Resigned or not, she was clearly distressed.

"You, sir!" Mathias strode into the alley, blinking as his eyes acclimated to the dimness. "Is there a problem?"

The pair's progress came to an abrupt halt at Mathias's question and the woman—not even a year on maturity's side of childhood—turned giant, horrified brown eyes to him. She sported fresh scrapes on her cheek and temple and favored her right leg, but otherwise appeared physically sound. The man, on the other hand, showed no signs of physical impairment and the expression he flung at Mathias was much less welcoming than the woman's frightened gaze. Given that the man could have easily been assumed the girl's father, Mathias doubted he'd stumbled upon a domestic dispute, and any father who treated his daughter in such a fashion deserved what was coming for him.

"A problem?" the man asked with a bitter chuckle. "Yes, there would be a problem."

Mathias eyed the girl calmly, easily understanding the look in her eyes. He didn't bother to draw his sword. "Might I be of assistance, then?" he asked, adjusting his gaze to fit the instigator.

The man spat on the ground. "Only if you can beat some sense into this little whore." He grabbed the girl's wrist as she tried to twist free from him and wrenched her head to the side with the hand in her hair, eliciting a cry from her at last.

A deep bed of anger bubbled up in Mathias's core, but his thoughts were abruptly intercepted by Etha's worried voice in his mind. *Oh… Mathias… You need to get out of there…*

Confused by Etha's unusual degree of concern over such a mortal dilemma, Mathias took a moment to study the man's stature and energy. He certainly didn't seem like a danger to one of the paladin's abilities. Mathias twitched a brow, trying to navigate Etha's warning. *I'll only be a moment longer. Nobody will be permanently hurt. You have my word.*

Pulling his mind back on track, Mathias met the man's eyes with a frown. "It's not in my nature to hit ladies," he said. "It seems to be a lesson you would benefit from learning."

The man growled at Mathias, though his grasp on the girl remained firm. "Calling this one a lady is a bit of an over—"

The last bit of civility Mathias had saved for this encounter disappeared in a snap. One insult to this helpless woman was enough, and Mathias would not allow a second to go unpunished, especially with the intentions this man obviously had in mind. Striding forward with the force of a charger, Mathias ended the man's statement with a solid punch to the jaw, sending him sprawling to the ground. Limp fingers released their hold on the girl as he fell.

Taking her chance, not waiting to see what other bold moves Mathias might try, the girl spun and stumbled away. Catching her wasn't a challenge for Mathias, as she was trying to run on an injured ankle and didn't have the dexterity to avoid the debris and obstacles strewn in the alley. He couldn't allow her to go running through the streets, injured and frightened by herself at night, not if what he'd just intercepted was a common occurrence in Seaton's nightlife. Mathias reached her in just a few lengthened strides and grabbed her by the shoulders to turn her to face him.

She hadn't screamed when she was in the hold of the lecherous man Mathias had rescued her from, but as she faced him now, she emitted a feral shriek and threw a flurry of misplaced blows his direction. Her strikes were weak, as though the idea of hurting someone frightened her. None connected in a manner which threatened even minor damage to Mathias, but her squirming was quite the annoyance.

"I don't mean you any harm," Mathias insisted, dodging a fist so it flew past his head. "I only want to tend to your injuries and make sure you're alright."

His gentle tone succeeded in stopping her aimless strikes, but those eyes that had so recently been filled with fear scathed Mathias with a ferocity he hadn't anticipated from such an outwardly timid woman. "I'm fine," she spat. She glared at him a moment longer, lips pursed in frustration. As her fists hadn't done any good at forcing her way free from Mathias, she resorted to wielding her knees.

"Would you knock that off?" The girl's awkward attempts were becoming more than a mere inconvenience, and Mathias reluctantly used physical force to twist her arms so he could pin her hands behind her back and watched as much of her profile as he could from his position over her shoulder. "I want to help you, if you'll let me."

"What if I won't?" Despite her disadvantage, she continued to squirm in Mathias's grasp. The authority which her words tried to convey, however, was betrayed by a trembling in her voice and arms.

"Then you'll have to come up with an excuse for what happened to your face and your foot tomorrow morning when your friends ask you why you're hurt."

She quit struggling as she contemplated Mathias's practical response. Injuries were never an easy matter to explain. Though she had experience with brushing them off, his offer seemed genuine and like something she wouldn't want to pass by. "Would you let me go?"

"That depends. Do you plan to try running off again?" She tensed beneath his grasp, the muscles in her back knotting up. "Who was that man?" Mathias asked gently.

"I don't know," she muttered, the loathing in her voice too strong to have been directed at Mathias. "What're you going to do to me?"

Mathias had already pieced together much of this puzzle, and the implication in the girl's question wounded his pride on a superficial level. Given the situation he'd rescued her from and that she had no reason to trust him off a single action, Mathias didn't correct her assumption. "I plan to feed you, treat those scrapes, and give you safe board for the night. At the very least, I'll help you get away from that man."

The girl pulled away from Mathias to contort her body around and look him over as well as she could. No man was as harmless and honest as he was trying to act. "I don't want your charity," she said. "You've already done too much. Please go away."

Mathias was nothing if not a stubborn champion of justice, and he wouldn't let this young woman talk him out of helping her so easily. "You've clearly been through a lot. More than you ever should have. And I swear by Etha's name that no harm will come to you while you are in my care. Please, let me do what I can to right that man's wrongs."

She gave one last, stout tug against Mathias's hold, stumbling forward as he released his grasp at last. Her sprained ankle gave out from the unexpected freedom, and this time, she allowed Mathias to catch her elbow to keep her from falling and she turned back to gape at him.

Having given up faith in men, she couldn't comprehend the compassion in his eyes, but there it was. If he'd wanted to hurt her, he'd had several opportunities to do so. As it was, the throbbing in her ankle was getting sharper, and she doubted it would hold her weight all the way back home. Her stomach rumbled at the promise of food. It was against her better judgement, but this man encompassed all that she'd once believed a man should be. Surrendering at last, she allowed this stranger to escort her to the warmth of the inn. She could sort out her problems after he fell asleep.

SEVEN

Demons as a whole weren't well suited for waiting, thriving best off instant gratification and the ability to avoid the irksome bother of worry. But worry had been bothering Kol nonstop, there was nothing at all gratifying about his situation, and waiting was the only option he had.

He'd returned to his chamber as Annin had instructed, cleaning his wound and stitching it closed the best he could. The pain of his procedure pricked hot at his senses, slowly dripping adrenaline into his system to stave off the exhaustion which hung over him like a gloomy cloud. Once he was through tending to his wound, nothing remained to occupy his mind besides trying to come up with some way to escape his endless loop of fretting.

It was an impossible task, and he ultimately gave up, fanning his wings wide to sink into the chair Nessix had used during her studies. He'd left her books closed and stacked neatly to the side, waiting for her to resume reading upon her return. Kol couldn't look at them. Instead, he stared down at the wood grains of the desk, repeatedly asking himself where he'd gone wrong, what signs he'd missed, whether or not Nessix had ever been loyal to him.

His eyes burned from exhaustion, begging him to drop his head down to rest on the desktop, and his dismal thoughts of Nessix were only interrupted by repeating to himself that he wasn't allowed to fall asleep. So many tasks demanded of him by other people, mocking the past when he'd been the one in charge. Kol should have listened to Berann all those centuries ago. He never should have voted for war.

Annin could have been entertaining Grell's whims for an hour or three days and Kol wouldn't have known the difference. The wait seemed to bleed on for torturous ages as Kol toiled over fears he could do nothing about. By the time his chamber door opened, his ears rang, his extremities tingled, and he could hardly muster the energy to glance up from where he slouched at his desk, let alone offer a greeting. He couldn't decide if his disregard of Annin's arrival came from simple exhaustion or his lack of concern for his well-being.

Whether or not Kol cared about his fate, Annin did, and he closed the door behind himself, bolting it shut.

"You're doing yourself no favors, dwelling on this the way you are." Annin didn't wait for an invitation to approach Kol, and he wouldn't have even if he'd expected the alar to deliver one. "Get up. Let's get you to your bed."

Kol blinked at the mention of his bed, his fatigued mind immediately rejoicing at the promise of the physical and mental comforts he craved. He braced his hands against the desktop and shoved the chair back with his thighs. Leaning on the desk for stability, he staggered around to the open part of his room and dragged his feet forward.

Annin frowned. The alar was a mess, and in hindsight, it was a good thing Grell had excused him from the scrying session. Kol had never functioned well when impassioned, and adding exhaustion to the equation was the fastest way for him to make a bad situation worse. With the door securely closed, Annin walked over to Kol and grabbed his arm to support him, doing so under the cover of looking over the crude stitch work used to repair his torn wing. Expressing vulnerability was considered disgraceful among demons, and Kol had already done a fine job displaying his for all the hells to see. Annin had neither the desire to listen to any more of Kol's pathetic prattle, nor to deal with the ominous sensations his friend's concern raised in him. He'd concentrate on his duties and nothing else. It's what he excelled at.

By the time Kol reached his bed, he had taken to leaning solidly on Annin's support, his feet barely lifting from the floor as he shuffled forward. His knees buckled instinctively as sleep finally came within his reach, and Annin released his hold, allowing Kol to topple forward onto the mattress. The alar drew in a deep breath and closed his eyes.

"Are you comfortable?" Annin asked as he pulled a stool over beside the bed.

"Does it matter?" Kol's voice was muffled by how he'd buried his face into the coolness of his pillow.

"It might. I have no way of knowing when you'll wake next."

Exhaustion took a temporary leave and Kol turned his head and opened his bloodshot eyes. Studying Annin's expression for his intentions was much more difficult without his mind functioning at full capacity. "What are you going to do to me?" Until now, Kol had thought Annin was the only living being who still wanted him alive.

"Why do you care?" Annin asked, as cryptic as ever. "You enthusiastically volunteered to try killing yourself to bring Nessix into our ranks, yet you're too afraid to fall asleep in order to find her again?"

Kol tried to sort through reasons to demand more of an explanation, but even his best efforts were met with crippling difficulty. Either way, Annin was right. Kol was willing to die for Nessix. Trusting the oraku more than he trusted himself, Kol closed his eyes.

"I'm going to take her soul vessel from you—"

As Annin reached forward, Kol spun to his side, hand flying to the pendant at his neck and clutching it possessively. "You never said that was part of the plan."

Annin sighed and rolled his eyes. "You never asked what the plan was. All you cared about was that I had one."

Kol shook his head, regretting the action as dizziness threatened to overpower him. "You *hate* Nessix."

"I do," Annin admitted freely.

Kol ground his teeth and snarled. "And after what Grell just did, what he must have said to you in my absence… No. You will not *touch* her soul."

Annin withdrew his hands and placed them in his lap. "Grell's talk with his inoga brethren beneath Gelthin absolutely made me want to get a hold of Nessix's soul vessel, because that is the only way we stand a chance of finding her before they do. I have no interest in becoming the property of one of those beasts. I'd assumed you didn't, either."

It was a valid argument, one which Kol would have agreed with wholeheartedly if not for one fact. "But if you chose to destroy Nessix—"

"I couldn't end her without the soul that's inside her. You know that. Destroying the vessel you carry would do me no good and her too much of it. I need you to trust me now as much as you did when you had me bind her to you. Let me have her soul vessel so we can find her."

The mechanics of how akhuerai functioned made sense to Kol, and he knew the boundaries and limitations of how to end one. His argument had been based solely in his illogical insecurity; he hadn't parted from Nes's soul since the moment he'd laid his hands on it and the thought of giving it to Annin for whatever procedure he had in mind sickened him. But not quite as much as knowing Nessix was gone. Close to defeated on the matter and growing increasingly too tired to care, Kol's head flopped back onto his pillow. "What are you going to do with it once you have it?"

Explaining these details was tedious, but Kol was disinclined to cooperate otherwise. "My theory is that if I can directly connect her soul to yours, you'll be able to reach her once she's unconscious."

"Your *theory*?"

"I said it was a plan, not a solution. If sharing blood with her was enough to let her access your memories"—Annin was sure to emphasize those last three words, accusation running thick—"you tapping into her soul may allow you to access hers."

All of this talk of theory didn't ring with the sort of confidence Kol liked to hear before engaging in a struggle for his life. Of course, he was already in one. Per the Divine Battle's perversion of Etha's grand design, demons had resilient bodies but weak souls. If Annin did have a way to join Kol's soul to Nes's, she'd pull him to her easily. As Annin said, theoretically, it was a good plan.

"What harm will be done if you can't connect us?"

"Nothing. You'll be joined by a single thread, enough to secure a connection, but not enough to harm either of you when it breaks. It'll register as a minor wound, something you'll both be able to walk off when you wake."

"You sound awful certain over something that's just a theory."

Annin smiled. "I've been playing with threads for centuries now, Kol. Don't think this is the first time I've plucked important ones."

Even when functioning at full capacity, Kol had never understood much of what Annin said about these elusive threads, and trying to do so now simply compounded his headache. All he had to know was that this was possibly their last option, and that even if something went wrong, Kol would be unlikely to know the difference. Annin had no respect for Grell, and so Kol was more confident than not that his friend wouldn't surrender Nes's vessel to the inoga while he was out.

Kol grumbled and rolled over to unclasp Nes's vessel from his neck. His stomach clenched as his reluctant fingers gathered the chain, and he stared longingly at the swirling mist of her soul. He hungered for that intoxicating warmth it had once given him to return. "What do I have to do?"

"Keep her calm and get her talking. Get her comfortable with you and see if you can find out where she is and what she's up to. It should be no more difficult than how easily she'd been able to read you."

If Kol had been a bit more coherent, he'd have winced at the insult. As it was, he took Annin's instructions in stride. He enjoyed talking to Nessix, anyway. Wrapping his fingers around the vessel once more, desperate for a glimmer of warmth he never got, Kol extended a wobbly arm to deliver the pendant to Annin.

The oraku snatched it up quickly, too fast for Kol's liking and well before his tired mind had the chance to generate any second thoughts. With the hardest part over, Annin reached his free hand over to Kol's shoulder to push him back onto his stomach. The alar flopped over as though he was already unconscious.

"All you need to do is relax," Annin murmured, digging a fine pick forged of Affliction from his pocket. "You must be exhausted, with how hard you've thrown yourself at this search."

Carefully, Annin scraped at the side of Nes's soul vessel, metal gently squeaking against the crystal. He glanced up as he caught movement from the corner of his eye, afraid Kol was about to protest damage being done to his trinket, but it was only the flopping of his limp wings as sleep wrapped its arms around him.

"Tonight, I'm taking over your troubles." One last scratch and a faint wisp of Nes's soul crept free from the vessel. Grounding himself, Annin cupped his hand over it and leaned over Kol's prone form. "All you have to do is go talk to your pet."

Kol registered Annin's words on a subconscious level, comforted more by his quiet, even tone than the message it delivered. His body sank deep into his bed, tingling with how near he was to the sleep he so desperately needed. A sharp pop, like the sound made when dislocating someone's thumb, but without the accompanying screams, echoed through the stuffy stillness pressing in on Kol's head. He sank in an endless ocean of white, pain and fear erased from his mind. All he knew was Nessix, and once he caught himself to stop his descent, he righted himself and scanned the bright void around him until he located the pulse of her warmth.

Grinning, hopeful at last, Kol darted forward.

* * * * *

The concept of running had already grown old to Nessix, and she found herself wondering if it would have been easier to stay with Kol after all. Maybe she would have still been able to reach Zeal. Maybe she'd have been able to sway him to help her in that journey. She'd grown skilled enough at getting her way with him that it didn't seem like an impossibility.

The thought that she might be able to find some peace in the hells was all Nessix needed to tune out the burning in her lungs and legs. With a precious few hours to gain ground on a demon search party, she wouldn't let that bizarre fondness she felt for her alar master slow her down. Besides, he'd be most displeased with her when he found her and though he'd often claimed he hated the idea of hurting her, he'd done so more than once. If asking about an old friend of his had earned Nessix a beating, running from his authority was bound to come with something far worse.

Nessix was tired of thinking about Kol and what he would think of her actions. Instead, she thought of Mathias. She thought of entering the splendor of Zeal and testifying to an army of paladins what she knew of the demons and their methods of creating and managing the akhuerai. She'd reclaim her pride, be the hero she'd always dreamed of being. All she had to do was reach Zeal, and this horror could end.

That mantra drove Nessix past aching feet and the threat of fatigue, carrying her to the point where the day ran thin. She slowed and tucked herself into a patch of grass patted flat by some large animal and plopped to the ground to unroll Zenos's map. It didn't do her much good without knowing which road she'd bolted down or which city was nearest, but as he'd promised, the roads were well marked and the cities and towns faintly traced in place. Nessix took care with rolling the map up again and grimaced as her stomach rumbled with the reminder that she hadn't eaten since her breakfast rations.

With daylight nearly gone, she had to find more substantial cover for the night. Her stomach complained again, but the urgency in Zenos's words as they reverberated in her mind were even louder. Reluctantly digging more food from her pack, Nessix hauled herself to her feet before her body convinced her that this patch of grass was tall enough to hide her from demons. She surveyed her surroundings, seeing nothing but open fields in front of her. If she took a chance and backtracked a couple miles, she'd have access to shelter in the form of some brambly bushes, but she preferred not to think about getting closer to those demons Zenos had sensed.

Nessix looked to the sun where it burrowed into the horizon and frowned. Her three hours had passed. If the god's estimation was accurate—and Nessix knew better than to doubt it—that city was very likely under attack. The philanthropist in her begged her to run back. Not only did she know how to fight demons, they couldn't even kill her. The general in her, however, demanded she stay her course. Reaching Zeal was her mission, for herself, for the akhuerai, and ultimately for all of Abaeloth. She'd have to trust that Seaton had someone able to defend it.

She trudged on, physically and mentally drained, but driven by sheer grit and determination. She couldn't afford to stop, but weariness begged her to go on no longer.

A warrior from birth, Nessix was accustomed to being worn out. She'd felt hunger on long campaigns. She'd often been deprived of sleep while managing her troops. But even when she'd been trapped in the hells, she'd had reliable access to warm meals and shelter. Provided she didn't care enough to push for freedom, she had a certain degree of security in the demons' realm, knowing when her days would begin, where her meals would come from, and what was expected of her. For the first time in Nes's life, she wasn't bound by a set of expectations and while that epiphany should have been liberating, it brought an untimely shiver to her skin.

Stumbling along the narrow footpath in the rapidly diminishing light, it became increasingly difficult for Nessix to scan her surroundings for potential shelter. She passed nobody else as she walked, and at times wondered whether or not she was on a road traveled by people as opposed to a path forged by wild game. Just as the sun was about to take the last of its light from her, a solid structure rose on the horizon. Laughing in relief, not caring what she'd have to do to secure lodging for the night, Nessix tuned out the protests of her body and powered her aching legs ahead.

Thick vines climbed the walls and pulled the thatching from the roof of the shack awaiting her. The front door had fallen from deteriorated hinges, replaced by a thick screen of spiderwebs. Nessix frowned, having looked forward to the warm meal and clean blanket her imagination had promised were waiting for her, but even more distraught that she'd be sleeping alone. It wasn't from any overwhelming desire for companionship, but from not having a second set of senses surveying for danger. No matter what common sense and protocol told her, though, Nessix was too tired to care. On the road, the risk of collapsing from exhaustion was too high. Carefully ducking under the door's webs to avoid giving away her location by disturbing them, Nessix entered the derelict building.

Before she'd even appraised the simple room, she sank into a corner, overcome by her need to sleep.

* * * * *

Nes's dream was cold and dark, reflecting the fleeting images she recalled from the shack's shadowy interior and echoing the fear fluttering in her heart no matter how hard she tried to suppress it. By all accounts, it beat the nightmares of Kol's she'd faced over the past year, yet she still shivered and desperately sought out brighter, happier places.

She tried to concoct what Zeal and all its grandeur must look like, but she had few descriptions to build on past elegant lilies and strict knights. She tried thinking of home and the serenity of the Great Spring, but her thoughts always drifted to Brant and cast a depressing shadow over what should have been her fondest memories. There was one place left for her to go, one place she fought even thinking about. No matter what it took, Nessix would not let herself go back into the hells, at least not without an army of Mathias's knights of the Order marching with her. Yet the hells were the only other image presented to her besides this abandoned shack.

Outside the door, confident footsteps trod her way, and Nessix scrambled to her feet. There were no menacing rumbles of thunder or terrifying bolts of lightning for her to fear, but she'd quit trusting the world that resided in her dreams some time ago. The steps stopped on the other side of the spiderwebs and she held her breath.

Silence reigned between Nessix and her visitor for long

moments, the only sound that reached her the steady breathing from outside. She waited for what felt like hours and nothing came for her. No threats, no attacks, and the longer she stood staring at the door, no increasing fear. Perhaps she'd been viewing the situation wrong. Maybe the dark was that of comfort and safety. Whoever had come for her hadn't yet torn the walls down or demanded for her to come out. What if this was Brant's spirit or Mathias reaching out to her? As her thoughts brightened, sunlight began to shine through the holes in the roof, yet Nessix couldn't make out so much as a shadow of who stood outside through the thick webs.

"Who's there?" she called at last, craning her neck but not quite confident enough to approach the door.

For several heartbeats, nothing happened, and then a hand reached forward to swat the spiderwebs away. Kol stalked into the room, lip curling as his flaming eyes surveyed the filth of the run-down shack.

"And here I'd thought you had standards," he sneered.

Nessix crossed her arms and straightened, thankful this was only a dream. Kol looked different from how she remembered him, taller and more stern. He clenched his jaw in a manner that hollowed his cheeks and when he looked into her eyes, she saw an eternity of suffering writhing within their fiery depths.

"What are you doing here?" she asked.

Kol completed his observation of Nes's shelter and stopped before her, his eyes warming with a possessive light. "That's all you've got to say?" He smirked at her stubborn silence. "You don't seem particularly surprised to see me here. Do you dream of me often?"

Everything inside of Nessix wanted to scream and throw herself at Kol. This time she was in *her* dream, a world she could control. The thought of tearing into him and fighting back after all the pain and shame he'd inflicted on her elated Nessix on levels she'd never before imagined. Yet when she tried to muster the motivation to attack, she stared into his judgmental eyes—much less receptive to games than she'd ever seen them—and couldn't move. Besides, that traitorous knot nestled deep in her core still wanted to look after Kol and make him proud. Nessix scoffed and turned to leave through the shack's back door.

Kol followed without hesitation. "You've got nothing to say to me? Nothing at all after how you betrayed my trust?"

Nessix stopped in the warm sunlight, glaring up into the clear blue sky she'd spent so long missing, and Kol remained there, robbing her of the ability to enjoy it. She spun to face him, frowning as his eyes methodically swept across the sun-bleached field, the dark hint of mountains far on the western horizon, the hills that lay a day's march to the north… Everywhere but at her.

"I've got a lot of things to say to you," Nessix snapped, "but I suspect you already know them."

"Ah," Kol sighed, still studying their surroundings with a careful intensity. "I do know that you're afraid, that you thought running back to the mortal world would offer you some sort of salvation, yet you're as lost as ever." His eyes flashed to hers for a tense moment as they delved deep into Nes's resolve, and then returned to the landscape. "Am I right?"

Nessix crossed her arms. "The mortal world *does* offer me salvation."

Kol chuckled and shook his head, taking wary steps closer to her. "No, little one. This world hates you, just like it hates me. I suspect you discovered that even your Elidae hates you. In fact—" Kol clipped his words into silence, a tight frown consuming his smirk.

"In fact what?" Nessix asked, no longer afraid to challenge him.

"The flemans hate you so much that it was one of your own who told Grell about your plan to go crying to Mathias." Kol sneered, conveying precisely what he thought of Nes's hopes for that reunion. "You let that poor man's entire city fall to the most vicious of my kind, you know. Those are the sorts of memories that aren't easily forgotten."

Nessix frowned at Kol's taunt. Half of it, she'd known. The only fleman akhuerai other than herself had done everything he could to hinder her progress in raising the akhuerai army, never missing a chance to try turning the others against her. His hatred of her was both known and expected, but Kol's knowledge of her plans hadn't been. As quickly as her nerves were piqued, they faded away from one simple fact.

"You are a dream," Nessix said. "And I don't have to be afraid of you."

Kol cocked his head and took another step closer. "You don't?"

Despite her bold claim, Nessix swallowed hard. "No."

Another step closer. "You've never had anything to fear from me, you know. But I will advise you to fear those who are tracking you. You ought to be *very* afraid of them."

Uncertainty squirmed about in Nes's stomach in a manner she thought she'd left behind. "I've got the situation managed."

Kol turned around briefly to look at the shack then back to Nessix, wearing a skeptical grimace. "If this is how you plan to survive, you haven't got anything managed. It's open season on you, little one. There's inoga after you now. Lots of them. Ones you've never seen before. The smart thing to do would be to come home before they find you. Let me and Annin fix this mess, keep you safe, and we can all pretend it never happened. You know you're safest with me."

Why had Nes's dream of Kol mentioned Annin being willing to help her? Nowhere in the wildest stretches of her imagination did she ever think the grumpy oraku cared about her at all. Shoving aside the anomaly, Nessix gave a stubborn shake of her head. "I'm going to Zeal," she declared firmly. "And not even an army of inoga will be able to stop me."

In a flash, Kol closed the distance between them, his fingers digging into the flesh of her wrists as he pulled her closer to him. Nessix struggled against his grasp, unable to break it, and registering pain above all other sensations. Wings extended, Kol wrapped them around her in a barrier to contain her in case she slipped free and tried to run. He glanced down, saw the ring on her thumb, and his scowl deepened.

"You're smart, Nessix." His growl was deeper and more menacing than Nessix recalled him using with her before. "But you've made a terrible mistake. You've made Grell very angry, and that doesn't bode well for either of us. You don't have to come back to me if you don't want to, little one. But know that I am coming for you."

Nessix gasped and woke coughing for air inside the run-down shack. Scrambling upright, she cast her frightened eyes to the door to find the spiderwebs fully intact, but her sigh of relief was cut short by a burning ache in her wrists. Looking down in the dull glow of moonlight which slipped through the holes in the roof, she saw the precise marring of bruises from Kol's grasp wrapped around both wrists. She didn't understand how that was possible, but after all the impossibilities she'd faced, she didn't have to. Kol *had* found her, and he'd confirmed Zenos's warning.

Nessix sprang to her feet, not bothering to survey her surroundings for tangible signs of danger. She grabbed her pack and ran out of the shack, sprinting north precisely because her life depended on it.

EIGHT

Mathias escorted the girl to the safety of the inn, receiving sly smirks to confirm his suspicions of who she was as he passed with her firmly in his grasp. He glanced down to gauge her thoughts and frowned at the way her eyes glazed over in defeat as she plodded along beside him. The revulsion from this young woman probably should have been a blow to his pride, but Mathias had faced worse trials than this sort of judgment in his past, and he wouldn't be daunted by it now.

He booked a room for them, much more politely than the inn keep was used to for the sort of activity the patrons expected, and led the girl away from their lewd remarks. The room was a simple interior chamber with a modest bed and a bare nightstand, but it was warm and dry and protected from the cruelty of the public. Free of windows, it was illuminated by a solitary lantern. Mathias released the girl from his hold after he gently forced her to sit on the side of the bed.

The paladin treated his patient's injuries with the caution one used when negotiating with a wounded animal. Pouring water from his flask onto a clean rag from his pack, he wiped the dirt from the scrapes on her cheek, sneaking the brush of his thumb against the wounds as he worked to urge her flesh to mend faster than simple cleaning would allow. She watched him fiercely with a clenched jaw and tears on the verge of tumbling past her lower lids, but she'd given up on fighting him.

When he was through with her face, he knelt down to tend to her foot. She winced preemptively, but didn't jerk away. "My name is Mathias," he told her quietly as he unlaced her boot. Carefully, he freed her foot to assess the swelling in her ankle. She didn't protest his actions, but neither did she reciprocate on his offer of a name, and Mathias sighed. "I beg you to relax. You have my word that there's nothing in this room that will harm you."

She still didn't answer, and when Mathias glanced up to meet her eyes, he nearly wished he hadn't. She scathed him with accusations he was unworthy of, chastising him for the wrongs of men he'd never met, men he'd have punched in the nose all day long if he ever stumbled across them. Her glare stated clearly that Mathias Sagewind was a liar, because all men hurt women like her.

This time, the unspoken assumption did strike his pride just a bit, but correcting the girl would do him no good. She'd made up her mind about his intentions, and there was nothing he'd be able to do to force her to believe otherwise. Besides, Mathias suspected she'd long ago surpassed her limit of having matters forced on her. He resumed assessing her foot, wrapping his hands around the swollen joint as Etha's warmth seeped from him into her.

"I am a knight, hailing from Zeal," he said, ignoring the fact that the title was more than a few years out of date. This lie wouldn't hurt nearly as much as the truth would at the moment.

Finally, the girl relaxed enough to sink deeper onto the bed. "You're far away from home."

Mathias smiled, relieved to have her speaking, even if it was to judge why he'd been in town. "Yes, I am, but such is the life of my order. I've been questing for some time and fate led me to Seaton."

The girl scoffed and jutted her chin away from Mathias.

"How did that man get a hold of you?" Mathias had no problems with the willing form of this girl's apparent occupation, but he'd never seen the sort of abuse she'd fallen victim to pass unpunished by reputable operations.

The tension returned to the girl's frame and she turned from Mathias entirely. "I don't know," she said, a poorly delivered lie if

Mathias had ever heard one.

A gentle rap sounded at the door and the girl jerked. Eyeing her tense form, Mathias stood and answered the door to accept the tray of food he'd ordered. After securing the door again, he walked to the bedside table, intentionally letting the aroma of cooked meat and a thick stew permeate the air as he passed the girl. Keeping watch on her from the corner of his eye, he saw her brows lift and her demeanor perk up at the thought of eating. Mathias picked up a steaming cup of tea and eased it into her hands.

"Did he threaten you to bodily harm if you put up a fight?" The fact that she hadn't screamed for help continued to bother Mathias.

That temporary bliss which came from the arrival of food immediately flit from the girl's eyes, and she shoved the cup of tea back into Mathias's unsuspecting hands with such force that it sloshed onto his shirt and pants. Barely retaining a sharp curse, Mathias caught the cup before the entire thing drained on him and deposited it back on the table.

"If he wanted to hurt me if I fought him, don't you think I'd be *hurt* right now?" She spat the question, as if she'd expected Mathias to consider the struggle he'd intercepted as a full-out battle to the death. "You know, this is really kind of you, but I need to go."

Mathias stayed calm where he knelt before her. He hadn't meant to push her further than she was comfortable, but as with most dealings he had with women, he'd failed to do so. "May I ask where you plan on going?"

His question seemed to confuse the girl and she straightened sharply when he made no move to restrain her. He truly was giving her the option to leave, if she chose to take it. The offer seemed like an obvious win for her, yet she hesitated. Mathias hadn't so much as lifted a finger to harm her. In fact, he'd somehow made her ankle quit throbbing and when she reached her fingers to her cheek, she found her scrapes had faded. The better part of her gut told her she was safest with Mathias. She wouldn't complain about her life, but she was afraid of what would happen if she ventured out on the street by herself tonight. Maybe she could lift some coins from Mathias… find a way to rent a private room until morning. She quirked her lips as she appraised his patient gaze and capable arms. There would be no sneaking past him.

"I…" She paused again as Mathias brightened at her willingness to talk, and for some reason, her dying sense of shame strictly forbid her to tell him the truth. "I'm a traveler, myself." She'd have been better served to tell Mathias the truth she so desperately wanted to hide than to try delivering this obvious lie. Fortunately, Mathias was of the moral fiber that he wouldn't embarrass her by letting her know he saw through it. "That man must've seen me alone and decided to come after me. I was going to go home in the morning."

The girl beamed at her story and Mathias, accustomed to dealing with officers and politicians, refrained from calling her out on her poor delivery. She was frightened and doing her best. If telling bogus lies to him was necessary to raise her confidence, he'd allow her to use them until she figured out he didn't buy them.

"Well, then," he said. "If you plan to leave in the morning, it makes sense for you to get a good night's sleep while you can." Mathias smiled that affable smile of his as her expression faltered. "You're not from around here. You're on your own. And you're clearly a target for the less savory citizens of this town. You've got a knight at your disposal until morning, my lady."

This bastard was clever. She hated him for that, but didn't want to dig herself deeper into this lie than she already had. All she had to do was keep him believing her story for a few hours, and then she could be rid of him. She'd pretend to go on her way, and he could go on his, and she could forget all about this terrible brush with hope. Besides, once the man from the street regained consciousness, she was quite certain he'd waste no time lodging complaints against her. All of a sudden that lie she fed Mathias had a solid amount of truth in it. She could no longer stay in Seaton, not with that reputation following her.

Uncomfortable with the mess she'd found, wondering why she'd thought it was such a good idea to put up a fight against a customer just because he notoriously skipped payment, the girl's shoulders slouched. "Alright," she murmured, not knowing what else to do. "I'll stay."

Mathias gave her a satisfied nod. "Good." He opened his pack to rummage for a cloak to use as bedding. "In the morning, we'll head out—"

"I'm traveling alone," the girl said before sense could catch her.

Her debate, had it not been tied to the circumstances, would have brought a smile to Mathias's lips. "And have you seen the trouble you've gotten into?"

She wouldn't mention the trouble *he'd* gotten her into if the man on the street clearly recalled the incident when he woke up. "I know my way home," she insisted, watching Mathias as though he was an unpredictable beast as he laid his cloak on the floor. "I don't need anyone's help."

This time, Mathias let his smirk slip out. He stood and shooed the girl toward the foot of the bed so he could pull the covers back for her, and patted the mattress heartily. "Well, I'm a knight." He stepped back and she warily lay down. Mathias pulled the covers up around her shoulders, smiling at the confusion in her eyes. "I've overcome terrible foes like you'd never imagine, and I vow to you here and now that I will arrange for you safe passage to wherever you're heading. To forbid me to do so would be a great shame upon my honor." Even if he couldn't find a reliable third-party escort, he and Nessix would be more than enough to protect one young woman on her journey home. If this girl was allowed to stretch the truth, so was he, and the dread that welled up in those confused eyes confirmed that she had no idea how much authority his words carried.

"Well," she started stubbornly, though she had no idea how to debate with him over this. There was nothing remotely threatening about Mathias. In fact, the longer he exposed her to his grating positivity, the better she felt. Not just more comfortable in his presence, but as though there may still be a way for her to find happiness. She nestled deeper in the covers. "My name's Khin," she chanced on a murmur, not knowing or really caring what Mathias would do with her name.

Mathias smiled and sat down on the floor to remove his

boots. "I swear to you, Khin, on my honor as a knight of the Order, that as long as you are in my care, I will do everything within my power to protect you."

She didn't have a ready response for him, but when he closed his eyes and rolled to his side, back facing her, she figured he hadn't expected one. Gripping tight to the hem of the blanket, relaxing into the comfort of an otherwise unoccupied bed, Khin closed her eyes and fell asleep.

* * * * *

Mathias had drifted off, mulling over how to balance Khin's safety with his mission to escort Nessix to Zeal. He never fell into a deep enough sleep to lose his awareness of the room's activities, not entirely convinced Khin wouldn't attempt to bolt in the night, but he'd functioned reliably off less sleep than he'd had over the past day. Besides, even if he wouldn't have found Khin, his lingering excitement wouldn't have let him rest soundly.

Mathias?

A faint groan creaked in the back of his throat. There were too many reasons he wasn't asleep and he didn't want to add Etha to them. She never failed to chime in when his mind was already in knots, and she often tangled them into more complicated jumbles before he was able to sort them out. He lay completely still, banking on some ridiculous hope that the goddess might believe he was so comfortable on the floor that he didn't hear.

Wake up, you horrible liar! There's something you need to know.

Mathias heaved a quiet sigh and rolled to his side. *That Khin's not telling me the truth? I realize that.*

No, you dummy. The gravity in Etha's hissed reply made Mathias's eyes shoot open. *Demons are here. They've beat Nessix to Gelthin!*

Mathias sat up in a flash, blinking rapidly to adjust his eyes to the lantern's flickering light. Khin slept soundly on the bed above him, gentle snores announcing how grateful she was to relax, and Mathias was caught in a sleepy haze of indecision as to what he should do.

83

You're going to get yourself and that girl out of this town, is what you're going to do.

He rubbed his eyes with one hand and groped for his sword belt with the other. *Get out of town? But someone has to defend it... I have to make sure it's safe when Nessix—*

There is no defending against this.

The grogginess left Mathias instantly and his casual pace at mentally preparing for combat skidded to a jarring halt. *What do you mean?* Mathias had always been Etha's default for facing demons, and she'd routinely flung him against daunting odds. If there was something even she was afraid of, Mathias *had* to stay to protect the people.

Etha hummed a tense warning. *Let Zenos worry about the town.*

Bah, Mathias scoffed. *I'm every bit as powerful as the new children.*

Oh... Mathias...

Before Etha had the chance to elaborate, the sound of shrill screams on the street squeezed through the walls of the inn. Mathias jumped to his feet to strap his armor in place as quickly as he could. *Why didn't you wake me sooner? With enough time to prepare?*

I tried *to warn you that this was coming when you were busy playing hero.*

Mathias fought the urge to stop and think back on how foolish he'd been to overlook the fact that Etha had been offering him insight at that time. Perhaps their relationship had become a bit *too* friendly over the years. *That was supposed to be a warning about a demon attack?*

Yes! Etha snapped, offended. *And now it's too late for you to do anything about it. Though I doubt this is the sort of thing you could have done anything about, anyway.*

Mathias glanced at Khin. She groaned and shifted in her sleep, disturbed by the subtle clanking of his dressing. *Are you going to leave it that vague?*

There are inoga in the street.

Etha spoke those words so plainly that Mathias froze. He hated fighting inoga for all of the obvious reasons, which might have been why Etha hadn't pressed the issue upon her first address. If given the option, Mathias would always try to find a way *out* of fighting them, which made it strange that he was so determined to stand and face them now.

You said "are" instead of "is," Mathias said, resuming his final preparations. *That means there's more than one?*

Etha stayed still as he secured his belt, then murmured, *Roll up your cloak. Get your pack situated. Since you pledged your protection to that girl, get her up, and run.*

Mathias's blood ran cold. He could count on one hand the number of times Etha had begged him to flee from demons, and most of those were tied to his stupid decision to traipse into their realm where she couldn't reach him. He'd faced armies of the beasts on his own. He'd been slain by them enough times to no longer be fazed by it. He'd even launched himself on suicide missions to stop their forces and Etha had *encouraged* that. The fact that she chose to beg him not to face the most powerful opponents the hells had to offer shook the foundation of Mathias's confidence.

But what about Nessix...?

His question was pathetically small, more timid than Etha had ever heard him speak in the entire time she'd watched over him. Mathias had given up the past year of peace searching for Nessix. He'd given his all to track down clues of where she'd ended up, had accepted hardships no man should ever have to face to uncover the fate of his lover, and it had all culminated into Nes's scheduled arrival in Seaton. Mathias had waited his entire existence to find a soul mate, and he'd invested the past two years fighting for her once he'd found her. And now, Etha was telling him to flee from the city where he'd find her. She was telling him to abandon Nessix to the demons that were storming the town as she spoke.

If she shows up, I will do what I can to protect her, Etha promised, not knowing how she could do that. She'd been trying to locate Nessix since the moment Sazrah told Mathias she'd surfaced and had barely been able to catch glimpses of something familiar to chase. *But for now, you need to protect yourself and that girl. Please, Mathias. Hurry.*

Mathias trusted Etha explicitly, for he had no other choice. And if his goddess told him he had to run, that the odds of even him surviving combat unscathed were impossible, fear was a very legitimate emotion to fall to. *And the civilians?*

Etha didn't answer. Cursing, having forgotten what it felt like to not be able to save everyone, Mathias grabbed Khin's shoulder as the screaming grew closer.

She woke with a start, voicing a startled squeak as she clutched the blanket. Mathias frowned as he faced her terrified eyes, sick to his stomach that he had to make this choice. "Come on, we need to go."

Khin pulled the blanket tighter around herself. "...Go?"

"Yes," Mathias said, helping her to her feet as she staggered through grogginess. "I swore I'd keep you safe, and Seaton is no longer that. We need to go."

Khin rubbed her eyes and gathered the blanket around herself as Mathias hastened her toward the door. They emerged into the hallway, greeted by open doors and confused glances from a few of the other guests as the sounds of screams became more evident. Khin's eyes widened as the panic outside settled into her mind. With the blanket clutched around her shoulders, she pressed closer to Mathias, coveting the confidence his determination mustered.

"What's happening?" she asked, bare feet scampering to keep up with his quick stride.

"I'm hoping I won't have to tell you until we're well outside the city limits."

Given how little she trusted him mere hours ago, it defied logic that Khin couldn't get close enough to Mathias now. All she knew was that she was scared, and he had a sword and an idea of how to keep them both alive. Afraid to ask any more questions, Khin allowed Mathias to guide her down the stairs.

A fine haze of smoke filtered through the windows and beneath the crack of the door by the time they reached the main floor, and the inn keep huddled behind his counter, sending a desperate gaze in Mathias's direction, one that begged him for help. Tears stung Mathias's eyes, as he knew that wouldn't be the last silent plea he received tonight, but in the moment, he blamed the sensation on the smoke.

Stopping before the door, Mathias bustled up the tail of the blanket Khin clung to so her legs wouldn't tangle in its trailing length and shoved the bundled mass into her arms. He looked down at the floor, steeling himself for what he had to do next, and drew his sword. Khin gasped, stumbling a couple steps away from Mathias as the truth of their danger sank in.

"Keep as close to me as you can," he said firmly. "I'm going to move briskly, so you'll have to run. If I need to engage in combat, you dart for whatever cover you can find. Am I clear?"

Khin's lips trembled as she tried to answer him, but all that came out of her was, "M-Mathias... I'm scared..."

His heart plummeted, and his hatred for the demons grew an inch. "I swore I'd keep you safe," he repeated. "If I succeed at nothing else today, it will be that. We need to run. Stop at nothing until I tell you to."

Khin never replied verbally, but her shaking hand reached out and grabbed his belt. Praying her strength and nerve held out for her to hang on and keep up, Mathias drew one more breath and flung the door open. To the sound of the inn keep yelling at him to close the door and take cover, Mathias dashed out into the chaos of the flaming streets.

Imposing in stature and unparalleled in strength, inoga didn't often come to the surface for combat. Their efforts were typically used to maintain what passed for order in the hells, a daunting task for any other creature. Mathias had faced well over a dozen inoga in his time and only succeeded in slaying three. The others had in no uncertain terms succeeded in slaying him. Those had always been battles he'd charged into assuming relatively equal footing— twenty or so underlings of varying classes backing up a single lord. But as Mathias ran through the streets of Seaton, he knew there would be no heroic stands taken today, just as Etha had told him.

Hundreds of demons skittered across the streets, tearing terrified people from their windows, breaking into homes and businesses and infesting them like rats. Loud crashes echoed from every direction, suggesting the locations of the inoga Etha had warned him about, but Mathias didn't slow to assess if his speculations were accurate. Wishing his armor didn't stand out so clearly and that it wasn't a well-known artifact to these fiends,

Mathias grit his teeth and forbid himself to engage even the least threatening demon he came across. All the while, Khin clutched at his belt and kept pace as they ran.

Navigating through the frightened congestion of fleeing townsfolk took longer than Mathias had hoped. He didn't waste his breath trying to shout for the panicking crowd to part for him, knowing such demands would be ignored. Jostled by the rush of bodies around them, Mathias and Khin progressed as steadily toward the city gates as they could. Just as their exit came into view, though, Khin's momentum slowed, dragging Mathias to a stop. He turned to urge her on, but the heartbroken gawk of sheer disbelief with which she focused on the distance took the words from his mouth.

A massive cluster of demons swarmed over a building whose sign dangled helplessly off one hinge. As the commotion of the raid rattled its supports, Mathias barely made out the name—The Tarnished Maiden—and he understood Khin's concern at last. Whether or not she'd hated the life she came from, that had been the closest thing to a home she'd had. The women who shrieked in horror and agony as the demons did what they saw fit inside those walls had been the closest thing to a family she'd had. And that was where Khin would have gone last night if Mathias would have let her leave.

Mathias placed his hand at the base of Khin's neck, fingers gripping firmly to steer her away. "There's nothing we can do. Let's go."

Khin shook her head fiercely and flung her arm back to tear away from his touch. Immobilized by shock, she didn't approach the chaos that actively ripped apart the establishment, but neither did she move to bolt, as though she was ready to condemn herself to the same pathetic fate.

Mathias glanced about the hysterical crowd. Immobilizing Khin wasn't the most appealing tactic, but he didn't know what other options he had. Nobody here was focusing on anything besides their own survival and they wouldn't think twice about Mathias taking any sort of physical action against a woman they all disregarded as a whore. He raised his hand to press his fingers to

Khin's forehead, and froze as three inoga lumbered out of the brothel, one carrying a panicking woman under each of his thick arms.

"She's not here," the one in the front roared, putting a disappointed stop to the demons who scrambled up the walls to pour into the establishment's windows for their own fun. "Destroy it."

Within seconds, a thick column of smoke belched from the brothel's roof, rapidly climbing into the sky. The inoga chortled and turned down the road—turned toward Mathias—as Khin shrieked her horror and heartbreak. The inoga in the lead lifted his head to face the sound, expression falling as he saw Mathias standing beside her. In delayed time, a toothy snarl contorted the demon's face as he raised a meaty finger to point at Mathias and turned to tell his friends who had come to pretend to ruin their fun.

Mathias had been discovered by his foes, and he was certain they knew why he was there. With nothing else to lose besides countless nights of sleep for how he'd walked away from all of these people who needed help so badly, Mathias pressed his fingers to Khin's forehead, commanded her to sleep, and wrapped her in a tight embrace as he whisked them into the divine pathways to reach the safety of Zeal.

NINE

The effects of fatigue crept over Annin. Monitoring the serenity of Kol's slumber did nothing to help him stave off his own exhaustion, yet he wouldn't be able to catch any sleep for quite some time. He'd promised Kol there would be no lasting damage done to Nessix's soul from this procedure, and he would do everything he could to make good on that. Not so much to please Kol or to test the range of his abilities, but to make sure Grell didn't have any new reasons to get angry at him. Considering his friend was already in rough shape, Annin shamelessly fed off a bit of Kol's replenishing energy to keep himself alert.

The portion of Nessix's soul which resided in the vessel Kol kept had resumed its intriguing pattern of multicolored swirls that had captivated the alar so much, suggesting he'd been successful in rousing something through this spell Annin had concocted. If not for his predisposed hatred of Nessix and everything she stood for, Annin might have considered the display of lights appealing, but he quickly diverted such thoughts by attempting to decode the meaning behind it.

Hours into the silent vigil, a spark flashed between the pendant and the thread of Kol's which Annin had secured to Nes's soul, pulling Annin from his stupor. Kol jerked, brows furrowing in displeasure at waking from his deep slumber. He groaned, eyes clamped shut, and raised his hand to press it against his forehead. Quietly, Annin drew the soul vessel to himself, wrapping his own threads around the flaw he'd made in the crystal.

"Well?" he asked. "Did it work?"

"It was your idea…" Kol grumbled, nearly incoherent. "What do you think?"

Annin smirked as Kol flattened his palm against his face and moaned even louder. "Did you find what we needed?"

That was a fantastic question. The visit to Nes's dream—or wherever it was Kol had been delivered—had given him a lot of information, but none of it what Kol had actually wanted. *That* information, though, of how Nessix could have done this to him, Annin would have no interest in.

"She's no longer on Elidae." Kol hefted his weight in an attempt to sit up, but abandoned the effort after one halfhearted try. "And she's very clearly on the run. Squatting in some run-down shack in the middle of a yellow field."

Annin glowered at Kol's response. "That's all you got? Didn't you tap into her soul like I'd told you to?"

Kol peered an eye open to glare at the oraku. "Of *course* I tapped into her soul like you told me to."

"And you didn't gather anything other than that she wasn't on Elidae and that she was running from you?"

Kol glanced away and succeeded in sitting up, driven by the notion that he might have to soon defend himself. "She wasn't running from *me*."

Annin rolled his eyes. "Of course she wasn't. She wouldn't dream of leaving you. I remember. So where is she? In case you need to be reminded, our fates rely on you figuring that out."

"She's somewhere near Seaton," Kol muttered, looking away from Annin to scour his room to see if there was any food. There wasn't.

"Is this something you know for certain, or a speculation you're making because you don't want me angry with you?"

"Oh, I know it for certain," Kol said.

The effort the alar made to avoid his eyes raised all sorts of suspicions in Annin, and suddenly, he wished he wouldn't have asked these questions. "What aren't you telling me, Kol? You're not just gambling with your life. I will get this out of you."

Kol sighed and pressed his hands into his knees as he leaned forward. "I know she's near Seaton because at some point, she had a visit with Zenos."

Annin's lips parted in a silent gasp as he quickly began to work over the implications of that statement. Shand had been an easy goddess to manipulate. She'd been so driven by her objectives that she was blind to everything else. But Zenos? He was scholarly to a fault, intimately aware of the energy flows on Abaeloth, and one of the few gods who didn't have any interests of his own to conflict with his duty. He cared about balance every bit as much as his meddlesome mother did, and he was not an opponent that smart demons ever wanted to engage.

"Did Nessix tell you this?"

"She's wearing his seal of warding," Kol groaned.

"Damn it…" Annin looked away from Kol to keep from striking him in frustration. "She wasn't still with him, was she?"

Kol shook his head, chewing over his own fears. "Not that I could tell."

Annin nodded slowly. They might still have a chance if all he'd given her was a ring for protection. "Grell's inoga won't know she's got his blessing and will keep chasing her the conventional way. We can work this in our favor." He studied Kol hard, debating whether or not to criticize him for what was going to come next. "Did you tell her she was being tracked?"

"I did."

"Did you tell her *who* was tracking her?"

"Yes. And I gave her the option to come back to me."

A tiny puff of a laugh left through Annin's nostrils. "And I'm sure she leapt at that chance."

Kol ran his tongue against the backs of his teeth, shoving his irritation with Annin's sense of humor aside. "She told me she was going to Zeal," he said, "and that I wouldn't be able to stop her. Either way, she's flighty and frightened. She'll end up in our hands again."

"Not willingly, I hope you realize."

Kol shook his head. "That doesn't matter. She belongs down here. She belongs to me. I've told her she's in danger, and I'm choosing to believe she trusted that."

"The same way you chose to believe she wouldn't run in the first place?"

Kol shoved himself to his feet and paced away from Annin, through with having the blame crammed down his throat, no matter how much he deserved it. "I've done everything you asked me to do. Now do something with that information."

Annin stood, hiding Nes's soul vessel in his pocket. "I can't do any more with that information than I already have. We knew she was heading to Gelthin. We knew she'd be on the run. Grell's already got his allies sweeping the southern region of the continent."

"So come up with another plan," Kol sneered.

If only plans on tracking a fractured soul across Abaeloth were easy to come up with… "Have you still got connections in the mountains near Harborswatch?"

In all honesty, Kol didn't know. That tribe of demons had been loyal to him at one time, but he hadn't communicated with them since he'd been relocated beneath Elidae. Demons without an inoga overlord dictating their actions didn't often last long on their own, but if any of them were still independent, it would be the survivors of Kol's old clan. "We can try reaching them after I get some food."

Annin didn't answer, unusual given the course of their conversation. Kol turned around to find the oraku standing with his arms crossed, narrowed eyes sweeping back and forth as he plummeted deeper into thought. Half of the time Kol had seen Annin behave like this, brilliant things happened. The other half of the time ended in headache. Kol held his breath to wait on Annin to announce his brewing scheme, knowing it would come whether or not he wanted to hear it.

"If we can get a faction of demons more loyal to you than not, we might still succeed." Annin tapped his lips and nodded to himself in another moment of silence. "Were you fool enough to send Nessix away with all of her belongings?"

Kol huffed out an irritated sigh and cast his eyes toward the ceiling. It seemed as though Annin wanted to make problems out of everything. "Yes," he snapped. "I did. All she owned was her sword and armor."

Under normal circumstances, Annin would have criticized Kol for giving a prisoner access to weapons, but his back was against the wall in this situation. Bickering over who was at fault wouldn't get them any closer to reaching Nessix before Grell's connections did, and so Annin slowly turned a circle through Kol's chamber as he sought another option to suit his needs. The desk chair was too cumbersome to carry along with them. The books were too valuable to risk taking to the surface. The cot Nessix had slept on still sat sad and empty where Kol had left it, testifying his belief that she would come back to him. It was a pathetic reminder, but one Annin was grateful for today.

"Have you touched that since you set her free?" Annin pointed at the cot and turned his eyes to Kol.

Confused, the alar shook his head.

"Good. Don't. Prepare yourself for the road. I've got a couple... things to take care of, and then we're going to approach Grell, petition for an escort force to travel with us, and we're heading to Gelthin."

Kol always hated it when Annin took control over the course of action, but as he still struggled with which action was the correct one to take, he surrendered to the oraku's authority. "What... *things* have to be taken care of?" As deep as they were both buried in this mess, Kol was more certain than not that he could trust Annin, but clarification never hurt when dealing with an oraku.

Annin studied Kol a moment longer, imagining the tantrum he'd throw if he found out there had been damage dealt to Nes's soul vessel. For the moment, the alar was too preoccupied with the fact that Nessix was physically gone to recall that he'd handed over her soul. As long as Annin slipped away before that was remembered, he suspected there would be few problems to come of it.

"Things you don't need to worry about. I'm sure they'd bore you like everything else I occupy my time with."

Annin delivered Kol a smile that bordered on friendly, striking the alar with a fresh jolt of confusion, and turned to leave the room before any other questions delayed him. Kol stood in the middle of his chamber and stared at Nes's empty cot, wondering how it was supposed to lead him to her. As with everything else Annin conceived, the plan and reason behind it would be uncovered in good time. Unwilling to risk leaving his room, Kol turned to begin packing.

TEN

Mathias latched on to the strongest place he could ground to during his desperate teleportation from Seaton—the Citadel's temple. He arrived during the priestess's midnight prayers, and startled screams announced his sudden arrival, growing shriller once the young women saw the unconscious girl roughly gripped in his left arm. Having narrowly slipped past one unpleasant situation, Mathias had unwittingly dumped himself in a safer, but no more appealing, one as Julianna marched out of her chamber to scold him for this disruption.

She carried herself with conditioned grace, easing the startled priestesses with gentle words of comfort, telling them that all would be well and reassuring them that it was only Mathias and one of his impulsive games. As the young women allowed their senior's words to calm them, Julianna speared her brother with a vicious glare, a set jaw, and a deliberate shaking of her head. Mathias sighed, too tense from the situation he'd escaped from to do anything else, and let Julianna herd him to a private chamber off the sanctuary.

"*What* is going on?" Julianna demanded the second she closed the door behind them. "I thought you were supposed to be going to—" Her eyes widened and her hand covered her gasp. "Wait. Is this your Nessix? Did you find her?"

Mathias closed his eyes, begging Etha for patience and strength, as his was lacking at the moment. He knelt down and carefully laid Khin on the floor so he could put his sword away and stretch out his arms. "No. Her name's Khin. You can thank Sazrah for me not going into the hells, but to Seaton instead, and you can thank an effective task force of inoga for why I came here in the manner which I did."

Julianna slumped back against the wall, looking down at Khin, then back at Mathias. "Define an effective task force of inoga, please."

"I had eyes on at least three and their armies of underlings. If my ears are considered reliable, there were at least two other locations being ransacked by them." He held up a hand and ducked his head as Julianna drew in a deep breath to protest. "And before you ask why I didn't fight them and why I brought a girl back here with me, both are Etha's will."

That breath tapered out of Julianna's lungs through tight lips as she glanced through the sparse room to grab at something that made more sense than Mathias's words. "Etha told you to run from inoga?"

Mathias braced his fingers against his forehead and closed his eyes. "Jules, have you ever faced one of them?"

"No, but I've read—"

"Then you can shut your mouth."

Julianna gasped once, failed to gain Mathias's attention from it, and tried a second one. When he still didn't look up, she sank back further against the wall and tilted her head to try catching his eyes. "So what happened to the city?"

Mathias shook his head slowly. "The three I had eyes on recognized me instantly. I had to flee or risk them dragging me into the hells, and I know how badly you want me to only enter them on my own terms. My hope is that Zenos is safeguarding what he can."

It didn't make sense to Julianna why Etha would order Mathias to run away from any threat made by demons, and it made even less sense that Mathias would agree to do so. Whatever was happening in this rift between the realms and the blasphemy of stolen souls was far bigger than she knew how to handle. And based on Mathias's defeated posture, he seemed just as ill prepared to deal with it.

"Mattie…" she murmured. "What are we going to do?"

Free from immediate danger, strapped with the guilt of abandoning all of those frightened civilians and town guards who had likely never seen a demon in their lives, Mathias shook his head. "I haven't figured that out. Still trying to get over not being able to stop them." Not to mention how his heart mourned Nessix as much now as it had when she'd first died. If those inoga weren't gone by the time her ship arrived…

"Are you willing to talk to the Council about this yet?" Julianna had avoided revisiting the topic over the past several weeks.

Mathias hated dealing with politics, but he didn't know what else to do. With Etha herself openly admitting he was better off to run than charge into combat, it was time to swallow his distaste for the Council. "I don't think we have a choice. Calls for support are bound to reach us soon, and when the demons expand their—" He grimaced and cursed his thoughtlessness as Julianna cocked her head.

"When the demons expand their *what*?" Julianna asked. "Their search? Blessed Mother, they came here hunting after your girlfriend, didn't they?"

Mathias heaved a sigh and looked to the ceiling, arms crossed. "That's what it looks like, but we don't know for sure."

"You mean you won't admit it. Blessed Mother…" Julianna shook her head and turned to grab the doorknob. Before opening it, she spun to face Mathias and jabbed an accusing finger at him. "You'd better find a way to fix this."

Mathias frowned at his sister's demands. Hadn't she spent days trying to convince him that he didn't need to solve all of the world's problems? Etha herself didn't know how to fix their current crisis, so what was *he* supposed to do about it? It all boiled down to one thing, something Julianna couldn't possibly want to hear, and something Mathias was beginning to suspect was increasingly impossible.

"I will fix it," he said. "As soon as I can find Nessix, I will fix it."

"Oh, for crying out…" Julianna leaned her head back against the door and closed her eyes to search for her patience. "Mathias. This is bigger than her."

"You never knew her," Mathias said. "And you don't know the demons' patterns the way I do. You weren't the one in the field extracting information from gods and from Heiligate. There is no doubt in my mind that Nessix is the key to something crucial that will change the way Abaeloth looks at demons. And she knows it, too, or she wouldn't have told Sazrah she has to find me."

Julianna peered her eyes open and glowered at her brother. He was right that she didn't know Nessix. He was right that she knew little about how demons functioned in combat. She hadn't sought firsthand accounts of any of the attacks or disappearances, and she certainly didn't set foot anywhere near Heiligate. Mathias could very well be right, but that didn't mean everything would be alright. "And what if it's a change for the worse?"

"It won't be," Mathias insisted firmly. "It *can't* be. You don't know—"

"I don't know Nessix," Julianna said. "And you can't be sure you know the Nessix that has brought an army of inoga to Gelthin. Please, Mattie. You've given too much for Abaeloth to let it be destroyed while your eyes are closed."

Mathias grit his teeth, having never been so frustrated with his sister in all his life. "Can you shake all those buffoons of the Council awake at this hour so we can have that talk you're pestering me about?"

Julianna lowered her gaze and frowned. This hadn't been the way she'd wanted to spend the evening. "I can."

"Good," Mathias said curtly, kneeling down to gather Khin in his arms. "I'll be down to tell them the state of Abaeloth's security as soon as I figure out where to put her."

Disappointed in Mathias and herself, Julianna couldn't even form the words to agree with his statement. She turned and left the chamber.

* * * * *

Mathias wasted no time tucking Khin away in a private chamber in the Citadel's infirmary. He wasted as much time as possible, however, in reporting to the Council's conference room. Though it had been decided between himself, Julianna, and Etha to keep the circumstances involving stolen souls from the often dysfunctional governing body of the Order, he suspected their accusations would fall solely on his shoulders. After all, he was the one most likely to cause them headaches, and he'd never done much to hide his delight in doing so. He just wished they were of the propensity to believe it when he said this was one headache he'd done all he could to spare them.

Upon reaching the conference chamber, he was struck first by how quiet it was. Under normal circumstances, the ruckus of bickering penetrated even these thick doors when Mathias was responsible for their gathering, and he didn't know what to make of the stillness permeating the hall. Maybe Julianna hadn't been able to wake the officials. Maybe he could continue this quest by himself, evading the direct oversight of anyone other than Etha. He hadn't wanted to face the Council—or anyone, for that matter—about his current mission anyway, and he was willing to take the opportunity to excuse himself from this most unpleasant obligation.

Not quite at peace with his decision, but preferring it to the alternative, Mathias turned to leave and nearly tripped over Etha's youthful manifestation. Eyes wide, he held his breath and forewent the effort of trying to come up with an excuse the goddess might believe.

"You know as well as I do that they're in there." Though Etha's usual physical body was so tiny and petite compared to her champion, she might as well have been a solid wall that kept Mathias from leaving.

Mathias thought to argue that Julianna could handle this meeting on her own or to insist that his time and energy would be better spent in the field, but Etha's steady gaze and the authoritative lift of her chin barred him from either attempt. He'd submit to her will, as he always did, but he wouldn't be able to concentrate on anything discussed in the chamber without one question answered.

"Did they find Nessix?"

Etha's eyes flicked away from Mathias's pleading gaze. "They have not stopped their rampage, so I doubt they've achieved their objective."

Mathias breathed out his tension and closed his eyes. "Have *you* found Nessix?" When he opened his eyes, Etha had her lips tucked in a dissatisfied frown and Mathias's heart sank to his feet, barely allowing him to gasp. "Etha, what happened?"

She held up a strict finger. "First, do I have your word, your absolute sworn obedience and full compliance, that you will enter that chamber—here and now—to discuss these matters with the Council if I answer that?"

Mathias's heart raced faster and sweat beaded on the back of his neck. He ran a hand through his hair and tried unsuccessfully to swallow against a dry throat. Shifting his weight restlessly, longing to run in the direction of a danger he didn't know how to locate, his damp eyes met Etha's. She wouldn't have asked him to swear to stay put if something wasn't terribly wrong. "But if—"

Etha snapped her fingers. "Do you swear your obedience, Mathias?"

Shoulders sagging helplessly, Mathias rocked back on his heels and shook his head in defeat. "Fine. I swear my obedience to you. I will turn around and enter that chamber the second you tell me what I need to know."

A deep breath lifted Etha's tiny shoulders and she reached forward to grasp Mathias's hand. Not for support, as she normally would, but to keep him honest. "I have not found Nessix; whatever the demons did to her soul makes her unable to be tracked, even by me. But"—she raised her voice to stop Mathias's attempt to pull away from her—"she'd reached Seaton well before the demons did and left it in a hurry shortly before their attack."

Mathias's knees buckled and he staggered backwards to slam his back against the chamber's doors for support, dragging Etha with him. "Nes was there?" he asked. "And I *missed* her?"

Guilt devoured Mathias, consuming his hope without mercy.

Etha covered his hand with hers and glanced at the doors. It wouldn't be long before someone inside came to investigate that thump.

"She is safe for now," Etha said quickly, answering Mathias's question before he organized his stunned thoughts enough to ask it. "Zenos caught her trespassing in the Forgotten Histories and sent her away as soon as he felt the demons' disturbance. Not even he knew who she was until it was nearly too late."

Etha's explanation wasn't enough to restore Mathias's strength, and she gently pulled him away from the doors as footsteps approached from the other side.

"She's got a map from him and has the experience to put it to good use. Mathias, as long as you can keep the demons off her trail, she will reach Zeal. We'll find her. This is almost over."

Because keeping demons distracted when they're after something is such *an easy task…* Mathias thought bitterly.

Etha fit him with a stern frown but before she could respond, one door swung open. Despite Etha's support, Mathias fell backwards and into Julianna's startled grasp. It hadn't been the way Etha had intended to get Mathias into the conference chamber, but it successfully accomplished her goal. Satisfied that Mathias was where he needed to be, Etha slipped from the mortal plane.

Julianna huffed at the effort of keeping her brawny brother on his feet, nearly falling over, herself. "What is *wrong* with you?"

Mathias pressed a hand against Julianna's shoulder, not helping her stability at all, to force his knees to straighten. "I… I need to go."

"Oh, no." Julianna shoved him upright, frowning as he flailed for balance. "You're not pulling this. Not now."

Mathias dug his fingers into his eyes and released a tormented groan. "Jules, Nessix is here. She's running from… she's the reason… I… I have to go." Mathias lurched to leave, though Julianna caught him with little trouble.

"Who is Nessix?"

Henrik Caldwell's pompous voice rang from inside the chamber, dragging Mathias back to reality and the complications which came with Council business.

The paladin's hand dropped to his side and he clenched his jaw. He might have agreed with Julianna that the Council needed to know about the missing souls. He might have promised Etha he wouldn't run from this conversation. But he'd sworn to Laes that he'd protect Nessix, and he'd vowed to her that he would keep her safe. Lips curling back in a snarl, Mathias gathered his strength to tear free from Julianna's grasp, and then he saw her remorseful eyes. The guilt never left him, but a temporary cloak of patience settled on his shoulders, encouraging him to at least try delivering his report. He allowed Julianna to guide him into the chamber, the door falling closed behind them.

Stepping up in her flustered brother's defense, Julianna spoke before Mathias had gathered his thoughts. "Master Caldwell, she's the general Mathias was sent to help on Elidae."

Murmurs rippled through the three dozen officials—mostly humans, with three elves and a dwarf among them—gathered in the chamber, and the Council's Head of Court, robe delightfully disheveled from the haste he'd taken to don it, leaned over his podium. "What's she doing *here*?"

Julianna's frown deteriorated into a grimace and though she was the stronger of the two Sagewinds right now, she looked to Mathias for guidance.

"And why would she be running?" Eldon Blaxton added. The Regent of Plebeian Affairs asked his question in a kinder tone than his contemporary. "Sir Sagewind, explain why we were called to court at this hour."

Julianna's lips closed and her brows tipped sorrowfully, silently apologizing to Mathias for her inability to sort through this matter while he was out of sorts. Seeing his sister hurt, especially when her pain was tied to him, was among Mathias's greatest fears, and he shook his head to dismiss her worries. Etha had brought him back to life to keep evil at bay. He'd faced horrors and death without balking. He could handle talking to the Council.

"She... That war didn't go quite the way my report said it did."

None of the Council members voiced their surprise at Mathias's confession, though Thessia Hazlitt, the city's Director of

Finances, didn't hide her rude cough.

When Mathias didn't elaborate, Henrik crossed his arms. "That doesn't answer our questions."

Mathias frowned, his guilt compounded by having lied under official circumstances. Never again would he allow Julianna and Etha to convince him that these sorts of meetings were a good idea.

"Respected sirs and madams of the Council," Julianna said, jumping to Mathias's defense. After all, she was the one who had been groomed for court—and outranked everyone here. "The demons have begun practicing necromancy."

Chaos erupted immediately, and Mathias's feeble attempt to clarify her statement drowned a rapid death in a riptide of frightened speculations. Until tonight, Mathias had considered this group of officials to be among the smoothest functioning in Zeal's history. They'd had a good run.

As they bickered over the implications of this report, who they could blame for the leaked knowledge, and what they could do about it, that blanket of patience slid off Mathias's back. He quietly shifted to withdraw, but Julianna's hand struck out to grab him once again. He groaned, but didn't fight her. As much as he wanted to deny it, he'd been the one gathering reports from the field. He was the one who understood demons' tactics. He was the one who knew Nessix. Julianna might have brought about more complications, but this was Mathias's quest.

Finally, Henrik's voice punctured through the cacophony to reach the siblings. "And how did *you* come to know this, High Priestess?"

Julianna squeezed Mathias's hand and took a deep breath. "Mathias went looking for Nessix's soul after it was stolen on the field and we've only now begun to piece the facts together."

Henrik trembled in a tiny fit of arrogant offense. "It is your duty to report such events to the Council first and foremost!"

Beside her, Mathias sucked in a retaliatory breath, but Julianna beat him to a rebuttal. "Our *duty*, Master Caldwell, is to execute Etha's will, and you'd be a fool to forget that. You can distrust Mathias all you want; he's earned it rather well. But you have my word as High Priestess of your Order that we were operating under Etha's direct orders, instructed to bypass conventional protocol in the name of urgency."

One of the few powers none of the Council members had the courage or ego to debate was Julianna's word, but the blunt reminder of her influence didn't make a lapse in protocol any easier for the officials to tolerate. "So why come to us now?"

Julianna had bought Mathias enough time for him to regain his sensibilities, and he stepped up beside his sister. He had fewer qualms with angering the officials than she did, anyway. "War is coming, one potentially worse than Abaeloth has seen since the Divine Battle. With Etha as my general, I can lead the warfronts, but someone in Zeal must begin logistics for sheltering refugees and recruiting foolish souls to charge with me."

After countless years of trying, Mathias had never before managed to silence the Council's bickering. Too bad it had taken such an ominous message to accomplish. He'd conditioned everyone in the room to question his honesty in the past, but his words tonight hushed them and stole the color from their cheeks. For the first time in Mathias's recollection, they appeared willing to let him do his job.

Henrik cleared his throat, shrinking behind his podium as the abrasive sound filled the hushed chamber. "What does this Nessix have to do with it?"

And just as seamlessly, Henrik threw the stunned silence back at Mathias. Besides the fact that he couldn't answer that with complete certainty, the better part of the paladin continued to deny how deeply involved Nessix had been forced into this ordeal. Moments into Mathias's contemplation, Julianna drew a quick breath and opened her mouth. She was too honest, and Mathias could not allow her to be the one to answer. He couldn't stand to see Nes's name sullied.

"She will be who leads me to the demons' demise," Mathias blurted before Julianna's bias could further influence their audience. "If I can find her before—" He winced at his hastiness. It was too late to cover a second slip, and he knew the truth would come out eventually. "Before the demons do, we will win this war."

More murmurs bubbled up from the officials, and Henrik spoke above them all. "So, she brought this war. It has been noted."

Mathias clenched his teeth. The less he tried to fight this assumption, the smoother the exchange would proceed and the sooner he could get on the road again.

"And what happens if the demons reach her first?" Henrik asked, the arrogance of accusation spitting on Mathias.

"They won't," he said. "I won't let them."

Julianna glanced from Mathias and his finely netted irritation to the cocky official who seemed to derive pleasure in tempting fate. Her authority in the matter was quickly dissipating, as it often did when Mathias's opinions contradicted the Council, and she dropped his hand so she could wring her own. Hopefully, she wouldn't regret the action.

"What happens if they *do*?" Henrik pressed, thin brows tipped in a disapproving frown.

If Mathias hadn't been bound by the law, he'd have accepted this underlying challenge for control through physical means. Henrik's intention, however, was to take advantage of Mathias's recent lapse of coherence to make him snap. The Council had been looking for a way to tether him under stricter guidelines for decades, and being able to claim him unstable would be a first step in accomplishing that. Fortunately for Mathias, their previous blathering had given him just enough time to calm down and spoil Henrik's plans.

"I don't know," he answered at last.

Henrik stared at Mathias, having opened his mouth for some grand declaration the moment the paladin began speaking. Now, Mathias's honesty left the decorated official standing there, mouth sagging like a fool as his objection wheezed silently from him. That humiliation was enough satisfaction for Mathias.

While Henrik struggled to compose himself, Eldon stood. "I'd like to make a motion to allow Sir Sagewind this quest, provided he first leaves a report—an *accurate* one—of what he knows."

Not bothering to hide her shock, Julianna's head snapped to look at her brother. His brows were arched in surprise. Historically, it took the Council days to figure out what to do with Mathias, long enough that he often snuck out without their consent. That they'd thrown out a suggestion within the first ten minutes after gathering clearly stated the depth of their concern.

Another rumble of murmurs came about as one by one the other officials agreed to the motion. Though Julianna loathed the idea of Mathias being thrown into danger, it was the life he lived, and she looked at him hopefully. As the final agreement came from Henrik, Mathias's eyes narrowed keenly, and Julianna's hope shriveled.

"How about a vague list of details until I get back?" he asked.

"Sir Sagewind, do you think this is a game?" Eldon scolded.

On normal circumstances, Mathias would have let this discussion become just that, poking and prodding until he got his way. Today, however, he frowned. "I know this isn't a game, more so than any of you do. And if it's in my power to do so, I'll keep you from ever needing to think otherwise. Here is your report; Nessix escaped the demons. She's on the run, allegedly heading here, and the demons are chasing her. They've got enough bodies to torment in the hells that they wouldn't be trying to stop her if they didn't have a damn good reason. She knows something the Order must hear, and we'll never hear it if we don't ensure she reaches Zeal. Julianna can fill in a bit more. Don't let your petty reliance on paperwork ruin our chance to pull ahead."

His brashness was met with the same irritation as always, but nobody objected. They were too afraid.

"High Priestess," Eldon said, turning to face Julianna. "Are you able to relay a report as your brother says?"

Julianna retained her frustrated pout. "I can share all that the sisterhood has uncovered, as well as what Mathias conveyed to me."

"Very well," Eldon sighed. "Sir Sagewind, grant us this evening to discuss what you've presented, and you should be clear to ride out within the next two days. May Etha continue to bless you."

Mathias opened his mouth to deliver his opinion on his estimated time of departure, head cocking in an argumentative tilt until Julianna pinched his arm. This was not the time for him to press his luck.

"Of course, respected sirs and madams." She bowed her head slightly to the Council members. "Etha has heard your promise."

Before Mathias had a chance to sabotage his good fortune, Julianna hustled him from the conference chamber.

ELEVEN

Nessix pushed past the fatigue of having slept in her armor, past the aching of muscles that hadn't fully recovered. Rations running low, the only thing she struggled to push past was the hunger that gnawed at her stomach. Besides the physical discomfort, she risked succumbing to starvation's weakness, which would leave her just as vulnerable as injury. She'd seen no game on the road and, ever mindful of the demons chasing her, was reluctant to leave the path or take the time necessary to try tracking any. Fluffy trails of chimney smoke stretched into the sky ahead, and Nessix let her eyes drift closed as she directed a murmured prayer of thanks to the heavens.

She wandered into the village, acutely aware of her bedraggled state and the cautious eyes which followed her weapons. Trying to remember what it was like to soothe civilians, she sagged with exhaustion and greeted suspicious glances with a tired smile. Before long, a stocky man carrying a weathered pike walked up to her, stopping outside her sword's reach but well within his weapon's striking distance. Nessix halted respectfully and held her hands open before her.

"I'm not after trouble," she said. "I'm on an urgent quest to Zeal, was attacked last night, and am in need of food."

The man cocked his head from side to side. "Attacked, eh?

They steal your coin purse?"

Heart falling, Nessix aimed to deliver a placating smile, but it came out as more of a grimace. "They did." She hadn't had a purse to begin with, but understood the intent of his question. She didn't have money, and that was what mattered.

"Then shove on. We don't have the means for charity here."

Nessix's stomach screamed at her to challenge this man to see if she could earn charity through respect, yet her brain scolded her for how reckless such an action would be. She hardly had the energy left to stand, and she had no authority on Gelthin. Closing her eyes and wincing at her hunger pains, Nessix bowed her head. Her remaining rations would take her to the next town if she couldn't find any easy game on the road. They'd have to.

"Then please excuse my intrusion. I'm just passing through."

"Jordan!" The shrill voice of an aged woman cut through Nes's gloom, and she looked up. "Shame on you! The poor thing can barely stay on her feet, and you tell her we can't offer her *food*?"

Before Nessix could politely tell the woman that she'd been through far worse conditions and lie that it was no trouble for her to seek assistance elsewhere, the tiny woman—smaller than Nessix was, herself—bustled over and began picking leaves and debris from the tangles in Nes's hair, murmuring something about "you poor, poor thing."

Jordan pounded the butt end of his pike on the ground with a grunt. "Poor thing barely on her feet is armed to the teeth and has eyes that have seen death. She'll get nothing from us."

The woman stopped picking Nes's hair clean to grasp her by the shoulders. Leaning back, she gave Nessix a stern appraisal and nodded in satisfaction. Releasing her hold, she resumed tidying Nes's hair. "We've all seen death around these parts." She raised her voice to deliver the next. "And *responsible* youngsters would keep themselves armed in these times." The woman stomped her feet to turn around, wedged her hands on her hips and leaned forward as she continued scolding the man. "If *you* won't feed her, then I will. Now, come on, dear."

She grabbed Nes's elbow and dragged her toward a quaint cottage not far down the road. Concerned that she might have complicated a dispute she had no business being in, Nessix cast a glance over her shoulder to make sure Jordan didn't follow. He swatted a rude hand and spit in their direction, then trudged off as though someone told him the way he wore his hair made him look funny.

"Don't you worry about Jordan, child." The woman patted the back of Nes's hand. "He's just a little on edge lately. You know. Since the changes came."

Nessix cleared her throat and waited patiently as the woman pulled the door open and ushered her inside. "Changes, ma'am?"

"Oh! That's right. You're not from around these parts." The woman chuckled to herself and bustled over to a table where an assortment of baked goods cooled. "Well, I'll not trouble you with our little village's worries. Let's get you fed, let you rest, and see you on your way to Zeal. If you like the pie, you can tell that blasted Order that we could use their assistance."

Nessix was certain she'd like the pie, but was put off by the woman's apparent distrust for the Order. Mathias had told her it was Gelthin's beacon of justice. If a village of unskilled civilians was having trouble, wouldn't it be just for the Order to intervene? This wasn't the first time Nessix wondered if she might have jumped ahead of herself on this quest. Pushing aside that concern was becoming increasingly difficult, but the old woman distracted her from those thoughts by offering up a slice of apple pie with the promise of a more substantial meal once her boys returned from their work in the fields.

Irma, as the woman identified herself, was a charming busybody of a hostess, refusing to let Nessix do anything more than take off her armor to relax. It was an offer she leapt at, and even sitting in a wooden chair was a relief to her weary bones. Irma gave Nessix a change of clothes so hers could be washed— something Nessix couldn't remember the last time she'd had done—and she was able to forget the hardships of travel, at least for the afternoon. All it cost was being a polite audience for a lonely old woman's gossip, which beat the dark places Nes's mind wandered in silence.

As evening rolled around, a bell tolled from outside, calling the men in from the fields. Dinner of a roast chicken, fresh rolls, and tender steamed vegetables was served, and Nessix had to restrain herself from requesting a second portion after the bland diet she'd suffered through in the hells. She settled for an extra slice of pie upon Irma's insistence that it would go bad if left until morning, and then was tucked away in the corner of a back room on a makeshift mattress made of a pile of quilts.

Nessix woke in the morning to bright sunrays streaming through the window and tense whispers from the main living area of the little house. Rubbing her eyes, she sat up and concentrated on her hosts' discussion, an unexpected and unwelcomed ball of nerves settling heavily in the pit of her stomach. She reached out a hand to caress her sword and armor and released a relieved breath at their presence as she strained harder to listen.

The words never came clearly and Nessix resorted to holding her breath to try to hear them. Could they have figured out who— or what—she was? She pushed the covers off herself and prepared to defend whatever she had to, the subtle sounds of her movement drawing Irma's attention. The old woman rushed through the open doorway and knelt down to shove Nessix back to the floor.

"You stay right here, dear," she said, shooting a quick glance over her shoulder.

Nessix furrowed her brows at the tension in Irma's voice, those nervous suspicions rolling around inside of her. "Is something wrong?"

"Nothing's wrong. Just…" Irma frowned. "*Business* as usual." The little old lady popped to her feet with deceptive spryness and prepared to leave, but Nessix wouldn't be thwarted so easily.

She sat up again. "It seems that business is a cause of concern. Is it one I ought to be aware of?"

The woman cast a hasty glance toward the front door and glared back at Nessix, an endearing strictness struggling for authority. "Not if you want to live. You said you don't have any money? Then you're not in this town, at least not for the next couple hours." Irma spun and pulled shut the curtain which served as a door before Nessix could argue, rapid footsteps carrying her toward the front of the house.

Curiosity vying against concern, Nessix eased herself to her feet and picked up her sword belt to secure it to her waist as she crept forward to listen more carefully. Fed and rested, she finally felt as though she'd stand a chance if she had to engage in combat. The hushed whispers continued, now with clear footsteps scampering here and there, the clinking of coins and opening of jars. The accommodating nature her hosts had shown her yesterday did not match the frantic temperament displayed this morning. Something was gravely wrong.

Holding her breath, Nessix waited until the sound of the front door opening squeaked through the house, resulting in Irma's throaty cry of despair.

"Where's it at?" a rough voice spat, echoed by a vile chuckle.

"Here. It's right here." The trembling on Irma's husband's voice made it sound as though he was begging for their lives. "I'll count it out for you, if you'd like."

"Bah!" the voice sneered, answered by another round of laughter from at least two companions. "You don't have the nerve to cheat us. Give it here, and we'll be on our way."

By now, Irma sobbed quietly, her husband remaining silent. A collection of feet stomped out of the small house and the door slammed shut behind them. Irma wheezed a quivering sigh and Nessix pulled the curtain aside, eyes serious and cold. She'd only seen funds seized by force courtesy of one other person in her life, and he'd been a tyrant she wished she could have witnessed the end of herself.

"What was that?" Nessix asked, an air of authority gained from years of governing both Elidae and her small collection of misfits in the hells shining around her.

Irma gasped and looked up at Nessix, waving one hand frantically while the other dabbed at her tears. "I told you, it's nothing to worry about. B-business as usual."

"It doesn't sound like any business you should be part of. If you can tell me that whatever just happened is something you consider normal and just, I'll shut up and head on my way."

"Business as usual," the man replied, voice shaking in his attempts to deliver firmness. His eyes spoke of a deep anger he was too afraid to touch.

These people had been kind to her. Whatever it was that terrorized them was not something they deserved, Nessix was sure of it. This couple was unlikely to disclose what she was after, and she wasn't keen in getting in a fight over it. Pride wouldn't allow Nessix to forego a chance to repay Irma and her husband for their generosity, and anger wouldn't allow her to overlook their distress. It didn't matter if it was a simple group of bandits or a full-blown army waiting outside the tiny house; Nessix would face them. She drew her sword and strode to the door.

"Oh, no! Stop!"

Irma's cry was shrill and piercing, traveling easily through the door which Nessix had flung open and reaching the trio of demons as they resumed their predatory stalking down the street. Nessix froze for a heartbeat, her breath catching in her throat as they spun to face her. Before their smirks could grow into grins of anticipation, Nessix leapt into action. They were nothing more than average soldiers, but she couldn't afford to take the chance that they'd been told to watch for her, and she would silence them before she bothered to find out.

Darting forward, Nessix targeted the demon on her left, working from the side of the group to avoid being grabbed. Based on their plump bellies and greasy faces, these demons hadn't seen the hells—or the level of fitness required to survive down there—in ages.

Nessix struck her first target quickly, swatting her sword diagonally across his chest as she grabbed one of her daggers with her off-hand. She sank the smaller blade into the demon's gut before he could protect himself, but her preoccupation with him gave his friends time to react. The demon in the middle threw himself at Nessix, crushing her arms to her sides. The third turned and ran off down the road.

Cursing silently, unable to do so verbally with her face smashed against the demon's chest, Nessix squirmed, trying to twist her way to freedom. The demon held her tighter, squeezing the air from her lungs, and she stomped down on the bridge of his foot, prompting a swift kick back at her. Taking advantage of her assailant's movement, Nessix jammed her knee between his legs and though he maintained his hold, it loosened enough for her to rotate her arms and jam her knife into his side.

The demon grappled for Nes's arm, despite his wound. She sent a hasty glance at the one who rapidly fled down the road and cursed again, this time out loud. In a town full of unarmed, unskilled, middle-aged farmers and facing only one armed combatant, that demon wasn't running out of fear, no matter how pathetic he and his peers looked. He was running for reinforcements or to report this turn of events. Leaving her knife sunk in her current opponent's kidney, Nessix disengaged to pursue the demon running down the road.

Necessity had forced Nessix to embrace running, her body and mind resilient against the taxes it posed on her systems. It was something the plump demon hadn't taken into consideration when he decided to try escaping her. Bundling her momentum into a spring, she leapt and latched onto the demon's back. He paddled his arms out at his sides as he struggled to catch his balance, his efforts halted as Nessix swept the length of her sword's blade across his throat. Gurgling, he toppled forward, landing both himself and Nessix roughly on the ground.

Shaking off her daze, Nessix pushed herself upright to turn back to where she'd left the second demon, and found him face down on the road. Stunned villagers crept from their homes to peer at the dead bodies. Rightfully reluctant now that the people saw how efficient she was at killing, Nessix stood, already missing the comfort she'd restored from the previous night's sleep. She strode over to that second demon, hefted him over onto his back to confirm he'd quit breathing, and retrieved her dagger. Wiping the blood off on her target's pants, she returned it to its sheath.

Cautious eyes that had judged her from the moment she'd arrived turned bright with wonder. Death never came without some degree of remorse or pity for Nessix, and she'd never before seen civilians so happy to see dead bodies. Slowly, she put her sword away.

"You... did you *kill* them?" asked a nervous voice from behind her.

Nessix turned and wiped her sweaty palms on her breeches. "I did. And now will one of you *please* explain to me what business you're involved in?"

She didn't get her answer, met instead with cheers as the bolder of the men rushed forward to pluck coin pouches off the belts of the fallen demons to distribute among the other households in the village. Nessix stood by as each of them who passed murmured his awestruck gratitude.

"Someone, please," she begged. "I need to know what's going on so I can know if my job is through." She had to know if there were more demons lying in wait nearby to be alerted by the ruckus of the villagers' celebration.

"It's been what," one of the women said, turning her inquisitive gaze to the crowd. "Two years now? Yes. Two years, I think. These three showed up, rattled about a few of our men and told us if we wanted to live, we'd keep them paid. Have you ever tried to stand up to *demons* before?"

Nessix's mouth dropped open to respond.

"Of course she's stood up to demons before, Marta," another woman scoffed. "Would you look at what she did!"

Nessix glanced around self-consciously as awe blossomed into a sense of worship. The crowd inched closer, her presence no longer a concern among them. "I've fought demons before." The confirmation restored a bit of the confidence Kol's visit had stolen from her.

"You *saved* us!"

Cheers erupted around her, and Nessix prayed once again that there were no vile ears listening in on what was going on. "I did. And now the smartest thing you can do is get rid of those bodies in case other demons come around and find them."

That thought sobered the crowd, as they contemplated the likelihood of more demons stumbling across their tiny town, but it lasted for just a moment.

"There won't be any others," someone shouted from the group.

"Not with you around!" came an instant agreement.

Nessix's shoulders slumped as she soaked in the wonder and

trust in their eyes. "I… I can't stay here."

This time, the silence hung over them with an oppressive force.

"But you have to. You're our savior, our champion!"

"We'll keep you fed!"

"I'll introduce you to my son when he gets back from the fields."

Nessix pinched her lips tight at the desperate offers and the lower one quivered. Not long ago, there was another group of people who had begged just as passionately to a savior who showed up and killed a few demons. Her heart ached for those times, flooding with an empty longing she didn't know if she'd ever be able to soothe.

"Were these the only three demons that have been by your town?" Several nods answered, and Nessix blew out a sigh of relief. "Good. That means it's likely they're the only ones you'll have to worry about. Now, dispose of the bodies somehow. Clean up this mess. If you want to avoid future conflicts with demons, you need to trust me when I say that I must be on my way." Simply knowing that demons had targeted this town was enough to get Nessix's heart racing and skin crawling.

"Where are you going?"

It only occurred to Nessix now that every piece of information she left behind on her way to Zeal was a clue to her whereabouts. No matter how good natured these people were, they'd crumble like aged parchment to a demon's interrogation.

"She said she was heading to Zeal," Jordan grunted, though this time with admiration.

A smattering of murmurs rose from the crowd as the general consensus agreed that Zeal was a much more appropriate place for one of Nes's skills. But that didn't stop them from trying once more to convince her to stay.

"What is your business in Zeal?" one of the young men asked. "Perhaps we can offer an alternative."

Nessix bit her lip. After their generosity toward her, after the fear they'd lived with the past two years, after their relief in having been freed from that fear, she wanted to give them the honest answer. They deserved the honest answer, though she doubted they'd believe it. But she'd already burdened them with too much danger simply by coming through their town. She had no idea the means which Kol would employ to find her, and she had even less of an idea what this alleged inoga search party had in mind for anything that stood in their way. As the danger those brutes posed crossed her mind, Nessix was struck with an even stronger urge to get moving.

"You're safer not knowing," Nessix said at last.

The crowd remained hushed, staring at her with wide, disbelieving eyes. Nessix held her breath, waiting for the boisterous laughter that normally came from people assuming such a statement was a joke. That laughter never came, just more nervous shuffling as the money pouches quit being distributed.

"Are you... are you a fugitive?"

Women ducked behind their husbands and those near enough to something to wield as a weapon clutched nervously to their improvised defenses. Nessix sighed. Leave it to commoners to not fight demons for their livelihood but take up arms against the one person they watched slay three of them. Either way worked for Nessix, she supposed. She truly wasn't much less of an abomination than the demons were, these days.

"I'm not a fugitive of any of the laws you'd be familiar with," she said. "But there's a reason I'm comfortable fighting demons, and that's the same reason I need to keep moving. I'll let you make of that what you will." Hopefully, they'd think she was a great hero questing to cleanse other towns, as opposed to the ugly truth that she was running from reality.

Silence pressed on a moment longer before the first of the villagers crept forward and knelt at her feet, raising his coin pouch in offering. Nessix shook her head, but he shoved it into her hand and closed her fingers around it.

"You came here saying you'd been robbed. Please," he said, "if we cannot get you to stay and benefit from our hospitality, this is the least we can do. To never have our money stolen again? We'd assumed this was lost to begin with, but you gave us our freedom and our peace. You gave our children their security."

Several murmurs echoed this man's sentiments as others walked forward to thrust their pouches at her, as well. Nessix accepted the first two, and then held up her hand.

"I will not take all of your money," she said. "Or else my efforts today would have been pointless. All I need is enough to see me to the next town. I'll figure something out from there."

The villagers seemed on the verge of protesting, but equally determined—and relieved—to keep their money. Nessix begged them to spare her a fanfare and to let her slip from town quietly, and once they finally began to drag the demons' bodies off the road, she returned to Irma's house to gather her belongings and a satchel of food for the road, and departed from the village.

TWELVE

Annin was as pleased with the results of the plan he'd thrown together—and his ability to salvage his scraps and splinters of Affliction to seal the flaw he'd made on Nessix's soul vessel—as a demon could be about anything. Confidence thriving at last, he'd quit fearing the outcome of his next request from Grell. Certain that conversation would yield positive results, Annin took the liberty of packing his most essential belongings to expedite their departure once Grell gave them permission to go.

He didn't bother to knock on Kol's door when he returned to collect his friend, assuming he'd be welcome, but when he pushed open the door, he stared dumbfounded into the alar's room.

The desk had been overturned. The collection of books Kol normally took such diligent care of were scattered on the floor. Kol's bedding was shredded and strewn throughout the chamber as if a drunkard had been assigned to decorate for one of those silly mortal festivals. Annin gasped, fearing Grell had decided against allowing Kol his search for Nessix. That fear was quickly abated as the whispered gust of Kol's wings announced his rapid approach and the firmness of his fist met Annin's nose.

"Son of a—"

Annin wasn't given the chance to finish his curse as Kol drove him backwards and kicked his legs out from under him. The pair

DEFIANCE

tumbled to the ground with Kol bearing the definitive advantage as he straddled Annin, grabbed him by the collar, and jerked him close to his face.

"Where the fuck is she?"

Kol was among the more civil demons, slow to anger and calm when tasked with matters involving anything other than Nessix. It was a trait which had allowed him to thrive among the elite population. His obsession with the akhuerai, it seemed, had surpassed the damnable affection Annin often criticized to the point that such respectable control was escaping the alar's grasp. His slip, referring to Nessix's vessel as her physical entity, was an ill omen for the overall state of Kol's condition.

"Her vessel is safe," Annin said, snagging his calm before the reaction to fight back seized him. "If I could interest you in getting off of me, I'd be happy to return it to you."

Kol's eyes were wild and fierce, looking for excuses to tear someone apart and for a moment, Annin wasn't sure if his words had penetrated that insanity. The alar's arms trembled, his muscles bulging and tense as they waited for orders to escalate the confrontation. Kol seldom lost control of himself in combat, but if he did, it would not be a fight either he or Annin would walk away from.

"She is unharmed, Kol," Annin tried again. "I have her vessel in my pocket. I had to ensure everything was safe and secure with it."

Coherence seeped back into Kol's eyes and he released one hand from Annin's collar to pat over the oraku's pockets.

"My left," Annin instructed, gritting his teeth as Kol searched the opposite side in his maddened state. "*Your* right."

Kol scowled, though it was unclear if it was at Annin's correction or embarrassment that such a simple concept had escaped him. He crammed his hand into Annin's pocket, fingers entwining with the chain of Nessix's vessel, and he closed his eyes with a quiet sigh. Tension fluttered from Kol's posture, and Annin shoved the alar off himself to dab at the blood running from his right nostril.

"You're going to have to trust me more than this if I'm

121

supposed to lead your search on the surface," Annin said.

Kol stared at the crystal pendant with a nauseating affection. "I'd love to trust you if you'd bother to prove you cared about her fate."

Annin stood, brushed himself off, and stretched the soreness from his wings. "I care about her fate tremendously, thanks to how closely you've tied it to mine."

As Annin spoke, Kol ran his fingers over the pendant, expression softening until he turned it over and discovered the blemish Annin had sealed over. Face contorting, Kol glared at Annin, but before he could begin spouting his fury, the oraku raised his hand.

"It was the only way to tie your souls together. Not one wisp of her escaped, and it's been sealed up with Affliction itself." The reassurance wasn't quite enough to soothe the ire from Kol's scowl. "If nothing else, her vessel is stronger with additional support from the god spear."

That was the correct combination of facts, and the fire about Kol simmered to a warm glow. He put the chain around his neck and stuffed the pendant under his shirt. "You will not take her vessel from me again."

That still remained to be seen, but Annin settled for a brisk sigh and roll of his eyes. "Very well. Assuming you can locate your possessions in this mess, get packed. We'll need to move before Grell begins to suspect we're up to something and changes his mind."

Breathing in the comfort he gained from the nearness of Nessix's soul, Kol calmed himself and glanced through the destruction of his chamber. He knew he'd seen his pack in here somewhere... "You've already received his approval?" Kol pulled the desired item from beneath a toppled stool.

"Not yet, but he's too eager to see us fail to not let us try."

Kol's frown deepened as he salvaged a fresh set of clothing from the mess of his chamber. He'd have preferred Annin to have taken care of these arrangements sooner. "We will not fail."

"Of course we won't. You and Nessix are bound to each other, her soul should start calling for itself once we get close to her, and none of the inoga who are chasing after her know what she looks like outside of Grell's description. You tell me all the time how smart she is; and we both know Grell's contacts won't track her with finesse. She'll stay on the move and we'll let the inoga drive her to us." The plan almost sounded practical. Annin pulled the knife from his hip and walked to the cot—the only item in Kol's room that had been spared his panicked rage—and cut a square from its cloth.

Over the years, Kol had adjusted well to Annin's unusual actions, but this preoccupation he had with Nessix's bed stood out strong enough to distract Kol from his packing. "*What* are you doing?"

Lifting the square of cloth with his blade, Annin pulled a handkerchief from his pack. "It's my backup plan." Carefully, he draped the square of canvas into the handkerchief, folded it up, and shoved it back into his bag. "Get packed."

Too spent to pursue the matter, comforted by the thought that Annin was thinking steps ahead of him, Kol shrugged off his curiosity and did as he was told. As with most things, Annin was right. The longer Grell had to calm down and resume thinking clearly, the less likely he was to let them leave.

Packed with the essentials and equipped for combat, Kol took a deep, grounding breath and tried to ignore the frantic tremor of doubt beating behind his eyes. If any of this was going to work, from confronting Grell to capturing Nessix, he had to reestablish control—of the situation, of Annin, and of himself. Finding Nessix—the goal which surpassed his will to live—depended on him pulling himself together. Seizing this motivation with a death grip, bleeding into it with the intention to possess it, Kol shouldered his pack and strode past Annin to open the door.

"Are you coming?"

Annin stood stationary a moment longer, quietly observing the sudden shift in Kol's demeanor. Such instability was grossly unusual for the stoic alar, more reminiscent of Grell's unstable fits, though Annin wouldn't make such observations out loud. Silently, he traced Kol's threads, familiarizing himself with those he'd be able to snap in an emergency, then stepped forward to leave the room.

Kol strode ahead with his wings sprung up haughtily and head held high as he looked down at the underlings they passed. The news of his breakdown had spread quickly thanks to Grell, but the command Kol held in his eyes and the authoritative malice in his posture forbid them so much as snickers in his direction as they scuttled away or pressed themselves against the passage's walls, eyes hastily averted. Kol flourished under their reactions, reinforcing his dominance in the way he needed it most.

"You weren't planning on us going on our own, were you?" Kol kept his eyes ahead.

Pleased, if still wary, of whatever form of control Kol had tapped into, Annin answered with the obedience he'd always favored showing Kol. "Of course not. I've settled on the alar of the fifth wing and have already sent word to their elite. They're more loyal than most and have proven to think their problems through with sound minds."

Kol flicked a glance at Annin's backhanded jab, comforted that the oraku had resumed his dry humor in place of the pitying judgement he'd recently taken to using. "And you think they'll come?"

"Enough of them. I offered promotions and possession of a unit of akhuerai to use as they saw fit if they agreed."

Kol furrowed his brows. "We may not have akhuerai for much longer."

"They don't know that."

Of all the plans Annin had come up with through this mess Nessix had landed them in, this one seemed the least reliable. There was only a slim chance that the entire operation wouldn't be scrapped after how phenomenally it had blown up, and if it did survive, Kol was sure there would be a new list of regulations to accompany it. Lying to other demons didn't bother Kol, but the thought of them figuring out they'd been deceived did. The last thing he needed was for his reinforcements to turn on him.

Annin and Kol didn't risk talking over how they'd aim to trick Grell into complying with their request; they had to pass too many curious ears in the halls. Those same demons who knew of Kol's shame were also of the impression that a shift in their hierarchy was near, and any chance to pull ahead would be taken. Now that Kol seemed to find his head, Annin was more comfortable with the idea of twisting the subject to their advantage; there was nobody in all the hells who wanted Nessix back more than he did. Any place Kol might stumble, Annin would be able to cover. The next time they spoke was when they rounded the corner before Grell's chamber.

"I think it would be best if you were the one to announce us," Annin said quietly.

Kol curled his lip, too late to make the same suggestion to Annin. It wasn't worth the debate, and a display of confidence might do Kol good. And, if Grell was still on his smug quest to defeat him, he'd be more inclined to bite if Kol was the one requesting his own failure. Scoffing and shaking his head, Kol picked up his pace before self-doubt suggested he come up with another idea.

"Grell, Annin and I have come for an audience."

No disinterested grunt answered Kol. No sharp curse to order them away roared through the open doorway. Not even an amused greeting. Catching his breath in uncertainty, Kol's gait clipped to an awkward stop, Annin slowing as he reached him. Provided Grell was inside, it was unusual for him to not give some sort of response, especially considering where Kol currently stood on his list of prospective playthings.

Both demons stared at the open door, faces blanched and frowns contorted closer to illness as they contemplated what to do next. A shadow passed through the doorway, followed by a massive hand gripping the frame, and Grell peeked his head into the hallway, eyes bright and grin broad. Those frowns twitched even deeper. They'd have both preferred if Grell had been missing.

"Ah, Kol, Annin!" Grell greeted, his tone light and warm. "Do come in." He disappeared into the room, pulling his shadow with him.

"What has—"

"Shh," Annin scolded softly, too disturbed by Grell's cheerful demeanor to humor Kol's whispered concerns. When he'd last left the inoga, it hadn't been with the feeling that he had any reason to be so happy, and even if Grell had means of contacting his Gelthin-bound connections without Annin's assistance, there hadn't been enough time for them to have found Nessix. Something else had put that smile on Grell's face, and that was unsettling.

Neither Kol nor Annin were eager in the vaguest sense of the word to accept Grell's invitation, but they didn't trust his patience to hold out for their reluctance. Figuring none of this would have happened if not for Kol's gross negligence, Annin gave the alar a shove. Kol moved forward without so much as an irritated glare, and he scraped together enough of his confidence for Annin to comfortably follow. The sooner this conversation started, the sooner it would be over.

They rounded the doorway, uncertain what they would find, but not expecting the amount of blood smeared across the walls and pooled on the floor. Kol stopped abruptly, Annin holding an arm out to keep from slamming into him.

The akhuerai who Grell had taken such a liking to was sprawled broken on the floor, jaw dislocated and eyes barely beginning to regain the faintest glimmer of life. A crushed finger twitched in the blood as his soul dutifully weaved his threads back together.

"You never told me how entertaining these creatures are," Grell said, wiping the blood from his hands on a cloth too saturated to do him any good.

Kol stared at the akhuerai's mutilated body a moment longer before mustering the nerve to look at Grell. "Had he quit talking for you?"

"Not at all." Grell caught his stool with a foot and pulled it from beneath his desk. He plopped down on its seat and leaned forward. "He's been incredibly insightful, giving me everything I want. But it's fun to see him squirm as he thinks about how he'll never be strong enough to fight me." Grell let those words hang between them for a stuffy minute, his expression igniting with a cunning neither Kol nor Annin trusted. "Now. What do you want to talk about?"

The one thing Grell hadn't accounted for in this ploy to frighten Annin and Kol was that Kol already considered himself a dead man. That wasn't to say Kol *wanted* to die, especially by Grell's hands, but it was something he'd accepted. His only regret would be that he wouldn't see Nessix again, which was why this meeting was of such grave importance. Shaking off that tremor of fear, whether or not doing so would register to Grell as defiance, Kol cleared his throat.

"I'd like to take you up on your offer," he said.

Grell's smile faltered as he struggled to remember what offers he'd thrown at Kol over the past few days.

"To try to find Nessix before your inoga do." Before Grell had a chance to register the confidence with which Kol made his declaration, he added, "I'm optimistic of my odds. I am, after all, best equipped to hunt her down."

That cocky addition narrowly saved Kol from Grell's suspicion and a smile stretched across his scarred face. "*You* are better equipped to find a woman you've already lost once while she hides on Gelthin than a force of highly motivated inoga?" Grell looked over the modest packs slung over Annin and Kol's shoulders and chuckled. "Have you stowed some secret lure for her in your overnight bags?" He laughed again, rather pleased with his execution of humor.

Annin hadn't been joking when he said Grell was too entertained with the idea of seeing them fail. "No lure, sir," Kol said. "Only the desire to prove I can finish the job I started."

That delighted Grell even more, and he slapped his meaty hands on his thighs, stood, and lumbered up to the two demons. From the floor, the akhuerai seized consciousness, murmuring a weak plea for something that implied mercy.

"Quiet, you!" Grell stomped a foot in the man's direction, eliciting a horrified yelp as the akhuerai cringed into a ball. With a swift hiss of a laugh and shake of his head, Grell turned back to Kol. "I did say you could try to find her, didn't I?"

Kol swallowed the desire to beg Grell to honor the offer, knowing well that would be the fastest way for it to be revoked. "You did. And I'm confident it can be done."

"Confident, huh?" Grell leaned back and put his fisted hands on his hips. "That's a strange attribute to see in Kol these days, isn't it, Annin?" Grell flicked his gaze to the oraku, only now narrowing his eyes at the idea that the two of them might be hiding something. "You sure you want to risk your welfare following him on this fool's errand?"

"He will need an oraku's assistance to make it back here, with or without his target." Annin delivered his statement with such indifference Kol nearly doubted his loyalty. "And if my understanding is right, you want him back alive, should your connections reach Nessix first."

Grell snickered and swung his attention back to Kol, jabbing his thumb in Annin's direction. "Are *you* sure you want this oraku going with you, Kol?"

Annin was the last person Kol truly trusted and he invested that trust in the notion that this was part of his plan. "Not entirely," he said, playing to the inoga's eagerness to watch him fail. "But he said he refused to let me out of his sight. Something about liability."

Grell's grin lifted wickedly as he inclined his chin. "You really think you can do this, don't you?"

Kol met the gesture with a firm jaw. "I do."

"Is that because you think you're better than my kind?"

"I'm willing to give it a try to find out."

"Annin, you've got your work cut out for you with this one..." Grell shook his head, scenes of the tortures Kol was destined to face actively playing in his eyes.

"Sir, might I make a request?" Annin asked, since Grell seemed to favor him to Kol.

"You can do whatever you'd like."

Annin nodded once, respectfully, and stepped up beside Kol at last. "I am requesting permission to bring a guard unit from the fifth wing. I could use the extra hands to keep Kol managed."

"You know what I appreciate about you, Annin?" Grell asked. "You're an *honest* demon. You speak your mind, no matter how deeply the one you're acting against trusts you. For that, I'll give you your unit of guards."

"Thank you, sir."

Grell smirked and sent a glance at the akhuerai who had begun to crawl away from him in the hope of finding someplace to hide, his interest moving on to more immediate forms of entertainment than waiting on Kol's imminent demise. "If you're going to out pace my friends, you'd better get a move on," he said as he clomped through sticky blood to approach the terrified man.

Not waiting to see if Grell would have second thoughts about granting his permission or who he wanted to target for his fun, not bothering to thank him for his lenience in case it drew attention back to himself, Kol turned and left Grell's chamber. Annin followed close behind, and together, they strode down the hall as the akhuerai pled for help.

THIRTEEN

A generous yawn broke Khin's sleep, and she allowed herself a luxurious stretch, the terror of the previous night barred from her mind by the wonders of divine grace. Her legs sifted through the sheets, the weight of bedding offering to harbor her longer, if she desired. It was a delightful thought, one she hadn't entertained since she was a child, but a resilient brightness streamed through an open window, beating against her eyelids until she couldn't stand keeping them closed any longer. Peering through the slightest crack, too comfortable to care that she wasn't sure where she was, Khin was shocked into full consciousness.

The chamber she woke in was pristine and perfect, untouched by anything Abaeloth might demand of her. She had no recollection of entering the room, barely able to scratch together details of the cramped lodging where Mathias had held her captive. Could he have upgraded their accommodations? He'd called himself a knight, which meant he must have been a noble, but that didn't explain why she didn't remember moving to these new quarters.

Her brows furrowed, eyes pinching shut, and in less than a breath's time, Khin relived the screams of the townsfolk, saw the brothel catch fire, and those enormous beasts charging toward her. She'd been too afraid to move, too afraid to think, and then

Mathias had touched her forehead. Her eyes shot open again, putting a stop to the scenes flashing through her mind. If it was real, she didn't want to remember it.

Khin sat up and cast her bewildered gaze across the room. Pushing the covers off of herself, she discovered she was still in the filthy, torn dress that had been assigned to her at the brothel. She wiggled her toes, pulling open the scabs her frantic flight through Seaton left on the bottoms of her feet. Most notably, there were no screams outside this room, only the whisper of a gentle breeze and the occasional chirp of a passing bird.

And somehow, Mathias had played a role in all of this.

It was easy to think of him as a blessing, considering the attack he'd rescued her from, his generosity and ability to alleviate her pain, and the fact that he'd kept her from falling victim to the same fate as the other girls at the whorehouse. If not for Mathias's intervention, Khin would have died, but here she was, sitting in this plush chamber full of comfort and bliss, even if she couldn't shake her worries away. No matter how chivalrous Mathias had been, there was something not quite right about him. The way he moved so calmly through chaos, how he had the ability to knock her out with nothing but a caress…

A light scratch sounded from the other side of the door, interrupting Khin's cascade of thoughts. Moments later, the door cracked open to produce a petite middle-aged woman holding a modest tray of food and tea, a pail of steaming water in the other hand. A towel was draped over one arm, and she was dressed in a simple skirt and blouse, clean and pressed to perfection. Tawny hair was pinned up in a loose bun, and amber eyes spoke gentle volumes, tugging Khin's mind back toward her first thoughts of comfort and peace. Etha stepped through the doorway and let it swing softly shut behind her.

"How did you rest, dear?" Etha set the items on the nightstand and dipped her towel in the bucket of water.

"Very well." Khin watched as Etha wrung the excess water from the cloth and chewed on her questions. She tried valiantly to enjoy not needing to worry, but not even her best attempts were able to quell her concerns. "I'm sorry, but where am I?"

Etha handed Khin the towel and urged her to wash her face. "You're in the kingdom of Zeal, safe within the infirmary of the Citadel. No better board in all of Abaeloth, if I can be so bold to say."

Khin scrubbed her face, breathing deeply the scent of lavender and mint. "Do you know how I got here?"

"Mathias brought you," Etha said. "Surely, you remember that?"

"No," Khin said, her voice troubled and small. She lowered the towel to her lap. "Zeal's *weeks* away from Seaton and I… we were just…" Her lips puckered in frustration and she shook her head. "Mathias said he was a knight. A *simple* knight. But he's not making much sense."

"Oh?" Etha smiled, eyes twinkling. She always loved to hear others' impressions of her favorite son. "How's that?"

"Well…" Khin suddenly felt ridiculous speaking her concerns out loud, but figured she'd never see this woman again. "His generosity's disturbing. *Nobody* helps strangers without expecting something in return. Only he…" She silenced herself. Whether or not she'd ever see this woman again didn't matter. Khin had escaped Seaton, somehow, thanks to Mathias, and the life she'd had there was one she was content to leave behind. "He never asked me for any sort of payment. And we were in the middle of a… a *war* or something, and he marched right through it as though he was going to the market. Then whatever he did to make me forget how I got here… I…" She looked into Etha's soft eyes, lost and confused. "I don't understand."

Etha laughed gently and eased the towel from Khin's hands to replace it with the cup of tea. "That sounds exactly like our dear Mathias."

Khin furrowed her brows and stared harder at Etha. "How do you know him?

"Oh, I've known him all his life." Etha lifted her hands as though drinking from the cup, and nodded at Khin to follow her lead. "He's a good man with a good heart. It's a blessing he found you."

The color drained from Khin's flushed cheeks at the thought

that the man she'd just declared the greatness of might have gone spouting the nature of their meeting to the population of Zeal. It seemed out of his character, but the more Khin thought about it, the more she realized she had no idea what Mathias's character actually was. This elegant room was not something some questing knight should have been able to casually afford. Everyone in Gelthin knew of the kingdom of Zeal and it only took a moment dwelling on what Khin had learned to remember the importance of the Citadel.

"Why was he allowed to bring me here?" Khin asked at last.

"The Citadel holds her doors open to the whole world," Etha moved to go dig through the contents of a nearby armoire. "No one is turned away if they have a need to enter."

Khin sipped her tea and watched Etha's search over the brim of her cup. "And every beggar and pioneer gets to stay in fancy quarters like this?"

Etha smiled and drew an olive-hued dress from hiding. "Dress, dear, and I'll show you around. The answers you seek aren't mine to give, but I might be able to take you to where you'll find what you need to know."

Khin didn't move, besides sipping another drink of her tea, studying Etha suspiciously. She seemed unthreatening enough, but so had Mathias for the most part, and look where that had landed her. *Yeah, in the nicest lodging you'll ever set foot in…* Khin shook that thought from her mind and tried to stay on track, grasping at those reservations that made so much more sense than reality. As it was, all of her options funneled down into complying with those who offered her help. Maybe this time, charity would work in her favor. Timidly, Khin slipped out of bed, accepted the dress, and tucked herself behind the dressing screen.

Her mind continued to rattle off questions to ask, but she feared knowing more would only further complicate these already confounding matters. Instead, she absorbed herself in admiring the delicate cleanliness of the gown. Her fingers slid across the fibers, and she wanted to waste the day caressing the richness of the soft folds of velvet. She couldn't remember ever having anything new, and it was almost a shame that she would have to start this fine garment on its road toward becoming a ragged old dress like those she'd always worn. At last, the temptation grew too strong, and Khin dove into the dress, savoring the way it danced about her legs and embraced her arms.

"Is everything alright?" Etha asked from the other side of the screen.

"Quite!" Khin chirped, forgetting all about her previous concerns as glee swept over her and coaxed out her innocence. "It fits perfectly!"

Etha grinned and handed Khin a matching pair of slippers as she flit back into view. It warmed the goddess to see her able to feel like a girl, and Etha could rest assured that Mathias would make sure she was treated like a lady in his care. Etha gave Khin a moment to slip her feet into the shoes and finish twirling about before clearing her throat.

"I'm glad to see the dress meets your approval," Etha said. "Now, if you'll come with me, I'll take you to the Hall of Histories so you can gather the information you seek. I think you'll find it quite enlightening."

Reservations now pushed aside all because of a pretty dress, Khin readily followed Etha from the room. Too many terrible things had tarnished her life, and if this encounter was destined to do the same, at least she had new clothes to show for it. It was better than her consolation prizes for anything else she'd lived through. Khin followed Etha through the halls, humming chipper melodies and completely oblivious to the fact that Etha was anything more than a kind woman.

Etha guided Khin around a corner and pulled open two massive, polished doors to reveal a marble floored hall which stretched several hundred yards in length. Elaborate murals lined the walls of both sides, spanning from waist height all the way to the vaulted ceilings. Below each picture were engravings, likely explaining the importance of each depicted scene. A gentle hand guided Khin by the shoulder, leading her a few murals down the hall.

"Who painted all of these?" Khin asked, gaping in wonder at a picture of four warriors of gigantic proportions hurling the elements at each other.

"Many people of great talent and promise come to Zeal to study here in the Citadel." Etha frowned at the same picture in which Khin expressed such amazement. "Among them are scholars and artists. They apprentice in hopes of leaving a mark as important as these in the Hall of Histories."

Khin turned to face Etha. "And what does this have to do with Mathias?"

"Possibly more than it should. Certainly more than he'd like. Take some time and browse through this hall. See if these pictures answer any of your questions. A great wealth of knowledge lies in them."

Khin wasn't thrilled with the assignment; she wasn't educated in reading and had rather enjoyed the convenience of Etha explaining everything to her, but she wouldn't push any further. This woman had been generous so far, and if these paintings held anything interesting, she might as well take a look at them. She turned to thank Etha for her kindness, but found her gone. Confused, having not heard her companion leave, Khin turned her wide eyes back to the murals.

* * * * *

The longer Mathias and Julianna walked together, letting their minds settle from their discussion with the Council, the more weight shed from the oppressive force driving against their hearts. Despite the hardships lurking on the horizon, it wasn't long before their previous tension gave way to the juvenile pestering which often occupied their spare time. As they neared the Hall of Histories, Mathias saw the doors hanging open and groaned.

He understood the need to remember tragedy. He knew there were endless lessons to be learned from the past. He did not, however, enjoy being hailed as the great hero he may or not be.

Etha had blessed Mathias to serve the land and execute her will, and she could have done that to absolutely anyone. The paladin doubted he would ever consider himself worthy of the honors which had been given to him, and thus, he hated this hall.

He hastened forward to pull the doors closed, Julianna following absently as she chattered, before spotting a girl in green intently studying one of the portraits.

"Etha, no…" Mathias groaned, a pinch of color draining from his cheeks.

Julianna peeked through the doorway, glanced at Mathias, and grinned wickedly. "You're telling me you magicked her out of a city under siege by demons and didn't even tell her who you are?"

A pathetic whimper creaked from Mathias's throat. "I didn't think I'd have to."

Julianna couldn't allow herself to pass up an opportunity to humiliate her brother. Giving Mathias a playful jab on the shoulder, she darted into the hall.

"Jules, stop—" He shot a hand forward to try grabbing her, but was too late. She'd cleared the doorway and was approaching Khin with growing enthusiasm.

"Can I help you?" Julianna trilled to Khin, louder than necessary. "I know these old paintings can sometimes deliver confusing messages."

The girl turned quickly from the picture of a dashing blond knight surrounded by a ring of snarling demons she'd been studying to look at Julianna, then to a mural depicting the High Priestess, and back again. "Yes," she spoke from numb lips. "I don't think I understand any of this quite right."

Julianna smiled that patient smile she used with the little girls fresh to Etha's teachings and rested a hand on Khin's shoulder. "What are you struggling with?"

"I know—well, that is, I thought I knew—" Logic rapidly fled from Khin's mind as she scoured the murals for anything that added up. "Who is Mathias Sagewind?"

"Oh!" Julianna gasped, pressing a hand to her chest and knocking herself back two steps. "The great and mighty White Paladin! Why, he is the hero of heroes, the defender of the divine. He could single-handedly wipe out an entire army of the fiercest—"

"Julianna, that's enough!"

Her mouth snapped shut and curved into an impish smile at her brother's exasperated order. She turned to face him, folded her hands before her, and fearlessly met his stern expression as he marched toward them.

"Is this…" Julianna gasped in mock surprise and spun back to face the timid girl. "Oh, dear *me*! You must be Khin. Mattie told me about you. Please forgive my lack of manners for not introducing myself, or have you already heard?"

Khin was no longer interested in Julianna or anything she had to say. Instead, she watched as Mathias came closer, her confusion enhanced by an overwhelming sense of awe and humility. Heroes weren't meant to rescue whores.

Mathias shuffled to a stop a few strides from the two women, safely out of Julianna's reach, and focused his disapproving glower firmly on his sister. Silent threats were sent her way, and they were eagerly accepted by eyes that glittered with their own challenges.

"Is this true, Mathias?" Khin asked meekly, barely finding her tongue.

"Exaggerated—"

"Completely," Julianna interrupted with a helpful smile. "Otherwise it wouldn't be history."

"Jules, please." Mathias rubbed his forehead. Debating Nes's fate with the Council had already sapped him of his patience. When he met his sister's spoiled pout, he continued. "I am the Sir Sagewind depicted in these murals, yes," he sighed. "But I am not a man of any exceptional greatness."

Julianna snorted at his modesty, but Khin's dark eyes welled with confusion. "Why didn't you tell me?"

Her tone was bewildered, but not hurt or angry. Mathias had intentionally wanted to hide these tales from her to keep her from thinking he could cure all the evils in the world, and if he'd been able to deposit Khin someplace safe before any of this had been uncovered, before she began to develop these stars in her eyes, he could have saved her from the drawbacks of being associated with him. That was, of course, assuming there would be a safe place to deposit a troubled young woman when this was all through.

"I did tell you," he reminded her. "I told you I'd faced unimaginable foes."

"That was supposed to be a joke!" Khin insisted.

Mathias hoped Julianna was having a riot with this, because the survivor's guilt erupting from Khin stung him like a whip. "I wish more than anything, for those who have fought alongside me, that it had been a joke," he said. "I do not lie, Khin. It was your choice to assume my words were in jest."

The information began to sink in, connecting the feats she had witnessed Mathias execute. It all made sense now, but she was reeling too hard from the past day's events to act on this startling news.

Mathias watched the thoughts process through Khin, relieved by her apparent maturity, and decided to turn the attention to his boisterous sister. "Now that we've established that, Khin, this is Julianna. She's the High Priestess and will be taking care of you in my absence—"

Julianna's jaw dropped at Mathias's liberties. She raised a hand to launch into her protest, but Khin beat her to retaliation with a hushed question.

"Where are you going?"

Mathias met Julianna's eyes for the briefest moment, threatening her in no uncertain terms that it was time for her to be serious. "I have to go find the reason the demons have come to the surface so we can put them back where they belong and keep them from hurting anyone else."

Khin's respiration rate picked up and she glanced between the paladin and the High Priestess, more lost than ever before. "I… I don't want to stay here." She covered her mouth as soon as she'd blurted the words, blushing and backing a step away. "I… I don't mean to disrespect, but I'm alone here. I… I want to go back to Fieldsdeep. I want to go *home*."

"I think that's a splendid plan."

"Shut up, Jules," Mathias instructed. "Khin, these murals showed you that I've fought demons before, right?" She gave him a feeble nod. "And I've been around for a very long time to do just that. For whatever reason, they're up here"—Julianna coughed, but Mathias kept speaking—"causing trouble again. Traveling will be dangerous, even for those skilled at fighting. I made a promise to keep you safe, and leaving you here is the best way to do that."

"Then teach me how to fight," Khin begged.

Mathias gave a dry chuckle. "We might have *days* before we reach combat on the road. Maybe not even that long. That's hardly enough time to teach you how to properly wield a blade, much less how to fight demons. You're staying here."

"I'll learn quick." The heat of demand crept into Khin's words.

Mathias hadn't pinned Khin as the kind to argue, and that, along with the humored arch of one of Julianna's brows, flustered him. "Even if you learn how to fight, you won't have the experience for what I'll attract once the demons catch my scent. I can't be distracted watching over someone else, not if I want to stay alive."

"I thought you were supposed to be immortal?"

Mathias coughed and Julianna curled her lips between her teeth to keep from laughing and looked away. "I can be slain," he said, confidence rattled for the stupidest reasons. "And if that happens, it will be because I'm fighting something of insurmountable power. That means whoever is with me will likely die, too. The difference is, I'll eventually come back. If I'm lucky, it'll be here on the surface and not in the hells."

Khin's nostrils flared and she scoured the murals for something she could use in this argument. All she had left at her disposal were tears, but as they leapt to her eyes, she was shocked to realize they weren't the tears of the tantrum she'd expected; they were tears of sheer determination, tears that promised she'd go running out into the open all on her own if Mathias refused to escort her. "Mathias, you are a man of greatness," she said solemnly.

"A man of greatness," Julianna murmured with a sage nod.

Mathias speared his sister with a glower which she shrugged off as though she didn't know why she'd received it.

"Please help me," Khin said.

Pinned between Khin's pleading and Julianna's goading while simultaneously crushed beneath the weight of Abaeloth's fate and Nes's salvation was a most uncomfortable place. Mathias sucked in a slow breath. "The road I must travel will be dangerous, even for me. You've never seen battle before, and I want to do everything I can to keep it that way."

"I've seen death," Khin murmured, those tears rising to line her lower lids. "I need to go home. I need to be with my family at least for a little while before we all die in this war."

Hearing words so blunt from a girl as outwardly subdued as Khin shocked both siblings, and suddenly, Julianna's eyes weren't laughing anymore. She softened her expression, discarding her mischief, and turned to Mathias with the gentle suggestion of granting this girl what could be her final wish. Even after all these years, the memory of a time when Julianna longed for one more day with her family still hung vividly in her mind. She reached out and squeezed her brother's hand.

"You wouldn't stand a chance in a dress," Mathias said stubbornly.

"Mathias, her clothes can be remedied." This had built well past Julianna's aversion to being used as a babysitter. Khin needed to find peace while there was still a chance it could exist for her. "I think she's made up her mind."

"You'd have to kill me to keep me from following you," Khin confirmed.

There wasn't one part of this debate Mathias enjoyed, the two women having stripped his determination from him and bent him against his better judgment. For being the great champion this hall claimed him to be, Mathias certainly fell hard in defeat. If they ran into trouble on the road, he could always whisk Khin away and deposit her in the Citadel for safe keeping. It would be at the expense of energy he couldn't wholly afford to waste, and the loss of time he suspected Nessix couldn't afford for him to lose, but at least his point would be made and proven indisputable. Mathias lowered his head.

"While I'll do what I can to ensure no harm finds you, if you come with me, I must revoke my promise that you'll be safe in my care. Do you understand?"

Khin drew a shallow breath and nodded, blinking back the tears that had now become more frightened as quickly as she could.

"Very well," Mathias said tightly. "Go with Julianna to be fit with something better suited for travel, and get some rest. My time is limited. We're heading out in the morning."

* * * * *

Determined to avoid the complications of Mathias sneaking out of Zeal without his young friend in tow, Julianna spared neither time nor expense in outfitting Khin for her journey. Equipping the girl with sturdy trousers, heavy boots, a thick blouse, and a woolen cloak, the priestess deemed Khin fit to travel.

The garments rubbed Khin in uncomfortable places and she blushed at how awkwardly she moved in them. She'd never worn such clothing before, having always thought them for men, but Julianna assured her that travel would be easier without the worries of managing a dress.

The only thing Julianna refused to provide Khin with was a sword, citing the very accurate observation that it was an unnecessary weight that the girl didn't know how to handle, anyway. Arming her would have only fanned temptations that were best left untouched.

Khin slept well that night, dreaming of home as she remembered it from a lifetime of fouled memories ago. When she woke, she was more enthusiastic than she'd been for anything in her life. That enthusiasm faltered as a priestess fetched her from her room to escort her from the Citadel to the street where Mathias was securing packs and bedrolls onto a pair of horses. Khin had demanded to go on this journey, unknowingly derailing a quest that carried massive importance to both Mathias and the fate of Abaeloth, but she hadn't realized it would come with *horses*.

"I hope you slept well." After his initial smile of greeting, Mathias turned back to his preparations. "If we keep a good pace, we should only be a few days from Fieldsdeep, but it'll be rough and with few comforts."

Still awkward in her atypical mode of dress, Khin rubbed at her pants leg and glanced away. "A good pace?" Her village was just a week from Seaton, which was nearly half the continent from Zeal. How fast did Mathias intend to ride?

With a final tug on the strap that held his bedroll behind the saddle's cantle, Mathias patted his horse's bay neck and turned to Khin. "We'll be pressing the horses hard and changing them out for fresh mounts in the cities we pass through."

Khin's stomach flopped and she gripped the straps of her pack a bit tighter. "Is that really necessary?" she asked. "I mean, I want to go home more than anything, but we don't have to risk our health or safety... do we?" It sounded like a good excuse.

One which Mathias wasn't biting. "Remember the attack on Seaton?" He waited for Khin's wide-eyed nod. "Those were demons, and the reports the Order has received imply these attacks are going to become quite widespread very soon. You learned who and what I am yesterday, so you know that I am obligated to address these matters. I'll see you home as safely as I can, but duty demands I'm quick about it."

Shoulders drawing close in a timid hunch, Khin looked at the ground. She'd been selfish to demand Mathias's escort with such perilous times lurking so near. "I-I'm sorry... If you don't have the time to take me home, I can wait until another trustworthy knight is available."

Mathias cocked his head, brows furrowing at Khin's sudden change of heart, and held his hand out to gesture for her to hand him her pack. "I'm heading south, anyway. Might as well take you home while I'm at it."

Khin let the pack slide off her shoulder, but didn't move to hand it to him. "Wouldn't a carriage be faster?"

"Ah." Mathias understood at last. He stepped forward to take the pack and secured it to the chestnut horse's saddle. "Have you never ridden before, or have you just had a bad experience with it?"

"My big brother was crippled in a fall while racing one of his friends. I was just a little girl."

Mathias nodded, his eyes sympathetic but confident. "Conditioned saddle horses like these will move much faster than cart horses can, and carriages attract trouble from road hazards and bandits. These horses are well trained and tolerant; if you can hold on, they won't drop you. You have my word."

"Yeah, but I don't have *its* word." Khin nodded in the direction of the sorrel horse who stood dozing with his head lowered and hind leg cocked.

Mathias stood back and looked over the horse before sneaking a glance in Khin's direction. He carefully kept the humor out of his eyes, but had to briefly roll his lips between his teeth to hold back a smirk. "That's because horses can't talk. You were so full of determination yesterday, not batting an eye at the risk of being captured by demons. Are you really going to be defeated by a horse?"

Khin frowned at Mathias's badgering and crossed her arms. "Do we really have to ride *that* fast?"

The faint hints of humor sagged from Mathias's expression and he rested an arm over the horse's withers. Khin didn't need to carry the worries of his mission. She didn't deserve the fury that would come from knowing that the reason Mathias was in such a hurry was directly connected to the massacre in Seaton. If he could do his job right, she might still be spared any direct knowledge of the horrors tied to demons, but to reach such an outcome, they had to move with haste. He'd been foolish to get himself duty bound to Khin when he was already devoted to finding Nessix.

"I will be riding hard," Mathias said, unwilling to lie to Khin's fears, but equally unable to compromise. "I am your best bet at getting you where you want to go in a safe manner, but I will not fault you if you want to stay behind. I warned you that this wouldn't be a gentle trip."

Khin had never been good at defying authority, a trait repulsively capitalized on in her recent past, and though she trembled at the scenarios her mind played out, a greater part of her refused to let go of the aid Mathias promised her. "But I don't know how to ride."

It hadn't been another attempted excuse, but a timid confession. Mathias held out his hand and gently beckoned Khin closer. "All you have to do is hang on and I'll take care of the rest." Without requesting permission, Mathias grabbed Khin's arm and touched her fingertips to the saddle flap to measure her stirrup length.

"How are you going to ride for me?" Khin jumped and squeaked as the horse behind her snorted.

Mathias smirked, walking to the other side of her horse to adjust the next stirrup. "Oh, you're going to ride the horse. I'll take care of steering."

Her brows tipped gloomily as it seemed increasingly likely that she had no way out of this conundrum.

Mathias walked back over to her side and wiggled his fingers under the horse's girth to try giving it a tug. "See? Girth's tight. Stirrups are the right length. You won't come off this horse unless you jump."

Her tiny frown and glistening eyes suggested she was still unconvinced.

Irritated by the delay and running out of patience to continue being polite, Mathias sighed, linked his fingers together, and held his hands low. "Come on. It's up you go, or back to the Citadel. Either way, I have to get moving."

Khin thought back on how far she was from home. She reflected on how, though she'd only known Mathias for a couple of days, he was the first person in nearly a year to show any concern for her well-being. In her mind, she recited the nuggets of information she knew about this man called the White Paladin. Safety and peace may never be hers, but a significant part of her knew that if either existed, she'd find them through Mathias.

"You promise I won't fall?" she asked meekly.

"Not as long as you hang on."

His eyes were so warm, comfort reaching out to her in his smile, and Khin stepped forward at last. She hadn't been prepared for Mathias to throw her into the saddle and when she gripped her mount with her legs, it swished its tail and danced from side to side, threatening to topple her off its back. Mathias steadied both horse and rider with a calm hand and soothing words, and before Khin knew it, she'd settled enough to let him instruct her on the appropriate places to hold onto a horse.

Khin had no less fear after the brief lesson, but she did have a mote more confidence as Mathias swung into his saddle with admirable grace and grabbed her horse's reins. They proceeded at a walk as they departed from Zeal, the horse's strong stride tossing Khin from side to side as they climbed the hill through the field of

144

lilies. Just as she'd begun to think that riding wasn't so bad, able to relax with the steady movement of her horse's gait, Mathias glanced over his shoulder.

"Sink your weight into your heels and don't pinch with your knees. If you feel like you're losing balance, grab some mane."

"What—"

"Let your horse move your hips."

Before Khin could protest what she knew was coming, Mathias cued his horse to a brisk canter, dragging Khin's along behind him. She clutched desperately at the saddle's pommel, fingers locked around its smooth leather until her arms ached from the strain. Her body fought Mathias's instructions, hips locking against the rocking motion of the horse's strides, the asymmetry of the gait pitching her forward and to the right. Her grip tightened and her breath came in sharp, quick little puffs as she tried to clamp her fingers even harder. And then, Mathias's voice reached through the flurry of panic spinning through her mind.

"See? It's not so bad. Your horse is in a good mood. Look at his ears."

Khin peered her eyes open. Sure enough, the horse's red neck arched gracefully, tiny ears pricked forward as he effortlessly powered down the road. Watching the steady bob of his head helped Khin accept the movement, better able to determine when the next jar from a hind leg tried to launch her from the saddle. She was still convinced she'd fall, but at least she felt better equipped to fight back against her mount's motion. Unable to answer Mathias for fear of biting her tongue as the horse bounded along, Khin was at least able to catch brief moments of relaxation as her hips rolled with the horse's strides.

She couldn't tell how long they raced along, knowing only that when Mathias slowed the horses to a trot to allow them a reprieve, she found the two-beat bounce even more disrupting than the canter. Mathias instructed her to stand in the stirrups to rest the tension in her upper body, uncovering how weak her legs were for this sort of activity. By the time they entered the first town to switch out their winded and sweat lathered horses for fresh ones, Khin could hardly stand. Climbing into another saddle was an unwelcome proposition, but not half as unwelcome as the idea of being left behind.

The next leg of the journey progressed in a similar fashion, but with no more hazards than before. Though Khin was still timid and afraid and her body ached to the point that she wondered if she'd ever be able to walk regularly again, she was inwardly impressed with herself for surviving this trial. Her complaints tapered and though she was sore, her body no longer fought against the motion of riding. The day pressed on toward retirement and Mathias slowed the horses. They hadn't yet reached the next town, but Mathias stopped their horses and dismounted with a spry hop which Khin envied, and led them off the road to where a lone oak tree stood watch over the fields.

Khin fidgeted in the saddle. "What's wrong?"

"We're losing light and I'm sure you're worn. We'll camp here for the night."

That tension Khin had so recently let go of crept back to her. "How far until we get to the next town?"

Mathias stopped beneath the lowest branch of the tree, eyeing its height before retrieving a rope to tie the horses. "I'm not sure, but we'll be better off stopping to recover."

He secured the horses and helped Khin slide to the ground. She wobbled on exhausted legs, groaning as her muscles protested her attempt at standing. Leaving the girl to fuss over the aches of travel, Mathias scavenged for fallen branches and dead brambles to build a small campfire. He pulled down their bedrolls, laid them out, and dug through his pack for rations. Handing Khin a parcel of cured meat, day old bread, and cheese, Mathias watched her scoot closer to the fire.

"Is this your first night on the road?"

Khin chewed on the thought of honesty before shaking her head, slowly unclasping her hands to flex the ache from her fingers and warm their joints by the fire. Mathias might have been helpful this far, but she didn't *know* him. He didn't deserve more of her past than he'd already pilfered from her. But then again, neither did she.

Mathias smiled tightly. He hadn't believed her story of being accustomed to travel when she'd first uttered it the night they'd met, and her reaction to the road so far did nothing to support otherwise. "I wouldn't usually impose on a lady to take a shift of watch unless she knew what she was doing," he said, hoping to coax honesty from her. "That's all."

Khin stared at the tiny flames as they licked at the air, too tired to put up a fight. "I've never been on watch," she answered at last. "I don't even remember stopping to rest on my travels."

"Oh?" Mathias asked. "I'd assumed as a seasoned traveler far from home, you'd have camped at least a few times."

Khin quickly recoiled her hands and tucked them into crossed arms, food untouched. "I traveled by carriage." She jutted her chin, hoping to convey more pride than poor showmanship.

It didn't take Etha's blessings for Mathias to see through the poorly constructed lie. "You do know that I have no intention to hurt you, right?"

He watched her struggle to sort out what to do with his words, and almost wished he hadn't started this conversation at all.

Bluntness had always served Mathias best and entertained him far more than carefully picking his way through conversations. Nessix had bit every time he'd approached her this way; being gentle with her had been a complete waste of his breath, and so he'd gleefully met her on her terms. On the darkening road, huddled before a tiny fire and bound to a mission he hadn't planned to take, a sharp jolt of longing struck Mathias like a knife. He missed the debates he'd had with Nessix. He missed her fiery retorts and the way she'd kept his old mind young and sharp. He missed her passion and drive. And he'd missed finding her in Seaton. Mathias fell so deeply in his cascade of nostalgia and guilt that he only barely heard Khin sigh.

"I'm not from nobility like I told you, sir." A strange take on bitterness drove Khin's murmured explanation. "My family's poor, barely able to pay our taxes, just like the rest of our village."

"Then how did you afford travel?"

Khin looked away from both Mathias and the fire, fingers absently picking apart her roll. Discarded crumbs fell onto her lap. "We're farmers. Or at least we were until the land quit producing.

Ma taught me my way around the kitchen and with needle and thread. Pa showed me how to handle pigs and goats, even butcher chickens." Another span of silence soaked her up until the snapping of the fire gently encouraged her to continue. "A girl from down the street, Marissa, went to Cedartown and found herself a wealthy bachelor, so she could send money back to her family. It sounds horrible, but it saved her family from the tax collectors."

"And you thought to do the same," Mathias said. "Was that man you were with in Seaton the one who was courting you?" He almost hoped that was the case, if only to dismiss the more likely scenario.

Khin's mouth fell open as she fumbled over how to explain how she'd ended up being manhandled by a creep in a dark alley in a city so far from home. Unable to come up with a story that stood even a slim chance sneaking past Mathias's knowing eyes, Khin settled for the truth at last.

"Me and two other girls left Fieldsdeep to find our rich husbands, and a caravan carrying a few other girls showed up. The driver offered us a ride and said the men in Seaton would pay our ways once we arrived." She gnawed on her lower lip, a nervous habit poignantly familiar to Mathias. "We were all so dumb that we hopped on and counted our blessings."

Mathias prodded the fire with a stick when Khin stopped to gather her thoughts. "There were no wealthy bachelors waiting upon your arrival," he concluded at her inability to do so. "Am I to assume that your fare was ever paid?"

"Oh, it was paid," Khin spat with a fierceness Mathias had not imagined coming from the otherwise timid girl. "There were eight of us, all about the same age, and we were sold like pigs to the highest bidder."

Mathias bristled, the stick snapping as he jutted it into the ground. Sparks spun into the air. He understood and, on most days, accepted class systems, but that didn't justify slavery. Worse than that, the form Khin had been victim to was the most depraved kind. If Mathias wouldn't have witnessed the establishment's demise, he'd set back out for Seaton when his more pressing duties were through to teach whoever had put a price on these young women's heads how ladies ought to be treated.

Through the haze of contained rage, Mathias listened as Khin explain how the man who purchased her had put her to work. She told him of how she learned to shut herself off in the presence of men, and how she managed to scrape enough of her earnings together to send back home with notes of encouragement so her family didn't have to know the horrifying truth. She was ready for Mathias to cast her aside like she'd learned society did to whores, but his jaw never unclenched and the repulsion never extinguished from his eyes.

"That's it." Afraid of her tale and what Mathias would make of it, Khin hardly squeaked her words. "That's the story of my travels and—"

"How late was I?" Mathias asked.

"W-what?" Khin stammered.

"How long were you forced into this?" he asked.

Khin looked away, hating that she'd mentioned anything at all. "About a year," she said. "But after the first day, what did the rest matter?"

How could she ask that? Each day of that imprisonment had torn her gentle soul down to this frightened, defensive girl which luck had led Mathias to rescue. What had started as a journey to aid her family had ruined Khin's life. These sorts of evils had no place on the Abaeloth Mathias fought for. His quest to find Nessix would not end until she was safe in his arms, but he was ashamed of himself for concentrating so wholly on that one task when there was still so much suffering in the world.

"Eat your food and get some sleep, if you can." Mathias needed time to himself to think things over. "I'll keep watch until morning."

Khin was too exhausted, both physically and emotionally, to argue. "Aren't you tired?"

"I'm a hero, remember?" He wanted to smile, but it never reached his lips. "One night of missed sleep isn't enough to defeat me. This is a new life for you. You need your rest."

Mathias was right. Khin could hardly gather the strength

needed to finish her meal, and according to Mathias's earlier assessment, they still had another couple days' worth of this rigorous routine ahead of them. If he was willing to let her sleep, she would do her best to accept the offer. It had been so long since she'd been near a just man that she felt compelled to flee from his virtue and honor to spare them both the humiliation of associating with one another. It was a pity, then, that her aching legs promised to betray her if she tried to stand. Silently, having no idea what to say next, Khin lay down.

As she rustled in her bedroll, Mathias delved into his brooding. Somehow, he would find a way to ease the damage that had been done, and he hoped that would begin with seeing Khin home and arranging to have funds sent her family's way. Khin was a sweet girl, and she deserved her break. Nessix was strong and skilled. She knew the demons were after her, and she knew how to fight them. Nessix could wait a few more days.

FOURTEEN

Nessix prayed as she ran. She prayed to her Inwan and to Etha, to Zenos and any other god who had half a mind to listen to her. She prayed for those poor souls she'd left behind in the village to stay safe from the demons. The image of Kol's disappointed scowl visited her each time she blinked, driving her harder down the road. She wouldn't be able to evade him forever, and she suspected he'd mercilessly sunder each town she passed through until he found her. The fewer interactions Nessix had with innocent men and women on her way to Zeal, the better.

She finished off the first root of dream stop and ate the food given to her by Irma within the next half day, leaving her once again with barely two more preserved rations. Night settled quietly over the road, bringing with it fresh concerns. Nessix fingered the pouch of coins given to her by the villagers, knowing the funds wouldn't last forever. Handling finances meant to balance a kingdom came effortlessly to Nessix, but her grasp on what small coins bought in the civilian world was lacking at best.

The simple concern occupied the majority of Nes's fretting through the darkest hours of the night and carried her into the city of Bessemar. The guard stopped her briefly to study her face in the flickering light of a single torch, opening a lengthy scroll before nodding and motioning her into town.

Spirit dragging, she located the inn, where she reluctantly exchanged half her finite wealth for a room. Despite her exhaustion, sleep evaded her for some time, assisted by her fear of poverty. She refused to let her ignorance of surviving a mundane life defeat her. Born and raised a soldier, she had only one marketable skill, one which had few employment opportunities for a lone woman on the move. At least falling asleep with that thought in mind provided her nightmares unrelated to Kol or Berann.

She woke to a warm, sun dappled morning and indulged her stomach's protests with the hearty, but plain gruel included with her board before heading out. Much less boisterous than Seaton, the streets of Bessemar made Nessix feel more at ease. There seemed to be little to no risk of unplanned encounters or difficult citizens, but the relative vacancy of the streets did leave her quite exposed.

Searching for means of replenishing her funds was Nes's priority. She was a seasoned officer, trained to find tactical advantages wherever they might be, and she hadn't missed the implications of the gate guard consulting his scroll upon her arrival. Either this town was rife with criminals—a theory which seemed relatively unlikely, given the quiet streets—or the entire city owed its peace to how seriously the authorities took security measures. Asking the next passerby where she could find the guards' headquarters, Nessix was directed to a modest stone building which stood out from its neighbors only because of a pair of weathered stocks and a rusty guillotine arranged on either side of the door.

A bulletin board was mounted behind the stocks, displaying several sketches of villainous faces. Bounties were more honorable work than any alternative, and Nessix picked her way around the devices to study the board. Her talent for reading foreign scripts was limited, but had been improved from her brief stay with Zenos. She stumbled through reading the posters well enough and settled on the one among the listings of produce thieves and drunkards which contained words she thought meant they'd prefer the subject to be killed.

The man depicted had no name, labeled simply as "the deadly letch," and the varying shades of ink on his portrait suggested he'd been sighted several times, requiring frequent updates to his appearance and list of crimes. All Nessix could gather from her limited understanding was that he was dangerous and hunting women on the road between this town and the next. Nessix smirked. That sounded perfect. Straightening her sword belt, she walked inside the guard station.

Four bored men in leather armor lounged around a table too small to comfortably accommodate them all, playing a game of cards. They didn't look up as Nessix entered, likely assuming she was one of their own or perhaps the local nark stopping by to report another petty crime. Bracing herself to receive their reactions, Nessix cleared her throat.

"Does the bounty for the deadly letch still stand?" she asked.

The four men looked up quickly, scanning Nes's slight build and noble face. Almost on cue, they began to laugh.

"So he's been caught?" she asked, undeterred by their response. "And I can assume you're just too lazy to remove the poster?"

The insult tapered their laughter, but didn't seem to strike any nerves. "Look. Lady," said the oldest of the four. "Don't travel at night and you'll be fine. Leave his fate to the professionals if you value your safety."

"The same professionals who have yet to stop him?" Nessix challenged, a fist to her hip.

The humor left the group now as bitter glances were exchanged across the table. The oldest of the men stood and walked toward Nessix.

"Ma'am." He reached an arm out with the intention of wrapping it around Nes's shoulder to turn her toward the door. At the strictness of her frown, he halted the action before he'd touched her and instead looped his fingers in his belt. "The letch is a dangerous man. How much do you know about him, anyway? You look and sound as though you're from out of town."

"All I know is what's scratched on that poster."

"Right. Well. He targets women travelling by themselves or those with a single escort. With one exception, he's killed every man in these situations and caught every woman he's known to have targeted. And he gets to know them pretty well, if you catch my drift."

Nessix crossed her arms. She knew exactly what this guard implied but had survived worse. "Have the women lived?"

The guard frowned. "Look, lady—"

"Did the women live through these attacks?"

The guard sighed and met Nes's crossed arms with his own. "Yes," he snapped. "Though I'm not sure how many of them are grateful for it."

"Has he ever attacked a man travelling by himself?"

"I see where you're trying to go with this—"

"And if you're smart enough to be the man speaking for your entire office, you must know that I'm speaking sense," Nessix said. "None of the men who have hunted this beast have succeeded because that's not what he's looking for. He's after women, so you'll need a woman to hunt him."

A second, younger guard stood. "Ma'am you really must be commended for your sense of justice, but we, as honorable men, simply cannot permit you to go after this criminal.

Nessix flicked her gaze to this new speaker. "You cannot permit me to walk out of town? Am I a prisoner in this city and not allowed to leave on my own accord?"

"Well, no, but—"

"Great," Nessix said. "Then be prepared to pull that poster down and spread the word that the roadways are safe again."

By now, a third guard was on his feet, the fourth slowly rising for good measure, though he looked disinclined to join the debate. "With *our* honor, we cannot permit you to go alone."

Nessix rolled her eyes. "You said he's killed nearly every man involved with these attacks, and I won't have your deaths on my conscience. I'm walking into this willingly and with my eyes open. If I fail, well, I'll have to live with that. But if I succeed? That will be justice for his victims. That will be open roadways for your town. It will be one less complaint you'll have to field. If I screw up, I will hold no one but myself accountable. As all four of you as my witnesses, I swear it."

The guards exchanged nervous glances, one of them humming a shrill sound as though he was about to be sick. The oldest of the group flung his hands in the air and strode two strides away from Nessix before turning back to her.

"Your plan is dangerous."

"I don't wear this sword because I'm afraid of danger."

He pointed to her mentioned weapon and swept his hand at the overall effect of her armor. "And what if that deters him?"

"Then I'll leave it with you," Nessix said. "I *can* trust you with my valuables, can't I?"

Trapped, as Nessix had smooth answers for all of his debates, the senior guard sank into his chair. "So now you're planning on facing him unarmed and in your undergarments?"

"Of course not," Nessix said. "One of you must have a wife or a sister or something that would have more traditional women's attire for me to wear? Something they wouldn't mind being ruined? You're welcome to deduct compensation for the clothing from the bounty I'll earn."

"Yeah, but what if you *fail?*" the third guard asked. The fourth promptly swatted his chest with the back of his hand.

Nessix was confident she wouldn't, but it was clear these men assumed otherwise and wouldn't take any of her efforts to reassure them to heart. "If I fail, you may keep my sword." It should have disturbed her how willing she was to put her blade on the line. Besides her armor and her mangled body, it was all she had left of the life she'd loved. "I'm sure selling it would buy more than a few dresses to replace the one I borrow."

None of the men smiled at Nes's matter of fact reasoning, grim frowns creasing their faces in a manner which she found most unattractive. Were they preparing to turn her down? She'd still go after this man if for no other reason than off principle. Maybe she'd be able to loot some money from him in the process. Even armed and dressed like a soldier, Nessix believed she stood a better chance luring him from hiding than the guards did. Finally, the second guard sighed.

"I've got a kid sister about your size," he said. "But all's she's got is one nice dress. May I see your sword?" He flushed at the blunt way in which he delivered his question. "You know. Um. Just in case?"

155

On nearly any other occasion, this lack of faith might have offended Nessix, but right now, it drove her harder. She truly believed these were good men doing their best to protect their civilians, but the idea of proving them wrong delighted her almost as much as the thought of earning honest money did. Reverently, Nessix drew her sword, laying it across her open palms as she stepped forward.

The guard's eyes opened wider as he looked over the old blade's perfection. Master smiths were expensive in any country, and Nessix owned one of the finest blades ever crafted on Elidae.

"May I?" The guard raised his hand, though he made no attempt to reach forward until Nessix nodded.

He grasped the hilt gingerly, as though he expected the sword to bite him, and the idea of this man commanding her weapon turned Nes's stomach. If he was afraid to simply hold it, he couldn't possibly be bold enough to wield it in a manner worthy of its splendor. As he tested its balance, a lopsided smile crossing his face, Nessix spun her gaze across the other three men. They seemed trustworthy, but too in awe of her sword's perfection for her to be completely at ease that they wouldn't make off with it while she was out. Either way, she had to hope that once they witnessed the results of her skill, they would reconsider any less than honest thoughts that might have flit into their minds.

Her worries soon softened as the guard turned the hilt back to her. "That *is* a fine piece of steel," he murmured. "Worth more than a whole chest of dresses, if you ask me."

The older guard crossed his arms. "So where'd you get it?"

Nessix lovingly sheathed the blade and turned to the men. "It was given to me by my late father. Had been in the family for several generations." She rolled the taste of bringing up her father through her mouth, less than comfortable about mentioning him after the path her life had taken. "It's been with me all my life, so I hope my offer conveys my sincerity."

The last two guards murmured sounds that aimed at respect and the man in the running to claim her most prized possession lowered his head. Only the old guard guffawed and crossed his arms.

"It's clear you're going to do whatever you want," he grunted. "I've given my advice, but your mind's set. You're going to go after this man with or without our clearance."

"I am," Nessix confirmed.

Picking at his teeth for a moment, the old man flung his arms down to his sides. "Very well. Randall, if you think you've got a way to pretty her up, get to it. You can't stop foolishness."

The young guard pressed his lips tight and gave Nessix a polite nod before rushing out of the building. Confident in her skills, if nothing else, Nessix pulled out a smile of her own and walked to the table to straddle a chair. Picking up Randall's hand of cards, she glanced up at the remaining men.

"So," she said, tone chipper at last. "What are we playing?"

* * * * *

Perhaps Nessix should have listened to the old guard's warning and skipped this mission. Randall returned with his irritated sister in tow, carrying a yellow dress. The young woman was coaxed into helping Nessix dress, an act accomplished with bitter sneers and judgmental jabs at Nes's less than feminine physique. Shoulders too broad, abdomen too toned, and chest just a touch too full once unbound, Nessix felt restricted and vulnerable wrapped in the gaudy fabric.

Slipping a dagger into her pack and irritably kicking at the flowing length of the skirt, Nessix reluctantly left her sword belt and armor locked in a cell with the guards she only mostly trusted, and headed down the road. The guards watched her try to appear ladylike on her way out of town, and she swatted away the gazes of the curious public as irritably as she swatted her loose hair from her face. Evening pressed in quickly, and Nessix had trouble trying to walk faster through the dress's hinderance. She hoped to encounter this man before darkness obstructed her vision.

The sun glowed dimly on the horizon as Nessix left the town and she put on her best attempt at an innocent and delicate expression. She'd often wondered what it felt like to be a normal woman, to wear dresses and paint her face and giggle over silly gossip. As she tried so desperately to act the role her life on the field had forbidden her, she realized it was far more work than she'd imagined.

Nessix marched along, so eager to prove her worth that she nearly forgot that a proper woman's stride wouldn't cover quite so much ground and that a single traveler would move with more caution. She fumbled with implementing both changes and settled for wrapping one hand tighter around her pack's strap. She continued until a gentle rustle from the wooded side of the road to her right caught her ears, and even then a little longer. It sounded again and Nessix fought a smirk as her tactical side clapped its hands in anticipation.

Disappointing her instinct to immediately spring toward her target, Nessix stopped in the middle of the road, huffing a frustrated sigh an octave higher than she was comfortable with. If she tried jumping off the path, there was a chance that the man would bolt, and she doubted he'd come after her a second time if he was as clever as she'd been led to believe. He'd frequented this road for some time, knew the terrain, and there was always the chance that he'd set traps. If she engaged without care, she'd lose her chance at success.

Feeling more foolish than ever before, Nessix fussed a high pitched and drawn out, "Oh..." and stuck the knuckle of her index finger between her teeth as she turned to look down the road behind her. She let her hand drop to her side and turned around again, pulling her lips between her teeth. Humming a temperamental bout of frustration, Nessix spun her pack to her chest and removed her map. The rustle came again, this time accompanied by the faint crunch of dead undergrowth.

It was all Nessix could do to retain her desire to leap forward and end this right now, but she repeated to herself over and over again that she needed to lure the man out of hiding to decrease the odds of complications. She didn't want a struggle. She wanted victory.

Unrolling the map, Nessix exaggerated her confusion, tilting her head back and forth, lowering the page to peer down the road ahead of her, even going as far as to turn the map upside down, a look of excitement popping across her face before she let her expression fall. She heaved another sigh, wishing this brazen fool would hurry up and assault her. Pride wouldn't allow her to fake this ignorance much longer.

Several more moments debating with the map passed before Nessix was rewarded by the sound of a throat clearing from behind her. Tucking away her victorious smirk, she spun, clutching the map to her chest as she jumped. Hopefully, her reaction came across as natural.

"Having some trouble with your map, miss?"

The man stood three paces from her, well dressed and clean shaven, wearing the same tousled brown hair depicted on the poster. His hazel eyes held the devious depth characteristic of troublemakers. Wishing there had been some sort of scar or grotesque disfigurement to confirm his identity—she didn't want to kill an innocent man honestly trying to help a lost woman—Nessix held her actions a bit longer. She beamed a grateful smile and lowered the map to provide an unhindered view of her chest.

"Yes," she said, aiming to keep her voice laced with ignorance. "I must have gotten turned around during my stay in Bessemar." She held the map out to him. "Is this the road to Longmont?"

A roguish smile swept across the man's face, exuding confidence and dripping with charm Nessix assumed came either from immense practice or some sort of enchantment. He sauntered up to her, stopping one step closer than she'd have allowed most people she liked, and plucked at the corner of her map to gain a better view of it.

"Oh, you did get turned around." The aroma of sandalwood and rain-soaked moss accompanied his nearness as he bent closer. "Look, this is the road you're on, heading to Cedartown. You should have taken the southern gate to get to Longmont."

Nessix slouched her shoulders as she pouted and fussed a repressed tantrum. "I just *knew* I'd get lost without a guide! If I go back to town to find the south gate, I'll be fine?"

She glanced at him for the first time since he'd stepped so near, his face close enough that she had to restrain herself from slapping him. The arch of his brows and the glint of lust in his eyes steeled all of his intentions, and Nessix fought hard to hold back her impulse to grapple him now. She needed to get to her knife before she engaged.

"You're already fine." His lips curled into a smile Nessix had learned from the demons—one which meant he was about to take something that was never meant to be his, and confident he'd succeed in doing so.

Here came that tittering laugh she'd hoped to not screw up. It felt as fake as it was, but he didn't seem to notice. Rolling up the map, Nessix opened her pack and rummaged around to clear a space for it inside. "Thank you so much for your help, sir," she said. "Is there any way I can repay you?"

In the time it took him to raise his hands to grasp her forearms, Nessix had pulled her dagger from her bag. His eyes widened at the flash of steel and recognition of Nes's firm scowl and judgmental eyes as she slashed through his throat. He staggered a step back, one hand reaching his neck as he sputtered an attempt to plea for his life, then collapsed to the ground.

Nessix stared at his body as his blood drained, morbidly intrigued by the similarities between his death and her own. Had she died looking as shocked as he did? Sighing, having expected more excitement from a man who had caused so much grief, Nessix was at least grateful that she didn't have to brawl while dressed like this.

Wiping her knife clean, she shoved it back into her pack, slung the bag behind her once again, and strode forward. "You should be ashamed of yourself," she sneered, snagging a hold of his collar. "I was told you'd be a challenge."

Squaring her shoulders, Nessix braced herself and dragged the man's corpse back to town.

By the time she reached the gates, dead letch in tow, the sun had long since dipped below the horizon. Rumor of Nes's foolhardy intentions had reached the gate guards, and so they didn't question why a frazzled woman in a blood-spattered yellow dress was hauling a dead man into town. Instead, they greeted her with wide eyes and slacked jaws—expressions Nessix would have to get used to, it seemed—and offered to assist her with delivering the corpse to the guard station.

Nessix graciously accepted the offer. She was tired and hungry, and more than a little anxious to collect her sword, her armor, and her reward. When the sun rose, she could resume running from Kol and the inoga with enough money to keep eating. Nobody had asked her name, she'd neither seen nor smelled a demon all day, and she'd rid the world of a villainous man.

A certain degree of fanfare from the few civilians still out and about followed Nessix and her prize, her first sign of concern for the night. She'd wanted to avoid commotion, and didn't want to be slowed down by curiosity or gratitude or any other hindersome emotion. No longer burdened by the need to pretend she was a proper woman, she lengthened her stride, hunched her shoulders forward, and kept her head ducked to avoid feeling obligated to respond to the awed gawks coming her way.

Word spread far ahead of Nes's progress and by the time the guard station came into view, the older guard and Randall stood out front, gaping. Respectful of the hour and slumbering population, Nessix refrained from shouting ahead, waiting until she stood before them where she gestured for her escort to fling the letch's corpse at their feet.

"Please tell me I got the right man."

The younger guard didn't answer—he couldn't have past his sagging jaw—but the older knelt down and grasped Nes's victim by the hair, tilting the corpse's startled gaze toward the moonlight. He grunted in a sound that couldn't quite count as satisfaction. "Yeah," he said. "That looks to be him."

Nessix breathed out that reserve of breath she'd been carrying. "Then I believe you've got a few things of mine."

The old guard grunted again and turned to go back inside, leaving the dead body on the steps. Randall continued to gawk.

"How'd you do it?" he asked at last.

Nessix kicked a leg in her skirt, trying to situate her foot to scratch the back of her calf. She jutted her chin toward the disgrace on the ground. "Slit his throat." She politely left out how obvious that was.

"No, I see that," Randall said, flustered at his inability to clearly express himself. "But we've been tracking this man for *months*."

"I told you," Nessix said. "He wouldn't show for a man."

"But where'd you learn how to do that?"

A smile wriggled its way to Nes's lips. "Come now, you don't think it takes all that much skill to slit a man's throat, do you?"

"But to stay so calm before a beast like him? And you're so… so…"

"So what?" Nessix asked, crossing her arms. At any other time, this young man's awkward marveling might have been charming, but Nes was tired and uncomfortable and just wanted the guard in charge to return with her belongings so she could go to sleep.

"Well, ma'am… you're not the most *imposing* woman I've seen…"

"I'm sure this thing thought the same." She shoved the letch's limp shoulder with her foot for emphasis. "Underestimating me was his last mistake." That comment staved off further prying and Randall gave her a tight smile before dashing inside after his superior.

Nessix stood and waited, doing her best to maintain her patience. She suspected the older guard was now cultivating reservations about the threat she might pose to his quiet town, but there had been more than enough witnesses to the actions she'd taken tonight that she doubted he'd be able to short her easily. Finally, the pair of guards came back out of the building, carrying Nes's sword, her preferred mode of dress, and a small purse stuffed with her earnings.

"You got a name, lady?" the older guard asked as Nessix instantly retrieved her beloved blade from the younger of the two and slung its belt around her waist.

"I avoid putting down roots for a reason." She held out her free hand to accept the balance of her possessions.

The man grunted. "Sounds to me like you're a trouble maker."

"Trouble solver, by the looks of it," Nessix corrected. She went ahead and snatched her bundle of armor and clothing, but didn't quite have the nerve to claim the coins from this man, not with him already so suspicious of her.

"I don't much appreciate any sort of trouble in my town," he said roughly.

"I'll be on my way first thing tomorrow, so there's no risk of me causing any." She left out the part of her being chased by demons, suspecting that was exactly the kind of trouble he'd want to avoid.

A contemplative nod bobbed from the old man as he plopped the pouch in Nes's hand.

Nessix lowered her head in acceptance and looked back up at Randall. "Has compensation for your sister's dress been taken from this?"

He nodded, tongue still tied over his awe of Nes's performance.

"Fantastic." Nes tucked the pouch in her pack. "I trust you have some sort of method for dealing with bodies? May I consider my side of the bargain through?"

"Not. Just. Yet," the older man said, pulling Nes's attention, which she'd resigned to retiring, back to him. "I don't quite trust you, lady, but you did good work. Clean, effective work. My force could benefit from your talents."

Nessix tried a polite smile that felt more like a grimace. "As much as I love helping where I can, I'm on a rather time sensitive assignment to deliver a message to Zeal."

"For Zeal!" Randall beamed. "She works for the Order! I knew there was something special about her!"

"Bah!" the older guard grumbled. "Then be on your way." He turned and disappeared into the building, calling over his shoulder, "Randall! String up the letch to let the town know they're free and quit gawking at that lady. She said she needed sleep."

"Of course, sir!" Randall called back, flashing Nessix a sheepish smile. "Please accept the gratitude of Bessemar," he said with an awkward bow. "You are an amazing woman."

There had been a time when such compliments meant something to Nessix, but as the highly functioning monster she now knew herself to be, the gushing praise seemed less flattering. She accepted his gratitude, wished him well, and turned to head back to the inn.

Retrieving her key, Nessix tripped her way up the stairs. The moment she closed and secured the door, she began to twist and squirm in the dress, trying—but failing—to reach her arms behind her to pull at the laces of the bodice. A wave of claustrophobia swelled around her and she resorted to bending over and pushing her shoulders forward. The seams protested at the flexing of her muscles, unaccustomed to a body objecting to its restrictions in this manner, and at her second, sharper attempt, they popped free at last.

Breathing in deeply, enjoying the feel of freedom easing over her, Nessix peeled the dress from herself. She stepped out of the skirt, leaving it in a dirty yellow puddle on the floor. Exhausted and eager to put the risky task of sleep behind her for the day, Nessix climbed into bed to dream up more clues about Berann.

FIFTEEN

The morning dew was cold on Khin's nose and she sniffled in the chilly air that welcomed her to a new day. Her muscles burned, but these aches beat waking in the warmth of a stranger's bed. Grateful that she didn't need to hurry back to her master, especially since the restrictive soreness in her arms and legs wouldn't allow her to hurry anywhere right now, Khin took her time coming back to the world. When she felt she'd gathered enough strength, she hauled herself upright into a seated position and blinked away her grogginess to focus on Mathias.

The previous night's anger had resolved into a motivated light in his eyes. He smiled warmly as Khin sat up, and she returned the gesture without fully understanding what they had to smile about.

"Did you sleep well?" Mathias asked.

Khin consulted her tight muscles and the knot between her shoulder blades but didn't know whether or not those pains came from the previous day or the hard ground she'd slept on. Either way, she'd slept, which beat most of her usual nights. "Yes, thank you." She looked around for a moment, unsure how to start the morning. Though Mathias outwardly appeared as chipper as ever, she couldn't quite silence her guilt that he'd stayed awake all night. "Did watch go well?"

"Every night on watch without trouble is a good one."

Mathias handed her a serving of rations and stood. "Get your things together and let's go."

Even with her mouth stuffed with bread and cheese, Khin managed a groan. The sun had barely risen enough to give the land a gentle glow, and her legs preemptively ached even more at the thought of climbing into the saddle. Despite this, she refused to complain. The confession she'd spurted for Mathias the previous night had freed her in ways she'd never be able to repay him. Whatever this great quest of his was, he'd chosen to put it aside for something as petty as seeing a whore back to her family. Mathias deserved her compliance, and though motivating her arms to roll up her bedding was difficult, she managed with nothing but minor grumbling.

Mathias didn't rush Khin, giving her time to eat her cold breakfast while he secured her belongings to her horse and grazed their mounts. Khin finished her meal, heaved a labored sigh, and hefted herself to her feet. She wobbled on legs that lied about their stability and staggered over to Mathias and the horses.

"We're still riding fast today?" she asked meekly.

Only allowing a hint of his smirk, Mathias nodded. "The sooner we get you home, the better, remember?" He positioned himself to give her a leg up and was pleased when she accepted his aid without debate.

As Khin settled into the saddle, her muscles relaxed into place, more comfortable than they'd been standing just a few moments prior. "You're sure I won't fall, even as much as I hurt?"

Mathias let his smile out in full now. "You've proven you can stay on. I think you'll have an easier time of it today." He reached out and grabbed Khin's hand, pulling it toward him to plop a hefty pouch of coins in it. Without a word, he turned to mount his horse.

Khin stared at the plump pouch, blinking several times and mouth agape. She hadn't peeked inside, but was reasonably certain it held more coins than she'd handled in her entire life. "What—" The coins weighed her mind down too much to finish the question. "Mathias, I can't take this."

Settling in his saddle, Mathias turned his horse to face Khin. "Of course you can. All you have to do is tie it to your belt."

Cheeks pale, Khin shook her head. "That's not what I mean. It's… it's *wealth*, Mathias. I don't deserve this."

Mathias tucked his lips in a short-lived frown and bent forward to grab Khin's reins. He wouldn't embarrass her by laughing at how little surrendering such funds would hurt him, and he wouldn't shame her with the reminder that she deserved far more compensation for the roads her life had dragged her down. Besides, it was a small gesture, considering the blessings he planned to pray over her village's farmlands.

"I've not done much to earn it, either," he said. "And I've no immediate need of it. It'd be a pity to just leave it out here on the road, wouldn't it?"

No amount of levity could restore the color to Khin's cheeks. Men like Mathias were myths, at the very least too good for her. He'd saved her life. He'd seen her fed and comforted. He'd changed his own path to suit her selfish demands, and now he insisted she take his money. A week ago, this would have frightened Khin, but now, it simply confused her. Longing fingers caressed the fullness of the pouch.

"Are you serious?" she asked at last.

Mathias turned in his saddle and smiled. "I'm always serious. Fate led us together, for whatever reason. I'll help you where I can."

Her confused wonder snuffed out in a pathetic flurry of disgust. "If it was fate that we met, I'd prefer my life to luck."

Mathias frowned. He hadn't meant to dredge up those memories. "Tell me more about your family," he said, hoping the change of subject would pull Khin from the gloom of her past.

"There's not much more to tell," Khin said. "My ma worked raising us kids. Pa raised the pigs and goats for the nearby villages until the land dried up. It was a simple life, just like I told you, until…" Modesty silenced her words.

"It doesn't sound too different from my childhood." Mathias didn't often think back on his days before Etha, finding them largely empty and wasted, but was content to revisit them for Khin's benefit.

The girl's skeptical glare swept across Mathias's glistening armor and the impressive sword slung at his waist. "I find it hard to believe you started out like me."

Mathias chuckled, though it wasn't with humor. "When I let myself think back on it, I find it hard to believe, too. But it's true. I was born an average farm boy, working alongside my father with dreams of becoming a knight until Julianna was recruited for the priestesshood. I escorted her to Zeal and stayed to chase those dreams. My persistence found me a knight to apprentice under, the demons struck, and I earned myself the title of Sir." Mathias stilled himself for a moment, to this day unsure how he'd impressed Etha enough to end up where he was now. "I wasn't born into this life, but I found it. We can all change our destinies."

It was a lovely story, but Khin wholeheartedly disagreed. "If it was that easy, every little boy would grow up to become a knight."

"But not every little boy had what I did."

Mathias spoke the words softly and with such inner reflection that Khin's defensiveness instantly cooled to curiosity. "What's that?"

"I had hope. Not just dreams and desires, but a genuine belief that I'd see them achieved. I had the faith of those who were in the position to help me and those I sought to help. I never said I accomplished any of this on my own."

Hope. Faith. They were words Khin had forgotten over the past year, first from her family's hardships, then when the faintest glimmer of them was pissed upon as she tried to make things right. Even in the security of Mathias's care, both seemed unreachable to her. She was so exhausted from being helpless; maybe overcoming that was how she'd find this elusive hope once again.

"Could you teach me something knightly?" she asked.

Mathias cocked his head at the unusual request. Khin hadn't struck him as the kind to care about chivalry, and he didn't want to bore her with tradition. "Like what?"

"I don't know…" Her confidence waned at how ridiculous she sounded. "Something… useful. Something helpful. Something to give me hope."

Mathias nodded in understanding. "You want to learn self-defense."

It seemed like such a bold idea for one of her stature and past, but one she had to conquer to get back on the road to her life. "Yes, please."

As much as Mathias had hoped peaceful times waited in Khin's future, knowing a few combat skills never hurt anyone. "How about at our next stop?" he asked. "I'll teach you how to use a knife."

Both timid and excited by the prospect, Khin nodded enthusiastically.

"Then secure that pouch like I told you, and let's get going."

Heart opening just a peek, Khin did as she was told and they started the day's riding, pressing ever closer to the peace she missed so dearly.

SIXTEEN

Even with a demon's superior regenerative traits, it would have taken several days for Kol's wing to heal enough to not risk opening the tear and a subsequent plummet into the ocean if they flew from Elidae, and so after he and Annin gathered up the ten alar who had deemed it worth their time and safety to assist them, they'd hastened down the Undersea Pass. Kol had hoped for a greater number of soldiers to back them and Annin had fully expected it, but all things considered, their disappointment was a fair trade for gaining extra bodies at all.

They travelled briskly through the passage, thankful for their racial stamina and Gelthin's relative nearness to Elidae. Where it had taken a reluctant and disorganized army of akhuerai nearly a week to traverse the tunnel, Kol and his men reached Gelthin in three days. Exhaustion and hunger shortened the demons' tempers, but this meager brotherhood was committed to their task. If they didn't succeed in finding Nessix, the hells—or at least the reaches Grell had contact with—would be even more perilous than they were accustomed to.

The route they took opened into the caverns beneath the town of Harborswatch on the far western coast of the continent. Well out of any probable reach of Grell's search party, it was also far from their goal of Zeal. Ancient trails wound through the mountains, whispering distorted memories to Kol and calling him up into their peaks with welcoming murmurs. He followed their promises with determination, grateful for the dry warmth of the season.

"Damn alar's gone mad…" one of the soldiers muttered between heavy breaths.

Annin sighed and shoved his weariness aside to trudge after Kol. "He has," he agreed, waving the grumbling unit along. "But he's no less clever. He knows where we're going."

"Yeah?" a second scoffed. "But do you?"

"Of course." Annin turned to face the group, his confirmation slowly motivating them to move forward. "He's taking us to Vesper."

The soldiers exchanged confused glances, shrugging at the question none of them had the answer to.

"What's a Vesper?" the first asked at last.

Annin opened his mouth to answer, but Kol beat him to it. "It's the homeland of my ancestors. If we can find allies anywhere, it will be there."

"*Homeland*," a third sneered. Of the group, only Kol and Annin were ancients of the first wave of demons, but the hatred of mortal connections pulsed strong in every demon's veins. "He *has* gone mad."

"No," Annin corrected with a reluctant sigh. "This time, he's thinking clearly."

The debating demon planted his feet, the soldier immediately behind him stumbling to get out of the way. "Maybe you've *both* gone mad."

Annin's abrupt halt pulled Kol to a stop, as well. The oraku gave their critic a moment to reconsider the stance he was attempting to take before slowly turning to face a stubborn scowl. "Is there going to be a problem?"

"If you've got us relying on mortals, yeah, there's a big problem."

Kol spat, disdainfully shook his head, and continued on. He trusted Annin to sort this out, whether it ended in the unruly demons' compliance or death.

"He said our homeland was involved. He never said a word about mortals."

"But what's that—"

All it took was the deliberate raising of Annin's hand and the threat which existed in the snap of his fingers to silence the debate.

"You had no way of knowing, whelp," the oraku sneered, "but not all of us who voted for war were content adapting to the hells. Some of us reclaimed our homes by force, the way it should have been. I'd frame my arguments with a bit more care, if I were you. The demons we're seeking haven't learned to deal with whining." Annin speared each of his subordinates with a strict glare. "Your options are to come with us or go back to Grell. I won't tell you which I'd choose."

Lines drawn, Annin turned and resumed following Kol up the path toward their old home.

Preferring their odds with a half-mad—but still reasonably predictable—Kol over Grell's instability, it didn't take long for the group to follow their leaders. Associating with demons as damned as Annin and Kol had been what deterred a greater number of alar from joining them on this quest. The dangers and implications hadn't bothered this particular group before, but they did now.

The fresh air and increasing determination which came from being in the same realm as Nessix revitalized Kol, and though he still ached for her, he was no longer defeated by that longing. He'd reach her. Drinking in this flood of enthusiasm, Kol hastened his unit up the mountain and as plumes of smoke twisted between the peaks, he pushed his men harder toward the village he'd left lifetimes ago.

Hours into the trek, a full procession of demons bronzed by prolonged exposure to the sun met Kol's band of alar, keeping a wary watch on the hell dwellers and their hands near their weapons as Kol's group entered their territory. Instantly, the group of alar ceased their skeptical judgement of Kol's plan as the promise of danger hung thick in the air. Kol raised his empty hands, fingers splayed to show he was not a threat, and Annin irritably gestured at their soldiers to do the same before holding his own hands low at his waist. The soldiers, humbled at last, complied with their leaders' examples, comforted, barely, by their confidence.

"Well I'll be Kalina's bastard," a deep voice zipped through the wary crowd. "Is that really you, Kol? Come all the way up here to chat with a commoner like me?"

A wistful smile eased Kol's face as the crowd parted to reveal a stocky demon wearing a patch over his right eye. If he hadn't been so short, he could have passed for an inoga, but with his comparative physical weakness, it was a good thing he wasn't any taller. "Lorrin," Kol greeted, warmer than any of his underlings had ever heard him speak. "It's been some time. Looks like you've done well for yourself."

Lorrin spat and flashed a toothy grin, the runes etched into the sides of his neck now visible to Kol's companions. They lifted their hands farther from their weapons.

"Tossed around a few mortals for the right to keep struggling for survival in the mountains. If you consider that well, sir, I won't argue." Lorrin stopped before Kol, his chest puffed out as he appraised the rest of the party. He snapped his fingers in excitement—gaining instant flinches and gasps from Kol's soldiers—and pointed over the alar's shoulder, grin widening. "And you've brought Annin!" Lorrin's excitement held a moment longer, and then he drew his arm back to himself, expression falling. "Wait. You've brought Annin…"

That hadn't taken long. "It's just the two of us for now, and we've come with friendly intentions."

Lorrin's eye narrowed. "But intentions, nonetheless?"

It wasn't often that Kol willingly released his hold on pride, but being back in the land of his birth, the only place he'd ever truly loved, after living in the drudgery of the hells allowed him to disregard his reservations. Lorrin had always been content beneath him, and had openly idolized Annin long before the Divine Battle had been a giggle in the back of their damned goddess's mind. Kol banked on the hope that this surface-bound oraku's calling him sir suggested such respect remained.

"Is there someplace private you and I can discuss a sensitive matter?" Kol asked.

"I've got a place," Lorrin answered.

Kol glanced at the wary eyes of the small army that watched his unit of soldiers. "Your men won't make problems for mine, will they?"

Lorrin looked over the group of his disciplined men, then back at Kol. "You think they're looking for trouble?" When Kol's glare remained strict and even, Lorrin scoffed and waved a dismissing hand at his army. "Blasted hell dwellers... scared of a couple of their kin. I thought the likes of you would be a bit more courageous."

The guarding army eased their stances, but maintained their careful watch, hands never straying far from their weapons. Kol could have just as easily criticized their paranoid response to a twelve-man force but he was here to ask for a favor, something respectable demons of any realm weren't known to do.

"We've had the need to learn to use caution lately." Kol wasn't about to ask forgiveness for this fact, but figured explaining the situation would hasten them to his objective. He took a step closer to Lorrin and lowered his voice to pique the oraku's curiosity. "Annin and I have caused a bit of trouble for our old friend Grell, and it's made my men rightfully wary."

Lorrin chuckled at the mention of angering the inoga, erupting in a brief bout of laughter after the first couple bursts. "Yes, yes. I see how that would do it." He slapped a hand on Kol's shoulder and craned his neck to address his troops. "Stand down and give none of these demons trouble. They're my guests and of no threat to us."

Kol didn't flinch from Lorrin's hand the way he'd taken to shrinking away from the same gesture from Grell, soaking in the warmth of camaraderie it was meant to convey. For once, it seemed, Kol had chosen the correct path. "May I leave Annin behind while we have our discussion?"

Lorrin patted Kol's shoulder once more then wiped the dampness of laughter from his one functional eye. "I'd prefer it."

Kol looked over his shoulder, meeting Annin's patient expression with a curt nod, and followed Lorrin through the mass of soldiers as they dispersed per their leader's orders. Lorrin brimmed with curiosity, a trait thriving among oraku, though

Lorrin hid it more poorly than most. It must have been liberating, having the freedom to express emotions here on the surface, without fear of ridicule or an inoga's judgement. Working his jaw as hatred for the demons' hierarchy steeped, Kol's desire to overthrow Grell increased tenfold.

They walked in silence, Lorrin respecting Kol's request for privacy and Kol not risking a slip until he had it, and soon reached a blue tent constructed of sheets of oiled leather. Discolored from the wear of harsh weather and sun, the very sight of it roused the dull ache of distant memories in Kol. Perhaps if things went south in his search for Nessix, he could stay here. Lorrin interrupted those thoughts before the fear of never finding Nessix took control of Kol by pulling open the tent flap and ushering the alar inside.

Plump woolen pillows scattered across the floor, a thick, faded rug the only barrier between the ground and where the two demons would sit. Centrally located beneath a vent in the roof was a smooth stone table raised half a foot from the ground, a pit carved out of the middle filled with ashes. The day was warm enough that no fire had been lit today. Etiquette stated that Kol should wait to seat himself until he was invited to do so, being the guest of Vesper's current leader, but he wasn't here to be polite and had to establish his authority before it became an issue. Taking his chances at offending Lorrin, Kol sat.

Lorrin didn't even blink at the control Kol had just claimed for himself, and sat down at the opposite side of the table. "So, these intentions of yours. I take it they have to do with the trouble you made for Grell?"

"They do." Tip toeing around the truth wouldn't do Kol any good, but the drive for self-preservation had conditioned him to hide unnecessary details. "Have any rumors about what Annin and I have spent the past century working on made it to your corner of the surface?"

Lorrin shook his head. "There's a reason me and mine haven't moved into your cozy caves. We've got no interest in your politics and games."

Kol kept his smug smile at bay. Lorrin's hatred for inoga burned just as strong as he remembered. "We've been building a sentient army of the undead."

Lorrin's eye widened with intrigue and awe, and he leaned forward, eager for Kol to elaborate.

"Based on what we've gathered of how our own souls work, we found a way to bind souls back to their bodies. This gave us a force of unparalleled potential, undying and resilient, but intelligent enough to think through their problems."

Lorrin's brows rippled closer together. "What's that supposed to mean?"

"It means..." Kol drew in a slow breath and streamed it out through puckered lips. "It means that they're prone to bouts of disobedience and unpredictable behavior."

A pinch of respect dwindled from Lorrin's expression as he sat back and cocked his head. "So what's this got to do with Grell?"

Lorrin might be an oraku, but the ability to see and access threads didn't inherently make one sharp. Keeping himself calm, commanding the variables at his disposal, Kol stuck to the lie that had taken him this far. "It took us years to fine tune our techniques to the point that we were ready to seize a general for this army. We chose the general of Elidae—"

Lorrin slapped his palm on the table. "I *did* hear about the disaster your lords made of that war! I guess Grell didn't learn anything the first time he thought he could trust a goddess?"

Kol frowned tightly, memories he'd have preferred to avoid coming back to him at the reminder of the ancient air goddess, Kalina's, role in his life. "Grell doesn't learn from anything."

"You got that right."

Unwelcome traipse into the distant past shoved aside, Kol pressed toward his objective. "We seized the general of Elidae to forge her into the leader of this army, and she exceeded our expectations on every front." He'd have to find a quiet moment to tell Annin of the liberties he was taking to ensure the oraku's opinions of Nessix didn't contradict this story. "But during their first trial here on the surface, she went missing."

Lorrin narrowed his eye and crossed his arms. "Went missing or ran off?"

Kol opened his mouth to demand she'd been taken from him,

but stopped. To a demon, a hunt was a hunt. The idea of Nessix actively trying to evade them might be more enticing. "We don't know," he said instead. "Combat started and when it ended, she was gone, no sign of her body on the field."

Lorrin rolled his head back and forth on his rune-etched neck, humming as he waded through his interpretation of the report. His gaze flicked back to Kol's. "You still haven't told me what this has to do with Grell."

Pleased that the oraku's preoccupation with his hatred of inoga prevented him from getting hung up on the details of Nessix's disappearance, Kol capitalized on this thriving grudge. "Grell is furious that she's missing and wants her back so he can do to her what he does to those he dislikes. We cannot afford to let him get his hands on her if we want to achieve our primary objective."

"Which is?"

Kol hesitated. Outwardly, the akhuerai had been designed to march against the mortal world, but Kol and Annin had spent several sleepless nights enthusiastically discussing how to use the undying force to establish a new order within the hells. Kol didn't know which option would be safest to tell Lorrin, but he knew which one the oraku was most likely to support.

"I don't need to tell you that the hells are run backwards," Kol said. "The inoga are not the best equipped to manage any sort of functional society, but they've got the strength and temper to claim that role."

Lorrin leaned forward again. "I'm listening."

"This woman is imperative to ensuring the army can stand against the inoga and any underlings who refuse to defy them. If Annin and I cannot secure her, the entire operation will fall apart. Grell's permanently neutralized her second in command, and nobody else has stepped forward to fill the position." Kol watched Lorrin carefully, pleased to see his lips twitch with distaste. "Grell believes this army has been designed solely to strike the mortal realm and he's taken personal offense that the general who controlled it is gone, so much so that he's recruited his peers beneath Gelthin to search for her."

177

Lorrin grunted, nose wrinkling in the pout of a child. "And what happens if they find her?"

Kol looked away. Vulnerable emotions had more of a place here than they did in the hells, but he'd spent so long covering them up until recently—and those cases had exhausted him—that he felt exposed doing so. Either way, it was a fair question and one Kol knew he'd have to address.

"If Grell's men find the general before Annin and I can, we will be assigned under the winning party's command and Grell will in no uncertain terms force her under his control. This will permanently end the goal to overthrow the inoga."

"And if you find her first, what then?" Lorrin asked. "You mean to tell me Grell will just stand back and let you keep her like nothing happened?"

Kol's fist clenched where it rested on his knee and he sneered at the thought of Grell's arrogance and the image of the inoga's mocking grin. "If I find her first, Grell won't have a chance to make that decision. I worked closely with this general"—Kol brushed right past Lorrin's presumptive snort—"and she's cultivated a healthy hatred of Grell. If I tell her she needs to rally her army to deal with him, she won't hesitate."

Lorrin nodded slowly, accepting what sounded like feasible reasoning. "She and her army could handle Grell, but what of the louts he conspires with?"

"We would take Grell quietly, by surprise. He's alienated himself from his peers frequently enough of late that it wouldn't be a problem. We'd have to strike Inek next, before he caught on to what we were up to, then Turit. I'm debating whether or not we'd be able to negotiate with Ehsmil."

"You seem rather confident in these creations of yours."

Kol raised his chin, the fragments of his shattered pride pulling back together at last. "Annin and I haven't devoted ourselves to this path blindly."

"So you're asking for manpower in this hunt for your lady general."

At least Lorrin spared Kol the humiliation of making the request. "I am. Grell has five inoga and their associated underlings scurrying about Gelthin. We were barely able to convince him to let us bring the ten alar we have. He's certain we'll fail, and I've not seen him so excited over such speculations in ages. He seems to have forgotten of your tribe's existence and that you and I have always been on cordial terms."

"Tss. Typical Grell." Lorrin uncrossed his arms and gripped his knees. "You got a plan to evade the Order?"

Kol slowed his breathing, accepting Lorrin's questions as his inclination to cooperate. "My plan was to find her before they do." He left out Nessix's ties to Mathias, banking on Lorrin overlooking the connections of her past due to his limited knowledge of the war on Elidae.

Lorrin narrowed his eye, not entirely pleased with that answer, but not quite willing to voice as much. "Under normal circumstances, I'd ask what was in it for me. Past relationships only go so far toward solving other people's problems. But if finding this woman will let us overthrow the inoga?" Lorrin grinned, bearing chiseled canines. "Why, that's not normal circumstances at all, is it? If we can humble even one of those churls, especially if it happens to be Grell, I'm in."

Kol kept his relieved sigh to himself. "And if you're in, are your men?"

"Look at what the hells have done to your understanding of loyalty." Lorrin shook his head, his words sorrowful, but his tone laced with a subtle jest.

"The hells have torn down a lot of concepts our kind would be stronger to embrace," Kol said.

Lorrin slapped his knees and stood, extending a hand to Kol to help him to his feet. "And it was those damned inoga who took them from you. You've got my tribe's help, brother. It's been too long since we've hunted worthy prey."

* * * * *

Annin had expected news of the tribe's compliance when Kol emerged from Lorrin's tent, though the other ten alar were pleasantly surprised at the surface dwelling demons' willingness to assist in the hunt. As Lorrin had so bluntly pointed out, the ability to network and cooperate with others was a dead concept among demons of the hells, but after a day spent recovering under the tribe's hospitality, eating their fills of warm food, sleeping in comforts greater than a dirt floor, and enjoying agreeable banter about their mutual hatred of inoga, Kol's troops warmed up to their new allies.

The following day, they broke into task forces, each band of Lorrin's men led by one of Kol's, since they knew Nessix's description and mannerisms. Besides Lorrin and Annin, the joint force only had two other oraku at their disposal, and they were assigned to the forces working farthest south with the intention of hindering the inoga's progress.

Assuming that Nessix would have fled north from the inoga pursuit, the units skirted from fifty miles north of the latest reports of inoga movement around Gelthin's coasts. Where inoga capitalized on brute strength and the ability to cripple the world through fear, Kol had tactics and intelligence in his favor, now that he'd calmed down enough to use them. They'd gradually push their search parties inland, driving Nessix to where she had nowhere else to run but back to him.

Kol and Annin took position on the outskirts of Zeal's territory, declining a robust unit in favor of a pair of Lorrin's most effective rangers. Their proximity to the Order and the potential of Mathias's vengeance made this a risky station, but it was Nessix's destination. If she managed to evade all of the parties chasing her, Kol would be waiting for her, and he would not let her escape him a second time.

The moment they landed in the forest flanking the fields of lilies which ringed Zeal, Annin insisted they go exploring the woods to the east. Kol went along with the mission for half the day, assuming they were scouting the region's safety. When it became apparent that Annin didn't care at all whether or not the Order watched for them from the trees, Kol drew the line.

"We're venturing too far from our station," the alar growled, holding out a hand to stop the two rangers who quietly tracked behind them.

Annin stopped and faced Kol, shoulders drawn back and brows arched in dissatisfaction. "We won't find what we need if we stay close to it."

The rangers exchanged cautious glances. This entire time, they'd been led to believe, by both Kol and Lorrin, that Kol was the leader of this operation, yet how sharply Annin corrected him—and the manner in which Kol accepted it with nothing more than a tight frown and temperamental tilt of his head—threatened to countermand that assumption. Fingers twitching closer to their weapons, the rangers remained silent.

"Would you mind telling me what it is we need to find?" Kol asked, his words snapping irritably.

Annin brushed Kol's ire aside, turned, and resumed walking. "I'll know it when I find it," he said over his shoulder. "And the faster I find it, the faster we can get back to our station. I cannot tell you what to do, but I can advise you that it's best not to waste time."

Kol bit down on the insides of his cheeks, and the rangers balked at the rage flaring in his eyes. He wanted to argue with Annin that all that mattered was manning their station. He wanted to demand to know how Annin knew he'd find what he was after when he, himself, had admitted to not knowing what it was. But what all of his wants boiled down to was his need to find Nessix and to do that, he had to trust his oraku's instincts. Cursing under his breath, Kol gestured the rangers to follow and trudged after his companion.

Ever conscious of the demons behind him, Kol was torn between maintaining an air of authority and stubbornly demanding answers. He often tolerated this sort of behavior from Annin, having learned that the oraku's mind worked faster than he was able to explain to those who didn't understand how magic functioned, but he'd let Annin play long enough.

Driving the rangers back two steps with a stony glare, Kol lengthened his stride to catch up to Annin. The oraku didn't acknowledge him, systematically sweeping the area with a precise gaze. That only ruffled Kol further.

"You have been of great assistance to me this far, but this is *my* operation," Kol said through his teeth. "You agreed to the plans we'd laid out. I have been patient with you. I've let you help Grell get his peers on Nessix's trail. I've let you paint me a mad man. I've allowed you to influence my dreams and risk the safety of Nessix's soul, and now you will tell me what you're planning."

Annin's brows tipped closer to each other, his nostrils flaring. He wouldn't deny Kol's claim of responsibility for the situation they'd landed in, but he wasn't about to let him try to be the smart one. "You are not in a prime spot to be demanding answers of me," Annin replied, his eyes not faltering as he scoured the woodlands. "You've put me in a rather perilous position that I am far better equipped to sort out than you are. You're welcome to try stopping me, if you think you can, but if you succeed in doing so, your task force will be down an oraku you can't afford to lose."

Kol snarled at Annin's reply, but didn't debate. "You've been acting strange lately."

Annin snuck a glance at Kol, one judgmental brow lifted. "*I* have been acting strange?"

Kol didn't wince at the insult. This was the only chance he would have to save himself, and he wouldn't let Annin's stubbornness and secretive propensities get in the way of that. "Yes, you have."

Annin shrugged with a speculative hum. "If you think so. It has been quite some time since my fate has been in the sort of jeopardy it's in now."

Kol drew in a deep breath, his chest trembling with forced restraint at Annin's passive aggressive taunts. "Have I not been open with you this entire time?"

"You waited to tell me about your stupid plan to bind yourself to Nessix until you declared it to Grell. You ignored my sound suggestions against doing so. And you haven't bothered to tell me what she knows." Annin paused his searching to give Kol a steady stare. "That last bit's the part that's driving me now, more so than the threat of a few inoga coming after me."

Kol gulped down his guilt and misgivings over Annin's accusations, tempted to try convincing the oraku that Nessix didn't know anything worth worrying about. Annin had likely caught on to the notion that Nessix had gathered forbidden information well before Kol allowed himself to admit the same. More concerned now as he stalked through this open forest than he'd ever felt nestled in the caves of the hells, Kol faced the problem he'd denied for some time.

"If I tell you what she knows, will you tell me what your plan is?"

Annin stared at Kol a moment longer before rolling his eyes and pressing on. "You don't need to tell me what she knows, only confirm that you're aware she knows it. Which, I'll inform you, you just did."

Kol's lips twitched somewhere between the urge to sneer at Annin's cocky assumption and that to cry for what might happen if anyone other than Annin figured out this secret. That concept of trust which Kol had invested in Annin shackled him even tighter to truths he'd been happier ignoring. Kol crossed his arms, chilled despite the warmth of this summertime forest.

"She only has a name," he said, voice dropping even softer. For a moment, he fancied the notion that it had been soft enough to evade even Annin's ears and he could forget he'd even mentioned it, but luck, as it was so fond on doing of late, didn't smile on him.

"And what has she done with a name?"

Kol rubbed his arms. "She got a swift beating from it and never brought it up again."

Annin glanced at Kol again. "Not to *you*. But how many akhuerai do you think she mentioned it to?"

That was a thought Kol had avoided thinking about. "She didn't like speaking of her dream. I doubt she shared its details with anyone."

"She shared it with you," Annin said.

Kol shook his head. "Even if she did ask around, it would have been to Auden, and he's as good as dead now."

They continued on in silence, feet unaccustomed to traveling the upper realm loudly crunching dead leaves and fallen twigs. Behind them, the rangers made so little sound that Kol glanced over his shoulder twice to ensure they still followed. The guilt

Annin had laid on Kol held his irritation at bay, allowing him to consider the secrets they kept from one another even. Just as he let himself believe Annin had moved on, the oraku spoke again.

"Does she know what to make of this name?"

Facing that last conscious terror of the Divine Battle for the rest of eternity was difficult for Kol to accept even in his sleep; willingly drawing up the memories burned into his psyche was even worse. He dug his fingers into his biceps to keep them from trembling and lowered his head. "If she sees what I saw, she'll know he was a magic user."

Annin frowned, jaw clenching.

Kol briefly appraised the rigid draw of Annin's shoulders and the spark of fury igniting his pale eyes, and hoped to point that energy in a safe direction with his next words. "And she'd know he worked with you."

"Son of a bitch…" Annin muttered, the anger warping closer to fear, just as Kol had hoped. "So if she goes talking…"

"There's a chance you'll be part of the conversation."

"Fuck!" Annin struck a fist toward the ground. "You never thought I should know this?"

"I…" Kol twisted his lips, reluctant to repeat the empty excuse which so routinely had failed him. "I hadn't thought it would be a problem."

Annin hissed and shook his head, stopping abruptly. "I'm beginning to think you don't think much at all anymore."

Pride begged Kol to retaliate, but Annin had made a good point earlier that he couldn't risk losing his oraku—and the only demon he could truly depend on. He stopped beside Annin, turning as he did, and the other two demons staggered to a stop.

"You're rangers, right?" Annin asked, not bothering to hide how thin his patience had worn.

The taller of the two bit down on the inside of his cheek to keep a rude response to himself, but the shorter spoke freely. "That's what you brought us along for."

Annin nodded, swung his pack around to his hip, and began to dig around inside of it. "So you're skilled at hunting and tracking? Not afraid of wildlife, I gather?"

"We've brought rations if—"

"I'm not hungry," Annin snapped, pulling a length of rope from his pack. He shoved it toward the more compliant of the two. "I need you to go capture a wolf."

Brows furrowing, the shorter ranger accepted the rope.

"And it must come back to me alive and likely to stay that way. If it dies before we reach our next stop, you'll have to find me another one."

The taller ranger crossed his arms and glared at Annin for a moment before looking to Kol for guidance. Even Kol was at the point where he wanted to correct Annin for his increasingly outlandish requests, but he no longer felt he had the leverage to do so. He gestured at the rope as if this had been part of the plan all along.

"Lorrin told us you were the best rangers he has," Kol said. "Catching a wolf shouldn't be a problem for you, should it?"

Neither of the rangers looked any more thrilled with the idea than one receiving orders to clean chamber pots, but they didn't object.

"Grab the strongest adult you can find," Annin added, as though it was a simple request. "Skilled and efficient enough to survive without its pack."

The two exchanged dubious glances, then cast their doubt toward Kol. Lorrin had claimed these two demons were the sharpest he'd known, but it seemed as though the ages had worn on them. Regardless, they'd promised their leader they'd do what was asked of them to see this mission succeed.

"Go on, now," Kol instructed, waving them along. "Our objective is on the move and we cannot allow hesitation to make us miss her."

Shaking their heads and muttering rude opinions neither Kol nor Annin could quite make out, the rangers disappeared into the forest. Kol waited until he was sure they were gone and another moment still, and let his shoulders slump away from their authoritative rigidity as he turned to Annin.

"Alright. I've humored you long enough. Why do you need a wolf?"

Annin sighed and shifted his bag around again to pull out the handkerchief wrapped around the fabric of Nessix's cot. He briefly waved it in the air, then shoved it back in place.

Kol stared at where it had been crammed away. "You're going to train a wolf to track her scent?" he asked flatly, puffing a dry laugh at the ridiculous notion.

"Of course not. Even if I had the patience, we don't have the time."

Kol shook his head, clearly several steps behind Annin. "So what is the plan?"

Annin pulled out his sly smile, turned about until he located a fallen tree, and walked over to sit on it. "My plan is to wait until our rangers get back with a wolf." He retrieved a handful of rations from his pack and began snacking. "Then, I'm going to try to make us a servant."

Caught up dealing with the consequences of the disaster that had become of the akhuerai, Kol wasn't thrilled with Annin's course of action. But what other choice did they have? However the oraku planned to pull this off, if it worked, they would benefit greatly from the advantage. Tired of debating logistics, Kol sat beside Annin and pulled out some food of his own as they waited for the rangers to complete their task.

SEVENTEEN

The next three days Mathias and Khin spent on the road passed by light and enjoyable, all circumstances considered. During their brief breaks, the paladin taught his young friend the most resourceful basics for a woman with no martial background to use in self-defense, rewarded by watching her confidence bud after its harsh winter. The hesitant, ashamed girl he'd first rescued on the streets of Seaton quickly disappeared into the curious young woman Khin must have been before life tossed her aside. Not once did Mathias stop counting the hours he was leaving Nessix on her own, but revitalizing Khin's spirit was a worthy exchange.

Khin recognized the hills leading toward her family's village as they entered the region of Fieldsdeep, and lit up with excitement as she told Mathias that they were nearly there. He opted to let the horses slow and walk under the excuse of allowing them to catch their breath.

In truth, part of Mathias was disappointed to lose the girl's pleasant chatter and he frowned at the idea of continuing his journey without companionship. Then again, the roads he planned to travel were not safe in the greatest stretch of the imagination, and he'd never wish Khin the dangers that his journey was bound to uncover.

Mathias's horse flung its head in the air, strides becoming

choppy as its ears pricked smartly forward. Having taken for granted his mount's tractable nature, the paladin patted its shoulder and calmly asked it to continue moving forward. It did, though with great bellows from flared nostrils and soon later, Khin's horse began to dance to the side.

"Mathias…" The girl drew his name out with a frightened edge, the relaxation she'd found over the past few days of predictable riding immediately forgotten as she gripped tightly to the saddle.

Next came the distant sounds of shouting and screams, and Mathias pulled his tense horse to a stop.

"Is that… is that a festival?" The concept of hope was still relatively new to Khin, but the confidence Mathias had cultivated in her tried to keep it alive.

The first plumes of smoke twisted into the sky.

Each second Mathias wasted debating whether or not to tell Khin what was wrong cost her hometown lives. Duty insisted he dash to the village's rescue, that Khin didn't need any more of an explanation other than an order to stay put. But that would leave her—still far less skilled as both a fighter and a rider than she thought she was—alone on the road in the midst of a demon assault. He couldn't leave her here, but neither could he take her with him.

He wasn't even certain if it was wise for him to rush in.

If it's those inoga from back in Seaton you're worried about, you shouldn't be.

Amidst the devastating conditions, Mathias found a breath of gratitude. *I don't suppose Khin would be safe left behind?*

The only demons in the area are in her village.

Etha seldom gave Mathias straightforward answers about what decisions he should make, preserving his gift of free will whenever she could. It was the least she could do for the man who served her so devoutly. However, Mathias trusted she'd never lie to him or set him up for failure, and made his decision.

"Stay right here," he told Khin, tossing her reins back to her. "And if anything other than me comes over these hills, you do not fight. You jerk your horse around and kick him until you reach the next guarded town. Am I clear?"

Khin's big brown eyes grew wide, glistening with nervous tears Mathias had hoped were behind them. "Mathias, what's—"

"Am I clear?"

She gasped at the snap of his voice, clutched her horse's reins, and nodded mutely.

Wanting for the reliability and courage of Ceraphlaks or even an experienced charger, Mathias pressed his common saddlehorse toward the sound of slaughter. Well before he crested the hill, he already envisioned the houses in ruins, the indistinguishable jumble of corpses strewn across quaint roadways, the terror encompassing those who bolted to escape. Mathias had lost count of how many times he'd witnessed villages razed by demons, and each time looked the same. He'd never get used to it, and that was among his greatest motivations to see it come to an end.

The stench of smoke and blood reached Mathias's horse, spooking the animal in a flurry of panicking legs Mathias was hardly able to contain. When its efforts to escape failed, it attempted to rear, forcing Mathias to jerk it to the side. He'd lose the animal if he dismounted now, but the fit it pitched would waste time and energy Mathias didn't have.

Drawing a knife, Mathias cut his packs free from the saddle and let them fall to the ground. Still gripping the reins, he dismounted and turned the terrified horse away from where Khin waited; as new as the girl was to riding, she wouldn't stand a chance staying aboard if her horse fed off this one's terror. Mathias gave a shout and an aggressive wave of his arms, sending the horse bolting away.

He charged ahead on foot, sheathing his dagger as he crested the final hill before Khin's village. There were fewer bolting citizens than Mathias had expected to see and far more of them on the ground than he'd hoped to find. Unlike the usual tactics demons used to trounce whole settlements, though, it wasn't aranau berserkers skittering through the streets and collapsing buildings. Instead, a disciplined force of demons methodically swept through the village, investigating each building in turn, snagging the arms of people who tried to dart past them with a casual brutality before cutting them down. As Etha had stated, there was no sign of inoga in this group. Mathias wanted to be relieved by that realization, but this meant there were multiple parties chasing after Nessix.

Guilt flared inside Mathias—guilt for having put his search on hold while enjoying Khin's company, guilt for forgetting that his duty was to Abaeloth's safety first and foremost. Fueled by fury, Mathias placed his hand on his sword's hilt. The frantic pound of hoofbeats rushing up behind him stopped his action and he spun to see Khin barely hanging onto her horse. Mind overcome by fear, she tried to maintain her balance with the reins, her hands lifted almost above her head as she hauled on the horse's mouth, heels kicking into its sides to keep it running toward Mathias. If only because of her terrible riding, it hadn't yet been able to concentrate on the danger ahead.

Mathias snatched the horse's reins before it had the chance to dump the girl and run. There was no point scolding Khin for disobeying his order, not with how close they stood to a small demon army, and so Mathias tried one last instruction.

"Khin, dismount and stay low. Close your eyes, and shut out everything you hear."

Mathias had no idea what made him think she'd honor this request when she'd so blatantly disregarded the first, and Khin did the exact opposite of blocking out the massacre below.

Her wide eyes swept across the village's remains, searching too frantically across the homes of friends and neighbors to gain any information more relevant than terror. When she'd fled Seaton with Mathias, she'd protected herself by imagining the town's destruction had been a bad dream. Witnessing it a second time struck her with a surreal helplessness, tearing down each layer of confidence Mathias had so carefully helped her build. The sight of her home smoldering and limp bodies flung carelessly into the street pummeled her with a deafening force and for what seemed like eternity, all she could do was stare.

No stranger to the demons' wicked ways, Mathias saw past the shattered remains of the town, gathering intelligence on the field instead. Unlike the attack on Seaton, this was more than a senseless raid. This was an organized company of nearly three dozen demons, working more methodically than any inoga would have the patience to tolerate. A single alar served as their commanding officer. Mathias scanned the horizon for enemy reinforcements standing by. Finding none, he frowned and turned to Khin. He hated incapacitating people for convenience's sake.

Before he'd lifted his hand to reach for her forehead, the girl launched herself from the saddle and scrambled down the hill. Worn from exertion, her legs buckled beneath her as she charged ahead, and she dropped with a heart wrenching cry of fear and frustration, instinct convincing her to sprawl on the ground to prevent an uncontrollable tumble the rest of the way down the hill.

Cursing, Mathias sprinted after her, finding a pinch of grace to thank Etha that Khin had tripped before reaching the demons. Intentionally veering from Khin's path to direct attention away from her, Mathias drew his sword, the blade hot with anticipation. Welling a pool of Etha's grace, Mathias channeled divinity into his breastplate, letting the energy burst from him in a blinding flash that instantly caught every living eye in the vicinity.

He was near enough to see the snarling faces of his foes and hear them curse his name. A few dropped the dying civilians they'd been torturing to turn their interest toward him, and Mathias savored the rush of preparing for combat. Coming off a year of remaining politically polite to the likes of spoiled gods and demon informants, he'd waited too long to raise his sword. Power surged into his arms and legs, ready to carry him through this fight as the demons near him braced to pounce.

"Disengage!"

The order was spoken so sternly and with such authority that even Mathias hesitated. Unfamiliar with such discipline coming from a demon, lifetimes of training swore he must have an ally lurking in this defeated village.

"She isn't here! Disengage! We must report this to Kol!"

Rage ignited into a furious inferno at the mention of Kol's name, burning so hot it would have surprised Mathias if he'd been able to pull his concentration away from his first target. A brief wave of shock snuck past his focus as the demon he'd just reached fell back as instructed, reluctant to withdraw, but no less obedient to the order. The vile beasts scattered, and Mathias darted forward to grab one's arm and quickly saw it to its end.

For as organized as this particular force had appeared when Mathias first found them, they didn't fall into ranks, nor did they flee in the same direction. The village had no proper walls, only aged fences intended to keep placid animals contained, and the demons cleared them with little problem. As fast as the urge to destroy these beasts had hit Mathias, his chance to do just that slipped through his fingers. There was no way for him to catch them all, not with how they'd scattered, and it took a firm slap from experience to regain control over the desire to try. Right now, he had to concentrate on finding survivors. Heart falling, Mathias sheathed his sword and walked forward.

A devastated shriek pierced Mathias's senses, and he spun around to seek its origin. Khin had found her legs during his brief attempt at engaging the demons and, just as before, she'd ignored his instructions.

She swayed on splayed legs before a squatty stone cottage, chest heaving and eyes stricken with so much disbelief that Mathias's seasoned heart ached. The home had been among just a few spared by the fires, but its stone walls hadn't protected those who lived in it from the demons' claws. A woman and boy lay bloodied and motionless on the worn footpath that led up to the home, a third body cleaved in half at the waist in the doorway. Mathias abandoned his notion of searching for survivors, realizing that Khin was the only one.

He rushed to her as fat tears flooded past her lower eyelids, gently calling her name as her distraught fingers pulled at her hair. The color drained from her cheeks and she wobbled precariously. As Mathias's hands cupped her elbows, her legs caved out from beneath her, and he gently eased her to the ground as she sobbed incoherently in his arms. He cradled her head against his shoulder to shield her from the horror, hoping her tears would further obstruct the sights of the demons' massacre.

Mathias couldn't readily recall everything about his first demon encounter of this magnitude, but at least his had come with prior experience with the beasts' cruel ways. Those few aspects he did remember were the disgust and fear, the complete shock of what these twisted creatures were capable of, the confusion of why they destroyed the lives of strangers. Little boys never counted on this when dreaming of becoming knights.

He sat amid this death and destruction, holding Khin as her feeble hands clutched him. He let her cry out her confusion and fear, let her express her loss as hard as she needed to. This had been meant to be a joyous homecoming, a fresh start to her life and permission to walk away from her past. Instead, the final threads of stability Khin had dangled from had been snapped and tangled beyond repair. Mathias held her, devoting his all into giving her what little comfort she was receptive to until fatigue began to claim her.

Slowly, the past few days' worth of exhaustion caught up to the girl. The physical exertion of traveling and riding wrapped around her and smothered her will to fight. Emotionally whiplashed, spent to her core, her sobs gradually shifted to chokes and hiccups, and her arms went limp as she curled against Mathias's chest. Her head fell against his shoulder, every few breaths strained with a residual moan. It wasn't until he was certain Khin had fallen asleep that Mathias allowed his own tears to slip free.

Etha…

Warmth flooded Mathias's chest, though it didn't ease his troubles. *I know,* Etha murmured. *And I'm sorry.*

She wasn't apologizing for this tragedy, as it hadn't been her fault, but she did hurt for Mathias's position. He'd been so anxious to see Khin rediscover peace and happiness, to pass her along to her family so he could concentrate on Nessix before the demons found her. Not only did Khin no longer have her haven, but Mathias now had to figure out what to do with her. And come to terms with the fact that the demons might be closer to Nessix than he'd thought. Mathias had grown desensitized to the concept of misery over the ages, but even he risked falling apart when it piled up too steeply.

Blinking back his tears, knowing they wouldn't help him resolve any of this, Mathias pulled Khin close and stood, cradling her in his arms. Even without a mount and transporting an unconscious young woman, he should be able to reach the town of Brookhaven by nightfall. This was not the sort of burden he'd expected to carry on this quest.

EIGHTEEN

Thanks to a life spent never wanting, Nessix had underestimated the cost of supplies and the luxury of room and board. She'd taken for granted how her station had guaranteed her these basic comforts in the past, and now that she was unknown to those around her, her coins didn't stretch nearly as far as they once had. Regardless of these limitations, the threat Kol and this army of inoga posed was far too great a risk for Nessix to sit around and dwell over, and she pressed north as hard as a soldier on foot could.

She passed through two towns without stopping, determined not to spend her money unless absolutely necessary. Determination could only carry her so far, and as the sun crept to bed and torches were being lit on still-bustling streets, Nessix entered the city of South Bend, hungry, tired, and dangerously close to poverty as she exchanged nearly the rest of her coins for a night at the inn. She'd spent the previous days on the road contemplating how to use her combative skills to remedy her financial problems and trying not to think about how far she was from Zeal. Bounty hunting wouldn't be a reliable source of income, considering her need to remain moving, but it was better than any alternative she could think of.

Stowing her armor behind the safety of a locked door, Nessix slung her sword belt on her hips and braced herself for the task ahead of her. South Bend was a noisy city with a boisterous nightlife that allowed her to fall into the shadows and pass unnoticed. The guard station doors were locked when she found it, but it couldn't be the only place she'd be able to find information on current bounties. The market ran late, vendors crowing about their wares well into the night from banner-strung storefronts. With ample distractions, Nessix felt safer here than she had on the open road. She slowed her pace and ordered her shoulders to relax.

Wary eyes trained on her surroundings, Nessix followed a trail of eager pedestrians to where they met with a less coordinated group of drunkards flowing in and out of a flourishing tavern. The sign was painted with gaudy colors and lively music streamed through open windows, accompanied by the shouted lyrics of drinking songs. Nessix took a step toward the establishment, passed by a woman in a bustled purple dress adorned with lace and pearls. An equally well turned out gentleman with a monocle and cane led this woman toward the tavern. Nes's expression fell. This would not be where she'd find what she was looking for.

Sighing her frustration, she turned back toward the market and approached a weapon vendor hawking a cart of cheap blades.

The vendor eyed Nessix readily, made a quick appraisal of the weapons at her side, and scowled. "No need to waste my time," he grunted.

"May I have just a moment of it?" She followed him around to the side of the cart. "I don't have much in the way of money—"

"Then how'd you manage those weapons you've got?"

Nessix curled her fingers to keep from instinctively reaching for her sword. "They're family heirlooms. Like I said, I haven't got much—"

"If you haven't got money, I haven't got time."

Heart rate accelerating, Nessix glanced around the busy street. She hadn't made a scene yet, and so she persisted. "I need to know where to find the cheapest tavern in town. Run down and only frequented by the most desperate."

The vendor stopped and stuck his head around the cart to reappraise Nessix. Despite her nontraditional mode of dress, she looked of far better breeding than to socialize with the likes of scoundrels. He pinched his lips shut briefly before answering. "No time, lady." He bustled to the other side of the cart.

Frustrated but committed, Nessix turned and met him on the other side, digging in her pack for the knife she'd lifted off the demon guard she'd killed on Elidae. The man backed away, waving his arms as if to ward off aggression, and she met him with incredulous eyes.

"Would you trade me information for this?" she asked.

Demon weapons came in only two varieties—valueless improvisations scavenged from the field, or steel of superior quality. Their style was unmistakable, with serrated blades, plain metal hilts without crossguards, and etched with the markings of the owner's clan. Any mortal simply possessing one got to demand indisputable bragging rights.

The man balked, refraining from grabbing the knife. "Look, lady. It's clear you're well bred. So where in Etha's name did you get that?"

Nessix grimaced and opened her mouth.

"Wait. No. Don't tell me. I don't want to know."

"You're a smart man," Nessix said.

The vendor eyed her with a shrewd glare and held out his hand. "May I?"

Nessix's willingness to hand over the blade pinched his frown even tighter. She was confident he wouldn't try to make off with it and that if he did, she'd be able to stop him. His palms sweated as he accepted the knife and turned it over in his hands. Few mortals lived through seeing a demon's blade.

"What's the catch?"

"No catch," Nessix assured. "I just need to know where to find the local slum."

The vendor grasped the blade by the hilt and waggled it in Nes's direction. "If you're setting me up—"

"For what?" Nessix asked with a laugh. "If you don't think it's a fair exchange, I'll take my knife—"

"You'll find it three blocks that way." He jerked the thumb of his empty hand to the left. "See the butcher's just down there? Turn left, go three blocks. You'll smell it before you hear it, and you'll hear it before you see it. Now run off. Your sword's making mine look bad."

Nessix nodded with a polite smile, not quite able to thank the man for his assistance, and turned toward the butcher's shop.

With her hair pulled back and clothing better suited for a man, she blended into this atmosphere better than she had on the well-lit main street. The weapon vendor's observation of her heritage stuck with her, though. No amount of men's clothing or self-confidence would cover up her regal bearing and for the first time, Nessix almost wished Kol had disfigured her face. Eyes followed her as she walked, soon joined by crude comments a life spent among lonely military men and demons left her immune to.

The weapon vendor had been wrong in one regard; the roar from The Stuck Pig bellowed to Nessix just before the nose-curling stench of boiled cabbage and urine hit her, and she paused to let her stomach settle. Gritting her teeth, Nessix buckled down on her determination. She'd survived the hells. She could survive a rancid tavern.

Holding her breath, Nessix adjusted her sword belt as she entered, instantly gaining the attention of every eye in the establishment. Bristled, but not deterred, she strode forward, the soles of her boots sticking briefly as she walked across the floor. She reached the bar, folded her hands, and prepared to lean against it until she noticed the thick film atop.

"Pretty thing like you shouldn't be in men's clothes," a nearby patron said. "Unless, of course, they're mine."

Nessix paid the jeer no mind and waited for the bar keep to greet her. He was wiry and lean, and looked as though he hadn't bathed since his mother was able to do it for him.

"What d'ya want?" the bar keep asked, slapping his palms on the filthy counter.

Nessix glanced at his hands and swallowed her grimace. The weapon vendor had certainly delivered when she'd asked for the worst available. "I'm looking for work—"

The man perched on the stool beside her leapt to his feet and shoved Nessix forward against the bar. "Shoulda said so from the start," he rasped in her ear, the smell of alcohol and halitosis gagging her even before the feeling of his lips wrapping around the side of her neck did.

There may have been a day when this sort of attack would have frightened or offended Nessix, but as this man's right hand groped at her bound chest and his left tried to dig down her pants, she jabbed her elbow into his ribs. His arms wrapped tighter around her.

"Ah, don't be like that," he said, rubbing against her back.

Gritting her teeth, Nessix broadened her stance, enticing the man to lean over her as his hand succeeded in working beneath the waist of her pants. Sucking in a deep breath, Nessix heaved her weight forward and flipped him over her shoulder, bending him backwards over the top of the bar. The keep, unimpressed by all accounts, took a step back to let the brawl play out.

The letch groaned and rolled onto his belly, and Nessix took two calculated steps backwards.

"Feisty, feisty." He hauled himself to his feet, though he didn't stand nearly as straight as he had before. "What's the fuss about, sweetheart?"

Nobody present seemed to think much of their altercation, but Nessix didn't know what ramifications went with violence in the underbelly of South Bend. Her fingers twitched to grasp a weapon from her belt, but she held herself back. Was this truly how the civilian world functioned?

The man lurched forward, grabbing for Nes's shoulders, but she met him with an uppercut that snapped his slacked jaw shut. He bit his tongue, roaring a closed mouth scream as he spun to nurse his injury. When he turned back, he spat blood and his inebriated eyes raged wild as he rushed ahead.

Nessix aimed a kick at his groin, but he caught her leg, his hands sliding up her calf and to her thigh as he pulled himself closer to her. She grabbed a fistful of his hair and cranked his head away, twisting until his spine creaked and he dropped her leg. With his arms free, he grabbed Nessix by the waist and charged, slamming her back against the edge of a table.

Crying out at the impact, Nessix lost her hold on the man's hair as he shoved his bleeding mouth against hers. His hands fumbled with the laces of her pants, and Nessix allowed the distraction as she grabbed her dagger. A couple patrons gasped and shouted warnings, but the man didn't register them until Nessix had wedged the blade against the juncture of his jaw and neck. Even that didn't faze him until she added force behind it and slowly, he pulled himself off of her, raising his arms to the side. He straightened and took a step back, and Nessix spat out a mouthful of bloody saliva as she stood, holding her knife at the ready.

"What kinda tease is this, askin' for work, then puttin' up a fight about it?" the man asked. "I like my girls feisty as anyone, but this is *cruel.*"

By now, the rest of the bar watched silently, and Nessix held her ground. "If you had any sort of wits about you, you'd have realized I wasn't through with my request."

"Oh, I hear you, I hear you." The man nodded as he moved closer to his stool. "I've got my wits about me, just got a little carried away by a pretty face, is all."

With that last word, he grabbed the stem of his stool and swung it in Nes's direction. She ducked beneath the swing, and darted up to the man, punching him in the throat. His eyes bulged, the stool clattered from his grasp, and he staggered backwards before falling to the ground.

Blowing out her concentration, Nessix put her dagger away and secured her pants. She stepped over the man's unconscious body to approach the bar keep once more. "Let's try this again. I'm looking for work of the unsavory sort, but not *that* kind. Do you follow?"

The bar keep raised his chin, looking down his nose at her, and nodded slowly. "Yeah, I follow. But I don't got nothin' for you."

Tired, frustrated, and just a tad humiliated, Nessix wilted as exhaustion suggested she return to her room to wait until morning for the guard station to open. There, she'd hopefully find more reliable—and quite possibly more legal—information.

"So, you gonna order something or did you just come here to rough up my patrons?"

Even if Nessix hadn't been on her last few coins, she'd have to be much closer to starvation to willingly eat anything prepared in this establishment. Her lip curled at the very thought of it. "Perhaps if you ran a bit more hospitable house, you could convince me to risk it. I'll be on my way."

Turning on a heel, Nessix strode toward the door, amused at how quickly the patrons skittered from her path. As she passed the last table, a low voice cut through the rumble of drunkards resuming their evening. "I've got a way for you to earn some coin, if you're honestly looking."

Nessix stopped and turned toward a grinning man with a wide scar stretched across his forehead. Beside him sat a scowling woman with hatred in her eyes and a larger man who slumped over the table, head nestled in the crook of his elbow. A collection of emptied mugs was scattered before them.

Temptation and desperation whispered to Nessix about how easy it would be to swindle a group of drunkards, but of all the things Kol had taken from her, her morality wasn't one of them. Lips creasing in regret, Nessix shifted her weight to resume walking when the man spoke again.

"My friends and I have five silver that says you can't track and kill a boar before the sun comes up." When Nessix hesitated, he added, "Five silver would stretch quite a ways around these parts."

She should have known better than to respond to this sort of goading, but five silver *would* stretch quite far, given her recent experience. She turned back toward the man and he kicked the chair beside him away from the table, gesturing at it for her to sit. On this second appraisal, he appeared far more sober than Nessix had first thought, and the woman went from a simple scowl to a shrewd glower as Nessix cautiously approached them. She declined the offered seat.

"You'd pay that much for someone to kill a boar?" She'd taken down ogres three times her size when she was barely an adolescent. A boar wouldn't be a challenge.

The man's grin broadened. "Sure thing. They *are* pretty mean, but you handled yourself so well just now that I don't think testy animals bother you that much. Name's Fletcher." He held a hand out to Nessix.

It had been so long since Nessix had received something akin to a compliment on her skill that she didn't care who it came from. She accepted Fletcher's hand, but still didn't take the seat.

Her compliance gained a glance from the woman, who swept her eyes over Nes's petite frame before shaking her head and flinging her glare aside. "How'd a woman with a face like yours end up as a combatant?" she asked, her accent thick and unidentifiable to Nes's limited knowledge of Gelthin's regions.

"My mother died when I was a child and my father and uncle were military men. The two of them raised me on the battlefield."

The large man, who Nessix had assumed was passed out, belted out an abrupt laugh, though he didn't bother to lift his head or open his eyes while doing so.

"So you're proficient at arms," Fletcher continued. "Just sword and knife?"

"Proficient with sword and knife, and an exceptional brawler." A long-missed swell of pride inflated Nes's chest "Trained across three cultures."

A smirk touched Fletcher's lips. "Are all of your brawls so noisy?" Beside him, the bitter woman snorted.

"Few are," Nessix assured. "I don't like to waste time, but have no desire to beat up drunkards who can barely stand."

"Oh, he'd been standing just fine. Threw you around a few times, too, if recollection serves right."

"Would you like me to shake him awake and challenge him to a rematch?" Nessix asked, an unintended edge of heat backing her words. "If you'd like to see me take him out faster, I'd be happy to show you."

Fletcher chuckled and batted a hand at Nessix. "Nah. I bet he's still out from that throat punch. Nothing exciting or challenging about killing a man in his sleep."

Nessix pursed her lips as thoughts of Brant crossed her mind. Avenging him was one mission she wished she could have claimed for herself.

"What were you just thinking about?"

Fletcher's voice jarred Nessix from her thoughts, and she shook her head, shoving the memory of her dear cousin into the crowded box where she contained Berann and Kol. She'd get her answers about Brant once she found Mathias. "Does it matter? You wanted me to hunt a boar. My life story shouldn't be any concern of yours."

"Alright, alright. Mantis?" Fletcher asked the scowling woman. "What do you think? You willing to give up a couple silver if our little brawler can pull off a boar hunt?"

The woman's lips twisted into a devious smirk, eyes glistening with a light Nessix didn't trust. "I *do* love a good boar hunt and sending her along will get her out of here." Nessix swallowed that one. "Treb?" Mantis shoved the large man's shoulder. When he didn't budge, she smacked him harder. "Trebuchet!"

The large man shot upright and groaned as he rubbed the back of his neck. He didn't need the time to blink the grogginess from his eyes, and looked Nessix over with a nod of approval. "Let's see what this little spitfire can do," he said, his words gilded with hints of a noble upbringing.

Nessix drew a deep breath that trickled out through puckered lips, suddenly doubting this party's intentions.

Trebuchet smiled at her, a kinder one than Mantis's and not as hungry as Fletcher's, but Nessix got the distinct feeling that she shouldn't trust it any more. "You'll want to take the east gate out of town to get into the woods. The boars aren't usually hard to find this time of night. If you can kill one and come back here with its tusks before the sun rises, we'll give you your silver."

"Boar tusks by sunrise," Nessix confirmed with a nod.

Mantis trilled a laugh and Fletcher continued grinning. "Night's not getting any younger," he said. "If you want that silver…"

Nessix didn't need any more encouragement. Killing a boar would be even easier—though less rewarding—than taking out criminals. "Stay where you are. I won't keep you waiting long."

Motivated by something other than fear for the first time in days, Nessix left the tavern and hurried toward the east gate, already imagining how long five silver would keep her fed.

* * * * *

Nessix tramped through the forest, straining to see clearly as the moon's dim glow filtered through the thick canopy. Fallen leaves crunched beneath her feet as she trudged along, and she paused when a low rumble intercepted the song of croaking frogs and chirping insects. It certainly sounded like a boar, though far deeper than what she associated with the animal. Drawing her dagger, ready to incite the animal to rush her, she crept toward the sound's origin.

Nessix had survived plenty of terrors in her time. From her unconventional childhood, to the unfair duties shoved on her. The demon war. Her death. Kol's manipulation and the thoughts of what he'd planned for her. Despite all of this experience, all of the bravery and grit she'd accumulated over the years, Nessix froze when the animal came into view.

This boar stood at least twice her height, hulking its stocky mass through the woods as it rooted through the loam, and Nessix murmured a quick prayer of thanks that it was alone. Even boars of manageable size were fierce and known to take down the occasional unlucky hunter. As she watched this behemoth toss chunks of earth with its snout, Nessix eyed those tusks she'd been instructed to gather, each the size of one of her legs. She'd boasted of her experience fighting beasts as large as ogres and as fierce as minotaur, but suddenly, neither of those foes seemed worthy of bragging rights.

The boar shuffled to a new tree, the old wood creaking against its rummaging.

A sour lump rose in Nes's throat and she swallowed hard to repress it. Calculating her options as best she could through this creeping dread, she traded her dagger for her sword, studying the nearby trees to search for means to vault onto the animal's neck. The coarse hair along its topline looked as though it would provide an adequate hold, and as long as she stayed low enough to avoid any branches, she felt reasonably sure she could hang on and hack away at it until it died.

The boar rammed the tree, and Nessix swore she saw it bend to the force. Slowing her breath in an attempt to calm her racing heart, she lifted a foot when a new rustle sounded from behind her.

Fearing there was a mate to this monstrosity, Nessix turned just in time to be tackled from the side and driven to the ground, the blow knocking her sword from her grasp. A pair of strong hands wrapped around her throat and crushed down. She should have known this was a set up. Deciding to give those lowlifes a proper scare once she woke, Nessix allowed the attack until a wispy voice filtered into her ear.

"You have been a terribly naughty girl. Kol is quite displeased with you."

Heart freezing, Nessix wheezed in a trickle of breath and kicked at the demon on her back. He outweighed her easily, crushing her against the forest floor and so she worked her left arm around to grab her knife and jabbed it into her assailant's side.

He howled, repelling from her to pull the dagger free as she crawled from him, rubbing her neck as she gasped for air. Before the demon could jump toward her again, a string of spoken words filled the night as an oraku stepped from around a tree. Yes, it seemed Kol was *quite* displeased with her if he'd gained clearance to mobilize those magic users.

Nes's legs grew heavy as the oraku continued his chant, rooting her hands and knees to the ground. A thick haze, comforting in the worst ways, wormed through her head and drew her eyelids closer to shutting. No! They couldn't have her! She tried to fight the sensation, tried to draw in the cool evening air to invigorate her body for another push, to drag herself out of the oraku's casting range, but her lungs sucked in air too slowly. Desperate, Nessix latched onto the only option she had besides giving up.

Grasping a hold of a rock, she forced her arm to raise, the weight of the stone wobbling her limb against this artificial exhaustion. Investing all of her remaining might in one action, Nessix expelled a weary bellow and launched the rock at the boar. Body succumbing to the spell, she collapsed to the ground.

An indignant squeal pierced the night, interrupting the oraku's words and giving Nessix a moment of clarity as the ground began to vibrate beneath her. The giant boar pounded her way. Still tingling, Nessix curled into a ball as the animal passed over top of her, and she whispered her gratitude into the night as feeling seeped into her limbs. Frantically patting the ground, she found her sword and rolled upright just in time to see the boar rake its tusk into the startled oraku's abdomen.

Screaming, the demon cast a final, desperate spell against the boar. The energy used to explode the creature's head overwhelmed the frail threads holding the oraku's life together and he collapsed instantly.

An enraged roar sounded from behind Nessix and she spun, instinctually raising her sword and allowing a third demon to impale himself. Mind scrambling, Nessix tore her sword free and pushed herself to her knees, assessing her surroundings. The first demon she'd struck was on his belly, clawing away from her, but so far, she heard no signs of backup. At least for the moment, she was safe.

Nessix stood and staggered to the first demon, stepping deliberately onto his path. "Looks like I *have* been naughty, and Kol's going to have to get used to that."

She doubted this demon had a reply left in him, and she didn't want to hear one, anyway. Swiftly, she grasped her hilt with both hands and drove it into the back of the demon's neck, the tip piercing between vertebrae. No other demons had come to the sound of their fight, suggesting this was a small search party, but they were enough to confirm that Kol was actively on her trail. Renewed urgency spurred Nessix past the notion of pausing to regain her stamina, and she strode over to the boar to complete her objective.

The oraku had done her the favor of obliterating most of the boar's head, its lower jaw torn mostly from its skull. That saved her the worry of how to remove the tusks from its massive body. She turned her gaze to the oraku, frowning at how close he'd come to taking her out. Either way, he'd failed at doing so, even if Nessix had to use luck and a wild animal to ensure as much.

She put her hands on her hips and studied her trophy. When she'd been told to return to the tavern, she'd assumed she'd be carrying back tusks easily stowed in her pack. Instead, she had the entire lower jaw of an animal that could have eaten her in two bites and was sure she'd raise concerns if she looked half as rough as she felt. She'd been set up for failure, and now her competitive edge was determined to ensure she succeeded.

Dragging the demon corpses to where the boar had rooted up around the tree, Nessix kicked dirt and dead leaves over them to disguise their obvious presence. Next, she twisted the boar's lower jaw free, slicing the charred flesh to mask the evidence of the oraku's explosion. Hoping her apparent ferocity would prevent undue prying, Nessix grasped the tusks and toted her trophy behind her like a crude litter.

Between exhaustion and the weight she hauled behind her, Nes progressed slowly back toward town. She cast her gaze to the moon as it hung low in the sky. Resilient and tough though she might be, her petite stature didn't loan her the strength to make light of this burden. Hunching her shoulders, she grit her teeth and pulled harder until the guard post's glowing torches came into view.

Releasing her hold on the tusks, Nes wiped her forehead on the back of a bloodied sleeve, then hydrated until her flask was empty. So close to being through with this nonsense, she blew out a slow breath, hoisted the tusks, and continued forward. The guards noticed her immediately and flagged her down before she reached the gates, jogging out to meet her. Nessix trudged toward them, braced in anticipation of complications.

"Lady, *what* have you got?" one of the guards asked, no judgement or anger in his voice, only an abundance of awe.

"Friend bet me I couldn't take out a boar on my own," she said. "I told him I could. Looks like he was wrong, huh?"

The first guard rocked back with a chuckle of admiration, the other leaning forward to look over Nes's handiwork with a low whistle. The second guard met her eyes.

"Have you been drinking?"

"Not at all," Nessix replied. "Just don't care to have my honor questioned."

The guards laughed and slapped each other on the shoulders, still gaping in disbelief. "You do know it usually takes a whole hunting party to take out a great boar, right? Your honor could have gotten you killed."

Nessix hadn't known that before she set out, but understood as much now. Besides, she *had* received some amount of help in the matter. She stuck that confession in her pocket for safe keeping. "Could have," she agreed, "but didn't."

The guards continued to stand there, jaws slacked in amazement and heads shaking. "You need help with those tusks?"

"Nah." Nessix adjusted her hold with sweaty palms. "It'll look more impressive this way, don't you think?"

"Looks impressive no matter which way you look at it."

Nessix gave them a weary smile and they let her pass with nothing more than a farewell, teasing one another as to whether or not either of them were bold enough to accept a similar challenge.

She dragged the tusks through the sleeping town, through the market that no longer hummed with business, and into the dank street leading to the tavern. With each step, she fretted over the choices she'd made. Running from Kol. Leading inoga to the surface. Leaving helpless villagers behind. This stupid mission...

Nessix couldn't help but think that it had been meant to kill her, more of a bet between Fletcher and his friends as to whether or not she'd return than anything else. With confirmation that Kol was after her—and close—she didn't have time for these ridiculous games. She should go back to the boar, butcher some meat off it, and skip town, forget she'd ever had this idea. But then the guards' enthusiasm came back to her. The fact was that she *had* survived, even when intercepted by demons. She had an impressive record of accomplishing the impossible. And she'd outsmart and outpace Kol, too.

Arriving at the foul tavern, Nessix kicked the door open and hauled the remains of the boar's bloody jaw inside. Most of the patrons had either stumbled back home or were passed out over tables or on the floor, but those who remained—Fletcher, Mantis, and Trebuchet among them—ceased their drunken philosophizing and goading to turn flabbergasted expressions toward her.

Had Nessix not been nearly trounced by exhaustion, she'd have laughed at the trio's dumbfounded looks as they beheld how she'd not only survived, but successfully executed their request.

Grunting, she threw the last of the day's strength into heaving the lower jaw between herself and where Fletcher sat.

"Here's your damn tusks," Nessix said, fighting the strain from her voice. "I believe you owe me five silver."

Mantis flung her hands in the air, a string of frantic words in a language Nessix couldn't grasp bursting from her as she shoved herself from her seat and stalked off to shoo the most coherent of the patrons out the door. Fletcher slowly rose to get a better look at the tusks. Trebuchet hadn't yet taken his keen eyes from Nessix.

"Where did you learn to take out a great boar unassisted?" asked Trebuchet.

Nessix stretched the burning from her arms. "In the forest out the east gates, apparently."

Fletcher pulled his gawk from the tusks to fit Nessix with a strict glower for her attempt at humor. "*Nobody* can kill a great boar on their own, experienced or otherwise."

Nessix opted against sharing that unintentional help *had* arrived, and crossed her arms. "You may want to reconsider that stance."

Trebuchet propped his elbows on the table and clasped his hands to rest his chin on his fists. He narrowed eyes that Nessix suspected hadn't seen a drop of ale all night. "You said you'd trained across three cultures in sword and knife and brawling. What people could possibly make a little thing like you so deadly?"

Nessix gnawed on the inside of her cheek as she weighed her options. It was obvious that neither of these men, nor the scowl-faced woman who was making her way back to the table, were simpletons throwing about drunken bets. They were scheming and sharp and quite possibly capable of their own amount of trouble if she pushed the wrong subjects. Either way, after the night she'd had, Nessix was determined to get her five silver.

"Like I said, I grew up in an army, under my father's wing, then trained a bit with a knight of the Order of the White Circle."

Both men studied Nes's features hard, to the point that she shrugged her crossed arms tighter to keep from self-consciously trying to cover her ears to mask the elven roots of her fleman heritage. Even those distant elven ancestors had hated their own

209

kind after their banishment, to the point that very little of their culture or lore had been preserved—much less taught—by the flemans. Nessix grasped for feasible lies she could use to answer the inevitable questions about which army she'd served with, realizing they'd never believe she'd come from Elidae.

"That was only two."

Mantis's snide comment halted all of Nes's excuses and her cheeks burned with relief and confusion. "I beg your pardon?"

"Whatever mercenary group your father worked for, and the Order. That's two, and neither strikes me as the kind to give you the skills to kill a great boar. Who else have you picked up tricks from?"

That heat flushed from Nes's cheeks and suddenly, the thought of making up stories about elves seemed much more appealing. Mantis's eyes narrowed, her scowl cutting deeper into her face, and both Fletcher and Trebuchet watched Nessix with the expressions of senior officers waiting for their green lieutenant to sputter her first report. Nessix cleared her throat and tried to hide her flicker of apprehension behind the proud lift of her chin.

"Does it matter?" she asked.

Mantis tsked sharply and Fletcher voiced a low chuckle. It was Trebuchet who spoke. "It could." He kept Nes's gaze firmly in his command as he slipped his fingers into a pouch to draw out the silver pieces one by one, pressing them down onto the tabletop in a tidy row. "Five silver can stretch a savvy traveler pretty far, but won't last forever. If you choose to work *with* us, we can arrange to have you work *for* us."

Nessix ripped her gaze from Trebuchet's long enough to glance at the coins. He said they'd sustain a savvy traveler, but she fell a bit short on that attribute, these days. She'd come here looking for work and though caution hummed its reservations about this particular trio, she was just desperate enough to pursue this hint of an offer.

"Working… for you. I need to stay on the move. Will this job allow that?"

Trebuchet's eyes narrowed as his smile broadened. "Oh, there's work all over Gelthin that would favor your skills. Lots of it.

It'd serve us all best if you *did* stay on the move. All you have to do is answer Mantis's question to get in on it."

Heart racing, Nes's gut twisted until the sensation rose up her throat and into her head. She'd trusted her instincts all her life, and right now, they screamed at her to proceed with caution. A rumble of hunger loosened that knot in her stomach, trouncing instinct's sensibility. She needed money and mercenary work—if that was indeed what she was looking at—beat thievery. This need for funds might have made the decision to agree to whatever this job was an easy one, but it wasn't enough to simplify her greater problem.

Nessix had never verbally confirmed her connection to or disgusting dependency on the demons. Among the akhuerai, she'd explained her intentions to delude Kol. To Sulik and Sazrah, she'd recounted stories of the demons' possession of her. But never had she credited the beasts for anything beneficial. Never before had she accepted her place as one of the fallen. Her eyes burned and a faint tremor in her jaw threatened to nullify the entire night's efforts at masquerading as confident. Nessix clenched her fists in her crossed arms to keep from withering away under the mocking eyes of her audience.

In all likelihood, any one of these three would be better traveled and more experienced in the greater workings of Abaeloth than Nessix was. Any lie she'd try to deliver stood too strong a chance of being sniffed out, and she couldn't risk losing the one lead she'd found. Pride wouldn't keep her belly full or shelter her at the end of a hard stretch on the road. She dug her nails into her palms.

"Demons," she blurted before the annoyance of uncertainty complicated matters further. The confession spoken, her heart rate plummeted, leaving her head spinning so she had to uncross her arms and grasp the back of a chair for stability. "One of the cultures I trained in was demonic."

The trio stared blankly at Nessix as she held her breath. After her claim processed past their shock and Nes's own, Fletcher and Mantis burst into laughter, but Trebuchet cocked his head as he studied her harder still. Nessix grit her teeth as they openly ridiculed her past spent pandering to Kol's whims and pushed herself away from the table as soon as she'd regained enough of her equilibrium to do so.

"You sure are a plucky one, demon lady," Fletcher said.

Nessix bristled but caught her retaliation before it got her in trouble. "If that's what you want to call it."

"How much do the demons charge to put little mercenaries through training?" Mantis asked. "Did you bribe them to come all the way up here, or did you have to go down into the hells to gain their expertise?"

Fletcher and Mantis continued to chortle and tears of rage and frustration burned Nes's lower eyelids. Humiliated and belittled by these petty lowlifes, her hand flew to the hilt of her sword, pride finally declaring that it had had enough. Trebuchet stood in the same instant, calmly holding a halting hand in Nes's direction as he spun to face his laughing companions.

"Silence. Both of you."

They obeyed the order immediately, all humor extinguished as though they'd never found it in the first place, and a chill cooled Nes's blood. Their prompt and respectful reaction uncovered a valuable insight to this group's hierarchy. Nessix turned her full attention to Trebuchet, no longer finding the other two worth her energy or consideration.

Trebuchet met Nes's eyes with the same calm authority with which he'd stayed her sword arm and, desperate and weary as she was, she met him well on equal terms. She was through playing games, through with their torment. Compelling evidence to her effectiveness and skill—skill they'd all implied lacking, themselves—laid on the floor between them. No matter what they wanted to make of Nes's past, they could not dispute that she'd be a valuable asset to any group looking to hire a competent sword. Trebuchet slapped his hand over the five coins and slid them over to Nessix.

"I told you what was asked of me," she said, staking her claim on the remainder of this conversation by speaking first. "Now you tell me what you have along the lines of work."

Fletcher sucked in a sharp little gasp and Mantis resumed that unattractive scowl at Nes's bid for dominance, but Trebuchet remained unmoved by her demand. He lifted his hand from the silver and straightened.

"As I said, we've got job opportunities all across Gelthin."

Nessix scooped up the coins as he spoke, eyes never straying from his. "To be clear, it's bounty work?"

"Bounty work," Trebuchet repeated, holding her gaze firmly. "Mantis, dig her out a crest."

"But, Treb—"

He snapped his head in the woman's direction and silenced her just as effectively as before. Eyes grumbling the complaints her lips didn't dare speak, Mantis hefted a burgundy canvas pack onto the tabletop and she rifled through it.

Trebuchet returned his attention to Nessix. "We've got eyes in most every major city on the continent, and those eyes have ears. You sign on with us and you're free to continue your travels where you will." Mantis flung a corded leather disk the size of Nes's palm onto the table. Trebuchet picked it up and rubbed his thumb across the stamp of two entwined triangles on its surface before handing it to Nessix. "Keep this visible on your person and the eyes will find you when a mission is available."

Nessix accepted the crude pendant, gave it half an appraising glance, then secured it to her sword belt. "How do I request an assignment if I'm in need of money and none of these eyes of yours come to recruit me?"

The tension left Fletcher in a short burst of laughter. "I suspect that won't be a problem once word gets around about you."

Part of Nessix wanted to glow at the apparent compliment, but her need to stay unknown and out of the demons' sights prevented her from doing so.

"Fletch is right," Trebuchet said. "There's no shortage of work for ones of our trade and if you can complete all assignments as well as you completed the boar hunt, your services will stay in demand."

"And my payment?"

"Our scouting fees are taken from the bounty and the balance given to you after completion of your assignment."

Nessix nodded. It wasn't the most ideal arrangement she'd been part of, but it was likely the best opportunity her circumstances would allow. "Then tell those eyes of yours to keep watch for me on the northern roads."

Trebuchet smiled. "I'll be glad to. Now, go on. For the love of Kenin, clean yourself up, and go make your fortune."

Nessix, having achieved her objective, didn't wait for anyone involved to throw in any surprises. She departed the filthy tavern and the judgmental patrons it harbored, relieved to have one of her problems solved.

NINETEEN

Mathias moved briskly. He still felt responsible for Khin, more so now that she had nowhere to go, but having witnessed two demon attacks tied to Nessix was the unwelcome reminder he needed to get back to his task. For now, he refused to acknowledge the faint resentment that came from Nes's apparent connection to this violence; he trusted she would have done everything she could to stop it if she was able, but the unconscious young woman in his arms was heartbreaking collateral to whatever was unfolding around him.

Pushing aside the guilt and blame, Mathias concentrated only on his march south, letting his mind drone on with the pattern of his footfalls like a good soldier. Well before the sun tucked itself away, the gates of Brookhaven peeked over the horizon, and Mathias enjoyed a fleeting breath of gratitude. The city still stood, evident by the pair of guards who glowered at him, taking their job more seriously than seemed necessary. As he approached the gates, the guards drew their weapons.

"Who are you and what have you done to that woman?" came what passed for a shouted greeting.

Mathias shifted his hold on Khin to let the crest on his breastplate peek around her body. He didn't know how deeply she slumbered in the divine peace of his arms, but wouldn't rob her of her recovery by returning the shout. If the guards wanted to fault him over a delayed answer, he'd give them the right to do so and let them deal with the ramifications of assaulting a knight of the Order later. Fortunately, the two men held their ground and tensely awaited his arrival.

"I am Mathias Sagewind of the—"

"*The* Mathias Sagewind?" The guard to his left blanched, lowering his spear. "As in the demon hunting paladin?"

Mathias smiled grimly. Current events had made recollection of his role on Abaeloth come too easily. "One and the same. A nearby village was just razed by demons and this girl is the sole survivor. I'm seeking information on the demons' movements and motives, if there is any information to be had here."

The guard to his right cursed quietly. "We'd hoped the village would be spared. Those poor folks had nothing of value to anyone… let alone demons."

The first guard coughed. "You don't *know* that."

Mathias glanced between the two men, waiting only briefly for them to elaborate. "I take it the demons passed through Brookhaven?"

The first guard glanced at the ground and grimaced. "They did."

"And it still stands?" This was an unusual development, both out of character for demons and contradicting the events Mathias had observed with their current resurgence.

"They didn't come as a typical raiding party, more… civilized than demons are supposed to be. In a fit of desperation, the mayor insisted we comply to their demands. We sustained damages, a few losses of life and innocence, but they departed after their search."

At least the report confirmed it was most likely the same group Mathias had encountered and not the one led by inoga. "Did they tell you what they were searching for?"

The second guard nodded. "A warrior woman with dark hair and pale eye. Said she'd be an outsider, likely scared." He craned his neck to better appraise the dark haired woman sleeping in Mathias's arms before quirking his lips and dismissing his curiosity at her flimsy build.

The first scoffed. "Anyone with sense would be scared if demons were chasing them..."

Mathias perked up. If Nessix had been turned into anything more than a warrior woman, he was certain the demons would have included that in their description. "I gather by the fact that they moved on to the village that they didn't find her here?"

"We haven't had any notable outsiders, matching that description or otherwise, pass through town in some time." The guard scratched behind his ear and glanced away. "That is, of course, besides yesterday's demons."

Though it was never a relief to hear of demonic presence in a town, Mathias was impressed at how the mayor handled it—his quick and calm thinking had saved the lives of his citizens—as well as the fresh bits of information the guards had given him. Nessix, though still unaccounted for, was on the run, and that meant he had a chance to find her before the demons did.

"Thank you for your time. I will do all I can to put a stop to the demons' search."

The guards exchanged cautious glances before the first nervously spoke. "You, ah… You don't plan on staying?"

"I have to report these attacks to the Order and get this girl to safety."

The second guard cleared his throat. "Our inn is still serviceable."

Mathias's torn sense of responsibility tattered to shreds at the guards' patchworked confidence. Whatever was happening, whatever war Nessix had catalyzed, few, even among the trained, were equipped to face it. He didn't know how fast the inoga in the south were moving or where their rampage was heading, but even Mathias was helpless against their strength and numbers. All he could do in defense of this city was offer prayers. Right now, he carried too many other burdens.

"I appreciate the offer of hospitality and understand your position, but my mission requires me to stay on the move. I'll personally put in a request for Zeal to send assistance if you feel your city needs it."

The compromise wasn't the grand solution the guards had

217

hoped for, but they accepted it without complaint, freeing Mathias to depart with his dismal thoughts. When he'd travelled far enough down the road to avoid alarming the residents of Brookhaven, he whisked himself and Khin away to her room in the Citadel's infirmary where Etha sat on the foot of the bed, awaiting their arrival.

Mathias didn't speak to her, still afraid of the only things there were to say, and busied himself situating Khin in the bed. She whimpered and rolled into the blanket's comfort.

"You've done all you can for her."

Etha's voice drew a slow sigh from Mathias and he pulled away from the bed to sink into a chair in the corner. "It doesn't stop me from wishing I could have done more."

"You kept her alive, didn't you?"

Mathias closed his eyes and leaned his head back, savoring this tiny slice of peace. He'd only give himself until Khin woke so he could personally explain that she had to stay in Zeal before heading out again. "Her and her alone," he muttered.

Etha fixed him with a dull glare and though Mathias refused to look at her, he felt it. "This isn't the first time the demons have beat you to tragedy, Mathias. I won't assume you're happy about any of it, but what's actually bothering you?"

Mathias opened his eyes at Etha's bluntness. He'd always been terrible at hiding things from her, and this time, he was shocked to realize he'd been hiding them from himself. The overwhelming weight of Etha's peace drew the truth he'd been trying to outrun from the cobwebs of his mind, and he leaned forward, propping his elbows on his knees so he could cram his face into his hands.

"It hurts." When Etha didn't reply, he blew out a slow breath and sat up once more. "Rescuing Nessix has been all I've cared about for... how long now? I'm closer to her than I've ever been, but at what cost?" He shook his head and glared through the sparse room for a way to vent his frustrations. Finding nothing useful, he bumped the back of his head against the wall. "If Zenos was honest, Nessix knows the demons are chasing her. She has to know that they're not going to simply ask people if they've seen her. She's a smart woman, Etha. Compassionate. She should have found a safer way…"

Etha mulled over Mathias's fears, soaking in his angst and despair. There was a vein of truth in his words, but he seemed to let the most important factor slip from his mind. "You know the limitations of the hells better than most. You're rendered nearly powerless down there. *I'm* rendered nearly powerless down there. Her only option was to flee, and I doubt she had much time to think through the consequences when the opportunity presented itself."

Mathias continued to bump his head on the wall, stubbornly brooding over Etha's excuses.

"Nessix *is* a smart, compassionate woman," she added. "She ran, likely knowing the dangers that might come, but she would have only done so if it was worth it. She'd have tried something this foolish if it only endangered herself, but to knowingly endanger innocents along the way? She must be harboring something more than her will to see you again."

Mathias stopped pounding his head. He'd been so wrapped up in his desire to save Nessix that he hadn't once stopped to think about the possibility that she might have some ulterior motive. With all of the people they'd imprisoned to play with, what made Nessix valuable enough for the demons to launch a continent-wide search for her? Wouldn't it have been smarter for them to let her be and wait for her to grow complacent and reveal herself to them? Nessix had to know something important that the demons couldn't risk the world discovering. Instantly, his bitterness seemed petty, and Mathias was—not for the first time this week—disappointed in himself.

"Where is she, Etha?" he murmured. Finding Nessix would end all of this pain, for him and all of the innocents in the demons' path.

"I can't tell you that."

Mathias frowned, hating that answer now more than ever. "You've bent your laws for me before during times of crisis, and I can't think of any other way to describe what's happening now. Please, Etha. Where is she?"

"It has nothing to do with my laws, Mathias." Her words

snapped sharply. Gentle or not, admitting her limitations was seldom easy for the Mother Goddess. "I have been doing everything I can to find Nessix, but I *can't*."

Nothing sucked the breath from Mathias quite like Etha telling him she was incapable of a task. "You *can't* can't?"

Just as Mathias hated accepting that Etha didn't always have the answers, Etha hated smothering Mathias's hope. She hesitated before delivering the unsettling confession she'd gleaned from Zenos, balancing Mathias's need for information with the damage it would deal. "I cannot track her. The demons didn't just twist her soul as Sazrah said. Mathias, they fractured it."

Mathias gasped at what that might mean. "Fractured her..." Vampires and demons still possessed the entirety of their souls, and with nothing but a little bit of warping, they'd become monsters. What would the complete fracture of a soul do? "Is she still Nessix?"

The pitiful tone of Mathias's voice broke Etha's heart almost as much as being unable to comfort his fears away from him. "Zenos didn't report any dangerous behavior from her and Sulik knew who she was the moment he saw her. If she'd been acting, she fooled both her commander and a god."

Mathias tried to let that soothe him, but his mind raced with fears of what had become of Nessix... and what he might have to do to stop her. "I need to get—"

Beside him, Khin yelped and jolted awake. Startled, Mathias jerked his hand toward his sword and Etha vanished. Feeling like a fool, Mathias leaned forward and waited to see what kind of support Khin needed.

Her tears had run dry and the puffiness beneath her eyes had receded a bit as she looked around the room. She didn't hunch herself in the closed posture Mathias had expected, but her eyes were dark and empty. She made no signs of opening the door for communication, so Mathias took that hurdle himself.

"Are you alright?"

His voice lacked the warmth Khin had come to know, reflecting his own gloomy thoughts. She didn't give him so much as a glance, staring at the wall as though it might deliver answers to make sense of a life that had gone so awry.

"Where am I?" she asked, her tiny voice swallowed up by memories she didn't want to accept.

Mathias choked down his guilt and despair. "We're back in Zeal. I never should have let you leave in the first place."

Khin's eyes dragged to meet Mathias's, her expression a chilling void. "Would me staying in Zeal have saved my family?"

It wasn't often that mortals—a child, no less—managed to make Mathias uncomfortable, but Khin did now. Life had left her bitter with good reason, more experienced than a girl her age ever should have been. He looked down at his hands, unable to provide an answer.

Mathias had been a puzzle to Khin from the moment they'd met, a man of atypical behavior, atypical desires, atypical compassion. She'd seen an array of baffling behaviors from him, but this was the first time she'd witnessed guilt, and that confused her even more. She'd been ready to throw away her life in her burning village, to be wiped from history with the rest of her family, but Mathias had wanted her to live, and he'd made sure she did. She wanted to hate him for that.

Wanted to, but couldn't.

He hadn't mentioned to her any details about the quest he'd postponed to save her from Seaton or escort her home, and she'd selfishly taken his kindness for granted. He'd withstood her tantrums and whining, patiently supported her while she tried to piece her life together. Weary wrinkles framed his tired eyes, and Khin knew that he'd continue overtaxing himself until he no longer had to worry about her. For that, Khin wanted to hate herself. That came a bit more easily.

Mathias wasn't fond of disappointing people and he was empathetic to a fault. Staring at his hands, he braced himself to disappoint Khin one last time. "I'll make the proper arrangements for you to stay here. The demons are on the move and Zeal is the safest—"

"No."

Mathias closed his eyes, fingers wrapping around each other as he rallied his patience to keep from snapping at the young woman.

"You *will* stay here until the demons have been quelled, and I'm the one who must do that quelling."

"Then I'm going with you."

Exhausted and beyond stressed, Mathias bit back his reaction. He couldn't keep Khin with him, not with the demons knowing he was on their trail. She had no home left, no family. For all Mathias knew, he might be her only living friend. She'd already expressed an unhealthy eagerness to develop combat skills and the little bit she'd learned had inflated her confidence to a degree dangerous in these circumstances. He never should have agreed to escort her anywhere.

"Mathias, please." Her tone softened from the entitled demands to a gentle pleading, pulling his glare to her stricken face. "Let me go with you. I *need* to go with you."

He sighed, trying to remember what it felt like to be on the mortal side of fear. "The demons have seen me on the field. They know I'm after them. That's going to draw their attention to me. Staying with me is no longer safe."

"I don't care if it's safe." Khin's mouth shrank to a stubborn pout, her eyes growing hard behind their remorseful glisten. "I can't stay here and do nothing."

Mathias caught his breath, recognizing that determination burning inside of Khin at last. Heart aching for the girl's loss and further disappointment pending his words, he shook his head. "Khin, you've got too much to live for."

She curled her knees beneath herself and popped upright, punching a fist into the blanket. "Like what? A job I never wanted that makes me a repulsive candidate for marriage? A home that no longer exists and a family who's dead to take care of me? What do I have to live for?"

Mathias hated to see such suffering in one so young, her innocence sullied by a world which had failed her. He'd give nearly anything to take that pain away, but the past was the one thing he'd never been able to touch, no matter how desperately nor how many times he tried.

"Hope," he said at last. "You've still got hope to live for."

Her frustrated tears ceased as she sneered at him. "*Hope?*

What's there for me to hope for?"

"For a brighter future. For the strength to move beyond the wrongs of your past. For the notion that what you've been forced to learn will help you help others from falling onto the same path."

Khin curled her lip and hunched her arms forward. "There's only one way for me to right anything about my past, and you know it. If you cage me in Zeal, if you imprison me here, you'll be no different than any of the other men who have used their strength against me. Is that what you want?"

That slap nearly hurt Mathias, but he'd been through worse. At least Khin had found her nerve. He just wished she'd chosen a different time and reason to let it out.

"Please, Mathias." Her tone softened now as her temper fizzled out from her previous outburst. "I know it's dangerous. I know I have no idea what I'm doing. But I won't be able to live with myself, hope or not, if I sit here and do nothing. I need this. Please."

The promise of vengeance was never a healthy attribute, but that aside, it was as if Khin had matured twenty years in the span of this one frantic debate. Everything about her—her tone, her words, her passion for justice—screamed with an aching familiarity. All that was missing was a suit of armor and demanding blue eyes.

"I couldn't promise your safety," Mathias said once more.

"I'm not asking you to."

"And I must resume my original quest."

"I just want a chance," Khin said.

Etha hadn't bothered to add her thoughts on the matter, but Mathias hadn't expected her to. Khin was expressing her free will brilliantly. Mathias sighed, chest restricting with the devastating premonitions of where that free will would land this girl if she was left to her own devices. She was too determined to throw herself at the demons; if Mathias allowed her to leave, she'd be dead within a day or two.

"You're staying here," Mathias said firmly.

Khin's eyes darkened in frustration. "You can't make me."

"No," Mathias said, patience wearing thin. "I can. I can and I will. It is about ten years too early for you to face demons on the field. I've got too many deaths on my hands as it is, and I won't add yours to them."

A heated jumble of curses burst from Khin as she sprang up and aimlessly swatted at Mathias. "You're going to abandon me, too?"

Mathias snatched her hands easily, confirming one more resounding reason why she was currently unfit to accompany him. "I am protecting you, child!" Khin shrank from his raised voice, wounded eyes brimming with tears, and Mathias took a moment to find his calm. "If I'd had the time to train you properly to stand against demons, I'd bring you with me. Etha knows I could use skilled backup. But time is something we don't have. I'll move more efficiently on my own and right now, my ability to do that may be the only thing keeping Abaeloth from war. Promise me you will stay here in Zeal so I can concentrate on stopping that."

Khin shivered with uncertainty, impulse and fear hindering all sensibility. "And what if I don't?"

"If you don't, I doubt anyone could stop you. But it would distract me, and that might be what makes me too slow to intercept the demons. I may already be too far behind."

Mathias hadn't meant for that last to harm Khin, but when her shoulders slumped and she dropped her head, he realized how it had. His efforts had been postponed to cater to her, and she had nothing to show for his sacrifice. Now, her selfishness might have permitted the outbreak of a *war*? Khin slouched down onto the bed as Mathias gently released his hold on her.

"I'm sorry I've been an inconvenience," she murmured. "I'll stay in Zeal. I won't cause you any more trouble."

Mathias stared at Khin, fighting to decide how genuine she'd been. Every other order he'd given her regarding the demons had been ignored, and those experiences warned him against trusting her now. This time, however, she'd given her word, and he liked to think that meant something.

"Thank you," he said, gentle and warm once again. "I'll arrange your room and board."

"You really have to leave?"

Mathias closed his eyes and released a gust of a sigh. "I do.

But this will be over soon. I promise."

He didn't wait around for Khin to try initiating another debate or for Etha to chime in that he had no grounds to make that vow, leaving the sullen girl alone in the room's safety.

TWENTY

Somewhere between ten and fifteen years ago, Talier had grown used to his brother's lies. They weren't the malicious type that got people hurt, but wild tales often elaborated on at Talier's expense. Liar or not, Marcoux wasn't a bad man, just a bored one. He'd been the one opposed to the quiet life nestled in the comfort of their village, the one to pester Talier to leave that comfort, the one to passionately claim that working as messengers for the upper class would lead them away from that stifling boredom. Talier hadn't been bored, but his older brother's enthusiasm had eventually worn him into compliance.

It was good work and Talier had once hoped the honesty needed for the profession would rub off on Marcoux. That hope was never quite met, and so Talier did as he always had and patiently tolerated his brother. He couldn't fathom how a man five years his senior had been given the more youthful soul, but perhaps he should have been thankful for it. The two made a good team; Marcoux charmed their way into lucrative contracts and Talier's reliability gained their clients' trust. They'd never get rich, but it kept them fed and clothed with sufficient funds left over to send back to their aged parents. For Talier, that was enough.

They were three days deep on a cross country trip and settled in for the night in the hills halfway between River Pass and

Deerfield. The countryside of Gelthin was generally considered safe, but Talier never slept soundly on the road. Too much could go wrong, he'd always claimed. Marcoux routinely combated those fears with his playful nature and uncanny ability to start a fire on his first try. Their current campsite left them exposed on every side, but after a full day's traveling, Talier was grateful to rest his legs.

As Talier unrolled his blanket and patted the ground to locate the least lumpy spot, Marcoux danced around the flames of their modest campfire, spinning some silly tale of ogres and demons and other frightening foes that lurked on the other side of reality. His antics pulled a faint smile from his exhausted brother.

"Marc, you *do* realize you're a grown man, don't you?" Talier asked when his brother stopped to pull out his water skin for a drink.

Marcoux's eyes glowed with mischief and he nodded as he finished drinking and wiped his mouth with the back of his wrist. "'Course I do. Why?" He already knew the answer; the two of them often shared this conversation.

Talier sat and stared into the fire, thinking over how much traveling wore on his body and his spirits. The constant movement, the never settling in place. It worked for Marcoux, but not Talier. He longed for the stability of putting down roots, and he'd played the messenger game with Marcoux for the entirety of his adult life. It might have been good work they were skilled at, but Talier was tired of it. He looked up at his brother's warm, innocent eyes, and sighed.

"Ever think it's time for us to find something else to do?"

Marcoux's brows ruffled close together and he cocked his head. "Tal, it's all we know how to do. How else would we survive?"

Talier shivered as a breeze passed over them and flared the fire. "We could move to one of the larger kingdoms. You could be a street performer with your theatrics. I could work your publicity."

Marcoux chuckled and laid out his blanket on the side of the fire opposite his brother. "A street performer? You really think that would treat us better than facilitating scandalous affairs and shady business deals between rich nobles?"

Of course, neither of them knew the nature of the letters they delivered, but they'd made a game of guessing the contents to occupy their time.

"It'd let us have a home again," Talier said.

"We've got a home."

"Not one you're content staying at."

Marcoux grinned. "But you think I'd be happy staying at some other home? In a place I don't belong?"

Talier shrugged. "If the money was right and the job entertained you, sure."

Marcoux shook his head and pulled a roll and some jerky from his pack. Blowing the fuzz from the roll, he took a bite. "My stories aren't good enough to find fame or fortune, not like the *real* performers. It's a miracle I can still pull smiles out of you."

Talier smirked. "Are you kidding? I've heard all the stories you've got so many times they should have gone stale, and you *do* still pull smiles out of me. You're good, Marc."

"You do know acting's just feeding people lies?" Marcoux gnawed off a bite of jerky. "Encouraging such mischief doesn't sound like the Talier I know."

"They're not lies if your audience expects to hear them." Talier picked up his own pack and blindly shoved his hand inside to search for food. "And being too modest... no, too *cowardly* to throw about such splendid tales doesn't sound like the Marcoux I know."

"Ah... you got me there." He raised his jerky toward his mouth as a muffled growl crept over the hill.

Abandoning their pleasant debate, Marcoux fished a flaming branch from the fire as Talier picked up a pair of rocks. It was unusual for animals capable of making such menacing threats to roam in the open, the one benefit of choosing it for camp. Another breeze pressed against the backs of the brothers' necks as they focused on the hill where the growl originated.

"I've got a job for you, if you're looking for work."

The brothers spun around, Marcoux gripping the stick with both hands and brandishing it like a sword.

Everyone who called Gelthin home knew the legends about

demons. Rumors floated around that they'd been managed, but not eradicated. Road-wise travelers like Talier and Marcoux even knew to avoid the city of Heiligate. But never before had either of the brothers imagined encountering one of the fallen. Marcoux's acting abilities faltered as fear dragged his heart to his throat, though the demon didn't twitch toward a weapon, massive leathery wings relaxed at his sides. His upper lip curled in refined disgust as orange eyes appraised the trembling humans. Talier's palms sweated and he clenched his hands tighter around the stones he'd grabbed.

"You're *sure* we're where we want to be?" The demon raised his voice to carry behind him.

Teeth chattering, Talier swept together the crumbs of his diplomatic skills and cleared his throat. "My… my brother and I were just on the road to… to Ironwood. If this is your campsite, we… um… we'll be on our way."

Fiery eyes snapped to Talier, expression cold, and the human cringed.

"It's better than the senile beggar and the twelve-year-old shepherd we passed earlier. We're running out of time." A second demon, also with wings but with pale eyes, crested the hill. He sounded grossly inconvenienced.

The first demon sighed, grimacing as he looked over each of the brothers in turn. Instinct begged the humans to turn and run, but terror and the certainty that the demons would easily catch them held them immobile.

Talier dropped his rocks and held his hands open. "We don't mean to cause you any trouble." He swatted at Marcoux's arm to encourage him to lower the makeshift torch. Marcoux refused the request, and the orange eyed demon stared harder at him, narrowing his eyes. "No trouble at all. You can keep our coins and rations, and we'll be on our way." The demon never pulled his gaze from Marcoux, and Talier coughed. "Put. That. *Down*," he whispered firmly. His brother still didn't comply, and Talier gripped his wrist. "We'll head south. We'll stay far from Zeal. I swear it."

The second demon stopped beside his companion and they both turned their attention to Talier. The young man gulped, mind numbing as he was struck with the overwhelming urge to cry.

"You know where Zeal is?" the first asked.

All Talier could manage was a feeble nod. Knees locked, he wavered on the cusp of fainting.

The first demon glanced at his companion, who shrugged, tilted his head, then waved a dismissive hand. "That one will do."

Even if Talier had the courage to ask what that was supposed to mean, he wouldn't have had the time. The demons had stopped ten yards from where the brothers stood trembling, but they cleared the distance between them faster than Talier could choke on his scream. Locked knees buckling as he tried to motivate himself to flee, Talier toppled to the ground. As he fell, he gaped in horror as both demons leapt on Marcoux.

Talier stared, morbidly transfixed as a flurry of wings and muscle enveloped his brother. Through the jumble of limbs, Marcoux swung his flaming club, a shower of sparks raining around them as the blow connected with one of the demons. Less than a second later, the makeshift weapon fell to the ground, Marcoux's scream and a nauseating crack chasing it.

"No!" Talier roared, fear for his brother surpassing fear for himself. He scrambled for one of the rocks he'd dropped, clutching it in his hand and imagining himself bludgeoning the demons to death with it. As he pushed himself to his knees, arm raised, his wrist was crushed in a firm grasp. Yelping as a wrench in his shoulder forced him to fall to his side, Talier looked up at the disapproving frown of a tall, sinewy man. This one had no wings, but Talier trembled at the malice in his luminous glare just the same.

"That would be very unwise of you," this third demon said.

Tears coursed down Talier's cheeks as he heard Marcoux cry out. He tried to roll over to see what was becoming of his brother, but the demon's hold only let him flop sideways to face a large wolf held at the end of a rope by a fourth demon. Far braver than Talier, the animal fought at the end of his tether, growling furiously as his front paws pulled at the restraint secured around his muzzle.

"Please…" Talier blubbered pathetically. "We're just trying to reach Ironwood…"

It took Marcoux losing the strength to fight for the demons to back off of him. Talier sobbed, slumped on the ground, no longer struggling for freedom. Marcoux was gagged, limbs left unbound since he could no longer organize them to move, and the two winged demons dragged him beside his brother, depositing him like refuse in the dirt.

Talier raised his head on a wobbling neck, choking as he looked at his brother's mangled limbs and broken face. "Let him go…" he begged, words barely coherent.

The orange eyed demon rubbed at the side of his face where burned skin had blistered, and kicked Marcoux soundly in the ribs. Marcoux was too spent to scream, but did manage a groan. He was still alive.

"I'd be careful what you ask of us," the other winged demon said, crouching down to meet Talier's eyes. "Our interpretation of such requests could be quite a bit different than yours."

The orange eyed demon turned and stalked a few strides away. The other glanced at his companion's behavior, then back to Talier.

"What's your name, boy?" the demon asked.

The faint memory of what it meant to be rebellious ordered Talier to deny the demon an answer, but his fear of what could happen if he did demanded he supply every bit of information asked of him. Conflicted and terrified, Talier couldn't even open his mouth.

The demon frowned and Talier cringed even farther away from him. "Do you have one, or will we need to carve one out of your brother's flesh?"

Talier pinched his eyes shut. "Talier!" He practically screamed the answer, desperate to do whatever he could to spare his brother any more torture. "My name is Talier Dalton."

"Very good," the demon said. "Look at me, Talier." He waited until defeated gray eyes peered open and the human tucked his chin to his collarbones. "My name is Annin, and that"—he jerked his head toward the other winged demon, who was slowly regaining his composure—"is Kol. Do you know what we are?"

Mind numb and exhausted from the terror he'd been plunged into, Talier gasped for breath to provide an answer. "You're demons."

"We are. And we've got a request to make of you."

Somewhere deep in Talier's core, resentment bubbled up like a plague, sneering over how this was not the proper way for someone to request assistance. He itched to try fighting, hoping his feistiness would pull the demons' attention from Marcoux, but what it came down to was that Talier was too afraid to fight. Even if he found a way to take out four demons, Marcoux was unlikely to survive without medical intervention, and the odds of anyone able to help them passing by at this hour were painfully low. Unable to think of a way out of this predicament, Talier fell back on the instinctual reaction of begging.

"Please... I'll do anything you ask. Just find my brother some help. Don't hurt him anymore..."

A touch of a smile lifted Annin's lips. "Comply with us and we'll see to it he lives." He didn't need to explain what would happen if Talier chose to resist.

"I will comply," Talier said. "I swear it."

By now, Kol had calmed enough to rejoin Annin. He didn't crouch down, but stood with his arms crossed, looking down at Talier as if he was the deformed runt of what was otherwise a superior whelping of fine-blooded hounds.

"Something quite valuable to us has come up missing," Kol said. "And you are going to help us find it."

A gutted breath pressed out of Talier's lungs. "I'm... I'm a *messenger*," he said, voice straining with panic. "I don't know how to track or hunt."

"So you're turning us down?" Annin asked. Kol shifted his weight to begin walking toward Marcoux, his hand moving to a blade at his hip.

"No!" Talier yelped. "I'm not! I'll help however I can, but I don't know how."

"You'll figure it out," Annin said. "Are you afraid of dogs?"

"Afraid of—?" Talier hadn't thought fear of anything other than these demons could register at the moment, but he suddenly remembered the wolf that the fourth demon had restrained. "I... I'm..." Facing murder was something Talier had never fathomed he'd have to do, especially in a fashion where Marcoux's survival depended on him. Overcome and helpless, he crumbled closer to the ground, wishing the demons would hurry up and kill him. "I'm afraid." He didn't specify what he was afraid of, mostly because that was everything.

Annin frowned. "That's too bad." He stared at Talier for a moment, as if giving him a chance to conjure up some courage, then shrugged and drew a metal pick the length of his forearm from his belt. "You're going to have to get over that."

Before Talier could respond, the demon holding his arm slammed a foot against his back, sprawling him prone on the ground. He thought to try pushing himself up again, but the sound of the wolf cursing its restraints as it was dragged closer froze him in place. Even in the most obscure tales Marcoux had concocted, nothing like this had even seemed remotely plausible to Talier. Demons were supposed to be quelled; at the very least, disinterested in simple men like them. How was he supposed to serve these demons and save Marcoux if they threw him to a wolf? Arms shaking in protest, Talier attempted to rise but was promptly shoved back down by a blow between the shoulder blades. His breath fled him in a massive gust.

"Do. Not. Move." Kol's voice was little more than a whisper in Talier's ear, raising a chill across his damp flesh. "Lay completely still or a very painful, very *prolonged* death awaits your brother."

Closing his eyes didn't keep the tears from flowing, and Talier pressed his face into the earth. He'd never wanted to be a messenger. He'd never wanted to travel or spend nights on the road. All he'd ever wanted to do was be a good brother.

A frantic yelp left the wolf, followed by a more frenzied string of growls, and Talier channeled his thoughts strictly on his own breathing. Whatever was happening didn't make any sense, but he wasn't in the position—in any sense of the word—to ask questions.

The wolf's weight crashed down on Talier's back, disrupting the rhythm of his breathing, and a humiliating whine escaped him from his efforts to keep from squirming. The animal thrashed violently, thick fur rubbing against the back of Talier's neck and sticking to his sweat. Its paws tangled in his sleeves, one hind paw hanging up in his belt as it scrambled behind him, but no teeth ever bared down. Suddenly, it dawned on Talier that the wolf was no less a prisoner to the demons than he was.

Poor thing… he thought amidst his own terror. *Neither of us ever stood a chance…*

Talier thought of Marcoux and how he'd never be saved. He thought of home and those dreams of settling down to find a gentleman's job. He thought of how it had been *his* weariness which made them stop out here in the fields instead of continuing on to Deerfield.

Marcoux's muffled scream cut through all of those thoughts, followed by a high-pitched yelp from the wolf. A burning pierce plunged through Talier's flesh and into his heart, and before he could scream, all of his thoughts stopped.

TWENTY-ONE

With confirmation that Kol was on her scent, Nessix knew two things; she had to move faster, and she could not risk sleeping by herself on the road. She'd spent four of the silver she'd earned filling her pack with basic supplies and rations and getting her armor serviced before leaving South Bend, and she continued her march north in earnest. Hunger satisfied, she sated her nerves with the rest of her second root of dream stop. With only one root remaining and nearly two-thirds of the route left to travel, she added this to her growing heap of concerns.

Three days and two towns passed at her rigorous pace where she kept her mind active with the nagging curiosity of Berann's identity and what part he'd played in Kol's past. Aided only by subpar naps which barely sustained her, exhaustion begged Nes to find proper rest at midday. Pulling out her map at a fork in the road, she rubbed her eyes and allowed herself a generous yawn. She traced a finger down the road she'd travelled so far, hesitating the closer she got to her current location.

The road to the right would see her to the next town within an hour and was a more direct route to Zeal. Following this route would put her through a dozen more cities than the course to the left, increasing the number of civilians who might be adversely affected by the demons chasing her. The left, however, would add a hundred miles to her journey and was another half a day's march to the next town. Grumbling her frustrations at her morals, Nessix rolled up her map and traded it out for a fistful of dried fruit before trudging down the road to the left.

She staggered into the town of Covington well into the night and wasted no time locating the inn. Too tired to care about privacy, and a pinch of her paranoia soothed by sleeping in a crowd, she was content to save money by curling up with her sword on the common room floor. She slept deeply, too worn to try delving for the secrets in Kol's past, and woke with nothing worse than a few knots in her back. Dining on a simple meal of warm porridge—the first hot meal she'd had in a week—Nessix left the inn to test Trebuchet's promise of job prospects.

The cobbled streets were swept, the buildings kept orderly and in admirable repair. The entire city breathed peace and cleanliness, and Nessix frowned as it began to look increasingly unlikely that any sort of criminal had a place here.

She never should have put her faith in that group of strangers. Their challenge had earned her a few days of food and means of caring for her weapons and armor, but she should have known better than to assume she'd actually solved her financial problems. Grimly accepting that her faith in the good will of mortals was drowning a slow death, Nessix opted to save the last few copper pieces she had to buy a spot on the floor of the inn in whatever town she stopped at next.

On her way toward the northern gates, a bright sign depicting a library caught her eyes, and Nessix paused, spinning the ring Zenos had given her around her thumb. There was no feasible way a god operated this establishment, and she doubted hidden rooms harboring secret, restricted histories were standard features in Gelthin's libraries, but it was her first chance to search for recorded evidence of the demons' past since she'd been chased from Seaton. She didn't want to waste time, but compromised with her curiosity by promising herself she'd be quick.

Closing her fingers over Zenos's ring for luck, Nessix entered the library.

The interior of the building was as cheery as the rest of the town, with the walls washed in a pale yellow and a fresh bouquet of pink tulips in a vase on the front counter. A kind looking older woman stood behind the counter, beaming a smile which Nessix did her best to return. As the tinkle of the bell mounted above the door announced another patron's arrival, Nessix squeezed through the crowded shelves and past a scholarly looking man browsing through the reading selections. She scanned each book's binding as quickly as she could, working her way to the back of the building for privacy as she tried to smother the glimmer of fondness that came from unwelcome memories of the hours she'd spent hunting for mysteries beside Kol.

Time passed with no luck, stealing Nes's patience along with it. Irritated and plagued with the dread of her insufficiency, she heaved a sigh and crouched down to hunt over the books on the lower shelves. Finding nothing of interest or relevance, she rocked back to her heels to prepare to stand when a young woman in a pink dress swept up beside her. Nessix glanced up, past a belt buckle stamped with the linked triangles of the crest she carried, and met the woman's pointed gaze. A quick chill blew across the back of her neck as she stood. Before Nessix could back away, the woman smiled sweetly.

"Trebuchet sends his admiration, Succubus."

Of all the greetings Nessix could have imagined, that had not been among them. She shook her head. "I'm sorry, what?"

The woman huffed and rolled her eyes. "Trebuchet sends his—"

"No," Nessix said quickly, not caring that word of her route of travel had spread among her employers. "I got that. But… the last part?"

"Succubus?" The woman stifled a giggle. "You know, the way you charmed that man in the tavern half to death… raised by demons… It's a perfect fit and beats what they gave me." She frowned and wrinkled her nose. "*Velvet*. Ugh. Anyway. That's your name now, at least the only one we care about. Does that bother you?"

It bothered Nessix very much, and the snide tone used to inquire as to her feelings about it only encouraged her desire to react. As it was, her light coin purse begged her not to make an issue of the matter. Repulsive connotations aside, having a name assigned to her beat needing to throw around her true identity while in transit. "No. It's fine."

"Good." The sing-song reply did nothing to ease Nes's growing nerves. "And I'm glad you're here, because I've found a job for you."

There was much about this interaction that hinted at danger, but Nessix was quick to blame her bout of discomfort on how little dream stop she'd allowed herself to consume. She'd made the arrangement with Trebuchet for this very reason, and she was silly to be worried over it. Forgetting about the books, having known her odds of finding one worthwhile and that she could comprehend were slim from the start, Nessix cleared her throat. "And I'm eager to take it."

Velvet's face lit with satisfaction and she laid a gentle hand on Nes's shoulder to steer her down the row of books to a table nestled against a window in the back. "Eager, you say?" She perched on the edge of the table.

Nessix crossed her arms. Despite her attempts at rationalizing the situation, Velvet unsettled her, but she couldn't quite determine why. The woman's arms were thin and soft, her full dress with its cinched waist would pose as a liability in a fight, and she carried no apparent weapons. Nessix shook off her persistent worry and tried another smile. "It's always good to feel needed."

"Indeed it is." A lofty sigh bubbled from Velvet, and she continued the conversation as though she was discussing plans for dinner. "Your objective is a man by the name of Carson Lander. He's a tall man, good looking. Honey colored hair and blue eyes. His house is five blocks west of the smith, with overgrown rose bushes all around it, and our intelligence says that if you're quick about moving, he's home right now."

A bounty on a man with a known residence in town? That was awful bold for someone with a price on their head... "What is he wanted for?"

Velvet cocked her head, brows rippling briefly before her smile chased the expression away. "Assassination."

Nes's eyes widened. Having grown up noble, even as a warrior, she'd known from an early age how dangerous and disgusting assassins were. "And he lives in town?"

"Where else would he live?"

"I'd assume he'd be on the run or something. Not cozied up down the street from the authorities." On Elidae, the local authorities would have tended to an assassin in their streets, not handed the responsibility off to a band of questionable bounty hunters and hoped the problem would be solved. Could this man be too dangerous for the town guards?

"*Oh…*" Velvet quirked her lips from side to side. "It sounds like you never heard…" She contemplated the situation a moment longer, then shrugged and flashed her smile. "You're being hired on behalf of authority from a neighboring town."

Nes's heart eased. So Carson *had* been on the run. Perhaps the residents of Covington knew him simply as a neighbor. Apparently, her relief in this revelation was clear on her face, because Velvet continued speaking as though there had been no cause for concern at all.

"You think you can handle him?"

Even with her life-long wariness of assassins, Nessix was pleased to discover that the thought of facing one—at least on her terms—no longer bothered her. If Carson ended up killing her before she could kill him, she'd wake again, assuming a demon didn't find her first. Eager to cleanse the world of at least a little bit of trash, Nessix nodded. "I can."

Velvet gave a dainty clap of her hands. "Excellent. When you're through, bring a lock of his hair to The Fork and Chalice and I'll get your payment. Don't make a scene about it and don't complicate things with the local jurisdiction. Remember, he's wanted by authority from another town. I'll take care of the administrative work."

"And that's it?" Nessix asked.

"That's it."

Nessix dismissed herself from Velvet's company and left the library, pleased that she was about to do some good—and be compensated for it—despite all of the terrible things Kol had insisted were in her future. She'd rid the world of one more monster, just like the one who killed Brant. It wouldn't be the justice she hungered for, but it would spare someone, somewhere, from suffering a similar loss.

The little house Carson occupied sat at the end of a quiet street. A sour-faced old woman aggressively swept the porch three houses down, glaring at Nessix before scampering back inside her home. Nessix hesitated a moment to see if the woman would reappear and, when she was more certain than not that her passage was clear, squeezed past those overgrown rose bushes to search for a rear entry point. She didn't know much about the intricacies of getting in and out of buildings she wasn't meant to be in, but she did understand ambush tactics. As she pressed toward the back of the house, a feminine voice begging for and—if Nessix could be so bold to assume—receiving pleasure confirmed her mark was not alone.

Nessix stifled a groan and looked back toward the street. Sitting around while the pair fulfilled themselves was no more appealing than the risk of trying to sneak back here a second time. Letting out that groan, Nessix sank to the ground and did her miserable best to tune out the home's activities. She needed the money. Assassins needed to be stopped. She kept telling herself both of these things to keep from dwelling over how much time was being wasted while she waited for her objective to wrap up his business. According to her map, it would take at least two more weeks to reach Zeal if she maintained her current pace, and she needed money to do that. Gritting her teeth and waiting for Carson to fulfill himself was only temporary. Getting caught by Kol wouldn't be.

The house grew quiet, not even the sound of residual giggles pushing through the walls. A few moments later, the front door opened and an immaculately turned out young woman departed. Nessix took a moment to marvel at how quickly the woman had put herself together, having always thought the fuss it took to get hair just right and make sure dresses were situated properly would take all day. No other sounds came from inside, and Nessix whispered a brief prayer that her mark had fallen asleep to spare her the inconvenience of a struggle.

She pushed herself to her feet and located a rickety door rotted halfway from its frame at the back of the house. Palms sweating, she held her breath and tried the handle, which gave to her timid request. Either this man genuinely thought he had nothing to fear in this town, or he assumed nobody would enter from this end of his property. No matter. Nessix entered into what served as the man's food stores.

Creeping out of the pantry, she peered down a short hall, finding a small room tucked to the right. As she stepped, a floor board squeaked and she froze.

"Back already?" came a lazy voice from the room. "I thought you needed to go home?"

Nessix held her breath. She'd survived several bouts against demon warriors; she would survive one against a mortal combatant. But that didn't mean she wanted the hassle of fighting one for his life. She pulled her dagger from her belt, fist clenched tightly around its hilt. She needed to live, and she needed money to do that.

"Fay?" the man called again, and this time, Nessix heard the rustle of his mattress shifting.

She was out of time. She could take out her mark quickly if he was in bed, but the second he was prepared to fight, she'd have a struggle that could easily involve the authorities.

"Inwan, guide me," she murmured.

Striding forward before she spent even a moment longer dwelling over the possible outcomes of her actions, Nessix sprang through the door, slamming into Carson's bare chest as she pushed him onto his back. Though his thoughts floated through the residual bliss of his recent encounter, the widening of his blue eyes confirmed he registered that Nessix was not the woman he'd been calling for.

Before her target could discard his shock, Nessix grit her teeth and slammed the knife into his throat. She ripped it free as he gazed up at her. His body sagged limply beneath her and Nessix gaped at the terror flawing his face. Taken by surprise or not, that didn't seem like the expression of a ruthless killer. She hadn't killed the wrong man… had she?

Rapidly swallowing the nauseating lump that rolled up her throat, Nessix grasped a handful of Carson's honey-colored hair and passed her bloodied dagger through it, clutching the freed lock tightly in her fist. She wiped her blade clean on his sheets and slipped off his bare torso, leaving him as exposed as his girlfriend had. Nes's frown deepened. That woman had left through the front door. Once Carson was found dead, she'd be the one blamed for his murder.

Velvet had said she'd tend to the administrative duties, and Nes's fraying nerves begged her to leave as quickly as possible. Slipping out through the back door, making sure to press it securely closed once again, she darted behind another half dozen houses before squeezing through an alley and back to the main street to head toward The Fork and Chalice.

Every time Nessix blinked, Carson's terrified eyes flashed through her mind and she couldn't shake the suspicion that something was wrong. She *knew* she'd had the right house. His physical description met the one provided to her. Shivering at whatever this eerie sensation was, Nessix travelled with quick, rigid steps, her eyes darting about rapidly. She hunched her shoulders to ward off passing greetings as she stalked toward the tavern. The closer she got, the faster she moved, until she ran up the steps and inside.

Early in the evening, the tavern was sparsely populated, and Nessix had no trouble spotting Velvet in her pretty pink dress. A second woman sat beside her, wearing a much finer blue gown and a strict expression. Nessix hesitated, palm sweating around the lock of hair, until Velvet waved her over. The other woman looked up at Nessix to sweep a judgmental gaze across her and that surge of confusion and regret returned to Nes's stomach. She walked over to the pair of women, eager to collect her money and be on her way.

"Your… *clothes* are rather clean, Succubus," the woman in blue said, her voice cool and stern.

Nessix gulped down her reaction to snap judgement back at this stranger and attempted to be obedient. "I'm efficient. I don't get dirty if I don't have to."

"See?" Velvet asked, pulling back the seat beside her. "Efficient. I told you it was fine to trust the new girl." She turned her devious eyes toward Nessix. "Have a seat, Succubus."

The refined curl in the new woman's lip adequately conveyed her disgust in Nessix, but that stoked Nes's irritation just enough to convince her to sit.

"A claim of efficiency isn't enough for my coin." The woman shifted a shoulder away from Nes's position.

Nessix unlocked her fingers from where they clenched tightly around Carson's hair, and she brought her hand to the table to reveal the fistful of honey colored locks marred at one end by the slightest streak of blood. "This was what I was told to bring back with me."

Velvet nodded in satisfaction and a broad smile finally lifted the glare from the woman in blue. "You did it," the new woman murmured, swallowing what tried to be a laugh. "You *actually* got rid of him."

That tremor of discontent resurfaced in Nes's gut. That didn't sound like a proper commendation from an authority figure. "That's what I was hired to do."

The woman promptly plopped a full coin purse in front of Velvet. "Forgive me for my doubt." She turned her gaze to Nessix again and that bright smile of hers faltered. "And thank you, Succubus, for saving me from a miserable future." She stood and smoothed out her dress, settled her composure with a deep breath, and saw herself out of the tavern.

All the while, Nessix gaped at her with pale cheeks and wide eyes, discontent maturing into a full-bodied nausea. "...What did she mean?" Nessix murmured, gaze slowly falling to the dead man's hair.

"Oh, she'd been the victim of an arranged marriage or something," Velvet said, as chipper as ever. "Neither loved the other, at least that's what she said. Fortunately, money can solve any problem, am I right?"

An arranged marriage...? That couldn't be right. "But you said he was an assassin."

"No." Velvet drew out the word to emphasize her assumed innocence in this terrible misunderstanding. "I said he was wanted for assassination. Assassination by you."

Nes's stomach coiled tight around that uneasy lump and her lungs threatened to restrict. There was no way she'd just killed a man for some spoiled shrew's convenience!

"Oh, cheer up." Velvet pulled open the coin pouch. "Look at the adventure you just came from."

What was *wrong* with this woman? An innocent man had just died by her hands! That wasn't an adventure. That was murder. Nessix wheezed in a slow breath. "I was... I was told this was bounty work."

Velvet smiled and pulled a palmful of coins from the pouch. "It is, more or less. Just... less well advertised." When Nessix didn't move or blink or breathe, Velvet heaved a sigh and feigned a tiny frown. "Sorry about misleading you. Fletch did say something about your morals getting in the way. But now that you've got one mission under your belt, you're already a criminal, right? No use beating yourself up over it now."

Hating herself for her ignorance and for letting her desperation get her into this mess, panic spurred Nessix into motion and she began to struggle with coordinating her fingers to untie the crest on her belt.

Velvet craned her neck to see what Nessix was doing and sucked her teeth. "I'd not try that if I were you."

"No," Nessix said shortly, repeating the word several more times as she succeeded in untying the knots. She slapped the leather disk onto the table and shoved it toward Velvet. "I'm out. Keep the money if you want, but I'm not the woman you and Trebuchet want me to be."

Velvet placed a delicate finger on top of the disk and pushed it back toward Nessix, a strict warning stealing the previous jest from her eyes. "Walking away isn't easy, Succubus."

"I've trained with demons," Nessix snapped. "The hard road doesn't frighten me."

"Then let me try again. Walking away does not happen. If you try, you will not leave this city. Am I clear?"

Even knowing that she couldn't permanently die, that threat chilled Nessix. She'd spent too long in this Inwan-forsaken town as it was; the time it would take for her soul to patch up fatal wounds was time she didn't have. Trapped between the threats of demons and mortals both, Nessix reached her numb fingers out to reluctantly drag the crest back toward herself, mind too fuzzy to sort out how to solve this problem quite yet.

"I'm pleased by your sensibility," Velvet said, though her expression didn't quite reflect it. She counted out five silver from the pile of coins in her hand and held them out to Nessix. "And here's what you're owed."

Nessix didn't reach to accept it, her shock from her previous actions compounded by this stingy compensation. "That is five silver."

Velvet nodded and flashed Nessix a grin that mocked the idea of generosity. "It sure is." She placed the coins on top of the crest to simplify Nessix securing them both.

Outrage bubbled up from around Nes's disgust, but she hadn't yet found the confidence to act on it. "Five silver is *it*? A man's life isn't worth any more than a *boar's*?"

Velvet dropped the remaining coins back in the pouch and pulled the strings closed. Clutching it tight in her hand, she stood. "The boar's might be worth more. There's a whole lot of meat on one of those beasts. Thank you for your time and expertise, Succubus. I look forward to tracking your progress."

She departed with a swish of her pink skirt and Nessix stared at those measly five silver pieces atop the leather disk, trying to figure out how to escape this trap she'd stumbled into. A pair of jovial men entered the tavern, one of them leaving a lingering gaze on her, and sense prompted Nessix to gather the proof of her employment at last. If she was forbidden to walk away from this job, she could only imagine what would happen if she let townsfolk figure out what she was.

A shiver struck between her shoulders, skating up her neck and into her scalp as she realized she'd just accepted this role. Whether or not she loathed it, she had to consider it as much a part of her as Kol was, at least until she reached Zeal. There, she'd find the answers to her troubles. She'd be free of needing to kill innocent men to survive. She'd be able to avenge her homeland and her army of akhuerai. She'd be able to repay Kol for all he'd dragged her through.

Gritting her teeth, not yet convinced these excuses justified this disgusting breach of ethics, Nessix rushed from the tavern to the market to gather provisions so she could get back on the road.

TWENTY-TWO

Talier dreamt of chasing rabbits and running naked through the forest, filled with carefree innocence and embracing a surge of self-confidence and power he'd never experienced before. Intoxicated by the sense of freedom, he savored every moment until sunlight beat against his closed eyelids, scattering the last of the rabbits back to their warrens and withdrawing the shadows he'd found so much pleasure in exploiting.

Groaning, Talier twisted his spine to alleviate the tightness constricting his chest and pressed each of his limbs out in a full-body stretch. Breathing deeply on the uptake of a yawn, the smell of sweat and dirt and dominance swirled up his nostrils like smoke fleeing through a chimney. The sweat and dirt made sense, but he'd never before smelled an emotion. Talier cut short his lazy reentry to the world and jerked awake.

Beside him, empty yellow eyes gazed at him, the grimace of a bloodied maw giving him a single order that shook him to his core.

The pack is in danger. Run!

Talier didn't register the appropriate fear of waking beside a predator past the instinct to escape whatever danger had killed it. Adrenaline punting him fully awake, Talier scrambled across the ground, arms and legs uncoordinated as they fought to determine how best to organize so he could flee.

I can't run! he thought frantically. *Not without my pack... Not without Marcoux!*

Memories a jumble, Talier swatted and scratched like a wild beast as a hand gripped his forearm. He twisted against the hold, free hand darting forward to grapple his captor's wrist as he kicked violently in hopes of a lucky hit that never came.

"Would you stop that?" The irritated voice dumped a barrage of terrifying memories on Talier. "If I let you go, you'll fall into the fire. I will not have that."

Chest heaving, Talier surrendered, sinking back against the ground. "Where's Marcoux?"

Kol couldn't quite decide what to make of Talier's apparent weakness. The human's fear of demons and his brother's fate would do much to keep him obedient, but he'd need to find a great deal more courage to race inoga in the chase for Nessix. Perhaps they'd chosen the wrong brother. It was too late to do anything about that now, and so Kol tossed a silver locket on the ground by Talier's face.

"You can assess his condition and remember why your obedience is so important with that."

Talier cast a bitter glare at the bauble to keep from looking at the demon towering over him. "I want to know where he is."

Crouching down, Kol snatched the pendant from the ground and popped open the locket. "He is secure, and that's all you need to know." He jutted the open locket back toward Talier.

Talier was slow to look, afraid of what he'd see, but morbidly drawn to it. A faint smear of blood marred the left side of the locket and beneath a crystal cabochon on the right side was a tiny animation of Marcoux, chained by his wrists in a standing position against a stone wall. His head weaved back and forth in the fashion of an animal that had been caged for too long and his fingers twitched now and again. More desperate than ever to fulfill this demon's desires, Talier gulped down his guilt.

"You said I'm supposed to hunt something for you?"

Kol smiled. "Straight to business, then."

"I just want to get my brother back."

The whining was getting annoying, but Kol would soon be rid

of Talier. "It's not some*thing* you're after, but some*one*. A woman named Nessix has escaped us and is running across Gelthin. Not only is she my property"—Kol smirked as Talier chanced a disgusted scowl at his word choice—"but she harbors some very valuable information that must be protected. You will find her for us, before she can reach her destination of Zeal. Her safe return means the release of your brother."

The hairs on the back of Talier's neck stood as the scent of irritation wafted toward him from the gust of a pair of wings. Annin landed behind his comrade and Talier scrunched his shoulders to his ears, wishing he was anywhere other than on the ground before two beasts of fairytales.

"Everything is situated and secure," Annin reported as he walked up beside Kol. Talier hadn't yet looked at him, but he could feel the arrogant pity skinning him from Annin's cold appraisal. "Is this one compliant?"

Kol smirked, those orange eyes more sly now. "He will be. I've given him the details he needs to know and he seems to understand our terms."

Talier coughed, drawing the attention of both demons. "The… details?" He lowered his eyes even though he hadn't been looking up. "Shouldn't I get a description or place she was last seen or… *something* to guide me in the right direction?"

Kol's lips parted to bare his teeth and he gestured for Annin as he rocked back from his crouch to sit. "This is where it gets fun."

"*Fun?*" Talier cried. "You're torturing my brother and call it *fun?*"

Kol brought out his smile once more as Annin took a seat beside him. "We *are* demons. Torture is one of our few joys in life. But the fun we'll have with your brother is an added bonus to what we have in mind for you."

Annin sighed, expression dull. "You want him to comply, Kol, not incapacitated by fear."

Kol arched a brow and glanced at his companion. "I'm pretty sure the fear's already come and gone after the other night."

"The other night…" Talier murmured, the burning in his

chest returning. The details trickled back to him, but they all seemed so ridiculous. Ridiculous or not, two of the four demons he remembered facing sat right in front of him, so part of it had to be real, whether or not he wanted to believe it. "What happened?"

Kol frowned. "Do you not remember, or do you not believe?"

Talier couldn't sort the answer out for himself.

"Do you know much about the Divine Battle?" Annin asked.

Talier shook his head.

"The different classifications of our kind?"

Another negative response.

"Magic?" When Talier hung his head, Annin hefted a sigh, though not one purely of irritation. At least this would spare him from needing to explain the chaos of Affliction, his being an oraku, and how magic could transform a man. "All you need to know is that the wolf over there sacrificed its life to lend you its senses, and it's those senses which you'll use to track Nessix."

Mouth open, but breath not coming fast enough, Talier gaped from Annin's bored gaze to Kol's cunning one. He wanted to accuse them of lying, or at least he would have if they were mundane bullies, but they gave absolutely no tells of dishonesty. Add the concept of trustworthy demons to the ridiculous notions of the day...

"What does this mean?" Talier murmured.

"It means," Kol said, "that your excuse of not knowing how to track is no longer valid." He wrinkled his brow and frowned, though his eyes maintained their cocky glint. "Maybe you shouldn't have tried so hard to convince us you didn't know how to hunt. You could have spared that poor creature's life."

Talier groped for a way to convince himself that this was all a terrible joke, for the nerve—and strength—to attack these two demons. More than anything, he wished he could go back in time and prevent any of this from happening. Before, he'd been a weary messenger, a normal man with a normal job. Today, he was supposed to swallow a story about being bound to a wolf so he could scour Gelthin for a single woman under the instruction of a pair of demons who had taken his brother captive. His head swam, and Talier was grateful he was already on the ground. Fear surpassed by shock, he rolled to his belly and hid his face in the grass. Maybe these demons would kill him and spare him from needing to sort through this nonsense.

"That's not very sportsmanlike of you, Talier," Kol said. "We've given you a generous gift seldom extended to mortals. All we want in return is to borrow your service."

Talier rolled his face to Kol, cheek pressed against the ground. "I don't know how to do any of this. I don't even know who this Nessix of yours is."

"You don't need to know that much." Kol spun a hand in Annin's direction, and the oraku opened his pack. "Sit up and quit groveling. Show some pride. Fabricate some confidence. We'll gain nothing from harming you and you have everything to gain by working with us."

Given how much they'd already forced him through, Talier didn't put much stock in that promise, but he pushed himself upright, coughing at the pull in his chest. As he did so, Annin drew a folded handkerchief from his pack. Subdued, Talier watched as the demon carefully unfolded the square of fabric. Annin jutted the handkerchief toward his face.

"What do you gather from this?" Annin asked.

Talier stared at the frayed square of thick canvas that laid across Annin's open palm, confusion growing past what he'd previously believed was his limit. His confidence that these demons weren't insane faltered, but he wasn't about to say as much. Rubbing his lips, he flicked a pitiful glance at Annin, and cleared his throat. This had to be a joke, though not one part of Talier could fathom how it was meant to be funny.

"It's um… white? Looks to be high quality. Maybe a piece of—"

Annin scoffed and rolled his eyes, immediately silencing Talier's attempt to answer. "I know what it is," he snapped. "I want to know what you can read from it."

Talier squinted, desperately trying to see if anything had been written on the scrap of fabric, wanting so badly to comply. "I can't see a—"

"Oh, for fuck's sake!" Kol struck quickly, grasping a fistful of

251

Talier's auburn hair and forcing his face nearly into Annin's open palm.

Talier gasped at the sudden attack, instinctively grabbing Kol's wrist to try prying his way free, but then, *it* hit him. A swell of information swept through his nostrils, tickling the parts of his brain that associated the smell of fresh candied almonds to the festival his father had taken him to as a child. Only this recollection didn't stir up fondness and a sense of excitement. This scent combined rage and refined temper, a deep sense of loyalty and sacrifice. It raised in him an eerie desire to run and an even greater urge to fight. She had no face, no physical features he could readily identify, but the distinct shape of a woman with a sword formed in his mind, binding itself to this scent and the uncertainty it awakened inside of him.

Moments later, Kol released his hold and, though he'd have felt foolish for it if he'd been of a more present mind, Talier pulled in a few more deep breaths of this scent, each one sharpening the woman's frame and aura. Slowly, he sat up, the reluctance in his eyes replaced by quiet contemplation.

"I'll ask you one more time," Annin said. "Could you read anything from that?"

Talier nodded slowly and licked his lips. "I could, but I can't explain it."

"You don't need to explain it, only recognize it. Can you do that?"

Talier nodded again. "That's the woman you're looking for, that Nessix. Isn't it?"

"Careful how closely you openly associate her with us," Kol warned. "If she suspects you've even imagined us, she'll bolt. And if she escapes you, that will render both you and your brother useless. I'm sure I don't need to elaborate."

The tiny flicker of confidence this strange reaction gave Talier flashed out. Marcoux had been the liar, not him. He'd seen his brother work crowds plenty of times, but that didn't mean he'd be able to do the same. "So when do we go find her?"

"*We* aren't going to find her," Kol said. "That was the entire purpose of finding *you*."

Talier's mind was hung up on the image of a lean woman with a sword. She'd stood firmly and with the bold air of a disciplined soldier. The one time Talier had held a full sized sword, his arm had succumbed to wobbling well before he'd raised it level with his hips. No longer fighting what happened last night, willing to accept it as truth, Talier stubbornly wondered why these skilled fighters who had taken out both him and Marcoux in a few rapid heartbeats weren't going with him to track this valuable prey. The thought that maybe all their skill and strength were outclassed by this mysterious woman popped into his mind, and the color drained from Talier's cheeks.

"Not meaning to complain, ah… sirs… but I'm not a fighter. Not by a long shot."

"I'm confident the wolf gave you more than a keen sense of smell." Annin kept his focus on folding his handkerchief over the square of fabric in his hand, careful not to contaminate its scent.

"But even if I did, I… I have no idea how to use it."

"You figured out one part just fine." Annin looked up, his blank expression chilling Talier more than the young man's ominous suspicions of the danger Nessix might present.

Talier cringed in anticipation of the fierce reprimand or ultimatum involving his brother's fate that would come from his pathetic question. "Why can't you hunt her down?"

Had the circumstances not been so dire, the two demons might have laughed at Talier's frightened request. For being so afraid of them, he certainly seemed eager to keep their company. But circumstances *were* dire and remembering the reason why he couldn't chase after Nessix personally did anything but make Kol want to laugh.

"She's wearing a charm that lets her know when one of my kind is nearby," Kol said. "And she's incredibly skilled at slipping through the cracks. You, though, are the most unassuming man I've ever seen, the sort of helpless dolt her morality would never let her walk away from on a dangerous road. Gain her trust, lead her toward the northeast coast, far from Zeal's eyes, and we'll relieve you there when we can organize a proper ambush for her."

Talier didn't flinch at the insult, already too taken aback with the realization that he was deep in an impossible mission now. The plan, as Kol presented it, sounded simple. But the simplest sounding plans very seldom were. There was a reason beyond a charm that these demons couldn't catch their Nessix, and Talier was certain he wouldn't be able to, either.

"What if I can't get her to follow me?" he asked.

Kol shrugged, expression indifferent. "Then your brother dies."

Surrendering to the fact that there was no way out of this arrangement, Talier hung his head. These demons had chosen the wrong brother and because of that, Marcoux would die. Talier would find a way to make this work. He had to.

"Do I at least get a heading?" he asked meekly. Gelthin was a sprawling continent and even with enhanced senses and his experience navigating the land, he'd need more guidance than he'd been given to locate a woman on the move.

Kol and Annin stood, obviously considering their task completed. Talier didn't trust his legs enough to hold him, so he stayed on the ground.

"She passed through South Bend within the past week or so," Kol said, "and should be heading north as fast as a woman on foot can travel. That's the last report we have of her. We've got several patrols scouting for her and will see to it they have your description. They'll make sure relevant updates reach you."

Talier's stomach twisted in knots, this grim situation growing that much worse. Without a word, Annin held the folded handkerchief down to Talier and it was accepted with trembling hands.

"If you can help it, stay where you can be found," Kol said as Talier crammed Nessix's scent into his pocket. "I'd like to keep aware of your progress."

Having delivered that last as an order, Kol trusted he'd be obeyed and launched himself into the air. Annin gave Talier one more critical glance and followed.

Left by himself in the peaceful hills between River Pass and Deerfield, his only company the bloating carcass of a wolf and his brother's spilled blood, Talier stared at the ground. He'd never hated anyone before, least of all someone he'd never even seen, but a gush of bitter loathing swelled inside him now. Everything he knew of life had been thrown on its head because of this woman. He'd learn how to track, and he would hunt her down. He'd learn how to fight, and he'd keep himself safe from her. He'd learn how to manipulate, and he'd happily lead her into the clutches of these demons. Talier had no idea where to begin his search, but knew he had to start somewhere. Gripping the locket Kol had given him, Talier stood on legs forged of determination, and marched south.

TWENTY-THREE

Guilt accompanied Nessix from Covington, and fear of being recruited for another job kept her from entering the next town she came to. The need for sleep required her to stop at the next one, however, and with a racing heart and unsettled stomach, she made quick work of locating the inn. Now knowing the value of the coins she carried, she was determined not to waste them and held her breath as she claimed a corner of the common room to recover her spent energy.

As though belittling her paranoia and shame, nothing but the snoring of another traveler across the room disturbed Nessix until morning. She ate her fill of a bland gruel, relaxing as she became increasingly confident that nobody was going to coerce her into criminal activity. When the rest of the town awoke, she spent half of her money on more rations, and by the time she was refreshed and restocked, Nes had found something similar to calm. After a brief consultation with her map, she left the town to continue north.

Half a day's march later, she'd shed the rest of her worries regarding the mortal scouts who watched for her so Kol's ever-present pressure could continue to drive her instead. She kept a rapid pace as long as she could afford and when the wooded road she'd been on thinned out, a dense cluster of thatched rooftops

256

framed the horizon. Nessix stopped to catch her breath and debate whether or not she should save her rations by stopping in town for food or continue soldiering on.

Losing the tree cover would leave her exposed to Kol's aerial advantage, and she'd stuffed her pack quite full at her last stop. She still had enough energy to press on until morning when she could find cover and sleep with the sun standing guard over her.

Mind made up, Nessix opened her pack to pull out a snack as a suave man wearing the mismatched armor of a second-rate mercenary walked toward her. With messy blond hair and deep brown eyes, he was attractive in a rugged way to those who were in the market. As it was, Nessix wasn't, and she gave him nothing more than a cordial smile and resumed digging in her pack. Seconds later, she realized he'd stopped in front of her and Nessix froze.

"Hands where I can see them, please."

That sense of calm Nessix had fostered over the past day slipped from her grasp as shock kept her hands immobile and her gaze lowered. Had Velvet turned her in? Had there been a witness to her crime, after all? A blast of heat struck Nessix in the face and stole her breath.

"I said hands where I can see them, Succubus."

Nessix gulped as chilled sweat rolled down the back of her neck. In terms of her freedom and longevity, this beat the alternative of being caught by the law, though she was no more pleased to deal with it. Wrangling the sense to do as she was told, Nessix pulled her empty hands from her pack and let the bag fall down to her side.

The man gave a slight nod of approval and grabbed Nes's left wrist with a firm hand.

She pulled against him immediately, narrowly stopping herself from reaching for her sword. "Take your hand off me," she warned.

"I cannot do that." The man turned and strode toward the town in the distance, dragging Nessix along with him. "Velvet corresponded to me that you might be hesitant to take your next job, but I've got one lined up for you and need to make sure you get it done."

Nessix attempted to stop, but her tired legs lacked the stability to stand against his steady pull. She gave a stout jerk of her arm and strained her shoulder against his grasp. Out in the open, near enough for the town guards to see her, trying to engage this man in combat was a poor option. Physical resistance wasn't working for her, so Nessix tried the other way out.

"I'm off duty," she said.

The man smirked and continued to plod along, grip unyielding. "You're *never* off duty, Succubus, unless we say you are. That is what working for us means. If it's any consolation, your next mark single-handedly dropped an entire family into poverty. This is a benevolent assignment." As the guard post came into full view, the man forcibly linked Nes's arm in his and tenderly covered her hand with his own. "Do *not* protest."

A bitter flare of humiliation swept across Nessix, contained in the trembling of her shoulders and the clench of her jaw. It wouldn't take a bit of acting skills to tell the guards that this man was controlling her against her will...

He patted her hand and spoke with a lowered voice. "You're just as much a criminal as I am. Don't be a fool."

The truth of this assassin's words struck Nessix a powerful blow and stifled her objections into silence. No more willing than before, but daunted into compliance, Nessix accompanied this man to the city gates. He engaged the guards in pleasant conversation, his deception of his intentions in the city casual and flawless. After he excused away Nes's sickened silence in a patronizing manner she'd have bluntly corrected in any other scenario, the guards welcomed them into the fair town of Midland.

As the name implied, the city was located centrally on Gelthin and provided a comfortable and convenient stopping place for cross country travelers. A vast array of people representing cultures Nessix was unfamiliar with passed through the busy streets, conducting their business but otherwise keeping to their own parties. It was a perfect place to pass along unnoticed. A perfect place to get away with murder.

Nessix attempted to pull her arm free again as her guide led her down the bustling streets of the business district, but he clamped his elbow around her wrist and grasped her hand. Even in the hells, Nessix had felt that she had more control than she did now. Trapped and on the verge of an untimely bout of panic, she concentrated on the aspects of this interaction that she could safely control.

"You said this family's impoverished." She kept her voice low to avoid the ears of the casual passersby. "If they've got no money, how can they afford this... service?"

Now convinced of Nes's compliance, the man loosened his grip to rub the back of her hand. "It's not your place to worry about where the money comes from."

Nes's insides squirmed at the heap of misgivings his answer dropped on her. The woman who had paid for her first assignment had been wealthy—or at least outwardly appeared so—and Nessix had been given a narrow cut of that fee in exchange for an inexcusable crime. A poor family wouldn't be able to offer a fraction of that rate, which Nessix fully suspected would impact her earnings.

She'd once been a proud general, killing to keep people safe. She'd become Kol's pet, teaching others to kill for their freedom. Now, she'd been degraded to killing for petty conveniences. What had become of her honor?

Desperation. That was what had become of it. And it was a filthier feeling than she'd ever experienced in her life. Desperation. It was what drove common folks to do evil and proud generals to stray from their morals.

"Pay attention."

Nessix blinked away her vile introspection and shook the immediacy of her self-loathing from her mind.

"Coming up on the right is the metalsmith's shop."

She glanced past the open storefront of a glassblower and the whitewashed shutters of a busy confectioner's shop to where a windowless two-story wooden building with a banner reading Filmore's Precious Metals was nestled among the artisans. She didn't let her gaze linger long, too afraid of being caught looking, and drew a long, deep breath.

"I'm assuming there's relevance in that?" she asked.

"There is." The assassin led her past the building where a jovial man's deep voice boasted through the open door about no finer wares in all of Gelthin. Though Nessix didn't try to peek in the doorway to locate the owner of the voice, her guide did. When he turned his attention back to the road, it was with a smug smile. "Remember that voice."

Nes's stomach clenched at the obvious connotations in the command and the cooling air of evening's approach suddenly felt balmy against her cheeks. "Is he guilty of a crime greater than running his competitor out of business?"

"I don't know." The assassin finally let Nes's arm slip from his so he could grab her wrist and pull her toward the inn at an extended gait. "And I don't much care. We cater to paying customers, just like anyone else."

Worn from both exhaustion and dread, Nessix didn't bother fighting the man's lead as he dragged her inside the inn.

The first floor was set up as a respectable tavern for road-weary travelers. As Nessix had observed in the streets, the pockets of people politely kept to themselves as her companion selected the most secluded of the two dozen tables in the great room. Continuing the guise of caring about Nessix, he pulled back a seat and, contradicting the same degree of affection, he gave a subtle twist of her wrist to force her to sit before taking the seat across from her for himself. Nessix kept her eyes active through the room, making quick appraisals of the quiet table of elves, the mixed group of sunburned loggers, and a human woman doing an admirable job juggling five young children while her husband negotiated prices with the establishment's owner.

Nobody here gave Nessix or her distasteful companion more than a second glance and that nagging fear that every lawful eye on Gelthin was watching her eased enough to allow Nes to breathe and find a believable smile as a serving maid answered the assassin's hail.

"Two of your house special," he said. "Ale for me. Wine for the lady. And see to it that the room reserved for Dirk has been prepared."

Nessix opened her mouth to protest, having not budgeted—nor even been able to estimate—the cost of a full meal and drink, but her companion passed the young woman four silver and she darted back to the kitchen before Nessix had finished drawing her breath.

Dirk sat, inquisitive eyes and lopsided smile following each of Nes's movements as she shifted under their weight. Through all of her fidgeting and notable discomfort, she didn't attempt to escape or argue, but neither did she sample her roasted game hen or wine when it was delivered. Shrugging, Dirk sank his fork into a wedge of potato, steam fogging the metal of the utensil as he raised it to his mouth.

"What's the problem, Succubus?" He bit down on the morsel, briefly venting the heat from his mouth before rapidly chewing. "Aren't you hungry?"

Nes's stomach groaned and she fought to will away the enticing smells that threatened her self-control. And no matter how appealing Dirk's physical attributes might be, Nessix wasn't eager to find out what she'd owe him for the room he'd booked. She glanced at the succulent meal then raised her eyes to his. "I'm trying to ration my funds."

Dirk chuckled and shoved the next bite into his mouth. "You think saving your money will make fewer jobs crop up?" When Nessix didn't respond, he continued. "Nah, people will always need our services. It's in our nature to be selfish and petty and cruel. If you hadn't learned that from the mercenaries you worked with, those demons you cozied up to had to have rubbed off on you, right?" He slid his gaze to hers.

Nessix trembled with restraint, that latent cruelty and pettiness Dirk had just mocked spurred on by the chaos which Kol had woven into her. Respect had always been a concept Nessix both understood and employed, even in regards to the likes of Veed and demons. She should have listened to her instincts when that virtue hadn't expressed itself when dealing with Trebuchet and his crew, but she'd been too hungry, too tired, too convinced that money would keep her on the fastest path to Zeal. Clenching her fists, she slowly drew her hands toward the edge of the table.

"Hands stay where I can see them." Dirk spoke his correction casually, as though he knew she'd comply, and Nessix hated herself even more that she did. "Relax, Succubus. Eat. Drink. Rest up a bit. This life doesn't have to be what you're making it."

She sneered and looked away from both Dirk and the tempting meal before her. "There aren't many other ways to look at it."

The serving maid returned with a key, a smile, and the promise that the room Dirk had reserved was prepared. He dismissed her politely and voiced a soft laugh as Nessix continued to avoid his eyes. Tapping the key on the table a few times, he finally slid it over beside her left fist and withdrew his hand to resume eating.

The gesture pushed past Nes's suspicion enough for her to toss a glance in his direction. "What's your game?"

"My game?"

"Trying to endear me to you so I'm more likely to comply with your orders?"

"Endear—" Dirk's brows furrowed and he placed his fork down as he studied Nes's guarded glower and closed posture. The darkness in her eyes was exactly the sort of viciousness he loved to see, but it spoke of suspicions and vile experiences he dismissed with a smirk. "Despite the connotations with your name, I have no intention of sharing the room with you." Through with his assessment of Nes's immediate concerns, he tore a leg off his game hen. "You're... not my type."

A wash of heat reddened Nes's cheeks and she flashed her eyes to Dirk's at last. "You expect me to believe you're doting on me out of the goodness of your heart?"

Dirk grinned and took a bite from the leg. "I'm not doing a damn thing that the guild hasn't told me to. You really think I'd waste my own coin feeding you like this and putting you up in private lodging?" He snorted, briefly choked on his mouthful of food, and cleared his throat with a swig of ale. "It's a gesture of good will from the masters. They see promise in you, provided you loosen yourself up."

"Good will," Nessix seethed, though the reassurance that Dirk had only been a means of obtaining her food did allow her to eye it speculatively. "Because I'm sure this guild is simply overflowing with the virtue."

Dirk heaved a sigh and lowered his half-eaten chicken leg to his plate. "I don't care one way or another what you make of the offer, but if you want my advice—"

"I don't."

His brows leveled and eyes narrowed in tempered rage for the first time. "If you want my advice, warm up to us. This is a dangerous field you've entered and having friends would do you some good."

Moral objections and longing for companionship aside, Nessix doubted she'd ever find trustworthy allies among this lot. "When one of you comes along who meets my criteria for friendship, I'll consider it."

Dirk cocked his head and frowned. "Have we been unfair to you, Succubus?" His voice was low and soft, armed with a biting edge that warned her against answering truthfully. "We've opened the roads you're so frantically travelling. We've stayed out of your business, as you requested. We've seen you fed and sheltered. What more could you want from us?"

Nessix scraped her fingers against the tabletop, splinters digging beneath her nails to remind her that she still felt. Besides the false pretenses which had been used to recruit her, this guild hadn't done wrong by her; she was the one choosing to do wrong all by herself. Dirk's knowledge of what she'd told Trebuchet and how she'd performed in Covington confirmed that this organization had elaborate lines of communication in place. She had no way of escaping what she'd so stupidly fallen into, not if she wanted to keep ahead of those pursuing her.

An argument or heated retort would only risk Dirk passing along more warnings of her insubordination, and she needed fewer complications. "Nothing," she muttered at last.

"Very good. And you're clear on tomorrow's assignment?"

She cleared her throat and looked down at her plate. "I am." Maybe this metalsmith was actually a terrible man. She could only hope.

Dirk stood and drained the last of his ale. "Then meet me back here when everything's settled. Same conditions apply as before." He tore the other leg from the chicken. "And do try to do right by us. There's no money in correcting bad behavior in one of our own."

Nessix couldn't come up with a response that wouldn't risk passing as bad behavior, so she stayed silent as Dirk turned and left the inn. Numb, she pocketed the key and finally allowed her aching stomach to motivate her to eat.

* * * * *

Despite Dirk's assurance that he had no interest in accompanying Nessix to bed, even after she'd double checked the door was locked and window barred, she still couldn't relax. Hovering on the border between sleep and awareness, she missed her chance to resume the quest of seeking Berann's identity, berated instead by the disappointed shake of her father's head, Brant's disgust, and Mathias's tears of sorrow. The sun peeked through the window and chased away their judgement, and Nessix stretched and groaned against the pull of muscles that hadn't quite recovered as she stood to dress. Not trusting her stomach's fortitude, she declined breakfast and departed the inn.

Birds sang their jubilations from ornamental trees lining the street of the business district, the sun's warmth beating down on the groomed pathways through the town as Nessix headed out to complete her assignment. She navigated the city with ease to the metalsmith's shop and stood outside the door for a few moments, hands on her hips as she cast a remorseful gaze to the heavens. This was a necessary evil to ensure her survival. After this hit, she'd spend all of her earnings on food to extend how long she could go without approaching another town and put off being snatched for her next assignment. It wouldn't buy the metalsmith his life today, but it would buy the next man his.

Putting on the best smile she could find in light of the darkness she carried, Nessix entered the shop. Torches lit the sales floor, the light of their dancing flames reflecting off rows of glistening silver goblets and bronze jewelry boxes. Shelves crowded the shop, creating a maze of narrow passages that promised to limit maneuverability.

"Good morning, love," greeted a pleasant woman behind the counter. "What can I help you with?"

Nessix grimaced at the dirt she tracked onto the rug-covered floor and a sour lump rose in her throat. "I'm here to browse. I'll have to consult my funds after I know what catches my eye."

The woman accepted her attempt with a warm smile. "Let me know if there's anything you'd like help with, and if you'd like something tailored more to your tastes, don't be afraid to ask. Fil is happy to take commissions."

That same wriggle of unease invaded Nes's stomach at this woman's offer as she wondered what petty offense her mark was guilty of to earn his death. She flexed her fingers and tried to silence her regret. Surveying for potential exit points to this windowless, torch-lit shop under the guise of browsing, Nessix hunched her shoulders when the rich tone of the metalsmith's voice affectionately greeted the woman from a doorway behind the counter.

Nessix glanced over her shoulder as Filmore stepped through the door. He was a large man capable of defending himself and his family, a man who would be most unpleasant to take on in a brawl. She'd hoped to finish this quietly in his shop, preferably away from his wife, but the more Nes thought it over, the more it seemed as though she'd have to sneak back in after hours to try to catch him alone. Her stomach flopped again as the bell above the shop door tinkled to remind her that she'd never be truly alone.

The wife's disgusted gasp of, "*Oh*," was followed by her clearing her throat and an attempt at a cheerful welcome.

Nessix looked up to assess what had caused the woman's discomfort and met the eyes of the group who had entered the store.

Five demons stood between Nessix and the doorway. They were among the fortunate ones capable of blending in to society when they wanted to, but Nessix recognized them easily. And, by their toothy grins and lustful gazes, they recognized her, too.

In an instant, the assignment Nessix had been hired for fled her mind in exchange for much more pressing concerns. Her minor scouting efforts hadn't uncovered any viable escape routes besides the front. No windows, no boards that looked like she'd be able to kick down. The demons blocked her sole path out of the shop.

One of the demons attempted to occupy the attention of the shop owners, instructing them to stay behind the counter. The woman clutched her husband's arm and pushed him in front of her. He folded his brawny arms and calmly told the demon—the demon he approached as though he was an average man—that this was his shop and any trouble they had with Nessix was to be taken elsewhere. Two of the others stepped outside to stand guard at the door, the last two fanning out to approach Nessix from either side of the shelf she stood behind.

Her only escape blocked, Nessix snapped with the need to survive. She'd come too far to be caught now; she was just a few weeks from safety and salvation!

"Don't try anything stupid," the demon to her left said as he steadily pressed forward. "The calmer you stay, the easier this'll be. Kol doesn't want to see you hurt."

Nes's heart raced at the mention of Kol, chaos and her unwanted connection to the alar suggesting this might be for the best. Sheer determination, however, kicked her in the shins and demanded she fight. From her peripheral vision, Nessix saw the metalsmith shove his wife more firmly behind him. Those people were scared. Innocent bystanders, even one she was meant to kill, were frightened because of her.

Nessix's eyes darted between the two demons as they approached. She couldn't quite grasp a solid plan through the conflicting inputs muddling her instincts, and she crept a step back, plunging her hand into her pack and grasping her final chunk of dream stop. The demons chuckled as she ate it, devouring the terror in her eyes.

There had to be a way out. Nessix took another step back. Her sword and knives would only take her so far outnumbered in the tight confines of the shop. The warmth of a torch kissed the back of her neck. Nessix frowned. This would not turn out well, no matter which way she looked at it.

Calming herself the best she could as the dream stop's influence slowly incorporated into her system, Nessix braced herself for the fight to come. She held her breath and sprang toward the demon to her left, hands reaching out for his neck.

He caught her with the ease she'd anticipated and she let him hold her wrists as she struggled against him. Predictably contained, she listened for the second demon as he rushed around the shelf to grab her from behind. As he neared, Nessix kicked backward and lodged her calf between his legs. The demon doubled over at her strike, and Nes kicked again, this time catching him under his chin. The attack didn't carry much power, but was enough to stagger him backwards into the shelf along the back wall.

"Little whore." The demon grappling Nessix lifted her from the ground and whipped her into a nearby shelf. She crashed through the display, the clatter of delicate wares punctuating her gasp for breath as she dangled at the end of the demon's grasp. "I told you not to fight."

Stuck in her opponent's hold, Nessix used the only tactic available to her. "Help," she begged the shop keeper. "Please, help me!"

The demons lowed their chuckles and her act drew the attention of the one containing the shop keeper and his wife. As Nes had hoped, the shop keeper used the distraction to usher his wife out of the way as he scooted toward the doorway he'd first appeared through. In the best case, he'd return with a weapon or hail the city guards. In the worst case, he and his wife would escape with their lives. One way or another, it looked as though Nessix was destined to fail killing him today.

She pulled against the demon who held her, throwing her weight at the end of his grasp until he was forced to try outmuscling her. Once she had him dedicated to her fight, Nes dropped to the ground as though she'd fainted. The resistance in the demon's arms gave way, and Nessix launched forward to catch him in the gut with her shoulder.

One hand fell free as the demon stumbled backwards, and that was all Nessix needed to grab her knife from her belt. A firm curse from the demon at the counter notified the two at the door that assistance was needed, and they spun to enter the shop.

It was too late for the demon who had grappled Nessix, as she swatted at him with her knife in furious chaos, slicing into his stomach, chest, and face. Dream stop not fully ingested, Nessix struck frantically, not aiming for any particular vital location, but trusting she'd hit enough to eventually take him down. A clatter from behind announced another demon's approach, and Nessix sprang aside.

The move landed her even farther from the door, but the roar of the metalsmith as he burst from the stairwell with a large pole announced that her makeshift cavalry had arrived. Demons weren't particularly worried over mortals and their efforts to resist them, but this group hadn't anticipated complications. Nessix didn't know how long it would take for their commotion to be noticed outside the shop, but it wouldn't be long. If she wanted to limit casualties, she had to make this fast.

With the demons momentarily distracted by Filmore's charge, Nessix strode toward the front of the shop as the man she'd been sent to kill launched his massive frame into enemies he had no way of appraising. He swung that metal rod and smacked the demon at the counter in the head, sending him to the ground, but not before it grabbed Filmore's collar to slam his face into the stone countertop.

Nes's actions were interrupted by the shriek of Filmore's wife as she rushed into the danger, trembling fingers covering her mouth as she scurried to her husband. Cursing the woman's stupidity and her own ingrained desire to protect innocents, Nessix dashed forward to intercept the demons from reaching her, but they grabbed the terrified woman before Nessix could fling her from harm, brandishing her as both hostage and shield.

"Think this over, Nessix…" the demon holding the woman said. "Getting people hurt? That's not like you. At least not the you Kol knows."

Ignoring the plight of the metalsmith's wife, no longer able to invest her concern in a woman who might have ended up a casualty anyway, Nessix snatched a chalice off the nearest shelf, and pelted it at the last demon's head. He dodged, but Nessix continued throwing items at him until he was forced to cringe and duck, arms sheltering his head. In the tight confines between the shelves, Nessix didn't have room to easily wield her sword, and when the shelves were emptied of improvised projectiles, she swung her pack at his head. He caught the pack and gave it a stout yank, pulling Nessix off balance and forcing her to slip the pack off her shoulder to avoid falling into his clutches.

Snarling, the demon holding the woman shoved his burden forward, trusting Nessix would try to catch her. Overwhelmed by the reeling madness inside and around her, Nessix deflected the terrified woman toward the demon she'd just attacked. Two were down, and Nessix had three more to deal with. She might still make it out.

The demon she'd assaulted with her pack repelled the metalsmith's wife. The woman lost her balance and cracked her head on the corner of the counter as she fell, taken out just like her husband had been. Nessix sprang at the demon before her, stabbing him in the gut, then spun on the one in the middle of the shop. Breathing heavily, Nessix crouched to brace for her next attack.

The moment her feet left the ground the first demon she'd struck voiced a brutal roar as he launched a flaming torch toward her face. She ducked just in time to avoid catching it in her mouth, and it clattered to the ground behind her, showering sparks and spitting fire as it caught the fine rugs covering the floor. Moments remained before the shop would turn into an inferno, but Nessix had to kill these demons to keep them from reporting to Kol. Darting forward, she plowed into the one she hadn't touched as he shook off his confusion at his comrade's actions.

Nessix took him to the ground and gouged his face with her knife until he quit fighting. Smoke billowed thick around her as the last demon darted toward her. She'd been prepared to hold her breath and kill him, but he shot past her, exiting the flaming building. Nessix turned to see the fire rapidly devouring the front of the store – including her only point of escape, and she leapt to her feet and dashed into the street.

Exposed to the fresh air, Nessix bent over and coughed, burning eyes sweeping the area for where the demon had run off to. He'd had a healthy head start on her, had inhaled less smoke, and had disappeared into the crowd. Her pursuer was concealed. The city's population cried for the authorities. And Nessix stood covered in blood in front of a flaming building.

Cursing, she bolted for the city gates. With a demon survivor, her location was compromised.

Shouts for her to stop chased her as she ran, but she couldn't stop. They'd want a report of what happened. As she continued running, they shouted of how she'd be arrested for obstruction of justice. She kept running. She wasn't afraid of the town authorities, or even Dirk, but she was terrified of what that surviving demon would report to Kol. She was too damn close!

Nessix ran, dodging prying eyes and grabbing hands as she raced from the city. She didn't have time to figure out where she was going, instinctively veering off her established course to bolt through fields and vault over fences in hopes of thwarting the demons.

She ran until her lungs burned, at which point, she grasped her side and let herself slow down. Her heart thumped fiercely, and her head swam from the effort she'd expended, but she didn't let that stop her. She groped at her side for her pack so she could pull out her map, but her pack—and her map—were gone, having been wielded as a crude weapon back in the burning shop.

This time, the curse came more firmly and was backed with a rush of tears. That had been her only form of guidance. Placing her hands atop her head, Nessix spun a slow circle as she stood in the middle of an endless field of wheat, casting her gaze to the sky to seek her bearing. She found her direction, still travelling north as she'd meant to, but she didn't know how far off course she'd gone. The demons had to know where she was heading; she'd made it too far across the continent for them not to.

And that one demon had escaped to confirm it all.

Fat tears of frustration rolled down her cheeks. After trying so hard to be careful, this was how it would unravel? Nessix could hardly believe it, but then a faint whisper of determination called out to her from the other side of her pounding heart. She hadn't been caught. Not yet. She still had time.

Lungs burning, Nessix turned and trudged north to seek the nearest road. She had no idea where she was, but at least this route took her away from Midland and, if she had any luck left, out of the demons' sights.

TWENTY-FOUR

It took Nessix two days to find another main road with nothing to guide her but the rising and setting of the sun. Another day on foot, stomach grumbling in a manner which she'd forgotten about over the past couple weeks of having money and means to buy and stow food, took her to the next town. She was in no hurry to hear what the assassins thought of the disaster she'd caused in Midland, but exhaustion and hunger begged her to stop.

She squeezed the coin purse at her hip, figuring she'd have enough for a meal, but would have to choose between a regional map or a night of rest. She closed her eyes and stuffed her tears of frustration back down, trying to dig up the memories of how much she'd loved roughing it when she still had a cushy fortress to return to.

Feet dragging, defeated and despairing, Nessix entered the next town she came to and collapsed beside the great fountain that greeted her just within the gates. Without the disposable energy to scout things out for herself, Nessix sat and waited to see if the assassins' eyes would find her. It wasn't long before a perky flower girl came up to her, handed her a half-wilted daisy, and said, "You will come with me."

Nes's legs ached, her eyes burned, and she'd run out of patience two days ago. The last thing she wanted to do was walk anywhere, but she suspected disobeying affiliates of this guild wouldn't alleviate any of her pains. Groaning, she pushed herself to her feet and followed the young woman through the street.

Each step she trudged behind her guide reminded Nessix of the trouble she was in. She knew she'd failed her last job. She knew word of her failure had spread among her employers. More importantly, she knew if she didn't come up with a viable answer for her mistake, she'd be on the run from both demons and assassins, and that was too many fronts to watch for on her own. She'd never missed companionship more in her life.

Exhaustion pulsed through Nessix as the young woman stopped to knock on a door at the back side of an herbalist's shop. It took concentrated effort to stay standing, and the mere concept of dealing with authority speared fresh needles into Nes's headache. The door was answered by a dapper man dressed and groomed as though he was someone's butler. He dismissed the flower girl and politely greeted Nessix, which she answered with a grunt as she followed him inside.

When she rounded the corner, a weasley aged man and portly woman seated at a table stopped counting their pile of coins and crossed their arms.

"The guild's been looking for you, Succubus," the man hissed.

"Let me be clear, I—"

"We know. You were jumped by demons," he said. "That isn't a valid excuse, not after your claims of knowing them and how they fight."

Too tired to argue, Nessix puffed a bitter laugh and looked away. "I did my best with what I had. Did my mark at least burn with the shop?"

The woman sucked her teeth and went back to counting as the man leaned forward and propped his forearms against the edge of the table. "He did."

"Then the job was done," Nessix said.

The man pressed his lips together in dissatisfaction and turned his chin to the side to look over Nessix through narrowed eyes. "You call that done?"

"Yes," Nessix snapped. "I do. The target was taken care of, as my orders stated."

"So where is your payment?"

"I—" Nessix croaked to a premature silence.

"So the contract wasn't fulfilled?" He pulled out a small red journal and sweat trickled down the back of Nes's neck as he opened it and dipped his pen in his inkwell. "Is that accurate?"

Nessix blinked, not sure why a formal reprimand bothered her so much. "It is," she murmured, cringing as his pen scratched across the page.

He flipped the cover closed once the ink dried and looked up at Nessix with the eyes of a disappointed parent scolding their unruly child. "You see, Succubus, we run a tight system here. I'd thought you were intelligent enough to notice as much."

Nessix bit her tongue to keep from retaliating to his goading.

"We fulfill our contracts in full, and we do *not* cause a scene in any part of the process."

"Sir," Nessix said, flustered that she'd used such formality. "Please let me explain—"

"There is no explanation!" the man snapped. "You go in, you do your job, you get out. To gain the notice of an entire *city*? You are sloppy, Succubus."

Had Nessix been thinking more like herself and less like a chastised school child, she'd have vented her thoughts about this organization, but all she could murmur was a small, "I'm sorry."

"It will not happen again."

"It will not happen again," she echoed.

The man stared at Nessix with an intensity she wanted to run from. The last time she'd been struck with this sort of fear was when Kol had first brought her on display for the inoga. She shivered, fighting back the urge to crawl under a rock and pray for death. The man's eyes bore into her, branding that shred of a soul she carried with shame. Nessix bowed her head, wondering when she'd stooped so low as to give others this much power over her.

"Your fine is ten silver," he spoke at last.

Nessix gasped, her eyes flashing from reluctance to a flare of anger at last. "But that's more than I've got."

He lifted one shoulder in an apathetic shrug. "Then I'll take all

274

you have."

"I haven't eaten—"

"Our records suggest you're an adequate hunter. And if you're so good at what you do, you could just take a job. One you'll do right this time."

Nes's hands trembled. If it wouldn't have been for that last job, she'd have still had her pack, food and map included. Her head swam from exhaustion and hunger and this fresh surge of emotion, and Nessix lost the will to protest any further.

"Fine," she spat, striding forward. She pulled the pouch from her belt and emptied it on the desk, watching as the man's nimble fingers collected her coins.

"Now, go on, Succubus. Know that the eyes have a fondness for you."

Nessix left the building, doing her best to keep from crying, trying not to think of how Kol would have laughed at her struggles and reminded her how easy she'd had it in his care. She strode quickly down the street, gaining far too much notice for her comfort. Her hair was tangled in disarray, as she hadn't done anything more than pull at it in frustration on her frantic run for safe harbor. Dried blood stained her blouse and breeches from her fight with the demons. She was filthy and tired and starving, with no funds to remedy any of it.

She needed to take a job; she had to recover her losses, but the assassin's warning of the eyes watching her twisted her stomach. She was through being watched. Delirious and with no way to soothe her nerves, Nessix hastened toward the city gates, too flustered to care whether or not she had money. She'd seen poor people survive, though she had no idea how to do it for herself. She'd always had what she needed handed to her and supplied readily. Even Kol had made sure her needs and comforts had been met.

For the first time in her life, Nessix was left wanting for more than the frivolous things she'd once longed for. She wanted a warm meal that would keep her full longer than a couple hours. She wanted the comfort of a blanket and clean clothes. She wanted a reliable source of drinking water and a good night's sleep.

Everything she'd taken for granted when she was revered as a general, she longed for now.

Kol had been right. She never should have run. At least with him, she'd been allowed to sleep, even if that meant wading through torments of his past. So what if she'd had to put up with dodging inoga and the dread of knowing she was building an army to strike against the mortal world? She could have met Mathias on the battlefield. Instead, she'd chosen to run, to subject herself to a corrupt world that had never wanted her. And she didn't know how to cope with it.

Unwilling to let any of the eyes see her tears of frustration, forbidding the assassins the pleasure of receiving that report, Nessix fled the town to continue her press east. Wanting to hide, needing to hide, she tore the leather crest from her belt and discarded it in the roadside weeds. She could outrun demons; she'd outrun assassins as well.

* * * * *

By the time she reached the next town, Nessix could barely stand. Exhaustion had nearly incapacitated her and she was dehydrated to the point of losing her voice. Bellview's guards rushed from their posts to help keep her feet beneath her.

"My lady, are you well?" one of them asked.

Nessix tried to croak an answer, but settled for shaking her head as the two men eased her to the ground. She gestured to her mouth with a feeble hand, and one darted off to grab his water skin. Nessix drained it, her stomach lurching as the cool water flooded into its emptiness, and she was gasping by the time she lowered it. She sagged against the stability of the guard crouched beside her.

"My lady, what happened to you?"

Nessix rubbed her forehead. "Attacked by demons. Barely escaped, but took the bastards down. Got robbed on my way here."

The guards frowned, the one Nessix wasn't leaning on shielding his eyes to scan down the road. "Demons?"

She nodded, but batted a hand his way. "I took care of them," she said. "They're dead somewhere down the road, nowhere near here."

The guards frowned and helped Nessix as she staggered to her feet, her stomach protesting loudly that water wasn't nearly filling enough.

"If a recently robbed woman wanted to find a place to work off food and rest, where would she go?"

"Oh, my lady, no need to worry about that," the guard said. "We can set you up at the station."

Nessix's urge to frown was quickly tucked behind a relieved and exhausted smile. She didn't need more connections with authorities.

The guard gripped her arm to help her stay standing and continued. "You've clearly been dragged through the hells and need help."

She laughed weakly. "Isn't that the truth…" Reservations drowning in fatigue, Nessix found a more genuine smile. "If you think your superiors will allow it, I'd feel safer nowhere else."

The two guards met each other's eyes and shared a nod before the one supporting Nessix led her into the city. She leaned on him and he eyed her as they walked, his curiosity thick enough to trip over.

"So…" he said slowly. "Demons…"

"Yeah," Nessix was too tired to come up with anything else.

"You fight them before?"

"I have."

That gained her a second glance and an impressed smirk. "How'd such a tiny thing get involved with learning an art few knights of the Order even know?"

Mention of the Order piqued Nes's interest and she raised her eyes from her feet for the first time. Maybe she was closer to Zeal than she thought. She'd pursue that when she had the means to deal with it. "The fact that I'm such a tiny thing is part of the reason I'm able to survive combat."

He nodded, lips twisting in consideration. "I suppose it is. If it wasn't for how rough you looked, I'd have thought you were just a meek lady playing dress up. But you really know what you're doing, huh?"

"I like to think I do." It wasn't a complete lie, though Nessix wished she could believe it a bit more.

"Well, you're safe here." The guard thumped a fist to his chest. "Best warriors this side of Zeal."

Nessix furrowed her brow and shook her head, trying not to think too far into his words, but unable to stop herself from doing so. "That's the second time you've mentioned Zeal. Is it nearby?"

"It's just over a week's casual march that way." He pointed toward the northeast. "Should be smooth travelling, if that's the way you're going." He was quiet for a moment before fishing for more. "*Is* that the way you're going?"

Nessix nodded, thinking over how fast she could cover that distance if she pushed hard. It was a pity she'd just lost all her wealth; she could have benefitted from a horse.

"You got business there?" he asked.

She shot him a hasty glance, suspicious of how many questions he was asking, but his pleasant expression and misty gaze reflected nothing more than a lofty dream of impressing someone who would carry his name to Zeal. "I've got someone waiting to meet me there."

He nodded. "Well, give the Order my regards when you arrive," he said with a chuckle. "Especially if you're meeting with someone important. Wouldn't mind a bit of attention directed toward our humble town."

Nessix didn't know how much influence Zeal had over the rest of Gelthin, but based on this man's behavior, the stories Mathias had told her, and the demons' revulsion of the city, she suspected it was a proper, uptight place. Of course this city was motivated to keep clean in light of Zeal. Perhaps they were looking for the greater city's support. Maybe they wanted to entice a branch of the Order to set up here. Whatever it was, Nessix suspected it was what had kept the assassins from establishing a presence in Bellview.

The guard gestured to the left and Nes's gaze followed his hand. "Well, here we are." He guided Nessix toward a pristine two-story building constructed of white stone, and puffed himself up with pride for his gallant deed of helping a lady in distress as he led her inside.

They were greeted by a chuckle and warm smile from a uniformed young man posted by the door. "You got a live one this time, Ben?"

"No, no," Ben corrected. "This one's not a prisoner. She's a demon slayer!"

The other man laughed again and crossed his arms as Ben pulled Nessix to a stop. His expression sobered as he looked over Nessix, appraising her disheveled appearance as it contradicted her noble profile. He cocked his head back and forth, growing less humored and more humbled, and shook his head.

"Damn, woman. What *did* you get yourself into?"

"Like he said." Nessix tilted her head toward her escort. "I got jumped by demons in the south and was robbed on the road here."

"Ah," this second guard mused. "Charity case?"

"Charity case," Ben confirmed. "All she asked for is food and sleep." He looked down at Nessix. "That *is* all you're after, right?"

"It's all I need." The idea of sleep danced about blissfully in Nes's mind.

"Right, well, are you comfortable sleeping in the barracks with a dozen off duty guards?"

Nes's lips twitched toward a smile. "It wouldn't be my first time sharing a bunk room with grumpy combatants. As long as they keep their hands to themselves, I'll sleep just fine." Possibly even better, considering how many able bodies would be surrounding her in case of an attack.

She followed Ben to a symphony of snoring and instantly shed her first layer of stress. He put a finger to his lips as he opened the door, and Nessix mouthed a thank you to him as he directed her through the darkened chamber to a free cot. Men sprawled on their backs, legs hanging off their beds, others curled tightly with their pillows. They were relaxed and content, and Nessix soaked in their ease. She gave her guide another nod and began to strip off her armor.

While she slept, she felt Kol's eyes on her, watching and waiting, but she'd come to anticipate these visits as means to slip into his psyche and grab slivers of truths he didn't want her to have. Secure in this room full of skilled men, Nessix slept hard through the bulk of the day, not even stirring at shift change. When she woke, she did so with a generous stretch and crept from the room, retracing her steps to where light from the setting sun filtered in through the windows.

A few disinterested grunts greeted her before one of the guards glanced up then smacked his companion with the back of his hand. As soon as the room's attention focused on Nessix, all of the men present stood and inquired on how well she'd slept.

"We were told you'd want food?" one of them asked.

"If you have some available," Nessix said. "But as I said before, I don't have any money."

"No payment needed for a demon hunter." The man rushed over to usher Nessix toward their unoccupied cafeteria.

"Demon… hunter?" Nessix asked, followed by a peal of laughter. "I wouldn't go *that* far." After all, the demons were the ones hunting her.

"Modesty's a charming trait," the guard said. "Eat your fill and swing by the office before you head out."

Nessix's brows furrowed, but she nodded her gratitude and pulled a plate off the stack waiting beside a modest buffet of food. Her reprieve here in the station was reminiscent of her days as a lieutenant, surrounded by the banter of her peers, treated as one of the troops. As much as she thrived off authority, there had been a sense of freedom in blending in with the masses, of getting to enjoy casual camaraderie. She sniffed back what she feared was the beginning of more emotions she didn't want to deal with and filled her plate, heading to one of two tables in the room.

If she'd been just a bit more confident, she'd have requested a fresh pack to stuff with leftovers, a water skin and, for Inwan's sake, a map to guide her to Zeal. If she'd been just a bit more confident, she'd have asked if she could take on any paying work so she wouldn't suffer at her next stop. That sobered her.

Eventually, one of those next stops would come with the expectation of another hit.

Appetite lost, Nessix forced down what was left on her plate.

As requested, she returned to the office where she was greeted by an enthusiastic gathering of guards who begged for sparring matches to test her skills.

When they'd established that she was determined to get on her way, the group of men presented her with a fresh set of clothing. Under the excuse that no demon hunter should look as though she went all the way to the hells to do her hunting—a comment Nessix allowed them to assume was made in good taste—they gave her a shirt woven of durable linen and a pair of breeches that hadn't been worn thin at the knees. It wasn't the pack or map she'd hoped for, but it was a comfort she'd neglected for too long. Thanking her hosts, wondering if they'd have been so kind if they knew her as the demon-perverted assassin she was, Nessix changed her clothes and departed the station into the evening.

She travelled the well-lit streets with the faintest whispers of hope now that she was alert and fed, comfortable for the first time in months as she headed toward the gate she'd been assured would put her on the road to Zeal. Relieved to be on her way, allegedly near a place monitored by the Order, Nessix soldiered on with renewed vigor.

Her departure from Bellview progressed smoothly until that nagging chill of someone watching her returned. The last time she'd ignored that feeling, she'd been tracked down by five demons. Drawing a deep breath, preferring to confront these foes while she had access to reinforcements, Nessix spun about to find a man inflated with an air of self-importance walking behind her. A hood obscured his face and he kept his head lowered so the cowl masked his features.

"Who are you and why are you following me?" Nes's voice rang through the evening air.

The figure stopped and tilted his head up, a piggish nose peeking out from the hood. "This is a safe town, my lady," replied a deep voice. "But a safe town that still has want of you."

Nessix glanced around them, praying this was some sort of set up. Unaware of this man's intentions or whether or not he was armed beneath that cloak, Nessix held her ground, prepared to bolt.

"I'll ask you again. Who are you?"

"A friend. And you're too broke to turn me down. Am I right?"

Nessix straightened and narrowed her eyes. "How do you know me?"

"There are eyes everywhere, even among guards in just cities. And you're going to need quite a bit of money to buy off your associates when they find you next."

Nes's heart raced, palms sweating. Besides knowing where this conversation was heading, this didn't feel like a safe deal. She must have made that concern apparent, because the man reached out and put a hand on her shoulder, a gesture she promptly swatted away.

A haughty snort mocked Nes's nerves. "I'm not what you think I am. At least not quite. A freelancer, if you will. And I've got a job for you, one that will pay what you deserve."

Nessix held her breath. One job off the records with a generous payout might be enough to see her to Zeal. She currently had energy and motivation, and was willing to compromise one last evil deed to be secure enough to put this all behind her. "What are you paying?"

"The going rate's what? Five silver per head?"

Nessix grimaced. Every reminder of how little these scoundrels valued life nauseated her a little bit more.

"I've never thought that was a fair cut of the typical fee," the man said to Nes's silence. "I'll pay you the full forty. But no more."

Nes's eyes widened. Forty was the going rate? It still didn't compensate for the value of life as far as Nessix was concerned, but uncovering how small of a cut her employers threw at her—just enough to keep her both hungry and fed—infuriated her all over again.

The man crossed his arms as shock worked across Nes's face. "Is that a fair deal?"

Choking down her disgust at the notion of verbally committing to this job, Nessix nodded.

"Fantastic. Now. I'm on Bellview's committee of allocations. There's five of us on the board, but only four can be trusted. I want you to make it so the whole committee is trustworthy. Can you do that?"

Desperate political mind jumping into action, Nes hoped this meant she was doing some sort of civic duty on this assignment. "I can," she spoke at last. "Where can I find him?"

A devious smile cut across the man's face, tiny eyes nearly disappearing as they narrowed. "He's a damn elf. Goes by Elric and rents an office above the cobbler's, near the main gates. You saw it when you entered town, I presume?"

Nessix clenched her teeth long enough to swallow a blunt reply. "I did."

He nodded shortly. "He goes up there around midnight and stays until the early hours of the morning, under the guise of balancing the books. Bastard knife-ears's just stealing our money and scheming ways to corrupt our council's fine name and hard work."

Nessix held up her hand, through hearing the details. Assuming this man was as honest as he was generous, she knew all she needed to. This was far more honorable than either of her last two assignments. "Is there a subtle way for me to get in?"

The man reached his grubby fingers into the folds of his cloak. "This subtle enough?" He dangled a key in front of Nessix.

It beat trying to break in. She quietly accepted the key and clenched it in her hand.

"It is. Forget about me until tomorrow morning. Meet me back here to deliver payment and know that I *will* hunt you down if you don't show."

The man smirked. "I'll be here. Don't you worry."

Coveting the funds more than she loathed the idea of backtracking, Nessix gave her client a generous lead and slipped back into town.

* * * * *

Nessix invited herself into her mark's office well before he was due to show and sat quietly in a corner, distracting herself by debating how to budget the money she was about to earn, when a heavy clunk from the lock announced Elric's arrival. As Nes held her breath, the door opened to reveal a tall, slender man. The torch he carried illuminated the cozy office, and he mounted it in a sconce before lighting a tasteful candelabra which he carried to the desk. Nessix stood, knife in hand as he met her eyes.

She expected him to run or pelt the candelabra at her. She expected a cry for help or possibly an infuriated demand to know why she was there. What she didn't expect was for Elric to heave a weary sigh, shoulders slouching as he set the candles on his desk and took a seat. He looked down at his books for a moment before bringing his eyes up to meet Nes's again.

"I suppose you're here to kill me?" he asked, his soft voice far calmer than made sense for a man in his position.

Nes's tongue snagged on the answer before she pushed past his solemn acceptance. "I am."

He nodded slowly, then went about sorting through the pages on his desk. Nessix lowered her weapon, thrown by his willingness to die.

"Are you going to go through with it or does watching a man balance the books entertain you?"

Nessix adjusted her grip on her knife. "You know what I am."

"Of course I do. I've hired my fair share of hits and figured I'd get one back one of these days. I'm not a skilled fighter, and won't offer you a struggle. If this is my fate"—he shrugged—"I might as well accept it, right?"

"I…" Nessix shook her head, not knowing why she was wasting her time talking to this man.

"May I at least ask *why* I'm being killed?"

Nessix cleared her throat. "I was told you are untrustworthy and have been stealing city funds."

He nodded as he jotted more notes in his book. "I have done that."

Nessix gasped at how freely he admitted the crime, drawing both his attention and slight smile.

"Are you surprised at this untrustworthy man's honesty?" he asked. "I suppose at this hour, there's no use hiding anything. If you'd like to hear me out, I've got a good reason behind my actions."

Nessix flexed her fingers around her dagger, torn. She needed to quit talking to this man. She needed to kill him and get out of here and be done with it. But the same instinct she'd trusted since childhood begged her to hear him out. She took a step closer to the desk, dagger still clutched in her hand. "Go on."

Elric shoved his book aside and bent down to unlock a drawer, pulling out a black folder that he plopped on top of the desk. He opened it and dealt out a collection of signed documents, ledgers, and crudely sketched city maps.

"You know what this is?" He spun the pages he considered most important to face her.

Nessix took another step closer and reached her left hand out to tug one of the maps closer to her. Some of the buildings were marked with red exes, as were several points along roadways. Her mind travelled back to the time when these sorts of symbols meant something to her.

"It looks as though those are positions meant to be attacked." Nessix glanced up.

Elric wore a somber frown. "That's exactly what they are. And it spans far wider than Bellview." He closed the folder. "These attacks are funded by a network of city governments trying to frighten their civilians into becoming reliant on them. There's a pact between twelve cities in this region to lay claim to the land, with plans to rise up in power and reign over the people who made them what they are."

Nessix frowned. If this man was trying to make excuses, he'd been planning them for some time; it seemed an elaborate way to try thwarting an assassin. "What does this have to do with you?"

"There are six of us, *six* individual men across twelve townships in a joint council of no less than sixty members, opposed to this notion. We're building an underground resistance among the civilians. This is where the missing funds are going."

Nessix straightened and pushed the map back onto the table. "You've put the funds back into the hands of the people to stand against their governments."

"*Corrupt* governments," Elric clarified. "I see nothing wrong with government as a whole, but I see a whole lot wrong with the way it may soon be run." He looked up and met Nessix's eyes. "If you're here to kill me, you can do so, but that will leave only five members to fight for the people. I understand your lot doesn't invest much value in life, but considering you did take the time to listen to me, I assume you have more integrity than your peers do."

Nessix tapped her dagger to her lips, knowing in her heart what was right. She'd grumbled in the past that managing the political state of Elidae had been a tedious hassle, but after spending so long wandering Gelthin, she'd begun to realize that Elidae, at least the version she'd known, was a far more stable place than the rest of the world.

"May I ask the price that's on my head?" Elric asked, interrupting Nes's musings.

"Forty silver," she murmured, distracted by contemplating how to best satisfy both herself and her contract.

"Ah, bugger," he whispered. It was too good a price. "Well, I won't fight you. There's no purpose in it. But perhaps you can spread the word of what's been going on."

Nessix stabbed her dagger into the desktop, screaming a curse in the process. She didn't want to kill this man! She didn't want to be the cause of this resistance failing. With such a significant network opposing this movement, they needed all of the allies they could get, and Nessix could easily be one of them.

Elric watched her as calmly now as he'd conducted himself this whole time. "No disrespect, ma'am, but you are the worst assassin I've ever encountered."

She looked up at him through tormented eyes, chest heavy as she tipped on the verge of breaking. Damn, she needed more dream stop… "I have no other way to make a living."

"Then how about you fight for a good cause?" he suggested. "Which of my fine colleagues hired you tonight?"

Nes's honesty locked with that strange sense of honor that tried to demand she was still under contract. She looked to those red exes meant to terrorize citizens, then up to this man, breathing in clarity at last. "A piggish man. Loud. He never gave me his name."

"Ah. That would be Bartram Welford. Yes. I can see how he'd

be the one wanting me dead. His sister and I were once involved. You said he put forty silver on my head?"

Nessix felt her heart flicker in anticipation of what was coming and nodded. "That's right."

"Would you take forty-one to spare me and take him instead?"

She straightened slowly. "Is he one of the ring leaders in these movements?"

"A rather influential one."

Nessix nodded. "I'll need a lock of your hair to lure him out."

Elric nodded and reached for Nes's dagger. "May I?" At her nod, he yanked it free and cut the raven lock himself. He handed both the knife and hair to her.

Nessix returned her dagger to its sheath and clamped his hair in her hand. "Make me a list of these other officials, the ones aiming to control the population."

He chuckled. "I've no doubt you're plenty deadly, but that's a lot of men for one woman to take on."

"Oh, it won't be me," Nessix assured. "I've got some friends in influential places in Zeal"—it was only partly a lie—"and I'm sure they'd love to hear about what's going on out here."

"I like the way you think." Elric pulled out a piece of paper and a nub of charcoal and began to scrawl out names. "Come by here once you're through. I'll have your payment gathered."

"Don't worry about the payment," Nessix said. "I've been promised funds from another source."

Elric provided Nessix with directions to Bartram's house and a list of those she'd report to the Order, and watched her leave. She was a terrible assassin, but she was quite the intriguing sell sword.

* * * * *

Nessix had always considered herself a bright woman, but she'd certainly been testing that with everything that had to do with this assassin business. Damn it, though, if there were civilians in need, justice demanded she do everything she could to help them. In the back of her mind, Kol laughed at her righteous determination, but she silenced him with threats of how she hadn't given up on uncovering Berann's identity.

She arrived at her original client's house sooner than he'd expected, evident by his tipsy state and the commotion from inside when he answered the door. Nessix didn't know the cause of celebration, but by Bartram's flushed face and disapproving frown, she understood she wasn't welcome. Either way, when she crossed her arms, his face sobered in a hurry.

"There a problem?" he slurred.

This would be too easy. "Is there a place we can talk about..." She rolled her eyes to indicate the building she'd just left, the one that still had a vibrant elf balancing—or more likely fudging—the books.

A lopsided smile lifted the man's lips and he backed away, slopping his drink as he waved her inside. "For that, I got any place you wanna talk."

Nessix entered the house, actively watching the halls for witnesses. "I think it's best our business is handled in private."

"Oh..." Bartram winced at the effort of concentrating on her request. "Right. Um. Come on." He turned and gracelessly made his way toward the sound of the unknown celebration, and Nessix grabbed the back of his sleeve.

"It's best I'm not seen."

This, too, processed slowly through the flood of alcohol muddling Bartram's reasoning, but he complied and turned toward the stairs. Nessix followed him quickly, hoping she could sneak out before the partygoers noted his absence.

As they climbed the stairs, his boisterous voice assaulted her ears just as enthusiastically as it had when he'd hired her. "You're earlier than you said you'd be."

"I'm efficient. If you don't trust me, I brought proof."

"Eh?" He turned, nearly toppling down the stairs and Nessix clung with her free hand to the railing. "What've you got?"

She held her other hand forward to reveal the lock of a hair she'd taken from Elric.

"Huh." Bartram lowered his head to peer at the dark hair in her palm. "Guess you did get it done." He turned and continued to clomp up the stairs, and Nessix followed as quietly as she could.

They reached the top and he grumbled as he led her down the hall, testing door knobs as if he didn't know what rooms they went to until his eyes lit up and he opened the door. "Here we are. Gotta get your payment."

Nessix followed Bartram inside a richly furnished—but poorly kept—bedroom as he walked over to a five-drawer chest and opened the fourth one. Holding her breath while he dug around, Nessix dashed forward and leapt onto his back, clapping a hand over his mouth. He tried to yell for help as he stumbled backwards, but before he gained momentum behind his drunken staggering, Nessix slit his throat. He was a large man, too large for her to adequately catch and ease to the ground, and so she let him tumble to the floor. Hoping the sound of the party muffled the brief struggle and noisy deposit of Bartram's corpse, Nessix retrieved the payment she was owed from the drawer and dashed down the stairs.

She made it out the door before anyone called for Bartram, and left the house behind as though she'd never been there. From a window overlooking the house, Elric watched and smiled. Perhaps there was something good in assassins, after all.

* * * * *

Armed with a full purse and a list of names, Nessix left Bellview in the night, unwilling to gamble on Bartram's connections hunting her down. When the sun rose, she broke one rule and made sure to speak to every passerby she encountered to confirm she was still on the correct path. Nobody was able to reliably tell her how far away Zeal was, but they kept her—hopefully—heading that direction. Discouraged with this reliance on an ignorant public and blessed, for once, with wealth, Nessix entered the next town determined to buy a map, fresh provisions, and means to carry them.

She explored the shopping district, pausing at the baker's shop to purchase some day-old rolls, when a homely woman with a shaved head thrust the leather disk she'd discarded after her flight from Midland into her hand.

"You are wanted, Succubus."

Fuming, Nessix stiffly completed her transaction, gathered up her little cloth-wrapped bundle of bread, and allowed this woman's steady glare to pull her away from the vendor. "May I inquire what for?"

"For an audience with the master," the woman said. "If you want to lighten the blow, you'll come with me quietly and willingly."

Nessix growled to herself, wondering what she had to do to keep these people happy, and gave a quick sweep of her hand. "After you."

The woman frowned at Nes's forward tone, but turned to lead the way through the streets. Nessix followed with rigid strides, wishing she could find a way to shed this ridiculous fear of her employers long enough to tell them to leave her alone.

The stony-faced woman brought Nessix to a blacksmith's shop, flicked the soot-stained man a copper, then continued past the forge to a nondescript door in the back. The heat of the smith's fire helped stifle some of Nes's rage and enhanced her dizziness as her guide pulled open the door to reveal a tiny room occupied by a one-eyed man twirling a knife and a woman in glasses holding a red book. Behind Nessix came the whisper of the bald woman's weapons being drawn, and she was shoved inside.

"You have been a busy girl, Succubus," the woman before her said. "Any idea why we called you here today?"

Nessix didn't care, but wouldn't say as much with one assassin at her back and another armed and ready to fight in front of her. Skill and tenacity aside, she didn't like her odds in a three to one skirmish in tight, unfamiliar quarters. "I haven't the faintest."

The woman in glasses kicked a chair to Nessix. "Sit," she ordered as she slammed the book on the table and thumbed through the pages. "It seems as though nobody bothered to tell you our rules or, if they had, you are too dense to follow them."

Nessix laughed bitterly and took the seat, crossing her arms. "I hadn't even been given an accurate job description. What makes you think I was given any guidelines?"

The woman glared at Nessix from above her spectacles and frowned. "Do you think this is a joke?"

Nessix rolled her eyes. "I don't know what to think about this organization anymore."

"Well," the woman snipped, snapping her fingers. The one-eyed man retrieved a pen and inkwell from the shelf beside him and delivered them promptly. "This is your final warning. One more infraction and you're eligible for termination."

Nessix swallowed a seething retort that wouldn't have helped her. "I assume by termination you don't mean simply let go."

"You are safe to assume it means an attempt on your life by one of the guild's choosing. The only escape from that is to execute your executioner."

"And if I succeeded in doing so, would I be punished for that, too?"

The shrewd woman gave her another scowl from above her glasses and Nessix tilted her head back with a groan. What was *wrong* with these people? What was wrong with *her* for putting up with them? A faint whisper in the back of her mind longed for the reliability of Kol's oppression.

"You don't seem to be taking to heart how serious this is," the guild master said, jotting notes in her red book. "We are an assassins guild. That means we are hired to neutralize targets as described by our paying clients."

"Right," Nessix said. "I've known what assassins do all my life. Trust me."

The woman's glare vied to peel the skin from Nessix. "Attempting an unauthorized separation from our employ was bad enough. Arson was worse. But you've engaged in one of the worst offenses one of our order can commit."

Nessix grabbed her urge to rant about how there wasn't much worse than killing for money by the scruff and threw it to the ground. "And what's that?"

"You killed your *client*."

Nessix bristled and would have jumped up to emphasize her case had it not been for the armed assassins in the room. "No... I *changed* clients. The second one paid better." She chose to omit divulging the differences in the two men's characters, fully believing that moral integrity meant nothing to the guild.

291

The woman's eyes narrowed and she straightened her posture. "We do not change clients." She enunciated each word clearly. "It is bad for business."

"What's bad for business is taking the deal that pays less," Nessix countered, rather proud of her command of economics.

"And what will be bad for your longevity is to continue debating a core tenet of our organization. Let it be known, Succubus, that you are hereby on watch. The next act of foul play you engage in could very well be your last. Your fine is thirty silver. Sign to confirm you've received your reprimand, pay what you owe, and get out of my hall."

Nes's fingers itched for her sword and she briefly contemplated whether or not she could overpower these three. She could rush the table and flip it to temporarily immobilize the first two. She could take the bald woman then, if she was quick. She'd attacked a raging inoga—three mortals shouldn't have daunted her. Yet, they did. She needed fewer complications to stay ahead of Kol and reach Zeal. Flinging herself to her feet, Nessix signed the book, slapped her payment on the table, and spun to shove past the assassin at the door.

"It was a pleasure," the shrewd woman called to Nes's back.

Nessix didn't merit the farewell a reply, not even a rude gesture. It wasn't worth her effort.

TWENTY-FIVE

The road north laid before Nessix clear blue skies and an open swath of farmland. Short, squatty homes with thatched roofs dotted the landscape, and cattle grazed peacefully in the fields. It was quiet and idyllic, peaceful and the sort of sight which mocked Nes's dreams of salvation after the roads she'd been forced to travel.

Every pound of her feet jarred awake another reminder of her vulnerability. Kol was after her. If she could trust him the way his influence over her longed to, an army of inoga were, too. The assassins watched her every move, constantly prepared to shove another murder plot at her… or kill her, themselves. Her plan to reach Zeal and put this madness behind her had been needlessly complicated by her want of a map. Logic and experience bluntly told her she had no hope of succeeding, but Nessix refused to acknowledge those doubts, latching on to her stubbornness.

She *had* to reach Zeal, and she would. Because if she didn't, the deaths she'd played a part in these past few weeks would have been wrong. The danger she'd put her akhuerai army in would have been wrong. Her vow to protect Abaeloth would have been wrong.

Her need to survive hinged on matters far greater than her desire to escape fear and pain. She'd been born with a greater purpose, one she used to believe revolved around Elidae. She'd finally begun to let go of that illusion and accept that she was possibly the only woman alive who could unravel the demons' hold on Abaeloth—with Mathias's help.

Thinking of the paladin roiled a pit of anxiety in Nes's stomach, and her old excitement at the thought of reuniting with him shriveled into a groan of dread. There was nothing forcing her to confess to him the evils she'd engaged in of late. Nothing besides his innate ability to draw words—most of them truthful—from her. He'd ask her what happened to her, how she'd managed to escape the demons and evade them for so long, and she'd have to tell him. He was too sharp to not pick up on it. Even if he wasn't, she preferred the notion of honesty with Mathias.

Nessix concentrated on the scuffing of her boots along the road, commanding herself to keep moving past fear and worry and not surrender to the urge to stop and bury her face in her hands or scream out in frustration. Stopping would let the demons get one step closer. Screaming would reveal her location. No, Nessix would keep going. She had to. And Mathias could judge her the way she knew he would.

Maybe he'd praise her for her ingenuity. It was a nice whim her subconscious threw her. Perhaps he'd understand that she was doing the best she could with the only skills she had. She could always attempt to spin it that she'd funded her journey as a bounty hunter. That, at least, had a degree of honor to it.

But that wouldn't change the fact that she couldn't lie to Mathias. Even if she could, he'd extract the truth from that goddess of his, the same goddess who still hadn't answered Nessix when she prayed. Mathias would know exactly what she'd been up to, and his disappointment in her actions would prevent him from being proud of her solitary survival and the grit it took to stay just out of the demons' reach. And Etha herself help Nessix when he learned the name she'd been given…

No, Mathias would scorn the crimes she'd committed, nearly as much as he'd scorn the abomination she'd become due to the demons' vile ways.

The simple answer was to stop running and let Kol catch her, to fall to her knees like she had when he'd first claimed her. At least in the hells, she knew when next she'd eat. She had people who relied on her. If she used her imagination, she had some amount of authority. Returning to Kol would let her escape the horrors she'd brought to the surface and forget her traipse into the evils of the world. Mathias was strong and knew how to make the difficult decisions. If Kol got his way and pushed her that final step to heartlessness, she trusted Mathias would see her to her end. Maybe then, peace would finally find her.

A cloud of birds fluttered up from the ditch, scolding Nessix for her wavering resolve as she passed, and she yelped, scuttling away from their abrupt departure. Had she become so pathetic as to let birds frighten her? Weeks without sufficient amounts of dream stop, she was too fragile and broken to survive a return to the hells; she was screaming over *birds*, for Inwan's sake!

If she let herself get caught, Kol's affection wouldn't protect her from punishment for her disobedience. He'd beat her well for her actions, if only to save face among his peers. His rage would pass and he'd forgive her, and if forgiveness was too generous a word, he'd at least let it go. Nessix didn't fear Kol, but she was terrified of the demons above him. She was terrified of the masses beneath him who would be encouraged to make sure she never thought of freedom again, who would force her to understand that she belonged to the hells. Kol had fought such assaults off her in the past, but not even his strength and experience or the respect he demanded from his ranks would be able to protect her from the punishment she'd earned.

Tears streamed down Nes's cheeks, the instinctual side of her wanting to jump in the ditch the birds had vacated and try to bury herself in hopes that Mathias found her. She needed safety. She couldn't go back. She *couldn't*. The tortured souls of the akhuerai depended on her. A trembling hand smudged her tears across her cheeks and she gave a firm shake of her head. That was why she was still going. Gritting her teeth, Nessix redoubled her efforts north.

* * * * *

Kol had paced a solid rut in the ground since the report of Nessix's last sighting reached him. Fists clenched at his sides, the limited amount of grace he'd scrounged up over the past few weeks of Annin's patience seeped away as rapidly as rain on a drought-parched field. His steady trudge irritated the oraku, pushing him closer to his own lapse of sanity. Annin had used every tactic he had in his arsenal and miraculously invented a few on the fly to patch up Kol to functionality. Seeing his hard work unravel disgusted him.

"Quit your pacing," Annin snapped, "or I will force you to sit."

Kol scoffed as he spun to face his friend, orange eyes blazing. "I'd *love* to sit down, but I'm a little preoccupied."

"And you think I'm not? I realize you're convinced that you're the only one invested in this search, but you're not."

Those furious eyes narrowed. "All you care about is whether or not your experiment is successful. If Talier fails, you get to make your notes and try again. I'm the one who will lose Nessix."

Annin rubbed his temple and closed his eyes. "How many days has it been since you slept?"

"That is completely irrelevant."

Annin opened his eyes again. "You're beginning to lose yourself again."

"I haven't lost myself," Kol muttered. "I've lost—"

"Shut up," Annin groaned. "You haven't lost anything. Talier's on her scent, and as soon as you manage to pull yourself together again, we can get in position to relieve him when he brings her to us."

Those words triggered a brief glimpse of clarity for Kol. He'd simply succumbed to impatience; Annin's plans always ended up successful, one way or another.

Nessix had proven difficult to catch, unwilling to risk her freedom for rest. She'd outsmarted and outpaced an army led by inoga, as well as Kol's mercenary search parties. Skill had landed one of those parties in Midland, and luck had allowed one of that squad to survive and quietly track her, despite rumors that Mathias Sagewind had actively joined the playing field. That demon deserved a promotion.

No matter how long Kol paced, there was nothing else he could do other than wait. He blustered a great gust of a sigh and sat beside Annin at last, flattening his hands against his face. So many of his perfect plans had gone awry at the last second; he couldn't shake the fear that this one would, too.

"You really have that much faith in this human?" Kol asked with a miserable groan.

Annin flushed, thankful Kol's frustration hid his eyes. "I've got faith in Nessix."

Kol's hands dropped from his face, his expression wiped clean by shock. Neither demon spoke for several heartbeats and Kol looked to his friend for confirmation. "*You*?" he asked. "*You* have faith in Nessix?"

Annin cleared his throat, having composed himself in those moments of silence. "I do."

Kol's brows rippled above confused eyes. "When did this happen?"

"Nessix hates us," Annin said, relief and confidence returning as he explained himself. "Not just you and me, but demons as a whole. Talier's useless in all accounts except for the senses which we gave him. Lorrin's rangers will stage their attack on him, and Nessix will rescue him off her blasted principles. His fear won't let her leave him by himself on the road, and she won't let him stay behind in any town she passes through because he can lead her to Zeal. Doubt Talier, doubt *me* all you'd like. But can you look me in the eye and tell me you doubt Nessix?"

Perhaps if he'd been thinking unhindered by this crushing anxiety, Kol would have thought Annin was manipulating him. Instead, the oraku's words pulled at his fondest memories of Nessix—her fearlessness, her instinct to care about him the way he cared about her...

Kol had personally selected Nessix for the role she'd filled because he had faith in her. He'd irreparably bound himself to her, unwittingly opened her mind to dangerous truths he had to trust she'd protect for him because of this faith. He didn't know why she'd run from him, but she had to have had a reason; it wouldn't have been a decision she'd made lightly.

"No," Kol murmured. "I can't."

"Very good," Annin said. "Now, convince yourself to believe it and stop your pathetic fretting. She'll be back in your hands in a week at the most."

Kol leaned back, allowing Annin's reassurance to soak through him and warm the chills of worry and doubt. *Soon, little one...*

* * * * *

Weary from nights spent weeping in the dark, Talier's hands tingled with numbness, his legs moving from muscle memory alone as he tracked Nessix's scent. He did his best to avoid thinking about the pair of demon rangers following him and what punishments awaited his inevitable failure, but the causal jokes and wicked laughter shared in that eerie language of theirs prevented him from forgetting they were there. And so, Talier concentrated on following where Nessix led him, his resentment for her growing with each dreary step.

It would have been easier to locate her if the demons behind him would shut up so he could benefit from his ears; the faintness of Nessix's scent suggested she was running, and he'd have appreciated the added insight. The breeze changed direction, slamming the trail to her location against Talier's face and, despite his fear of the creatures behind him, he stopped abruptly.

The familiar aspects of this strange woman were still there—strength, determination, ferocity—and he recognized her without a doubt from that swatch of canvas Annin had given him. Close to encountering Nessix for the first time, though, Talier now picked up the relatable strains of terror and helplessness, a desperation to survive before the whispered advice of giving up turned into an overwhelming scream. Nessix, too, was afraid of the demons. Unfortunately for her, Talier's fear of them was all he had.

"You find her?" the taller demon asked.

Talier gulped down a sickening cocktail of emotions warring between terror and relief. Afraid of his voice failing him, he nodded.

"Then let's get on with it," the demon ordered.

There wasn't much about this ordeal that Talier was particularly confident about, but this aspect of Kol's grand scheme had bothered him the most. Marcoux was the bold one. He'd have charged down the road after the scent of a crying woman to capture her for the demons without a second thought. He'd effortlessly charm her into accompanying him. Awkward, incompetent Talier was so scared of his captors he could hardly move to even confront her. Something sharp prodded the small of Talier's back, motivating him past his self-defeating fear.

"You going to stick with the plan, or do we have to force you to run?"

Talier didn't need more motivation; he was quite thoroughly frightened without needing to act. Locking on to Nessix's scent, he darted down the road, too panicked to entertain the idea of trying to escape his captors now. The pair of demons gave chase immediately, spurring Talier's flight instincts even more. By the time an armored woman—much shorter than Talier had imagined she'd be—came into view, his panting and racing heart were genuine.

"Help!" he shouted, gasping to replenish his breath. "I'm begging— Help!"

The woman spun, sword drawn before she'd fully turned around, and Talier staggered in shock. He'd been told Nessix was a general and the scent he'd committed to memory had conveyed to him several aspects to support that claim. Facing her now as he ran from these two demons confirmed none of the stories Kol had told him had been exaggerated.

Her eyes were red and cheeks flushed, but discipline set her brows and accentuated her jawline. She held herself with a sense of relaxation, treating a surprise assault as casually as a blacksmith would light his forge. Combat was routine to Nessix, a set variable of her job. Talier didn't belong here! Overwhelmed, fearing the demons on his heels, fearing the woman before him, and fearing for Marcoux, Talier screamed.

Exhaustion struck him between the eyes. Fighting had failed

him. Fleeing had failed him. With few options left, Talier's knees buckled and he crashed to the ground. This was where it would end. The demon rangers were close enough to Nessix now that they'd be able to grab her. Talier had served his purpose and, as Kol frequently reminded him, he was expendable. Crying out another plea for help, not knowing who would listen, Talier curled into a useless lump on the road.

Booted feet rushed up from behind him and Talier pinched his eyes shut, waiting for the pierce of a blade to end his life. Then, a ferocious growl raced from in front of him, and he opened his eyes as a cloud of dirt rose up from the road as Nessix charged past him. Her scent had changed, now enhanced with hatred and a flood of self-assurance.

There was a muffled grunt and a thud, followed by the scurry of limbs trying to organize themselves beside Talier. A second grunt, this one more guttural, came from whoever had been dropped to the ground, and Talier pinched his eyes closed once again, too afraid to watch his death close in on him.

The shorter of the two demons barked a brisk command and a stern, feminine voice answered in kind. Talier peeked open one eye and watched Nessix dash forward to engage the demon. She was supposed to be on the run from these beasts. Talier had been told she'd do everything she could to distance herself from them. Instead, he lay breathless as she used the advantage of her sword's length to run her opponent through with the grace and ease of a dancer. In that moment, Talier's heart stopped.

Nessix was brave and efficient. She'd come to his aid from nothing but his vague cry for help, and she'd freed him from the demons who had dragged him this far in a frantic scuffle that couldn't have lasted longer than a minute. For the first time since Kol and Annin had shown up to ruin his life, Talier felt a brief surge of hope. And then, he looked to his side where the taller demon bled out in the road and panic flooded him once more.

The plan he'd been ordered to follow included the two rangers slipping away from the scene to report back to Kol. Nessix had effortlessly foiled those intentions and all of a sudden, Kol's reluctance to confront her himself made sense. Talier was, allegedly, safe from this woman as long as she didn't figure out who he worked for, but she didn't waste time when demons were nearby. Plan disrupted in a way Talier couldn't fix, Marcoux's fate—and his own—suddenly became less clear, and he hated this strange woman all over again.

He didn't have long to process this resurgence of emotions, as Nessix turned to face him. She sniffed and rubbed her nose with the back of her hand, glancing over his prone form with a pitying, but compassionate, eye. "How many others are there?"

Talier's words snagged in his dry throat. "It was just the... the two."

Nessix gave a short nod and glanced around their surroundings; there was no viable tree cover to attempt hiding the bodies. She knelt down and wiped her blade clean on her most recent victim's pants. "I know demons don't have a problem looking for trouble, but what got them chasing you?"

This was the part Kol hadn't told him how to handle, the part Marcoux would have charmed his way through. Talier gulped and attempted to tuck his fear away with his brother. "I might have been the one looking for them."

Nessix stood and sheathed her blade, brows furrowed. "What in Inwan's name for?"

Talier opened his mouth, shock of Nessix's effortless brutality and distress over what Kol would make of his failure muddying his thoughts. As terrified of Nessix as he was of the demons, honesty would serve Talier better than lies he'd never excelled at delivering. Trembling arms pushed him to a seated position. "They... they attacked my brother. A while back."

Distinct lines of sorrow claimed the strictness of Nessix's brows and she lowered her gaze. "I'm sorry," she murmured, heart in her voice as only a survivor of the demons could express. "Did they kill him?"

Talier blanched at the question. It was nearly all he'd thought about since waking up at Kol's feet. He'd been warned that Nessix was keenly in tune with how the demons operated and to be careful how much information he disclosed to her, and so he nodded. "Yeah. They did."

A brief frown pressed across Nessix's lips, but she otherwise retained her regret. "That was more of a blessing than you know. I suspect he was luckier than you were."

Talier gasped at Nes's cold logic, but was too caught up on what her words implied. If Marcoux was better off dead, was Talier doing him a disservice in trying to placate the demons to keep him alive? His concerns flit from his mind as Nessix strode up to him and extended her hand to help him to his feet. He hadn't yet found the nerve to accept it.

"Since you *did* survive, let's get you to civilization. There's no way those two were out here alone. We need to get moving."

Despite her recent display of competent violence, Nessix's expression held a degree of warmth that defied the dead bodies on the road. This hadn't been part of what Talier had agreed to. He wasn't supposed to be truly alone with this woman. Without his guards, there was nobody to take word back to Kol that he'd successfully reached her, and without that report, it wouldn't be unreasonable for the alar to assume he'd failed. Palms sweating, Talier reached forward and let Nessix pull him to his feet.

Nessix was shorter than Talier had expected, barely reaching his shoulder, and her effectiveness chilled him all over again. Unarmed, inexperienced, and grossly underqualified for the assignment he'd been given, he rubbed his palms on the legs of his pants and waited to see what Nessix would offer next.

"Come on. We need to get you to the next town, preferably before dark."

A normal woman would have given a stranger a moment to decide for himself what he wanted to do, but Nessix snagged Talier's left bicep and pulled him along as she continued north down the road. She didn't spare her victims another glance, far more content to leave them behind than Talier was, and he bumbled along beside her.

"I um… the nearest city is that way." He raised a shaky arm to point behind them, toward Bellview.

Nessix's eyes darkened just enough to make Talier regret his suggestion and her fingers bit into his flesh. "I'm not heading that way."

Talier didn't bother with an attempt to pull his arm away, though he did reach his free hand up to wipe at the sweat running down his neck. "Greenville's still fifteen miles ahead," he said, voice trembling. "We won't make it before nightfall."

Nessix jarred to a stop, throwing her shoulders back with a disbelieving shake of her head. She looked at Talier, eyes alight with hope. "How do you know that?"

"I'm a messenger by trade. Navigating is a big part of what I do."

Those blue eyes he'd never trust widened as a relieved gust of breath left Nessix. "Do you know how to reach Zeal?"

Talier swallowed the fresh wave of nausea her question brought with it. "I do."

Nessix released her grip on his arm and took a step back to look him over. Her smile erased the edge of danger from her face, nearly negating the fear and loathing that warred inside of Talier. She finished her appraisal with a satisfied hum.

"I lost my map in a skirmish. In exchange for protection, would you guide me the rest of the way to Zeal?"

After how thoroughly he'd vilified Nessix, Talier hadn't expected such a cordial request.

Gain her trust, lead her toward the northeast coast, far from Zeal's eyes, and we'll relieve you there when we can organize a proper ambush for her.

One more look at her eager eyes, and Talier realized he might be able to pull this off, after all. She'd admitted to being lost without a map. If he led her far enough to the east that she was spotted by one of Kol's scouts… Talier nodded and delivered a weak smile.

"I could do that. There's no place safer from demons in all of Abaeloth, is there?"

Nessix's lips eased into an elegant smile, an attractive expression she instantly contradicted with a hearty slap on Talier's shoulder. "You're a good man…" She trailed off, waiting for him to provide his name.

"Talier," he said, awkwardly extending his hand. "Talier Dalton."

Nessix accepted the gesture with a firmness unusual to the

women Talier had known. "You can call me—" She cut herself off, a flicker of discontent sweeping across her face as she fumbled over what name to give him. Back on the road to Zeal, she was ready to leave Succubus behind. "You know what? You can call me Nessix."

Talier's initial impulse was to ask her what she'd been about to say, but his mental fortitude was depleted. Desperation had forced him to trust Kol and Annin, and he'd eventually develop the same for Nessix. Just as lost and alone as the woman who thought she'd found a troop to watch over at last, Talier accepted Nessix's lead as they raced the sunset to Greenville.

TWENTY-SIX

There were many things Mathias should have done before leaving Zeal. He should have informed the Council of the attacks in the south. He should have made good on his promise to personally request aid for Brookhaven's rebuilding. At the very least, he should have told Julianna what he was up to and see if she'd acquired any additional insight that might help him. Instead, Mathias had simply requested proper boarding arrangements for Khin and asked one of the young priestesses to relay to Julianna that the girl was now under her care. He'd wasted too much time as it was, and he'd let nothing else slow him in his search for Nessix. Slipping away without saying goodbye to Khin and without Julianna even realizing he'd returned, Mathias took his pegasus, Ceraphlaks, out of Zeal, unhindered in his search for the first time.

Knowing where Nes started her quest and that Zeal was her destination, Mathias returned to the south and followed the most logical road north. The course of his investigation uncovered a patchy trail of destruction, evidence that the inoga were still on the hunt, but they'd left the majority of cities untouched, implying they had some sort of method to their search. While Mathias was grateful for the towns spared the inoga's brutality, his skin crawled over what it meant that they were using such discipline. Doing his best to tune out the implications of this unusual pattern, Mathias landed Ceraphlaks outside the city of Bessemar to sniff out any reports that might lead to Nes's trail.

Means of execution and humiliation—both showing signs of rust and neglect—openly advertised the guards' base of operation in the otherwise peaceful town. With little more than a glance at the list of bounties posted out front, Mathias walked into the post.

A group of four bored guards sat around a tiny table, playing a game of cards. None of them looked up as Mathias entered, though he did catch brief glances his direction. He waited for the current hand to wrap up, but as the guards reached to draw fresh cards, Mathias cleared his throat.

The oldest of the guards heaved an irritated sigh and slapped his hand face down on the table before dragging his chair around to face Mathias. "Can I help you, knight?"

Ah. So that's what it was. Men of the Order seldom stopped by local agencies unless there were problems. "Not looking for trouble, and not bringing any with me. I simply want to know if you've seen someone."

"I've seen a lot of people." The guard pulled his chair back around. "Goes with the job." He picked up his cards and gestured for the game to resume.

"I'm looking for a woman of elvish descent. Dark hair and blue eyes. She'd be small, short, about this tall." Mathias held his hand up around shoulder height to demonstrate. One of the younger guards dropped his cards, no effort made to hide their faces, and looked up at his comrades, cheeks paling. Mathias cocked his head and pressed further. "If she was armed, it would likely be well, and she'd be stubborn if she didn't get what she wanted."

"Etha's tits…" a third guard groaned, throwing his cards down, as well. He slumped in his chair. "Is she a fugitive of the Order? She is, isn't she…?"

Mathias was too shocked, too thrilled, to laugh. After all of his searching, he had a solid lead, more than just whispers from the gods and secondary accounts from bitter connections.

"Well?" the older guard asked, his voice tight as he weighed what it might mean if she had been. "Is she or isn't she?"

Mathias shook his head to jar his mind back to functioning. "Not a fugitive, at least as far as I know. Just a girl in need of some help, one I've been trying to reach."

The third guard snorted. "That one doesn't need any help." He sent a hasty glance at Mathias, flushed, and grabbed his cards again, shoulders hunched close around his neck. "No offense, of course."

Mathias glanced back at the door, wondering if he should have stopped to read the bounties. "She didn't… she didn't cause any trouble here, did she?"

The older guard pushed himself from the table, forfeiting his hand. "Harmed nothing more than our pride. Took out a roadside predator we'd been hunting for months. Opened the roads north all by herself." His cheeks paled beneath his poorly maintained stubble. "*What* could be after her that she'd need the help of the Order?"

Rumors had to be spreading about the demons' attacks, and it was part of Mathias's duty to ensure military forces were aware of such dangers. Too often, these warnings resulted in panic rather than preparation, and Mathias still had to extract every last detail these men had of Nessix. Besides, the existing path of the inoga's destruction suggested they'd already passed Bessemar and had chosen to leave her standing. They might remain untouched. "It's best you don't worry about that yet. Is there anything else you can tell me about her? Did she tell you where she was heading?"

"She refused to give us a name, something about not putting down roots, and said she was on an urgent assignment to deliver a message to Zeal."

That relieved chuckle left Mathias now. He should never have doubted that Nessix was trying to do the right thing. If this guard reported accurately and Mathias's intuition served correct, she was carrying something Zeal needed badly. Answers. Nessix knew what the demons had planned, and she must have some idea of how to stop it.

Unable to mask his smile, heart skipping in relief, Mathias lowered his head in gratitude. "Thank you for the information, gentlemen."

The older guard grunted and turned back to his game, unwilling to take the chance of drawing any more of Mathias's interest. Around the table, the other three guards had settled into a tense silence. Taking their reactions as his cue to leave, Mathias departed from the station, a refreshing anxiety driving him back onto the road. He walked away from the gates to avoid the commotion that would come from summoning Ceraphlaks in the busy streets and was soon joined by the warmth of Etha's presence. A quick glance at her youthful face suggested she was perturbed, but not in a distressed manner.

"My *tits*?" she seethed, arms crossing tightly across her insubstantial chest. "Is that the sort of disrespect toward my name you find acceptable these days?"

Mathias smirked at her lighthearted ire, embracing the concept of jokes and laughter once again. "It was, in fact, unacceptable, Mother. But if I'd have smote them for their blasphemy, I'd have missed their report."

Etha gave an offended snort but slipped her hand into Mathias's and squeezed it to blunt her message. "Well then, I've got one up on you."

A sharp gasp nearly stopped Mathias's progress and he pulled his hand free to turn and walk backwards to assess Etha's silent tells. "One up on me? How so?"

"Zenos had sent Nessix from Seaton with his seal of warding. None of us may be able to track her soul, but a god can locate his artifacts if they're activated."

Mathias did stop now, reaching forward to stop Etha before she ran into him. "Zenos's seal... That means Nes found trouble."

"Ah, but his record showed that five demons entered Midland and only one escaped. The seal's song departed from town heading west. Which means..."

"Which means she might still be ahead of them." There was still no end to Mathias's uncertainties, but his hope was gaining ground rapidly now. Gripping Etha's hands, he dropped to a knee and kissed her fingertips. "Thank you, Mother," he whispered.

She smiled down at him, basking in the much-missed radiance of his happiness. "Remember this the next time some dirty men talk about my breasts and we'll call it even."

Pummeled by a gust of relief, Mathias bowed his head to conceal his grin. "Of course, Mother."

A melodic giggle danced on the air and Etha bent forward to kiss the top of her champion's head. "Now go get on her trail," she said. "We're so close!"

Etha's divine presence whisked away, replaced by Ceraphlaks's ready snort and steady hoofbeats. Recharged and confident, Mathias stood and mounted. Paladin and pegasus shot into the sky, bound for Midland.

* * * * *

Julianna had squirreled herself away in her study the moment her priestess had delivered Mathias's message. She'd initially wanted to accuse the young woman of lying to her, except for the fact that none of her priestesses would dare disgrace Etha's name in such a way. Not to mention that the entire situation reeked of Mathias's impulsiveness. Grace compromised by irritation, Julianna had reassigned morning prayers to one of her senior aides so she could brood in private. It wasn't the fault of any of her students that Mathias could put her in such a foul mood so fast.

The timid knock on her door would have slipped past Julianna unnoticed had she not been expecting it. Still stewing about in her ire, it took the High Priestess another pair of long, calming breaths to locate a warm smile and look up to greet Khin.

The young woman stood with her shoulders hunched forward and her gaze directed toward the floor, her flushed cheeks betraying her confusion and hurt. Julianna was far better equipped to manage such regret than her brother was, but that didn't make her any more pleased to accept the burden.

"You asked for me?" Khin mumbled the words, weary and timid in light of all of her recent discoveries.

Julianna's expression softened and she shoved her irritation with Mathias aside. No use adding that to Khin's troubles. "Yes, my dear. Please come in and have a seat."

Khin hesitated a moment longer, lips creased as she held her thoughts to herself, and then entered the High Priestess's study. It took Julianna gently patting the seat of the chair beside her to coax Khin to sit, and even then, the girl perched on the very edge, as though preparing to bolt. Julianna had some fierce words waiting for Mathias once he returned…

"I've been briefed on the current situation, and you have my greatest sympathy and full support in whatever way you need it," Julianna said.

Khin glanced up, meeting Julianna's eyes for the first time. "So you'll help me track down the monsters who killed my family?"

The ferocity in the timid girl's voice stunned Julianna. Perhaps Mathias had made the best decision, after all. "I'm afraid my duties keep me here in the security of the Citadel, a security you're now granted, too."

Khin shook her head and let her gaze fall. "I don't want security."

Julianna cocked her head, feeling out the gentle wisps of Khin's emotions, watching the way her threads pulsed with fear. It had been lifetimes ago since Julianna had last felt such pain herself, but she hadn't forgotten its sting. "Of course you want security. It's why you were so determined to stay with Mathias, wasn't it?"

Khin hunched her shoulders tighter to keep them from trembling. She hated that she had to depend on someone else for what should have been such a basic need. What the past year had taught her, however, was that it didn't matter what she wanted; her hand had been dealt, unfair as it was, and the sooner she accepted it, the sooner she could quit feeling sorry for herself. "I wish he'd have never saved me in the first place."

That was one response Julianna hadn't been prepared for, and her brow wrinkled. "If he wouldn't have taken you from Seaton, there's a very good chance you'd have been killed."

A shamed flush washed over Khin's cheeks, and the tremble pushed past her defenses at last. "But then I'd have never had to know… I wouldn't have seen…" Tears pooled in her eyes and she looked up at Julianna to silently plea for a solution that didn't exist. "Why did he have to make me *hope*?"

Internally, Julianna mourned for this little girl, despite her lingering frustration with her brother. On an academic level, she understood and agreed with the actions Mathias had taken, and for a moment, she regretted his talent for rubbing off on people. "If Mathias could have delivered on that hope, he would have without hesitation."

Khin shook her head and sniffled back her tears as bitterness seeped into her mind. "There was nothing stopping him from letting me go with him. I could have found my hope and peace out there."

Julianna pursed her lips to hold back the harsher reprimand that tried to come out. Even the youngest of the priestesses were well versed in the current political and wartime situations, and it was hard for her to remember that some people lived lives outside this delicate drama. Perhaps the time to get back to her humanitarian roots was coming due. Might as well practice on a captive audience.

"Mathias must have told you *why* he refused to take you with him?"

Khin scoffed and looked pointedly away. "He said I'd be a liability. After he trained me himself, he said I would only distract him."

Centuries fielding Abaeloth's trials had taken the innocent charm of such lofty claims from Julianna, and she smiled sadly. "You don't want to fight in the coming war."

"But I do!"

That smile shrank with the remorse reality had faithfully taught Julianna. "You're not a warrior, Khin. You're a survivor."

The girl snorted and slouched back in her chair, throwing her peevish glare aside. "What good is *that*?"

Julianna leaned forward. "The survivor's the one who has to build the tomorrow which the warrior gave his life for. It is every bit as heroic and admirable as taking up arms."

Khin opened her mouth to respond, but a quick flash of tears forced her into silence.

"The Council and Mathias's quest have already consumed too much time," Julianna explained gently as it appeared Khin couldn't continue her debate. "He's several steps behind where he should be, and needed to dash off to gain ground faster than even our most seasoned knights could handle."

Khin picked at her cuticles, balling up her courage for the one question she'd had floating in the back of her mind from the start. "He kept mentioning his quest, and now you have, too." Her timid eyes flashed up to the ancient wisdom in Julianna's and darted away before she faltered. "What's so important about it that he had to abandon me?"

Compassion eased Julianna's shoulders and she sighed, still sorting through the logistics of this same question. "There are others who need him. Yes, even more urgently than you do."

The answer didn't sit well with Khin as her troubles and stubbornness, that pinch of selfishness Mathias's kindness had coaxed to life, stormed about. She needed Mathias! He was *her* hero! "And why do *those* people get to be helped? Why aren't *they* liabilities?"

"Oh, child. The woman he's after is a great liability, for Mathias and Abaeloth both. Please do not think he's enjoying the quest he's on."

A woman? Jealously spun through Khin's core, dredging up a feeling she hadn't identified before. "Then what makes *her* so special?"

Julianna's frown returned, both from Khin's pettiness and the same judgement she'd made of Nessix. She trusted Mathias but continued to struggle with accepting the chaos that his lover from the past had brought about. One second looking at Khin's belligerent eyes confirmed that she was just as eager to hold this woman accountable for these crimes, and Julianna still clung to the unlikely hope that Nessix harbored more answers than problems. Encouraging Khin to proceed into the void she stared down would only complicate an already dire situation.

"If Mathias can find her before the demons do, we stand a very good chance at stopping the demons' movements before they start a war."

A gloomy cloud of frustration hung around Khin as she curled her lip. "One woman could stop a war?"

Julianna tilted her head from side to side as she balanced the facts of Mathias's reports against his biased opinions of Nessix's worth. "With Mathias's protection and the Order's backing, that's our hope. That's why it's imperative that nothing slows Mathias down."

Guilt should have humbled Khin, scolding her for how much of Mathias's time she'd already taken, how each day he'd spent babysitting her put him one more day behind in this search that even Julianna felt was important. But jealously squashed any sense of maturity. If it wasn't for this woman—a woman who had to be stronger and smarter than Khin to be considered so valuable—Mathias wouldn't have had to rush off. He could have trained her better, taught her how to safely face her foes. He could have guided her through combat and vengeance and, at least in this terrible moment, Khin would get to remember what hope actually felt like. She didn't know anything about this woman besides the fact that Mathias wanted her, and for that, Khin loathed her. She did her best to swallow this emotion, not yet willing to risk tarnishing Julianna's impression of her or losing what favor she might gain from the High Priestess.

"Then forgive me for getting in his way." Khin's words were snipped and did nothing to convey her sincerity.

Julianna waited a moment for Khin to elaborate or amend her tone, wary of the confusion and determination brewing in that young heart. Nothing else came as Khin stewed over her personal misery and misfortune, and Julianna hid her concern behind a practiced, patient smile.

"Mathias is a problem solver. We should trust that he'll see this through."

Khin nodded gloomily, and stood. "Thank you for talking to me, High Priestess. I'll take what we discussed to heart."

Julianna watched Khin keenly, easily seeing what matters had been settled, as well as those which had not. "If you have any other concerns, do not hesitate to seek one of my priestesses."

The girl gave an awkward curtsey and saw herself out, trailing a hand along the cool marble wall as she moped through the halls to the chamber she'd been assigned. She wanted to be more than a survivor, yet every time she'd tried to find a solution to her problems, her efforts made matters worse. With her record, maybe Mathias had done Abaeloth a favor. She didn't even know how to fix her own life; what did she think she'd be able to do in a war?

Khin had given up on praying to any of the gods the morning she woke up to find out that the man she'd gone home with wasn't a wealthy suitor, but that hadn't stopped her from casting devastated screams toward the divine realm. Most gods didn't bother to listen for mortals who didn't directly plead to them, but Ceredulus, god of the undead, always listened to the cries of the most desperate souls. And this one, he was thrilled to discover, was tied closely to Mathias Sagewind.

As the girl fumbled her way into her room and flopped on her bed to moan her frustrations into a pillow, Ceredulus slipped inside her mind, as uninvited as every other man in her past, and soothed her to sleep.

Content for the first time in centuries, Ceredulus left the pliable girl sleeping soundly in her bed and reached out to the loyal mind of the most patient and devout servant he'd left planted outside his prison of the Veil. When Ceredulus and his champion were through with Khin, Mathias would have no choice but to grant the god his freedom.

TWENTY-SEVEN

It had been too long since Nessix had been able to enjoy company. Talier wasn't an ideal troop in the conventional sense, but the akhuerai hadn't been, either. He was just as timid as those broken men and women, and perhaps that was what made Nessix comfortable giving him her name and sharing with him the mundane aspects of her past. He led her more toward the east than she thought made sense, but she'd recruited Talier to be her guide and trusted he was putting them on the fastest route to Zeal.

Be it by luck or their proximity to the holy city, the first two towns they passed through were clear of guild presence, sparing Nessix from explaining her occupation to her new companion, but paying for supplies and shelter for two—as Talier had no money—quickly emptied her coin purse. As with every inconvenience that had cropped up during the four days since they'd met, Talier took over the role of fretting over this problem, and Nessix grudgingly told him she'd resolve it, refusing to divulge how she planned to go about doing so.

The next day, the pair reached the city of Fulton, and the emblem of linked triangles burned into the bark of a young oak tree half a mile before the gates promised Nessix she'd be able to find work here. Looking forward to whatever assignment she'd be given even less than usual—Talier had proven himself to be a reactive companion—Nessix stopped just past the tree, drew the few coins she could spare from her pouch, and pressed them into Talier's hand.

"Go to the tavern and get yourself something to eat. Wait for me there."

Talier looked from the coins to Nessix, sweat beading on the back of his neck. "I can't let you go," he blurted before Kol's warning of hiding his involvement with the demons echoed in his mind.

Fortunately, Nessix laughed off his concern, the hint of a smirk lifting her lips. "You've seen me fight. I can take care of myself, you know."

He flushed and pocketed the coins. "I... um, yeah. I guess you're right."

Nessix, oblivious to Talier's mission and the skills he'd been given to achieve it, slapped him heartily on the shoulder. "And you'll be fine, too," she added, misreading his reluctance as more of the same nervous predisposition he'd displayed over the past few days. "Go on ahead. I shouldn't be long."

Trapped between his nagging fear of Nessix slipping away and what she'd do to him if he pushed her to suspicion, Talier glanced toward the east where Kol and Annin were supposed to be waiting for him, and nodded slowly. "Should I get you something while I wait?"

A touch of that humored confidence flit from Nes's grasp. She wouldn't be able to afford a second meal until after she got paid, and even then, she didn't favor the idea of jeopardizing Talier's safety by dining with him in a city with a blatant assassin presence. "I'll eat when my business here is through."

Talier's head bobbled uncertainly and he lingered a few moments longer before cramming his hands in his pockets and trudging toward the gates. Nessix busied herself by accounting for her weapons and mustering her patience to deal with whoever was sent to deliver her assignment. When she was confident Talier had cleared the gates, she stepped up behind an aged gentleman leading a content little burro hitched to a produce cart, and entered the city.

Thriving with commerce and the comforting aura of hard

work, Fulton would have been the sort of town Nessix enjoyed, if not for the fact that she'd explored up and down the main thoroughfare and no eyes had approached her yet. She scanned the crowd of townsfolk going about their business, no better at identifying who her hidden messenger might be than ever. A ball of nerves tumbled in her gut; with Talier in tow, she needed work, even if it came with the risk of catching that final reprimand they'd threatened her with. Gritting her teeth, Nessix spun on a heel and headed toward the first alley she'd passed on her way in. She'd find these bastards herself.

That had been an easy declaration for her confidence and frustration to make, but executing it was much more complicated. The alley was narrow, clearing her petite shoulders by little more than a hand on either side. Refuse and debris littered the ground and Nessix stopped as someone emptied a chamber pot from a second story window twenty feet in front of her. She hadn't passed a doorway yet, and a quick appraisal overhead unveiled a solid line of windows waiting to drop waste on her.

Pulling the hilt of her sheathed sword more upright to avoid catching the blade in the tight confines, Nessix turned around to leave the alley and found the silhouette of a sturdy man waiting near the main street. At least she already had a hand on her weapon. Trusting her skill and her armor, Nessix didn't hesitate as she strode ahead. Four strides later, the man's arms dropped to his sides and he approached. Adrenaline pooled in Nes's core, ready to draw upon, and she marched forward confidently, forced to stop as the man blocked her ability to squeeze past him.

She met his hard eyes in acceptance of the challenge he hadn't yet declared. "Pardon me."

The man loomed over her, reeking of smoke, steady gaze bearing down in an obvious attempt to intimidate her. "Are you here alone?"

Nes's heart rate kicked up, tough she'd yet to determine if it was due to fear or anticipation. If she had her way, she wouldn't have to find out. Swallowing the tick of apprehension, she squared her shoulders and met this man on his terms. "You're here, so I suppose I'm not."

His eyes narrowed, peeling at Nes's desire to appear strong. "Did you come to town alone, Succubus?"

The greater fear of needing to engage this brute in these tight quarters seeped from Nessix on a slow breath, but was immediately replaced by a sensation she hadn't experienced since she'd slipped free from Kol's grasp. Nobody affiliated with the guild had asked her about companions in the past, which meant they knew Talier was traveling with her. The fear Nessix had carried since the first day of her flight toward Zeal had come true; her association with an innocent had endangered him, and she didn't know if she'd be able to talk her way out of it—or get to him in time to keep him safe.

"That old man with the produce cart?" She wrinkled her nose in an attempt to mask her nerves. "Just because we passed through the gates at the same time doesn't mean we're travelling together. Was I supposed to kill him for his audacity of heading to the market at the same time as me?"

The man raised his chin, looking down at Nessix with a dark keenness, as though aware she was lying to him, but unable to prove it. "You weren't acting as a bodyguard for free food?"

Nessix cocked her head. She'd gone into this bluff expecting it to fail, but would gladly play off this assassin's questions. "I've learned my lesson about honest work. Do you have an assignment for me, or are you just wasting my time?"

The man scoffed and awkwardly backed out of the alleyway. Nessix followed him, mind rapidly churning through how to feign polite compliance so she could get her eyes on Talier—hopefully alive and well—as fast as possible. Her guide didn't make anything of how eagerly she followed as he led her through town, and her heart rate climbed even higher as it became clear that he was taking her to the very place she'd sent her clueless companion.

Each stride Nessix took awakened more of her anxiety. She wanted so badly to redeem herself from this twisted path she'd fallen down, and protecting Talier had been her foolish first step in trying to do that. She'd journeyed this entire time avoiding making connections with innocent passersby to protect them from being targeted by the demons. Now, she'd pulled Talier into the assassins' sights, subjecting him to them and the demons both. At least she wasn't alone in this plight any longer. The thought didn't console her the way she'd hoped it would.

By the time the pair reached the tavern, Nes's heart raced with the possibilities of Talier's fate. Her guide flung open the door and squeezed past a staggering patron to get inside and Nessix breathed out her tension as she spotted Talier seated by himself at a central table, contently cramming food in his mouth. It was a poorly defensible position, but he was alive.

The door closed behind Nessix and Talier perked up and looked at her. Before he could finish growing a smile, Nessix narrowed her eyes and gave a single, deliberate shake of her head. Air of authority still strong enough to impact the timid man, her subtle action held him wide-eyed in place, and she moved to the table the assassin claimed and took a seat with her back to the wall to keep both Talier and the door in view.

Savoring the aroma of a hearty beef stew and fresh bread, Nessix spent one of her last two coins on a meal for herself. Two bites into her food, a fire-haired halfling equipped with so many rings, knives, and garrotes that Nessix was surprised he had the strength left to move led a human man toward her table. The human's face was gaunt and wrinkles from several nights without sleep flawed what might have been an otherwise attractive face.

"Good day, Succubus," the halfling said, taking a seat beside the man from the alley as he gestured for his companion to take the one next to Nessix.

She watched the small man carefully, distrustful of his cordial tone. "Not interested in small talk. I just want my assignment and to be on my way."

The halfling's eyes narrowed. "*Small* talk? What's *that* s'posed to mean?"

If this had been one of Nes's first encounters with officials from this guild, the correction might have flustered her, but she was past the point of caring whether or not she offended them. "Inane drivel. Pointless conversations. Wasted time." She scoffed and swept a disappointed glance over the tiny man. "I thought those above me were supposed to be smart."

The halfling leapt onto the seat of his chair, snarl brandishing threats that were likely quite real, but a deep chuckle cleared the developing tension.

"Sit your tiny self down, Throttle," Nes's guide said.

The halfling shook in a bluster of outrage and jabbed a grubby finger at his comrade. "You best watch yourself, Lucky!"

"And you'd better sit yourself down," the bear of a man repeated.

The halfling eased back into his seat with a righteous grunt. "You said you wanted work. Well, we got you work."

Nessix used the shift of her gaze from the halfling to the human assassin to check on Talier's composure. Her poor companion had quit eating, his cheeks pale and wide eyes glistening with all sorts of assumptions Nes's pride didn't appreciate. She'd tend to his concerns after she tended to her assignment. Beside her, the human who had accompanied Throttle inside scratched at the wood grains in the table, his pain tangible and chilling Nes's stew before she'd finished it. A creeping despair clung to him, a loss of will that seized Nes's heart.

"Have you done this sort of thing before?" she asked quietly, spooning another mouthful of the stew, though she didn't taste it.

Throttle snorted but neither Nes nor her client reacted to it. The man remained focused on the table, digging at the grains that had been smoothed away years ago. "No. I haven't."

Nessix gnashed off a mouthful of stale bread. "And I'm not completely convinced you want to do so now."

He shook his head and looked up to meet Nes's eyes for the first time, his gaze broken, tiny and terrified. "I hate the thought of death," he murmured. "Nobody deserves their life destroyed, but…"

Nessix gave him a moment to continue. When he didn't, Lucky prodded the matter. "Don't waste our time. Either you've got work for her, or you don't."

The man folded his lips in a tight frown and nodded before he continued. "Last year, my wife and daughter were killed by bandits on the road to South Bend. We'd paid good money for a bodyguard to escort them. My girls… they were killed. That coward? He returned without a scratch and nothing but a few petty words of condolence. I'm a forgiving man, ma'am, but his lack of empathy, the physical condition which he was in… something didn't add up."

"I agree," Nessix said, ignoring the manner which the two assassins rolled their eyes and shifted impatiently. "Did you report it to the local authorities?"

"I did," he said. "And they said they couldn't do anything about it, said it happened outside their jurisdiction. My son—" The man's voice cracked and he had to clear his throat to press out the next words. "He wouldn't let it drop. It consumed him. That was his mother and baby sister. I begged him to let it go—the whole reason we'd paid a professional to guard them was because neither of us could fight. But he… he wouldn't listen…"

Nessix laid down her spoon. Talk of death didn't turn her stomach; being a soldier, she'd learned to tune it out. But this intimate suffering did. "He went to confront this guard."

"Last week."

"And things didn't go the way he'd hoped they would."

The man looked down at the table as Throttle snorted again, his hands falling still at last. "The son of a bitch was drunk when my son confronted him. My son, my wimpy, soft son, threatened a trained swordsman, a man who could have easily picked him up by the collar to drag him back home. Instead, that man, that great protector of peace, slaughtered my boy right there in the middle of the street."

While Lucky and his halfling companion whispered snide commentary to one another, Nessix gasped that such a violent action had been made in public. "With so many witnesses, this man was allowed to walk?"

Eyes vacant, her client nodded. "The witnesses all agreed on what they saw and the authorities believed their reports over mine. My son had threatened a man he knew out skilled him and who was obviously not in his right mind. They slapped the guard with some community service, and my son's still dead."

As were his wife and daughter. Nessix didn't have the heart to ask if he had any other family to go home to. A soldier first, a general second, all she wanted was to see peace for those who didn't ask for trouble. "Give me a description and a location if you've got it. I can't bring your family back, but I will see to it this man not only dies for his sins, but that he's aware of why he's been killed."

The man's gaze snapped up to Nes's, shimmering with tears of some sort of twisted hope. Fishing in his pocket, he withdrew a folded scrap of paper and slid it across the table. "That's where you'll find him. He's tall and pasty-skinned with a scar running down his left cheek. Name your rate. I am a man of means, and I'll stop at nothing to find justice for my family."

Before Nessix could flip open the paper, Lucky slapped his hand on top of it. "We'll discuss rates after Succubus is on the street."

Nessix bristled at the interference, but it was the human man who protested. "I am paying for her services. She is who I will discuss payment with."

"She works for us. If you want this taken care of, you'll work on *our* terms."

Nessix met the mourning man's eyes, pleased to see a ripple of indignation within them. She knew Lucky and Throttle planned to take advantage of them both, but as Talier's shock continued to bear down on her, she decided it was safest to let the matter drop before it escalated. Swallowing the disgust of her lie, Nessix pushed her chair back and swatted Lucky's hand off the paper.

"I'll see to my end, sir," she told the man. "We can both trust these two with the rest of the details."

Nessix would never escape the duties of justice, even if she succeeded in escaping Kol and the assassins. She'd been born to serve, and seeing that Abaeloth still needed her for that purpose warmed her weary heart. Taking two more bites of cold stew, Nessix made sure to pointedly watch random men throughout the establishment, hoping to thwart any hidden eyes from further suspecting her connection to Talier. Suspicions set at ease by the mundane activity around her, she gave Talier one last glance, firmly ordering him to stay put, and left the tavern.

Meandering through the streets, Nessix opened the scrap of paper to review her target's location. It would be a difficult house to sneak in and out of, situated just on the fringes of the noble district. Of course the two-story house was on one of the busier streets; it made no sense to appear pompous if there were no neighbors near enough to tell you how great you were.

She walked past the house, as if she didn't even notice it further than appraising how nicely the flowerbed was kept, and turned down the next street, surveying the best way to slip behind it. She hadn't drawn attention of the general population yet, but she didn't know how well guarded the streets in this distinguished part of town would be. Frowning, Nes crammed the paper into her pack and made a brief adjustment to her sword belt.

There were certain things that life as a warrior had conditioned into Nessix, responses which her time beneath Kol had only enhanced. When a flimsy grip closed around her upper arm, it triggered those reactions instantly, and she wasted no time whipping around to slap her assailant's forearm to break his grasp. As Nes's fingers closed around her dagger's hilt, Talier staggered away from her, empty hands open and waving before him.

Nessix shook off her hasty reaction at the sight of Talier's frightened eyes, though her nerves didn't quite settle. "What are you doing here?" she hissed on a tense whisper, rapidly scanning the street for anyone showing them too much interest.

Talier crossed his arms and fidgeted his weight back and forth, as though trying to decide how close to Nessix he truly wanted to stand. "What was I supposed to do?"

Nessix sighed. She'd deceived Talier so far and had no right to lose her patience with him because of it. "You were supposed to stay in the tavern until I came back to get you. Remember?"

It would have been hard for Talier to forget that if not for how loudly Kol's orders reverberated in his mind. Of course, he was quickly becoming more afraid of Nessix than he was of the demons, so it might not take much to change his mind. The truth—or at least part of it—would sound much better than any lie he'd come up with. He cleared his throat.

"I… I got scared, okay?"

Nessix frowned and glanced about once again before walking on to avoid suspicion. "I assigned you to the tavern to keep you safe," she said as he nervously shuffled along beside her.

Talier gulped his nerves. "No, I got spooked by… by those men you were talking to."

Her frown deepened, eyes hardening as she faced the inevitable confession. "You don't need to worry about them."

Talier rubbed his hands up and down his arms. "Not by *them*, but by what they were talking about…" He glanced around and lowered his voice, though he didn't venture closer to Nessix. "What they asked you to do."

The grimace Nessix had been holding at bay slipped out and she abandoned the whim to try passing the transaction off as a more scandalous kind of engagement. Talier was naïve and afraid of life, but he'd proven intelligent so far. He wouldn't believe such a lie. That left Nessix with the dismal option of admitting to her only companion what she was. A wash of sourness coated her tongue.

"And what do you think they asked me to do?"

"You know…" Talier slinked closer to her. "To kill a man."

Nessix looked at Talier, his eyes too haunted for his statement to have been a simple guess. She shivered, wondering if maybe he'd been planted by the assassins as some sort of test. Another appraisal of the glisten of sweat on his neck and his inability to hold her gaze shot down that theory. "What makes you think that?"

Talier coughed and folded his arms tighter. "I heard the mopey one tell you about the man who killed his family and heard you agree to avenge them. The other two were talking money with him after you left."

Nessix stopped abruptly, prompting Talier to skid to a stop and inch away from her. "We were halfway across a crowded tavern from you."

Talier's mouth sagged open, the last bit of color draining from his face. As cowardly as he was, he held his ground. It shouldn't have surprised Nessix, as he'd shown an unusual bout of courage to have encountered the two demons she'd rescued him from. Something didn't quite add up about Talier, but she was relatively certain it wasn't tied to the assassins.

"Well?" she asked, crossing her arms. "Who tipped you off?"

"No one." He scratched the back of his neck. "I have good ears..." He cast his gaze aside at that comment, avoiding Nes's speculative eyes.

"I'd say you do." She cocked her head in consideration. Whatever it was Talier felt he had to hide from her couldn't have been worse than what she'd hidden from him. She heaved a weary sigh, her odds of keeping him secret from the guild officially gone. "I've put you in a perilous position, Talier."

He coughed on his dry tongue as he formed a reply. "No more perilous than when you found me."

Nessix glanced at him, frown pulling deeper. "Don't be so sure. I'm not supposed to keep company—apparently. Those above me are already suspicious of you, and I'm sure those suspicions have been confirmed over the past few minutes."

Frightened or not of the strength and cruelty lying dormant in Nessix, Talier had been shown nothing but generosity and an ironic warmth from her these past few days. As far as he could tell, she hadn't caught on to his deceit and slowly, that strength and cruelty she harbored looked more and more like safety to him. He drew closer to her, desperate to shake the nagging loneliness which dumped so much insecurity on him.

"I'm going to have to ask you to do something you won't want to do," Nessix said.

Talier couldn't answer, spinning through how many unpleasant tasks he'd already undertaken for others. Nothing but a queasy whimper leaked out of him.

"I can't risk leaving you alone now." Nes walked forward again, a tether of fear dragging Talier with her. "There are too many eyes watching that'll want you dead. More, once the demons realize you're traveling with me."

A second whine, this one shriller, ineffectively answered Nes's statement.

"You won't be safe with me, but you'll be in even greater danger if we separate. We're still on the road to Zeal, right?"

Suddenly, Talier's brilliant plan of sticking to the eastbound roads to increase their distance from the just city seemed like a terrible one. He nodded mutely.

"Good. Once we get there, you should be safe."

"*Should* be?" Talier squeaked.

Nessix looked up at him, eyes no longer filled with that quiet certainty, but with the regretful hardness of a general condemning her troops to dismal odds. "I've never been to Zeal, but if I've gotten the right impression of the Order, they'll protect you."

There had been a brief moment when Talier had first woken at Kol's feet that he thought he stood a chance at carrying out this mission, but that had been before he'd known how complicated the matters surrounding Nessix were. Demons. Assassins. The Order. Who *was* this woman?

"You said you had something unpleasant to ask me?" Talier was eager to hear his sentence so he could succumb to it and be through with it.

Nessix clenched her teeth and looked forward, nostrils flaring with a resigned breath. "I have to complete this job. Unless we're only a day or two from Zeal, we need the money." At the shake of Talier's head, Nessix continued. "Since I can't let you stray far from me, I'm going to put you on watch."

Talier sputtered in shock and stopped. "You mean while you—" He cut his words off quickly, sense returning to him before he blurted Nes's plans for passersby to hear.

Nessix turned and walked back to Talier, grabbing his arm to drag him along again. "Yes. The man I'm after has connections, and you've got good ears. I'd be grateful for your assistance, and as soon as things are done, we can get out of town and put this whole mess behind us."

That was assuming Talier would ever be able to put *any* of this behind him… "But I'd be complicit in… in…"

"No," Nessix said tersely, her confidence and expectation of obedience silencing Talier's objections. "You'll be responsible for keeping me alive, just as I'm continuing to do for you." She let her gaze linger on her mark's house as they walked past it a second time.

Talier's twitchy eyes followed Nes's gaze and his flight response fought to kick in. If not for the demons' possession of his brother, he'd have abandoned Nessix and the trouble she was getting him into here and now. A hearty slap on the shoulder plunged Talier back into the present.

"Come on." Nessix's tone brightened with forced encouragement. "You were brave enough to go after demons unarmed; surely you're brave enough to stand outside a house while I take care of a little business."

She made that statement so causally, so certain he'd comply with her that Talier, having never questioned authority in the past, found himself nodding, despite the nauseating bubble rising from his stomach and into his throat. "Do people normally try to stop you?"

Nessix slowed her pace as they neared the back of the house and she kept herself from looking at Talier, knowing that he wouldn't want to hear the truth. "Not yet, but I've got a hunch they'll try to soon." She stopped and turned to face him. "I should have been up front with you about this from the start. I'm sorry for getting you involved."

Her apology sounded genuine and the slight tip of her brows suggested this truth did bother her. But a simple apology, heartfelt or otherwise, wasn't enough for Talier. If not for her, Marcoux wouldn't have been captured. If not for her, Talier wouldn't be facing criminal actions. If not for her… he might already be dead to the demons. Trembling hands swiped at the sweat trickling down his temple.

"And what if… What if the man you're here to… you know… gets to you first?" He hated to think of how to explain to Kol that he'd secured Nessix and then let her walk into her death.

"This man cannot kill me."

Common sense begged for Talier to argue with Nessix about all of this, but her authority and charisma kept his sensible debates lodged in his throat. She smelled of regret and desperation, but both of those were nearly obstructed by confidence. Whether or not her claim of being unable to be killed was true, she believed it. Talier, with no grounds left to question her, caved at last.

"All I have to do is stay on watch?"

Nessix's eyes drifted closed, a tremor of emotion rippling across her brow and lips before she opened them again. "Trust me when I say even that's more than I want to impose on you. Alert me if any danger shows up. I promise to be as quick as I can so we can get out of town."

Talier couldn't put his finger on why her request for his trust meant anything to him. What struck him more powerfully than this odd desire to comply with Nessix's demands, possibly what had subtly forced him to do so, was that brief flare of regret she'd passed along to him. He fully intended to turn her over to Kol the first chance he had, eager to be rid of this wretched responsibility and to be reunited with his brother, yet she'd blindly embraced him as a companion. Talier's only benefit to her had been his knowledge of Gelthin's geography, a skill he'd intentionally exploited to his benefit, and she'd selflessly kept him fed and sheltered, preparing to kill a man to ensure she could continue to do so. Talier had gathered enough from Annin and Kol to know that Nessix hadn't simply been misplaced. As much trouble as Talier thought he and Marcoux had landed in, Nessix, he was sure, was in even more. And she still worried about his safety. He could hate Nessix all he wanted, but he realized now that he did trust her.

"Please be quick," he murmured.

Nessix closed her eyes briefly and mustered her calm. "Thank you, Talier."

Before the dust of this unnerving revelation settled, Nessix disappeared between the houses. Talier swallowed the whimper that tried to crawl up his throat and timidly crept closer to the house to tuck into hiding behind a row of groomed hedges nestled close to its whitewashed siding.

Nessix had been gone no more than five minutes when the scent of smoke and malice choked Talier. A subtle whoosh of fabric rippled from behind, and he spun to find the furious little red-haired man from the tavern charging toward him, a knife grasped in each hand.

A seed of the wolf's aggression sprouted inside Talier, urging him to confront this threat, but that instinct was promptly stomped into the ground by the simple fact that Talier had no combat skills of his own. Hair raising on the back of his neck, Talier spun, ears trained on the halfling, and plowed through the door Nessix had silently slipped through minutes prior.

He flung the door closed as he cleared it, but a sharp slam announced his hunter's unhindered pursuit. What had begun as an assignment to keep witnesses from discovering what Nessix was up to had turned into a frantic scramble for his life, and the only person who could help him was the woman who had landed him here. Too panicked to worry about matters as trivial as shame, Talier screamed Nessix's name as he tore through the unfamiliar layout of the house, tracking her scent.

Past the pounding of his heart, Talier heard the thuds of a struggle from the second floor. He didn't spare a look behind him, relying on his superior stride length to keep ahead of the halfling. Nessix's scent led him to the staircase and he took the steps two at a time to gain even more distance. The thuds had since gone silent and Talier shouted for Nessix again, now more afraid of his immediate danger than that posed by Kol.

Talier was two leaps from the landing when Nessix appeared at the top of the stairs. Locks of her hair had come loose from where they'd once been pulled back, bruises beginning to show on her throat. Blood from the dagger she gripped had spattered across her greaves, but her eyes were focused and impatiently awaiting Talier's report. He gestured frantically behind himself, still plowing up the stairs. "Halfling!" he gasped, not caring how ridiculous doing so made the situation seem.

"Half—" Nes's eyes widened. "Shit!"

Fear and self-loathing seeped from Nessix, heightening Talier's own terror, but he didn't have the chance to dwell on this rapid change in her as she gripped his arm and shoved him into the first open door. He cried out as the empty gaze of a dead man pled to him from the floor, thinking briefly about leaping from the window before sense grounded him. He spun around, wringing his hands as Nessix squared her stance in the doorway.

The halfling had made it up the stairs, his tiny feet racing toward them. Though the numerical odds were stacked in their favor, Talier had smelled a cold eagerness in this little man which sang of death. Unable to control himself, he staggered backwards as Nessix crouched and launched herself into the hallway to meet her opponent.

Nessix had never fought someone smaller than herself, a fact that rushed up to her as Throttle snatched the upper hand by darting past her to latch onto her back. Having previously taken account of his choice of weapons, Nessix threw her weight backwards to crush him against the wall. The impact winded them both, but Throttle hung on tight and when Nessix lost track of the hand that had been tangled in her hair, she jammed her elbow back, connecting sharply with the tiny man's side.

A surprised "ooph!" left the halfling and Nessix didn't waste the time to assess whether or not that had been a sound of defeat as she jabbed her elbow back again and again. If not for her responsibility for Talier, she was tempted to let Throttle kill her to free her from the assassins' employ. Unfortunately for her sense of mischief, she knew if she was killed here, Talier would be next. Even if he managed to escape the raging halfling, he'd have the demons on him in no time. Another jab and Throttle fell from Nes's back, hitting the floor with a thud.

Before Nessix could turn around, Throttle scrambled toward the room Talier hid in, and Nessix dashed ahead as the assassin reached the doorway. Talier released a terrified roar of uncertainty and slammed the door closed on the halfling's wrist. The crunch Nessix had hoped to hear never came, but the agonized scream satisfied her well enough. Throttle pulled his hand back, shredding the skin from it in the process and by the time he'd gathered his bleeding appendage to his chest, Nessix slammed her foot into his face. The strike sent him to his back and Nessix stomped down on his throat. His eyes bulged and before he could cough for breath, Nessix stomped down again, this time crushing her weight down until he quit moving. Heart slowing, Nessix leaned her weight off the dead halfling.

"N… Nessix?"

Talier's voice squeezed through the crack of the door, but Nessix responded neither to that nor his cautious eyes peeking into the hall. She'd never known what it felt like to be in trouble, not the kind she faced right now. She'd been in over her head in combat, she'd been thrown about by the demons for asking the wrong questions, but she'd never known what it was like to be wanted for a crime, and that thought made her want to bolt every bit as quickly as she wanted to run from the demons.

"It's safe now," she said, strength waning from her voice.

The door creaked open the rest of the way, dripping splatters of blood and chunks of flesh at Talier's feet. All color drained from his face as he gawked at the dead halfling and back at Nessix. "You… you killed him?"

Exhausted, Nessix sighed and crouched down to loot Throttle's coin purses. "Yes."

"You killed him *dead*!" Talier's voice trembled and Nessix was surprised he hadn't fainted from how rapidly he hyperventilated. "You killed them *both*!"

Already worn and chased by the knowledge that it wouldn't be long before Lucky or any other member of this association grew suspicious of their friend's absence, Nessix stood and held the coin purses out to Talier. "Yes, I did."

"But they were *men*." *Men like me*, Talier thought bleakly, *men like Marcoux*. "Not demons."

Nessix withdrew the coin purses and crammed them into her pack. "No less monsters. Let's go. We don't have much time." She turned and rapidly descended the stairs.

Shivering with these revelations, nauseated by the results of Nessix's violence, Talier leapt over the dead halfling and hurried after her, more afraid than ever of appearing disobedient. "Where are we going?"

"We can't very well stay here, and I doubt it'll take long for someone to report our ruckus."

Talier gulped, clinging pathetically to an obscure sense of hope. "Are we leaving town?"

"Yes. We can pick up provisions at our next stop." She reached the bottom of the stairs and turned to wait on Talier. "Do I look presentable to a respectable public?"

Talier awkwardly pointed at her hair where it had escaped its bindings, then curled his hand back to his lips as Nessix quickly secured it. "And, um, your boots."

Nessix kicked her right leg forward and frowned at the blood splattered on it. "Well. I guess we'll have to be that much faster. Stay close."

Not waiting for the debate that might come, Nessix hauled Talier out the back door.

He squirmed in her grasp like a child trying to escape his mother dragging him to be switched, asking himself over and over again what he'd done to deserve landing in this position. Nessix walked with a brisk purpose, head bowed as though she was plowing through a torrential storm, and Talier kept close at her heels with choppy strides.

He followed her out of the noble district and into the back streets, trembling at how her adrenaline remained built and prepared for another round of combat. Too afraid to separate from Nessix, Talier's heart began to race to a different song. When she jarred to a sudden halt, it stopped entirely.

Lucky blocked their exit to the street. Nessix pulled a dagger from her belt and handed it back to Talier. He nearly choked on the stench of her rage and righteousness.

"If he gets past me or anyone comes from behind, you must use that."

Talier's jaw flapped uselessly at her hushed order, terror having seized his voice minutes prior. His sweaty fingers wrapped around the hilt

He was not an ideal troop and Nessix hadn't had the time to forge him into one, but he was all she had. "I'm counting on you."

Nessix drew her second dagger, the scent of her rage settling into a calm determination, an aroma which frightened Talier in an entirely different manner. Palms slick, he groped his dagger with both hands, heart pounding in his ears as the stench of the alley burned his nose and Nessix dashed toward the bear of a man ahead of them.

Lucky reached a hand inside his vest and Nessix sprang forward to plunge her knife into his inner thigh. Blood spurted with the strong beating of his heart, washing down Nes's arm. The wound would see him dead in minutes, and Nessix wasn't curious enough to know what he'd been reaching for to stay around and watch. Rapidly weakening from blood loss, Lucky didn't have the strength to fight for his balance as Nessix drove her shoulder into his gut to topple him backwards.

The moment Lucky hit the ground, a flash of steel zipped past Nes's head, a dull thunk confirming it struck wood and not Talier. Nessix ducked behind a rain barrel to avoid the next thrown knife and her long-repressed fear of taking wounds in combat pried itself from her heart. As much as she'd imagined letting the assassins kill her, now that she faced death as a valid consequence of her actions, she no longer thought it would be so entertaining. A third knife ricocheted off her pauldron and she located a greasy-haired man tucked in the shadows of an adjacent doorway.

Her opponent watched her with steady eyes as he drew a fourth knife from his belt. She'd have to get close to him to strike, and he still had a healthy supply of projectiles to send her way. Raising her left arm to attempt to use her metal bracer as a shield, Nessix prepared to lunge forward—

And Talier's timid voice cried out her name once again.

The assassin's gaze shifted from Nessix to Talier and the moment he began to raise his arm to flick his knife at her hapless companion, Nessix closed the distance between them and bashed her bracer into his face. Stunned or unconscious, the assassin crumpled to the ground. Nessix slit his throat, straddling his corpse while her heart slowed.

"There's a lot of shouting on the street."

Talier's voice shook with threadbare resolve, and Nessix wasn't quite ready to face the tears she knew would be in his eyes.

"Are they running toward where we came from?"

"Yeah."

Nessix panted over the body of the man who was supposed to be in charge of keeping her in line, smudging the tickle of blood across her cheek. They had to escape town quickly. Even if the authorities didn't stop her in her bloodied state, the assassins' eyes would be on her soon, especially after she'd killed three of their own.

"Do you know the closest way out of town?" Pulling her victim's coin purse from his belt, Nessix stood and moved to the rain barrel to splash water on her face and armor.

"Yeah, but it leads south—"

"That's fine. We'll find a different road."

Talier was through with all of this, but needed Nessix now more than ever. He doubted Kol would waltz into prison to bail him out of murder charges, but Nessix just might be able to get him to safety. Hoping this delay wouldn't impact Marcoux, Talier gave Nessix a subdued, "Okay."

It was his lack of a desperate debate that caught Nes's attention and made her feel like the terrible person she'd become. Instead of dwelling, instead of hating herself, she had to take action. Tucking a stray strand of hair behind her ear, she looted the final purse off Lucky.

With little more than his fear guiding them, Talier led the way out of town, consciously putting distance between himself and the goal he began to believe he'd never reach.

TWENTY-EIGHT

Among those of the divine realm, Kenin had never been commended for his generosity. He was, however, known for his curiosity and attraction to drama, and when Mathias had visited him several months prior to ask about the missing soul of a woman named Nessix, that curiosity had been hooked.

The paladin seldom made time for the children gods and even more rarely requested their help. Whoever this Nessix was, she must have had a juicy story tied to her, and Kenin was delighted when the sputtering soul of an enraged halfling popped into his realm, cursing a woman with the same name. Dismissing formalities past ensuring he'd heard correctly, Kenin took advantage of his godly might and dragged the halfling's spirit to do the unthinkable for one as chaotic as him.

He sought Etha.

The Mother Goddess had been preoccupied with the crisis threatening to shake apart the balance of her ideal world, but Kenin was too intrigued to let something as bothersome as respect deter him. After all, the only way he'd seen one of his peers lose her power was from her radical ambition to hurt Mathias. Kenin planned to do the exact opposite of that. At least that was how he intended to present himself to Etha.

Etha's focus skated rapidly across the far reaches of Abaeloth, snagging only briefly on curiosities that might be relevant to her search. It was unusual to find her so frantic, and Kenin had smugly assumed that his witnessing her discomposure would have gained her instant notice. He never received her attention or the shame that he'd fancied would be tied to it. She didn't even waste a glance on him, disregarding him as a concern altogether.

Kenin often enjoyed being ignored, gleefully capitalizing on the occasion to sneak around where he wanted. Now that he'd made pulling Etha away from her concerns over Abaeloth's activities and the multitude of jumbled prayers his objective, he found it wholly insulting.

"How's this gettin' me any closer to my vengeance?" the halfling hissed peevishly, either not realizing Kenin was a god or figuring that, being dead, angering one no longer mattered.

Kenin turned his glower to the halfling. If not for the fact that the angry little man might prove useful—and thus valuable—to Kenin, the god would have flicked him into oblivion by now. "Patience, or you'll be getting nothing."

The halfling scoffed but otherwise stayed silent and Kenin, tense and impatient, almost wished his charge would have disregarded the warning simply to postpone the dicey task of interrupting Etha's concentration.

"I've got no time to deal with you, Kenin." Etha still didn't look his way.

Kenin didn't often experience flagging confidence and he didn't care for the sensation one bit. Etha's words had carried a definitive warning. Thoughts of Shand's demise constantly plagued each of the remaining children gods, and Kenin glanced from the fuming spirit beside him back to Etha's firm shoulders. The entire divine realm had been abuzz with rumors regarding Mathias's desires and Abaeloth's plight. It was no great secret that answers were both needed and anxiously sought. And Kenin sorely hoped he had one of those answers with him now.

"Perhaps you'll have time to deal with the soul of my charge?" Kenin invested the entirety of his courage into that question.

"I'm too busy to be doling out favors right now."

The sensible thing would have been to accept Etha's terse

answer and leave her to her brooding, to try bringing his treasure to Azerick or Drao or even Mathias himself, all people who Etha appreciated more than she'd ever appreciated Kenin. But sensibility and profitability didn't always accompany one another. Kenin grit his teeth as he faced the potential of Etha's temper. Mathias better have given him the correct name... "He's seen that Nessix woman."

Etha whipped around and stalked up to the pair with such force that both Kenin and the halfling shuffled an involuntary retreat. Her brows were strict and a stern frown curved her lips, but her eyes glimmered with the hunger Kenin had hoped to see. He breathed out his accumulated tension and fit a sly smile onto his face.

"I didn't either say I saw anyone named Nessix," the halfling muttered, crossing his arms. Though he hadn't shown Kenin the appropriate respect a soul ought to give a god, he kept a wary eye on Etha as he raised his chin away from her.

Kenin cast a hasty glance at Etha and cuffed the halfling on the back of his head. "That's not what you were bitching about when I found you."

The halfling sneered at Kenin. "It sure was. I was bitchin' about the bitch who killed me."

"Right," Kenin snipped, eager for the tiny man to hurry the tale along before Etha lost her patience. "And Nessix was who killed you."

Etha's eyes narrowed in contemplation and she studied the halfling's rebellious soul for deceit.

"No, *Succubus* killed me. I don't know no Nessix."

Kenin gulped down his anxiety and shoved the halfling closer to Etha. "Tell her *exactly* what you told me when I asked you why I should help you."

The halfling's face screwed up in comical rage as he spun from Etha to spout off at Kenin. "Why I gotta tell her"—he jerked a thumb over his shoulder—"anything? She already said she wasn't handin' out favors."

Patience gone, Kenin's lip curled in a snarl, but as he began to raise a hand to properly reprimand the noncompliant soul, Etha intervened.

"Surely, you want your murderer to be found?"

The halfling swung around again. "Oh, she'll be found. My brothers'll see to that."

Etha cocked her head, unmoved by the soul's confidence. "If this... Succubus you speak of is who I think she is, she has been outrunning demons and slipping through the fingers of gods. Your mortal brothers won't be able to find her unless she wants them to. Now, if you were to give me her general whereabouts... I could be swayed to go hunt her down and deliver to her what she deserves."

Kenin was both pleased and appalled at Etha's honest manipulation of the situation. He'd never witnessed this sort of cunning from the Mother Goddess and wondered if perhaps they had more in common with each other than he'd thought. Her eyes flashed to his.

Don't count on it.

Humbled at once, Kenin lowered his eyes and shoved the halfling's soul again. "You heard her. The sooner you talk, the sooner your killer can be found."

Throttle twisted his puckered lips from side to side, trying to balance out if this hassle was worth his effort. He hadn't even been sent to deal with Succubus, just that awkward man she'd strolled into town with, and then she'd gone and stuck her nose in his business. She'd *ruined* his hit! He gave a shrill little growl and spat to the side.

"Succubus has got a real shit reputation, you know? Never playing by the books, always makin' more work for us. We shoulda booted her right from town the second she showed up with that wimpy man."

Etha disregarded the coarse language and scrutiny of Nes's flaws, perking up at the mention of her travelling with a companion. Nes's soul might be fractured and unable to be tracked, but a mortal man could be located with relative ease. "What wimpy man?"

The halfling regarded Etha's enthusiasm suspiciously. "What's in it for me if I tell you?"

"You'll be permitted a restful afterlife as opposed to those I typically grant rude assassins."

Throttle opened his mouth to protest, ready to demand to be resurrected so he could take revenge himself, when Kenin jabbed a finger between his shoulder blades. As it was, the entire adventure of chasing his mark, fighting Succubus, and being whipped about the heavens like the gods' plaything left more questions unanswered than the halfling was comfortable with. He'd pieced together who Kenin was, given how the god of mischief was the only one he'd ever considered worth trying to appease, and he actively fought his suspicions of who Etha was. Kenin seemed anxious to please this goddess and so Throttle figured it was in his best interest to do the same.

"I don't know who he was, never got a name short of Succubus's tagalong. Whoever he was, he didn't want any part of the life she'd chosen, was twitchy and tryin' to talk her out of her job. That's the kind of liability that'll go talkin', you know? We don't got time for that, so I was sent to shut him up."

"You keep calling the woman who killed you Succubus. Why?"

The halfling snorted at Etha's question. "'Cause that's her name."

Etha frowned as the dots began to connect. Mathias wouldn't be thrilled about this. "Then why did Kenin tell me she was called Nessix? Not even he is reckless enough to lie to me."

"'Cause that's what her blasted tagalong called her. He went runnin' after her when he heard me—damned if I know how he pulled that off—screamin' that Nessix name."

"Whatever you want to call her, what did she look like."

"Like a bitch," the halfling muttered.

Kenin shoved him again.

"Short. I mean, for a half-elf. Dark hair. Cold, pale eyes. She must have offed someone impressive to afford her armor and that shiny ring she wore."

It took a lot to knock the breath from a goddess, but Etha's cheeks paled and her mouth dropped open in a gasp that was afraid to hope. It sounded as though Nessix had gotten herself into quite a bit of trouble, but Etha would judge those actions once she understood why they'd been taken. Nessix couldn't have fallen completely if she was in the company of a helpless man who she would kill to protect. The assassin part was troublesome, but Etha could work with it. She just had two more questions before she could close in on her.

"How long ago did this happen?"

Throttle glanced at Kenin. "How long ago did I die? Does time pass normal here?"

Kenin looked straight at Etha, already imagining how her favor would benefit him. "No more than six hours ago. I brought him here as soon as he started yammering about that man screaming Nessix's name."

Etha nodded curtly and turned her attention back to the halfling. "And in what city did this happen?"

"Fulton. And—"

Etha swatted her hand as though batting away an annoying fly and the halfling's soul was sucked into the heavens to find the rest Etha had promised him. She turned from Kenin, prepared to start her search for a frightened man near Fulton when the clearing of a throat scratched at the thin barrier between her patience and irritation.

"Kenin?" she asked, refraining from turning to face the young god in case his conniving face pushed her to hastiness.

"Haven't you… forgotten something?"

A deep breath braced her tiny shoulders, fists clenching at her sides. "You have my gratitude."

"Your—" Kenin caught his belligerence before it had the chance to stoke Etha's ire. Her gratitude was a boon in itself, especially in such uncertain times. "Thank you, Mother," he replied instead, his voice stretched just tight enough to convey his disappointment.

The subtle arrogance in Kenin's tone didn't escape Etha and she turned now, expecting to find anger in his eyes. When all she found was his gaze still averted from her, proud shoulders sagging, she was struck with guilt. Kenin had single-handedly delivered the best lead on Nes's whereabouts that anyone had been able to provide this far.

"I'll be sure to tell Mathias what you did today," she said, disregarding how her paladin had previously bargained his services to this god. "He won't soon forget it. I regret that I cannot thank you more personally, but if I'm to track Nessix's frightened companion, I must make haste." The explanation was more than she owed Kenin, and she disappeared in the same instant.

The god of mischief now had Mathias indebted to him twice over. Today hadn't been a complete loss. Satisfied, if a bit disappointed, Kenin returned to his tavern to calculate just how he'd use the favors he'd been given.

* * * * *

Nes and Talier had slipped through the southern gates of Fulton as quickly as possible. Wealthy with coins but not provisions, and turned around in their haste to escape the dangers they'd left behind, both lost track of where they were. Nessix had insisted on skirting wide around the city, putting them on a westbound road and even farther off course from both Zeal and Kol.

Demoralized and lost, Nessix was content with her companion's relative silence. Though she didn't blame him for the disaster they'd escaped, she didn't yet trust her tongue to not make it sound like she did, and the poor fool was distraught enough without her adding to it. Besides, he was still her best shot at reaching Zeal and she'd vowed to protect him until they reached the holy city. She wouldn't fault him if he chose to part ways with her, but neither would she intentionally drive him away.

They kept a quick pace, and as an ache began to stab at Nes's side, she glanced at her companion, finding his eyes dark with trouble and glistening with tears he only barely kept contained. His attention darted frantically around their surroundings, as if waiting for another ambush, and Nes's heart fell. Her leadership skills had deteriorated further than she'd thought if she couldn't alleviate a single man's fears.

She reached out and grabbed Talier's wrist, launching him into a panicked retreat that she narrowly halted by tightening her grip.

He dragged her half a stride and, though he abandoned his efforts to escape once he registered who had grabbed him, a misting of tears slid past his efforts to hold them back.

"We need to rest," Nessix said softly, casting her gaze toward the afternoon sky. They had an hour or two to play with before they had to begin searching out shelter for the night. "It should be safe to take a break."

Talier's throat constricted against the desire to scream. Nessix had no idea the danger they were in! He was plenty scared of the mortals who apparently wanted them dead, and though he'd come to realize that Nessix was quite aware that demons were chasing her, she had no idea what would happen if Kol's men caught up to them now. Talier had fumbled every step of the way and he'd avoided punishment because he'd still been viewed as useful. But how long would that leniency last?

"We don't even know where we are," he argued weakly. "How do you know we're safe?"

A tiny sliver of Nes's heart eased at Talier's tone; he was frightened, but not angry. Confident that he'd listen to her orders, Nessix pulled him to the side of the road and dragged him down to sit with her in the grass. "The ache in my legs and side say we've put enough distance between us and anyone from Fulton who might suspect us of foul play, and you haven't heard anything that could be a threat."

That much was true. Talier's senses hadn't picked up anything more than passing wildlife and Nes's determination. Kol and Annin might be able to move close to silently, but Talier had imprinted their scents in his mind. If either of them were nearby, he'd have known it. So where did this fear come from?

He looked to the petite warrior woman beside him as she stretched and rummaged through her pouch. Her expression sagged with exhaustion and a world of trouble spun behind her blue eyes, but she still looked at him with a doting fondness, her vow of protecting him more important to her than her own safety. She handed him half a strip of jerky and the majority of a smashed roll. Tired and hungry, Talier wouldn't have been able to protest her offering even if he wanted to.

Accepting the meager rations, Talier's hatred and anger and fear were compounded by a growing well of guilt. He was using Nessix shamelessly as a means to get what he wanted, and she was selflessly giving of her limited possessions and her own well-being to keep him safe. He bit off a bite of the jerky, unable to savor it as his throat greedily propelled it into his stomach. Talier stared at Nessix as she carefully sipped at her water skin, wondering if she deserved to be in the demons' clutches more than his lying brother did. Cramming the last of the jerky in his mouth, Talier pressed his fingers against the pocket which held the locket of Marcoux. The roll no longer seemed appetizing.

"Here." Nessix pulled Talier's mind away from his confusion as she held out the water skin. "Try to ration it. I don't know when we'll come across a source to refill it."

Talier stared at the water skin until Nessix shook it at him, then pulled his fingers from his pocket, distancing himself once more from his brother to accept the drink.

"Do you think you'll be able to reorient yourself once we find the next city?" she asked.

Talier lowered the water skin, grateful for Nes's distraction to keep him from guzzling the entire container dry. "Is it safe to approach another city? I mean after…" He lowered his eyes and twisted his lips to keep the couple bites of jerky he'd taken in his stomach.

With the assassins' lines of communication, it was probable that descriptions of both her and Talier would soon be circulated. She'd have to take more care when entering cities from here on out, and even in those that lacked guild presence, it was not improbable to think that there might be an assassin or two waiting for her. She forced a smile. "All we'd really need to do is identify which town we find, right? Between that and the sun and stars, you should be able to get us back on the road to Zeal."

"I'm not even sure I want to get close enough to the next city to get its name," Talier mumbled, handing the water skin back to Nessix.

Her smile faltered. "We'll need to stop for provisions eventually. We can hide you outside and I'll go in—"

A cloud of dust puffed up in front of them, courtesy of the front pair of a horse's hooves. Neither having heard nor seen the animal's approach, Nessix fell back on her rear and Talier grabbed her arm, springing to his feet to prepare to run. Nessix scrambled quickly to her feet, hand flying to her sword as she looked at the stoic white pony carrying a pretty young woman. Thick amber curls hung from beneath a wide-brimmed hat and tumbled well down the woman's back, and she sat primly in a side saddle to accommodate a luxurious satin gown. Its rich green hue offset honey-colored eyes that studied Nessix carefully.

Behind her, Talier tugged at her arm and fiercely whispered, "We should run."

Etha only briefly flicked an inquisitive gaze at Talier and his unusual traits and unnatural attributes before scouring her delighted eyes over the familiarity of Nes's sword and armor. Divine law prevented Etha from disclosing who she was or interfering with what remained of the broken woman's free will, and that was all that prevented Etha from leaping from the saddle to embrace Nessix. Frustrated with herself for those rules she'd put in place when she was young and foolish, Etha smiled sweetly, resigning to leave Nessix in ignorance.

"Are you the one they call Succubus?"

Talier's fingers clenched tighter around Nes's arm, clearly conveying his fears that this petite woman was here to finish what the halfling had failed at. Nessix, on the other hand, glowered, displaying all of that haughty stubbornness Etha had come to know and admire when she'd still been a mortal. She shook Talier's hand from her arm and stepped in front of him.

"What would make you think I am?" she challenged.

Etha was just as pleased to see that the demons had done nothing to dampen Nes's ferocity as she was that the late general's morals still demanded she protect those in her care. "I'm in need of an assassin, did my research for the most efficient one around, and have spent a very, *very* long time trying to track you down."

Nessix scoffed and eased out of her preparatory crouch. "I am both financially stable and separated from that field of employment. Move along. Hire someone better suited for the job."

Etha cocked her head and tapped a finger to her lips, undaunted by Nes's short tone. "Hmm… You're the best woman for *this* job. I think I'll hire you."

Nessix shook her head and straightened to her full height. She'd gotten used to the demons telling her to do things she didn't want to do. She'd become accustomed to the assassins giving her threats without merit. But she'd never had such an ultimatum delivered to her. "I said I'm not for hire."

"Gold's not enticing enough? What *would* you accept as payment?"

Nes's eyes narrowed as she felt the blanket of obedience that had arrived with this woman slowly peel away from her, and promptly opened them wide again as she identified the sensation. This was the exact same soothing influence Zenos had slipped over her upon their meeting. Heart rate climbing, Nessix swallowed the reluctance of gambling with a god and stepped forward to meet this woman on her terms. "I'm in need of a map that can guide us to Zeal."

Etha's lips lifted in a small smile as Nessix struggled with the truth. The poor girl. She was bright and well versed in tactics, and though she had more experience with gods than most, she had no idea.

"Is *that* all?" Etha turned and opened a saddlebag, drawing out a rolled-up piece of parchment. She snuck a quick glance at her modest audience, finding two pairs of wide, eager eyes and retained breath. Nes's road must have been quite trying for her desperation to become so obvious.

Etha unrolled the map and in the same action, gripped the right-hand edge of it with both hands, and tore the treasured guide in half. Nessix gasped sharply as the goddess unceremoniously crammed the northern half of the map back into the saddlebag and proudly thrust the southern half forward. Neither Nessix nor her companion moved.

"Well?" Etha asked. "Do you want it or not?"

The past few weeks on the road had taught Nessix all sorts of terrible lessons she'd been happier left ignorant to, chief among them the value of an accurate map. Seeing this woman—divinely enhanced or otherwise—treat one with such disregard stunned her beyond comprehension.

"What have you done?" she murmured, lips numb and anger absorbed by shock.

Etha flapped the half of the map beside her pony's head. "Just a little guarantee that you'll track down the man I'm hiring you to find. This half will take you to Fairmont, where you'll find him. I'll meet you there when it's done and see to it you have what you need to make it the rest of the way to Zeal."

"Nessix…" Talier murmured, his fears openly apparent.

Nessix longed to heed his unspoken warning, but they needed a map to figure out where they were, and the only way to get one was to accept one more assignment. She clenched her fist, wishing she'd have been able to walk away from her guilt just as badly as she wanted to walk away from this job. She looked again at the map fragment and then to the young woman's patient expression. This was all she needed. This would allow her to reach Zeal, to reach her salvation. Clenching her teeth down on her regrets, Nessix strode forward and accepted the proffered map, despite Talier's squeak of protest.

"Who am I looking for?"

Etha's eyes lit up with excitement and she had to remind herself that she had to preserve a certain degree of Nes's ignorance to see this done. "I'm sending you after a man. He and I are um… close."

"I don't need a story, just—"

"Lately, he's been gallivanting all over Gelthin with *another woman*." She lifted her chin to give Nessix a shrewd appraisal; she'd never had a reason to hire a hit before, especially one on Mathias, and the idea was too much fun. "You're *exactly* the kind of woman he'd let close, and I want you to put a stop to his wandering. For good."

Nessix pressed her lips tight, hating the pettiness which plagued this part of Abaeloth. "I'll need more to go off of than that. I'm not going to risk killing the wrong man due to your lack of providing a name or accurate description."

So Nessix *hadn't* lost her authority! Etha nodded, smiling in satisfaction. "His name?" She hid her giggle behind a disgusted scowl. "Dogs like him aren't worthy of names. But—" she held up a finger and dug once more through her saddlebags, producing a yellow scarf embroidered in red with the head of a lion on one tail. "He's blond and will be wearing a matching scarf. Bland clothing. He's got a muscular build and will likely be carrying a sword but, knowing *him*, he won't be likely to use it against you. Do you need anything else?"

"May I keep the scarf?"

Etha nodded and handed it over for Nes to scrutinize. "Do what you wish with it. I've no need for it anymore."

"And you'll give me the rest of the map when this is through?"

The next nod was more enthusiastic. "I wouldn't miss this for *anything*." Nes's eyes narrowed. Maybe she'd pushed the enthusiasm too far.

"You don't plan on travelling with us, do you?" Nessix asked.

Ah. So that was what it was. Etha eyed the filthy, spent pair and how empty their packs hung at their sides, and suspected a third mouth was unwelcome company.

"With me on my pony and you on foot? I'd think not!"

Etha's arrogance was accepted in stride, much more readily than the suspicions that would have come from admitting that she had one more errand to see to.

"But you *will* be there." Nessix asked, swatting Talier's attempt to gain her attention to silence. "With the other half of this map?"

"You have my word."

The two women—fallen general and Mother Goddess—met each other's eyes, sharing between them an unspoken understanding which Nessix couldn't explain but wouldn't question. Another moment passed, the only sound interrupting their silent promises Talier's nervous shuffling, and then Nessix nodded and stepped back to her companion.

"Very well," Nessix said. "We'll meet again in Fairmont."

Etha lowered her head, relieved that Nessix had taken the bait, but hiding as much under the guise of gratitude. "Carry Etha's blessing with you, Succubus."

The goddess let those words confuse Nessix as she turned her pony and cantered off down the road. Nessix watched her disappear, her confusion snapping away as Talier timidly tapped her shoulder. Not yet pulling her gaze from the puff of dust that hung in the air from the pony's departure, Nessix absently handed the map to Talier.

He accepted it and stretched it open. "We're not actually going to Fairmont, are we? This is enough to put us back on track; I can get us back on the road to Zeal."

Nes closed her fingers over the yellow scarf, hating that she couldn't agree with Talier. She was through being an assassin, so worn from killing people who hadn't earned their deaths that she no longer knew if she was even comfortable being a soldier. It was ironic that pride forbid her to back out of this assignment, especially after how low she'd fallen, but perhaps it wasn't pride alone which bound her to this mission.

"Where is Fairmont on that map?" she asked, turning back to Talier at last.

"Here." He pointed at a city lying westward of the road they were supposed to take to Zeal. "But you didn't answer me."

Nessix blinked and looked up at Talier, pleasantly surprised by his subtle demand. "It's not like you to take that sort of tone, Talier," she teased. "Careful, or I'll start thinking you're up to something."

Talier flushed and barely kept his stammered rush of excuses contained by blurting out what he hoped passed for logic. "All we were missing was our location. Fairmont's too far southwest, besides."

He raised a valid point. Without knowing where Kol had scattered his troops, without knowing the path the inoga had taken, backtracking carried a substantial risk. Nessix dropped her gaze to the scarf and sighed, cursing how she still clung to the concept of honor.

"I gave my word," she murmured.

"But you said you're not an assassin anymore."

"I may not be an assassin, but I'm not a liar, either. I'm going to Fairmont, Talier. You can part ways with me if you feel you must."

Talier gaped at her. He couldn't claim to know Nessix well, but that was the first time she'd mentioned the idea of separating from him. Still unsure if he needed to stay with her for the protection she offered him from the demons or if he needed to stay with her so he could deliver her to Kol, all he *did* know was that he had to stay with her. He cast his gaze to the ground, surrendering, as always, to the fact that his opinions didn't matter.

"Alright. Let's go to Fairmont."

"That's a good man!" Nessix slapped Talier on the shoulder and snatched the map from him to study it, grinning. "Now, let's get going."

* * * * *

Mathias followed Nes's sparse trail to the town of Midland. He'd contently gone along with the theory that any lead was a good lead until he entered the town to find a hefty portion of the business district burned to the ground. A foreboding dread gnawed at his excitement as he poked around the locals for rumors of what had happened.

The specifics varied, as they always did when asking for stories from a gossipy public, but two aspects of the reports stuck with Mathias—confirmation of a dark-haired woman fleeing the scene, and that of a group of five unsettling men had confronted her prior to the fires starting. Some said the woman killed all five men. Others claimed they'd been trying to kill her and she'd started the fire in self-defense. Nobody could confirm how many of the men had escaped. The only thing Mathias *could* confirm was that Nessix *had* been here and she was tied to the disaster that had leveled the business district.

Dread singing a mocking song in the back of his mind, Mathias arranged a meeting with the sheriff over supper at the tavern overlooking the damage. Their conversation didn't begin well and Mathias suspected if it hadn't been for his station and bribes, the sheriff would have dismissed him completely.

"I've received a whole anthology worth of stories of what happened here," Mathias said. "What facts have you been able to confirm?"

The sheriff scoffed and crossed his arms, sneering at his full plate of food. "Fact is a third of the business district was burned to the ground, and another dozen buildings sustained heavy damage. Twenty-three of my civilians died in these fires, another handful of bodies are still unidentified. No offense intended, sir, but your Order can't fix that."

"No," Mathias granted, "but it can help find whoever was responsible so they can—"

"Good luck with that."

Mathias sat back and absorbed the sheriff's bitterness. "What makes you think I can't?"

"We've got old Rhett locked up in a cell. Guilt ate him up after the city burned, said he never meant for others to get hurt."

Mathias's heart fell. "So he's the one who set the fires? What about the rumors of the dark-haired woman?"

"Oh, those reports are real, and she's the one we're after. But you won't be able to catch her."

The challenge enticed Mathias, but not quite enough to overshadow his dread of whatever it was Nessix had been responsible for. "Why's that?"

"She's an assassin."

The rest of the sheriff's rant slid past Mathias as bubbling nonsense. Suddenly, he wished he hadn't been so certain the woman from these rumors was Nessix.

An *assassin*?

Mathias could justify most professions, honest and otherwise, but murder for hire was neither something he condoned nor something he'd ever imagined Nessix stooping to. Perhaps the demons had ruined her more than he'd thought. He reached forward to push his plate away just as a calloused hand slapped down on the tabletop, drawing the startled attention of both men.

"Is there room here?" a husky, feminine voice asked. Before either man could respond, their visitor answered herself with, "Good," and pulled a chair over to sit beside them.

Mathias soaked up Etha's comfort readily, dismayed to find it not making much of a difference in alleviating the burden which had just been dumped on him. He looked to his goddess to see what answer she had for his silent petition for help and coughed at the uncharacteristically plain and stocky features she'd adopted for this visit.

"Looks like the road's taken its toll on you," Mathias said, relieved to have a more innocuous form of shock to distract him.

Etha batted aside the tails of her yellow scarf and pulled Mathias's half-empty plate over to herself. Ignoring the sheriff's fuming glower, she began eating from it, speaking with her mouth full as she scrutinized the shield and lilies glistening on Mathias's breastplate. "Funny. I thought Etha's followers were humble and polite to their elders."

Mathias's tension settled at Etha's goading. "I'm sorry, my lady."

Etha twirled the fork in Mathias's direction, mouth still full. "And fix your hair. You look like a stranger."

Mathias raised a self-conscious hand toward his head, eager to ask Etha what game she was trying to play, but the sheriff beat him to speaking. "Do you know this… this woman?"

A delicate challenge glittered in Etha's eyes, promising Mathias that this was not some simple social visit. Disregarding the sheriff's question, having not wanted to continue talking to him, anyway, Mathias turned to Etha. "My road's been long and tiring and I seem to have lost myself along the way. Is there something I ought to know?"

The sheriff scoffed and attempted to interject once again.

"My own travels," Etha said, seamlessly interrupting the blustering man, "have pointed to a mighty valuable treasure in Fairmont. A treasure a man like you would be quite interested in getting his hands on."

Mathias stared at Etha mutely, too afraid to believe what she was implying after the bumpy road he'd just tumbled down. Fear mingled with hope, both of them gripped tight by a heartfelt longing that made his eyes burn with the threat of tears. While Mathias struggled to arrange his thoughts into any sort of coherence, the sheriff cleared his throat and turned to Etha to take advantage of the temporary silence.

"With all due… respect." A distinct lack of the virtue popped on that last word. "This man is a knight of the Order, not some treasure hunter. And he's—"

Etha spun her plain face to the sheriff, arching a menacing brow to silence his complaint. "Everyone's a treasure hunter when there's something they want badly enough."

The sheriff slapped his palms on the table and pushed himself to his feet. "Ma'am. A third of my business district has been burned to the ground. You and your rumors are interrupting negotiations to secure the Order's assistance—"

If not for the narrow timeframe she had to work with, if not for how long Nessix had been lost to them, if not for how Mathias had torn himself to pieces trying to find her, Etha would have gladly toyed with this man all day. As it was, she was ready for this terrible phase of Abaeloth's history to be put behind them. She, too, slammed her hands on the table and stood, ignoring Mathias's gasp and wide eyes.

"Sir," she snipped. "There are more pressing matters than your business district in Fairmont, ones that may have more to do with this tragedy than you seem to think. You will receive your assistance from Zeal, but for now, you will dismiss this man from your blathering so he can go do the job he vowed to do."

"Now see here—"

Urgency to prevent a scene—or offense to his goddess—pushed Mathias past his shock and he took his turn to leap to his feet. "Sir, I feel deeply for your plight and your city's loss, and I will personally petition for Zeal's aid to reach you in whatever regard you deem necessary. But if this traveler says there are matters I must tend to in Fairmont, then there are matters I must tend to in Fairmont."

"Do you even *know* this woman?" the sheriff asked again, cheeks red and voice trembling with his struggle between displaying and demanding respect.

Mathias gave the man a tight smile. "I've run into her several times in the past." Etha gave a curt nod. "And she's always come bearing official orders." Etha whipped the scarf from around her neck, draped it over Mathias's shoulders, and nodded again. "Your

352

concerns will neither be forgotten nor ignored, sheriff." Mathias smirked as he opened the door he often left closed when out gathering information from locals. "You've got Sir Mathias Sagewind's word on it."

"Mathias Sagewind—" All of the hot air deflated from the sheriff as he rapidly recalled the significance tied to that name. The claim itself bordered on blasphemy if it was a lie, but accusing the White Paladin of such a petty action would do nothing to help his case. Trapped in the situation, the sheriff sank silently down into his chair.

"The Order and all of Abaeloth thank you for your understanding." Mathias turned to Etha. "My lady, if you'd lead the way, I am only honored to follow."

Giving the sheriff a playful wink, Etha spun and flit from the tavern as well as her bulky frame allowed, leading Mathias to the road to Fairmont. The road to Nessix.

TWENTY-NINE

"It's not too late to turn around and forget about this. I can get us to Zeal from here."

Nessix continued to ignore Talier's persistent bargaining, concentrating all of her effort on investigating their approach to Fairmont for signs that the assassins might have a presence here. That one unknown variable was her greatest reservation as to whether or not she was comfortable with this arrangement and Talier eagerly mistook her careful search for second-guessing whether or not this was where she truly wanted to be.

"The guards will get suspicious if you keep snooping around like this."

That warning did merit Nes's consideration and she sighed and turned toward the gates. Convinced, if barely, that Fairmont was safe to enter, Nessix nodded to Talier and walked ahead.

Flustered at Nes's stubbornness, but not brave enough to tell her so, Talier flung his hands in the air and scampered after her. "How long will we be here?"

"About a day. I want to stock up on enough supplies that we won't have to stop until we reach Zeal, then I'll go scout out the lay of the city and its guard posts. We'll spend the night, get some quality rest, and I'll take care of business in the morning."

Talier frowned and dug at the cuticle of his thumb. "Are you putting me on watch again?"

Nessix lowered her head, regretting her companion's fears. "I'll need you close enough for us to make a hasty retreat and would appreciate any assistance you can give me in the process."

He groaned, remembering with a bittersweet fondness the days when he'd thought Marcoux put him in unpleasant predicaments. "I really don't like this… We should just buy our provisions and leave. If we managed to get a couple horses, we'd even be able to outrun that girl and her pony."

The guards hailed their approach and Nessix silently contemplated Talier's logic as formalities were exchanged. Talier ceased his verbal fretting as soon as they entered town and between his nervous silence and her half-expecting a confrontation—or a poisoned dart to her neck—Nes's heart rate steadily climbed.

They made their way to the market, where Nessix coaxed Talier into discussing what sort of supplies they needed to purchase in an attempt to soothe them both. Just as they'd resumed their casual chatter, exchanging coins for their basic needs without feeling like they were on the run, Nes's heart leapt to her throat and she choked on a sharp gasp. Dismissing herself from the current transaction as she retreated to catch her breath, she recognized that foreboding feeling of being watched.

Talier finished their business and walked up to her. "Is um… is everything alright?"

"Have you seen or heard anything we should be wary of?"

Nessix spoke quietly, raising the hairs on the back of Talier's neck. He chanced a couple of tentative sniffs to the air, uncovering nothing unusual other than Nes's heightened caution. "No, but I haven't been looking."

"I'm going to have to ask you to start." She motioned Talier to follow as she wandered toward the southern walls to where her caution warned her against.

He followed, but with growing reluctance. "I thought you said you wanted to do your scouting alone." He did not care for the rigid manner with which Nessix stalked ahead or how close she kept her hands to her weapons.

"I'm not scouting, I'm tracking."

Talier swallowed his fuss of discontent and scooted closer so he could lower his voice. "What are you tracking?"

"I'm not sure yet." She drew the statement out with a contemplative uncertainty that did nothing at all to soothe Talier's growing fears. "That's why I want you close. If nothing else, I'll be able to direct you to the best escape route."

That whimper escaped him now. "Escape route from what?"

"From whatever's watching us."

* * * * *

Using the divine pathways, Mathias and Etha arrived in Fairmont mere moments after departing Midland. Restless and eager, Mathias distracted himself from brooding over Nes's reported means of employment by investigating the city, asking casual questions to see if anyone had seen a woman matching her description.

Etha had politely excused herself from his investigation, leaving him alone to sort through the multitude of fresh information. Nessix was an assassin. It was likely she'd been responsible for trying to burn down a city. But she'd also been praised as a fearless hero. Combat was practically the only thing she knew, so Mathias shouldn't have had such a hard time accepting the turn she'd taken... except for the fact that no matter which way he looked at it, the champion of the people he'd loved wouldn't have ever gone down this road.

Angry for exposing himself to these thoughts when he should be staying alert for Nessix—even if it was to stop her from whatever job she'd accepted—Mathias wound through the city, making small talk with the locals. A dainty hand slipped into his, pulling even the most buried of his thoughts to the present. He looked down at Etha, approving of the refined face she'd assumed. The tumbling curls and tailored green gown suited her much better than the stocky build and rough garb of the traveler who had recruited him for this mission. He smiled at her, confused when she didn't return the gesture.

"Mathias," she said quietly, all mischief and enthusiasm

sinking in a trembling dread. "You ought to head toward the southern walls."

He furrowed his brows. Always welcoming Etha's advice, this particular direction, paired with the goddess's timid tone, rang of a danger she wouldn't have willingly pushed him toward. "The walls?"

"Yes." Etha wanted nothing more than to tell Mathias to turn and run with all his might out of Fairmont, screaming warnings of the impending danger to each city he passed on his way back to Zeal, but this close to reaching Nessix, knowing what would happen today if Mathias didn't reach her… The trembling seeped from Etha's voice and into her entire body as she squeezed Mathias's hand, her silent petition for him to find the strength she couldn't fathom him having. "To the walls…"

Mathias knew better than to ask Etha for more insight; she'd have given it if she'd been able to. Sense and logic were both things he'd abandoned long ago in favor of faith and obedience and, steeling himself against the soul-rending stream of reservations Etha transmitted to him, Mathias shook his hand free of hers and moved to carry out her wishes. His progress through the streets halted abruptly as Etha's presence stayed at a constant distance. He didn't turn to look back.

"Are you coming because you want to or because you need to?"

The plan Etha had embraced involved her tagging along to witness the reunion between Nes and Mathias, a momentous event she'd jubilantly looked forward to. Now, however, she was frightened to let Mathias go anywhere by himself, especially if that somewhere involved this long-anticipated reunion with Nessix. Afraid of the truths she couldn't quite tell him, Etha stayed silent. He'd know what to make of that.

"I see." Mathias batted aside the rapid rush of reluctance that came from Etha's trepidation. He'd been resurrected to serve as her champion and fear—no matter how sensible—would only hinder his ability to fill that role. Trusting Etha as he always did, salvaging faith that he'd survive, if only because she refused to leave him, Mathias weaved through the crowd, pressing toward the southern walls.

Etha's distress grew with each stride, an unusual and unwelcome sensation for Mathias to absorb, until a shrill scream from in front of him pierced the pleasant day. Etha gasped but stayed close to Mathias's heels, and that first scream was joined by a chorus of others. Moments later, the thuds of a crushing force striking against homes' defenses punctuated the terrified song, accented by the cries of splintering wood and eventually driven by the beat of menacing laughter.

Mathias had come to Fairmont by Etha's orders, confused but full of hope. He might not have decided what to make of Nes's alleged changes, but that hadn't made him any less eager to find her. After stopping a war on Elidae, after months spent questing and so many nights lost to despair, Mathias had come to Fairmont convinced this trial was almost over.

He'd never imagined it would end in an inoga attack.

Tears sprang to his eyes as Mathias swallowed concerns for himself and the aversion to pain that tried to rise at the thought of his typical interactions with these monstrosities. A town full of civilians aside, Nessix had slipped through his fingers too many times. He'd be damned before he let it happen again. Drawing his sword, thankful for Etha's backing, no matter how shaken, Mathias ran to the sounds of danger.

* * * * *

Two months ago, when Nessix still had access to dream stop, the screams of terror would have told her to run. They'd have confirmed the knot of being watched and urged her from town, trusting Talier could truly lead her straight to Zeal. Two months ago, she'd have been able to think with a calm, rational mind when adrenaline spiked. Her instincts to survive beat just as strong as ever, but now survival seemed far more likely through fighting than fleeing. She was through running from Kol and the assassins and would leave a bloody warning for them each time either force attempted to intercept her.

Talier begged her to stop, going so far as to try physically restraining her, but she swatted him aside and ignored his words. As the screams grew, accompanied by the tell-tale crashes of a demon raid, the man's growing terror stifled his courage to try stopping her and Nessix charged ahead.

Her charge came to an abrupt stop as sensibility squeezed past the cracks of the chaos raging inside of her.

In Seaton, she'd had a god to warn her of the inoga's search. She'd made her assumptions about this force based on her prior knowledge of how the beasts functioned, but no amount of experience could fill in all the blanks. Inoga didn't work well together. Nessix had assumed one of the overlords, two at the absolute most, had come leading an army after her. In her most ideal scenario, that inoga would have been Grell—who she'd engaged once before—or Inek—who she'd developed a special sort of hatred for. She'd convinced herself she'd be able to evade either or both of those monsters if she was careful, and she very well could have.

But it hadn't been Grell or Inek who came chasing after her. And it wasn't just one or two inoga who rampaged over the southern wall to pound through the nearby homes. Five of these brutes barked orders to their underlings who filed through the streets like worker ants.

"Find her! Search everywhere and spare nothing!"

Nes's mouth opened in a contrite gasp. In the back of her mind, she'd known both Kol's troops and these inoga's own were killing and pillaging in search of her, but she'd kept running, stuffing those thoughts in the same corner where she locked Veed's treachery and Brant's demise and her cursed affection for Kol. Witnessing one of the inoga reach through a window to drag a shrieking woman out of her home forced Nessix to face how she'd betrayed her vows to protect innocents. The inoga spun the woman in his grasp to appraise her features, tossing her aside to her demise after confirming she wasn't Nessix. And suddenly, that foolish urge to stand and fight against impossible odds rallied even the shriveled parts of Nes's courage, just as it had when she'd stood in defiant defense of that damned alar she'd never be able to escape.

Nessix ripped a dagger from her belt and flexed her grip

around it as she focused past the remnants of terror and intelligent tactics.

"Nessix…" Talier plucked weakly at her arm. "What're you… we need to…"

Perhaps if he'd been able to complete his plea, Nessix might have reconsidered her actions. Instead, his helplessness only pushed her closer to certainty. "Talier," she said calmly, her doubts and fears squashed flat by duty. "Run."

He couldn't have run, even if he'd been able to inspire his legs to move. Kol and Annin had been terrifying enough. Even their lackeys who looked nearly identical to common folk frightened Talier. Kol had told him that there were demons more terrifying than him hunting Nessix and that he was to do everything he could to keep her away from them, but he'd thought the alar was being facetious. Now, too late, Talier understood. Whether or not he wanted to honor his debt to Nessix or obey Kol's threats, he simply couldn't let her engage in whatever foolish move her squared shoulders and firm jaw conveyed she was thinking about. Heart jammed in his throat and senses half numb, Talier reached for Nes's arm again, missing it by a fraction of a second as she raised it and sent her dagger sailing through the air.

It sank into the thick muscles of the nearest inoga's left breast, pulling his attention from ripping the door off a house as he looked down at the blood running down his chest. He lifted his bemused gaze to the frantic and scattering crowd, struggling to comprehend how any of them could have been so bold. His answer found him all on its own as Nessix stepped forward, the only being to willingly move toward their assault.

"I'm right here, you yeasty codpieces!"

The carnage paused as every demon spun to the taunt. Through the mass of fleeing civilians, Nessix stood as a tiny beacon, buying the mortals time to run and tempting the demons toward blind madness. The inoga she'd struck gaped at her as his four comrades lumbered closer to stare with him, disbelieving their luck.

"Nessix, what are you doing?" Talier squeaked.

"What I should have done months ago." Rationale shed,

Nessix darted forward, taking advantage of the demons' hesitation.

Behind her, Talier screamed her name as she flung herself at her first opponent.

* * * * *

It was difficult to maintain a good, heroic charge against the steady flow of people running against him, but Mathias persevered, reciting mantras of courage and duty in his mind. A bold declaration delivered in a woman's voice rose above the clamor, a challenge spoken in a manner his memories grappled to believe, and Mathias pushed harder. A man's voice followed the taunt in a definitive scream, this one delivering a name Mathias had longed to hear as a direct address for months.

"Nessix!"

Mathias had no idea who shouted that desperate plea to Nes, but he didn't have to. That scream had just confirmed Mathias's hope that Nessix was the great treasure Etha had referenced in Midland. And the cry of shocked terror that Nessix was about to do something reckless assured Mathias that she had not been changed as much as he'd feared. His only concern now was how close these realizations came to one another.

Mathias abandoned his efforts to slip unobtrusively through the panicking population, now shoving terrified men and women out of his way as he pushed ahead. Those mantras of courage faltered as a new fear, that of losing Nessix for good, grew.

Is she alright? he asked Etha.

I don't know.

He growled at the reply but didn't question it. They'd been through how Nessix couldn't be tracked by conventional means, but he needed to hear that she was okay. She had to be. He'd lost her twice to the demons already and was certain that the inoga would not be as tidy or quick with her as Kol and his Spirit Binder had been.

The rush of fleeing bodies tapered at last to reveal a tense crowd huddled at one end of the street, facing an army of demons which fanned around a group of five inoga. The massive beasts

361

muscled their way through the living arena, grappling with one another. Every few heartbeats, one would belt out an enraged roar and dive into the rest of the group. All five bled from their faces, shoulders, and torsos. Skirmishes among inoga were common occurrences and though Mathias should have been grateful they'd spared the rest of the city due to this distraction, he was still wrapped up in his concerns for Nessix. Without knowing her location or state of physical wellness, he had no choice but to hold his action. He didn't have to wait long.

Mathias had loved watching Nessix in combat. She'd learned to use her petite size to slip in and out of situations that would trap the average soldier. She'd had a beautifully tactical mind which always shone so brilliantly when engaging her foes. He'd watched her best the fiercest opponents, misleading them into underestimating her capabilities and for the briefest second, as he watched her spring off one inoga's shoulders to wrap her arms and legs around the next one's massive bicep, Mathias gaped at her in awe, hardly believing he was witnessing her take on a group of the beasts on her own.

You'd better start believing it, Etha warned grimly. *They are unlikely to stay confused for long.*

Nessix plunged her knife into the inoga's armpit, riding his arm as he jerked it in response to the pain. One of his comrades rushed to grab her, and she released her hold, tumbling to the ground to roll under their feet. She sliced a calf of that first inoga and sprang up to jab her knife in its groin, and Mathias stared in shock as the great demon bellowed in fury... and crumbled into a roaring mass of demon flesh onto the bloodied ground.

Don't mistake luck for skill, Mathias! Etha urged. *Look at her. Look at her! She won't stand much longer.*

While Nessix was quick to dart out of the reach of the next sweeping arm, her pace dragged from what would be necessary to keep up with this set of opponents. Mathias wanted only one thing more than to not have to engage these demons, and that was Nes's safety. Backed by Etha, here by her orders to ensure just that, Mathias swallowed his tears of terror and awe, and pushed aside the frustration that his reunion with Nessix hadn't been the joyous occasion he'd prayed for.

Will the city be okay if I grab Nes and run? he asked.

They've begun evacuating. I'll buy what time for them I can. Do not lose her again, Mathias.

Nessix slipped out from beneath the inoga's feet, eyes turned upward as she gauged her next leap, but before she could coil her energy to spring, the demon to her left spun, crashing his shin into her chest. The blow pummeled the breath from her and she flew backwards, reaching an abrupt stop as she collided with another inoga. As the brute's arms closed around her, crushing her arms against her sides, her name pierced the air from two voices— Talier's horrified shriek and another, deeper, much more reassuring voice she'd heard often in her dreams.

She squinted past the pain of her creaking bones to where the young woman who had hired her restrained Talier, and then at Mathias as he rushed her way, sword raised and yellow scarf billowing around his neck. Uncontrolled tears ran down her cheeks, washing trails through the demon blood spattering her face, and she shouted her defiance as she pushed against the inoga's grasp. Mathias closed in on them fast, an aura of righteous fury illuminating him. Nessix had come too close to fail now! She kicked to try catching a kneecap as her head grew fuzzy from oxygen deprivation, but then a greater terror roared between the remaining inoga.

"Grell says death won't kill her. Take her out and let's go!"

On a subconscious level, Nessix braced for the pain of however the inoga planned to end her struggles—with the amount of trouble she'd given them so far, she should have been grateful that Mathias's proximity would force them to find a quick method—but she refused to accept this fate. Mathias was *right there*. She'd escaped the hells to reach him. She'd journeyed across a foreign continent to reach him. She'd taken part in unforgiveable sins to reach him and now that he was here, the demons would *not* take her.

If they expected to see her dead, she'd humor them.

Nessix weakened her struggles, utilizing all of her will power to fight her instincts against doing so. Savoring a slow, deep breath, she let her head bob and then slump over the inoga's arm, surrendering her strength and praying the beast was as slow to make connections as Grell was. Ignoring Mathias's pleading was the hardest part of this ruse as her heart ached for his sorrow and desperation. Unfortunately, breaking his heart now seemed to be her best chance at alleviating both their pain in the future.

The inoga holding Nessix grunted his pleasure at her apparent defeat and hoisted her limp body over his shoulder. Mathias roared his fury and frustration, driven by duty and determination and his unfaded love for Nessix. He would not be too late to save her. Never again would he be too late.

The demons turned and began fleeing the city. Long, muscular legs launched the inoga away from Mathias, and he pushed to the extent of his limits, too focused on Nessix's unconscious face to form coherent prayers. Coherent or not, they seemed to be answered as Nes's eyes flashed open. She cast Mathias a rallying glance and an exhausted smile, and before the inoga who carried her could distinguish her movement from the jostling of his gait, she pulled her last dagger from her belt and gouged it into the behemoth's side, driving it between his ribs.

Had the situation not been so dire, Mathias would have stopped to marvel at Nes's feisty tactics and hope she truly was more Nessix than not; he'd never fancied the idea of engaging her in combat, and it had little to do with his fondness for her. Instead, he continued to drive himself forward, refusing to allow Nes's gambit to go to waste.

The inoga bellowed and dropped Nessix. She slid down his back, catching herself awkwardly on his belt to strike again, lower this time. The demon's allies stopped to address his curses as Mathias reached them at last. He grasped a hold of Nes's gorget and pulled her free from the beast, dragging her back from the inevitable storm of the inoga's rage.

Neither paladin nor general had envisioned their reunion being so perilous, and they'd both dreamt of it for so long that even their immediate danger wasn't enough for them to not quietly acknowledge that they once again stood beside each other. The searching could stop now. The fear and pain and ceaseless longing could be over.

As long as they could defeat these inoga.

Neither warrior took their focus from the threat before them, and Mathias was both pleased and dismayed at how calmly Nessix had learned to face demons. That she continued to fight them assured him in all the best ways that she had not surrendered to their rule. If they both made it out of this, it would be the best day of Mathias's unending life.

Nessix broke the steady rhythm of their panting as the demons spun to close in again. "Oh, I've missed you, Sagewind." Drawing her sword now that she had the range to use it, she darted forward, revitalized with her paladin at her back.

Her words sang months' worth of belated promises and reassurance to Mathias and though they faced such steep odds, he felt as though the two of them could conquer the hells together. Nessix finished off the inoga who had been carrying her with a quick slash to an artery, and Mathias joined her in combat. After all, he was supposed to be the one rescuing her.

He rushed the nearest inoga, but a swarm of mundane demons closed over him, driving him away from where Nessix had resumed her struggle against the three remaining inoga. The overlords snarled threats and orders at her, keeping her on the run so she had no window to strike. Inoga weren't as adaptable as the rest of their kin, but these three had learned from Nes's previous attacks. Her glow of enthusiasm was soon overtaken by frustration as she fought to concentrate on their movements, forced to forget about the army that backed them.

Mathias was tired, but he was impassioned. Summoning Etha's grace into his sword arm, he commanded his blade to elongate into a halberd. "My fight is not with you," he told the group of demons standing guard between him and their lords. "You will let me pass."

A wiry demon in the front swatted his sword at Mathias's halberd. "Or else—"

The taunt was never completed as Mathias twisted his blade around and beheaded his critic. "Anyone else?"

You don't have time for this, Mathias... Etha's voice shook with warning.

The demon mass growled and grumbled, closing in on Mathias steadily, but wary.

I'm not sure I have a choice.

From over the heads of his opponents, Mathias saw Nessix fly into the air, her limbs scrambling as though she'd be able to find purchase on nothing before crashing to the ground. She'd already expended much of her strength, and Mathias knew her landing would sap what little she had left. Trusting Etha's orders, having full faith that she wouldn't abandon him now, Mathias erupted with divine might, a concussive force blasting from his core to send his enemies sailing yards away from him. He didn't have time to assess if they'd been dazed or killed. He had to reach Nessix.

As he leapt over fallen demon bodies, Mathias watched in horror as the inoga formed a tight circle around Nessix where she groaned on the ground. They took turns stomping down at her and though Mathias couldn't see her, her screams conveyed their strikes were connecting. But those screams also promised that Nessix was still alive.

From where she restrained Talier, Etha could clearly see how Mathias's plan was going to end, and it wasn't in a way that any of them—besides the inoga, of course—would be happy with. They'd incapacitate him and Nessix both and drag them into the hells. Etha had to break this nasty habit of bending the rules for Mathias's sake, but would justify doing so once more today since the demons had done the same.

Drive them back with another concussive blast.

Etha's instruction almost slowed the paladin's charge. Almost.

I won't have the energy for much else if I do.

That's fine. All you need is the energy to throw Nessix out of the way.

Mathias seldom had trouble trusting Etha, but this, possibly the most urgent situation he'd ever faced, was one of those times it was a struggle. Experience told him inoga weren't always driven back by bursts of power and shining lights. Common sense reminded him that he had a finite amount of power left in him, and he needed to ration it for the rest of the fight.

But Nes's screams…

Her screams pulled him back to a past he'd do anything to

change. They ran him through with guilt and determination. He needed to stop those screams, and he trusted Etha's assistance would get him closer to doing that than he'd be able to do on his own. Never again would he reach Nessix a second too late.

Mathias slid to a stop as one of the inoga turned toward him, still several paces from Nessix. The stomping halted as the other two looked up, leaving Nessix whimpering and wheezing on the ground. Smug smiles contorted the inoga's faces and as one lifted his great leg for a final blow, Mathias bellowed the past year's worth or rage and fear and aggravation.

Etha's might burst from him, nearly blinding him. The inoga's mass and steady foundations prevented them from being flung aside as their smaller comrades had been, but the blast was enough to make them stagger backwards as they spun their curses his direction.

Throw Nessix to me.

The choice of Etha's words were too precise for Mathias to interpret any other way than literally, and though he hated the idea of manhandling Nessix after the beating she'd just taken, he'd do as he was told. For whatever reason, Etha needed him on the field a bit longer.

He reached Nessix in heartbeats, and her blue eyes glowed with joy and pain through a mask of blood. Her breastplate had been crushed around her torso, dented and digging into her in unnatural ways which impaired her breathing. Mathias longed to stop and help her, but Etha had implied she'd look after her and the inoga wouldn't stay stunned for long. Nessix gasped to try speaking, but before she could petition for Mathias's sympathy, he grasped her under the arms and hefted her with all of the force he had left in him in Etha's direction. He swung back toward his opponents, grimacing at the muffled whimper that accompanied the thump of Nessix striking the ground.

I have her, Etha said, allowing Mathias to devote the entirety of his concentration on his next task. *Take your hilt with both hands and raise your weapon above your head.*

Mathias's muscles felt as though they'd burst. He'd only known exhaustion like this once before and that had been what killed him. This, though, was worth dying for.

Quit being dramatic and do as I said!

Too tired to argue, Mathias supported the wavering strength of his right hand with his left and raised his halberd overhead. His arms shook with strain and stars flashed across his vision, but he grit his teeth and waited for Etha's plan to come to fruition.

Hold it tight!

That instruction didn't make a bit of sense to Mathias until the blade, raised mightily in the air and held by fatigued arms, suddenly took on the weight of all of Etha's resentment for the demons. Mathias cried out as he fought to keep the blade vertically in place, dizziness assaulting him as his knees threatened to buckle. The inoga shook the daze from their eyes and snarled at the weary paladin.

STRIKE THE GROUND! NOW!

Mathias was only too happy to obey and he let the weight of the sacred weapon plummet downwards. The impact drove it blade-deep into the ground and the moment metal touched earth, a bolt of holy fire cleaved the ground, tearing a fissure twenty yards long before them. Mathias invested everything he had in keeping hold of his blade and as the three inoga waved their arms in comical shock before tumbling into the rift, Mathias sank to his knees, panting and spent.

The blessed blade, compassionate to Mathias's plight and exhausted in its own right, shrank down to a miniscule boot knife. Mathias moaned against his aches, closed his eyes, and slipped his old friend into place. A gentle hand squeezed his shoulder and just enough strength to stand flowed into him.

"She's asking for you…"

Mathias was on his feet faster than his head was prepared to accept, and he staggered the first few steps toward where Nessix wheezed, a young man timidly trying to wipe the blood from her face. Mathias quickened his pace as well as he could and knelt down beside her as Etha stood watch.

"Two inoga, all on your own…" Mathias said softly, pushing Talier's hands away so he could unbuckle the obliterated breastplate. "You've always amazed me, Nes."

Her eyes were delirious with pain and blood loss, and a clumsy hand plucked at his sword belt then flopped to her throat where her fingers scratched weakly. "Kill… me…"

Talier sobbed audibly and covered his mouth, but Mathias continued working. "I can't do that. Goes against my principles."

He pulled the breastplate off and retrieved his knife-sized sword to cut her shirt open. Her hand tried to catch the blade, but evading her efforts, even as worn as he was, was no challenge. A mess of broken ribs greeted Mathias and the degree of bruising across Nes's abdomen and torso implied significant internal bleeding. With Etha physically with him, those injuries were of little concern to him, but the small metal ring driven flush with her chest, just above her breasts, was.

Brows furrowing, already forming theories of how the demons must have tried perverting her, Mathias touched the ring, gasping the moment his blessed flesh came in contact with it.

A torn, mourning soul reached out to him, begging him to make her right again. It was unclear if that would come from rejoining the torn halves of her soul or a final release from this world, but Mathias read one thing clearly. It did not function as a soul ought to. Shaking, on the verge of tears, he snuck a glance at Etha.

Her face was grim and her brows strict. "Do not try to heal her," she advised gently. "She may not be able to be mended like that, and I don't know what might happen if you try."

"What do you mean don't try to heal her?" Talier shouted, coughing on phlegm. "You're just gonna—"

Mathias reached forward and pressed his fingers into the young man's temple, shaking coherence back into his own head as Talier slumped to the ground. The paladin met Nes's eyes, sorrowful for her pain, both physical and spiritual. "The inoga said something about you not dying. Does that mean you're immortal?"

The question was distorted through the din of agony and lingering death, but Nessix managed a brief affirmative.

Mathias stared into those beautiful eyes, so full of confusion, so full of pain, so full of trust. This wasn't how either of them had envisioned they'd find each other, but that didn't change the fact that they were together at last. Shock had dulled many of the injuries Nessix had sustained, and Mathias gently pulled her shoulders into his lap. He'd do everything he could to fix this, still blaming himself that it had happened at all, and if it began with delivering mercy to the woman he loved, he'd do so.

A faint sigh left Nessix and she closed her eyes. "Stay 'th me..." she murmured.

Mathias's heart broke, despite the swell of closure that folded around him. "I'll never leave you again."

As Mathias slowly reached for his knife, tears of relief and victory ran down Nes's cheeks as she lay, safe at last, in her paladin's arms.

The Afflicted Saga

Despair

Tale of the Fallen: Book V

DEMONS HAD BURIED A LEGEND…

Nessix lay on the same bloodied ground she'd come to know so well, the same bloodied ground which had always caused her so much fear and sorrow. It wasn't a grief she owned, but one she'd had forced on her when Kol had taken her captive.

Screams of terrified and tortured men petitioned to the heavens for mercy. A deep, rolling rumble rushed beneath the singed earth, as though laughing at the frantic efforts of the mortals who struggled to accept their impending doom. Bolts of wicked lightning crackled and hissed through a sky so saturated with smoke that only those broken on the ground stood a chance at breathing, and even down there, it was contaminated with the vile stench of blood and waste from the dead and dying. No stranger to battle and intimately familiar with this precise one, Nessix allowed the tainted air to flow in and out of her lungs with each of her wracked breaths, welcoming the sensation as she closed her eyes and smiled.

This time, Kol could keep this terror for himself. This time, Nessix was safe.

Gone was her urge to sift through Kol's memories for wisps of information which might help her defeat her position beneath the demons' rule. The instinct to push through agony and terror in her desperate race to figure out who or where she was no longer launched her to her feet. Not even her persistent longing to uncover the mysterious Berann's identity and worth motivated her to move this time. Horror rained down on the age of Abaeloth's innocence and crashed all around her, and Nessix relaxed into the blood-soaked mud of the battlefield and into the peace of lingering death. This would never be her nightmare again.

The mortal version of Grell screamed for her—for Kol—through the heartrending din of the dying battlefield. In her past detentions in this dream, his hoarse cries had stirred in Nessix the overwhelming need to answer his call, to let him drag her toward their ultimate demise in the hope that safety might be found. Never before had she even thought of attempting to ignore his frantic efforts, but she did today. Her smile broadened at this subtle jab of defiance against the man who would soon become an inoga.

Get up... You must get up!

The whim crept into Nes's mind, trembling past the raging chaos of the field around her, and her brows wrinkled as she contemplated how thoroughly it contradicted her decision to stay put.

Get to Grell. You must find safety.

Moments after addressing her delight in avoiding just that, her eyes flashed open.

I am safer here and now than I've ever been, she calmly told the rogue thought to stave off the manner which it tried to seep into the peace she'd found. *If I get up, that's when the end begins.*

When the... The words clipped short and the snap of a sharp gasp came from the back of Nes's mind. When the next words came, they had shed their rattling fear and chilled her through to her bones. *The end has already begun, little one. Where are you?*

It was Nes's turn to gasp and she actively had to fight the reaction to leap to her feet and push past her broken hip to drag herself, screaming, toward the friendlier, mortal version of Grell. The sooner she was with him, the sooner the dream would end. And the sooner this nightmare ended, the sooner she could once again escape Kol's presence. The notion that the alar had breached her defenses to slip into her mind—though perhaps it was more accurate to say that she was in his—frightened Nessix worse than any threat of lightning bolts or the agony of being twisted and torn into a demon. And if Kol had found a passage into her mind...

Scrubbing her thoughts clean of her recent memories of Mathias's rescue, Nessix engaged her demon as boldly as she could. *I am where I need to be. Far from the hells. Far from you.*

You are assuming you know where I am. Despite the playfulness of Kol's word choice, his tone was grave and terse.

I know you haven't caught me, Nessix countered, gaining courage. *So you can't be that close, can you?*

Wherever you are, little one, you are not safe. Quit with this nonsense and come back to me. I can protect you. There are—

Inoga after me? she finished for him. *You've told me that, and I've seen it for myself. And I will tell you now that I'm not worried about them.*

Not worried *about them?* Confusion ran as thick as the carnage of the battlefield in Kol's words, laced with faint hints of outrage. Everyone was afraid of inoga. Kol suspected even Annin, despite the boldness which he used when addressing them, was afraid of inoga. Nessix had tried to fight Grell once before and failed miserably, and she'd been killed by Inek on her first day as an akhuerai. *What has happened to you that you no longer fear inoga?* It'd be a nice trait to develop for himself.

Nessix hesitated, conflicted as to how much she could risk disclosing to her old master. She knew this was a dream and that several miles must still remain between her and Kol. She knew that if she could trust Mathias—and she liked to think she could—that she would remain well out of the demons' grasp. But she'd also learned long ago to not underestimate Kol's tenacity or intelligence. He'd be quick to share any insight he gathered on her whereabouts with Annin, the damned oraku would find a way to fill in any missing information, and Kol would keep on his hunt.

Nessix might be safe in the conventional sense, but her problems were far from over.

Inoga don't frighten me anymore. She stuck with the bold claim, despite how ridiculous it sounded. The ground rumbled beneath her back and a fresh wave of screams covered the sound of Grell's desperate calls.

They don't frighten you anymore. Kol could have repeated this statement ten thousand times and it couldn't have sounded more ludicrous. *Tell me where you are, little one. I can get you out of whatever trouble you've found, but only if you quit this silly rebellion.*

Nessix smirked, wondering if the intentions of her expressions were conveyed to Kol as clearly as her thoughts to him were. She suspected the alar did have the desire to protect her, but she also knew that he wasn't looking out for her half as much as he was looking out for himself. Grell must have been livid that she'd escaped, and demon hierarchy would place the blame heavily on Kol's shoulders. In all honesty, Nessix was surprised the alar was still alive. A niggling fear squirmed about in her belly at the thought of the punishment her actions would ultimately earn Kol and she pressed the conversation forward to escape the emotions that thought tried to rouse in her.

I got myself into the trouble I'm in, and I can get myself out of any more I find, she said, savoring how it felt to finally talk back to Kol without the risk of repercussion.

I don't think you understand the trouble you've found.

I've got a good enough idea of it.

Kol snorted in the back of her mind. *You think you're that clever? That just because you slipped between my fingers you've escaped your troubles? I know you're in Gelthin, but I suspect you've put that much together.* Another bolt of lightning streaked across the sky and this time, both Nessix and Kol recognized the timbre of Grell's agonized scream. Kol hastened his words. *I know you've gone seeking Mathias Sagewind.*

So what if I have? Though Kol had hastened his demands of her, Nessix remained calm. In just a few more moments, she'd be awake, Kol gone from her mind so she could tell Mathias everything he needed to hear. *As kind as you've been to me, that shouldn't frighten you so much.*

Nessix, you need me.

Are you sure it's not you who needs me, Kol?

Wherever you are, whatever you're doing, turn around—

Through Kol's frantic delivery, Nessix heard a tinge of desperation. It wasn't the same arrogant demand which he'd used at the start of this conversation, but it bled with a very mortal longing, dredging up feelings which Nessix had tried to fight for months now. So long without dream stop, even trapped within this nightmare, Nessix easily recounted the way which she'd stood defiantly against Grell in Kol's defense. She equated her own longing for Mathias to Kol's pleading to her now, and that connection to him which she'd never asked for begged her to take pity on him. There was a great chance he'd die because of her disobedience—if Mathias didn't kill him when Kol's hunt for her led him to Zeal, Grell would once he crawled back into the hells. Even Annin stood the chance of being Kol's demise if the oraku finally lost his patience with him.

Before Nessix had the chance to react to this deluge of fear, the bolt destined to strike her diverted its natural path to slam into her and her demon where she lay on the ground. The surge of the strike coursed through her body, burning its corrupt power through her veins and snapping at parts of her she didn't know how to describe. Kol had silenced his objections to her, his fear for her fate and his longing to see her again echoing in the silence of her agony as divine might reforged the vessel she currently wore into what would become a demon.

The sensation raked through Nessix and, with a brilliant flash cast against the back of her eyelids, this nightmare and all of its horror ended.

Keep up to date at www.katikaschneider.com

ABOUT THE AUTHOR

A lover of literary adventure and notorious breaker of writing rules, Katika Schneider's been an obsessive writer for most of her life. She started out writing for herself before surrendering to her characters' demands, and began pursuing publication in 2014. She's a firm believer that everyone has a story to tell.

Holding her degree in Animal Science, Kat planned on attending veterinary school until incisions started making her faint. She lives with her husband and their abundant family of critters.